THE TRUTH
ABOUT A GIRL

JANA WILLIAMS

PRINT ISBN: 978-1-9994086-6-4
eBOOK ISBN: 978-1-9994086-7-1

Printed in Canada

Edited by B.K. Editorial Services
Cover design by Arjuna Jay
Interior design by TeaBerry Creative

The Truth about a Girl is a work of fiction. Although some real people and events are portrayed, all situations are fictional.

*I acknowledge that I live and write
on the unceded traditional territory of the
Musqueam, Squamish and
Tsleil-Waututh First Nations.*

For
Barbara…
Her support, her patience
and generosity.

THE TRUTH ABOUT A GIRL

CONTENTS

the
truth
about
a
girl

ONE

Summer: hot, dry and with a cloudless sky. Ten-year-old Scooter Wells sits atop her father's shoulders as he walks them along a bluff overlooking the South Saskatchewan River. Scooter's mother, Janie, and her older sister Hayley follow them along the narrow dusty trail. Twelve feet below, a deep bend in the river wallows up against the base of the bluff.

Hanson stops and peers over the edge. Scooter looks too. Below her, the water is as green as a grape arbor—and looks as cool as the iced tea at Mona's Highway Diner.

Hanson whispers to Scooter. "You ready for a cool dip, Scoot? Damn it's hot, ain't it?"

The screams of the cicadas announce the heat. "Lemme down, Dad." Scooter wriggles a bit in excitement. "Lemme down."

Without warning, Hanson takes both of her hands in his and pulls her straight up. "Take a deep breath, Scoot."

Hanson hauls her over his head and tosses Scooter in an arc into the river below.

TWOOOSH.

Beneath the surface, the unremitting scream of the cicadas is silenced, the blowtorch heat of the day obliterated.

The sudden impact of the shockingly, cold water clamps Scooter's mouth closed. She plunges down, down, down into a suddenly silent world. Helpless against the sheer velocity of her fall, constrained by the press of water surrounding her descent, Scooter is imprisoned by the depths.

Her skimpy white cotton shorts are plastered against her abdomen; her torso is bare, as her t-shirt rides up over her chest. One thin arm is flung up through a halo of stringy blond hair.

The moment she is able, Scooter's arms and legs begin to flail, pitifully at first. Her eyes open wide with the shock of her sudden descent into the river's depths.

Atop the bluff, the incessant scream of the cicadas in the cottonwood trees is nearly muted by the screams of Scooter's twenty-eight-year-old mother, Janie. On the bank, ten feet above the pond, Janie is babbling incoherently with shock. She fights with all her might to free herself from the two wiry arms wrapped around her torso.

"Hanson, you son-of-a-bitch, LET ME GO."

Six-foot ought, and forty years old, Hanson holds Janie

tightly in a bear hug; her feet barely touch the ground in his embrace. Hanson calmly peers over the lip of the bluff. "Stop it, Janie. If the fall didn't kill you; the water would. God knows you can't swim a stroke."

Janie turns angry, horrified eyes on her husband and pounds him on his shoulders and chest. "Neither can Scooter, you bastard. Let me go."

Suddenly, a couple of young teenaged boys below them shout up from an outcropping on the river's sandy beach. "You want us to dive in and get her?"

Hanson pulls a cigarette from behind his ear and jams it in his mouth before Janie can capitalize on his lapse of attention.

The boys continue to scrutinize the surface of the water. Janie overhears their offer and begins struggling anew.

"YES, YES. Dive in. Go get her (begins sobbing). Please."

Hanson talks around the cigarette in his mouth. "Don't you dare, boys. If either one of you moves a muscle, I'll wail the tar outta you."

He peers down again at the unruffled surface of the pond. "Just give her a minute, will ya, Janie."

Janie is heaving huge wracking sobs now. She's slipped from his arms and lies piled at his feet. Hanson uses the moment to pull a flip-top lighter from his t-shirt pocket and lights his ciggie.

Janie holds out her arms to her oldest daughter, Hayley, who has been silently watching the entire family drama at a safe distance. Dressed in a pink ruffled two-piece swimsuit, Hayley shakes her head "NO" at Janie's insistence that she come comfort her.

Hayley is understandably hesitant to go too near either of her parents at the moment. She looks from Janie to Hanson and wisely decides to stay put, right where she is, outside of harm's reach.

Deep in the river, her descent comes to a halt. The moment she can move, the look of terror on Scooter's face is transformed to a fierce mask of stubborn determination. She flails her arms and kicks her legs, pushing herself upwards towards the shining light of the surface.

For a long moment, the tableau of concerned family and interested bystanders is frozen in time at the edge of the river. Each face is riveted on the spot in the river where Scooter disappeared.

Then, Scooter erupts like a geyser from the center of the pool of green water and spews the mouthful of river she almost swallowed.

The two boys call out shrilly, "There she is. THERE SHE IS!"

Hanson takes the cigarette out of the corner of his mouth and peers over the edge of the cliff again at the pond below. Seconds later, the blond halo of Scooter's hair floats to the surface for a second time, just before she shoots out of the water and screams bloody murder.

"Daaad-dy. You bastard."

"Now you can help her, boys. 'Cuz as far as I know, Janie's right—Scooter can't swim a stroke."

Hanson flips the cigarette into the bush nearby and scoops up Janie. He grabs a picnic cooler in his other hand and kicks a couple of empty beer cans into the brush.

Below him, both boys dive into the water and race for the screaming towhead bobbing up and down in the middle of the pond.

Hanson strides back down the path, towing Janie along by her arm. "But by god, our Scooter can bob like a damned cork."

Hayley follows behind, paying careful attention to the distance between her and her dad.

Scooter watches the boys progress, pumping her legs up and down like a bicycle in the water. She can just make out the silhouettes of her dad, her mom and Hayley scrabbling down the hill towards her.

The scorching sun blazes off the droplets of water thrown up by the two boys racing through the water towards Scooter. Each boy grabs one of Scooter's arms and hauls her towards the nearby beach.

Scooter stands, upon landing, and flings the wet from her hair like a shaggy dog.

Suddenly the *sound* of a piercing whistle and the crack of a whip echoes across the water from the other side of the river.

Scooter jerks her head around and watches as a herd

of twenty horses gallops down the far riverbank and churns into the water up to their chests. A lone rider quickly follows but stops at the water's edge. The horses continue to mill for a long moment and the whip cracks again. The horses immediately begin to churn the water to foam as they extract themselves from its depths and gallop away.

Scooter is mesmerized. "Bloody hell, what was that?"

The boys are impassive at the sight. "The ranch herd being brought in for the fall roundup. They run free all summer until time for us to bring in the cattle."

Scooter huffs her disbelief. "They run free… and then they come back?"

"Yup, the cowboy rides their leader. And they always go where she goes."

Scooter watches in amazement at the sight of twenty river-soaked horses galloping back onto the prairie. The cowboy follows, whip-cracking incentive to the herd.

Scooter stands and watches until the cloud of dust they kick up makes them disappear. She mutters to herself, "Not me. I wouldn't ever come back."

• • •

Hayley and Scooter's blond heads are pressed together in the middle of the spacious back seat of a crumbling old family sedan. Scooter's hair is still tangled in damp strands from the water.

She is reading aloud and utterly focused on an old, dog-eared picture book. "Sable Island, in the Atlantic Ocean, has a rep...a repu..."

Hayley glances down at the book and inserts a word smugly. "Rep-U-ta-tion, Scooter." Unfazed, Scooter continues, "Has had a reputation as a graveyard for ships for over 500 years."

Scooter looks up, beaming. When no one acknowledges her reading genius, she plows back into the text. "But Sable Island also can suc...suc.."

This time Janie interjects. "How is it spelled, Scooter?"

Scooter rattles off the spelling. "S-u-c-c-o-r."

"Ah. That's an old word that means to aid or assist — 'Succor'. Janie half turns in the seat to look back at Scooter. "So, they're saying Sable Island destroys ships but helps something survive. What does it help Scooter?"

Without missing a beat, Scooter dives back into the story. "But Sable Island can also succor life. For 500 years, horses have roamed free on Sable Island."

Suddenly the ancient sedan begins to sputter and steam begins to rise from beneath the hood. Hanson carefully guides the car to the side of the road and parks.

"What the hell?" Hanson pounds the steering wheel in frustration. He climbs out, approaching the steaming hood with caution. He uses his shirttail to pad his hand while he raises the hood and props it open. More steam billows out.

Scooter leans out the window. "What is it, Dad? Is it broken?"

"No, not broken, dammit. Just riled up." He lifts the canvas radiator bag off the front grill of the car. "Like a woman, she needs a minute to cool off, Scoot."

After a few minutes, he pulls off his t-shirt and uses it to twist the hot cap off the radiator. Clouds of steam burst forth, but then the vapor tapers off.

"Now, we'll just give her a little bitty drink." He pours a bit of water in the radiator. When that doesn't boil off immediately, Hanson pours in a bit more. Once he's sure it's full, Hanson replaces the cap and rehangs the bag, then closes the hood.

He eases back into the driver's seat. "That should do 'er till we get home. Okay, now where were we?"

Scooter opens the book one more time and begins to read again.

"The horses have prosp...prospered on Sable Island, where men have failed to thrive."

"Right-o. Let's see if this damn car can thrive long enough to get us home."

Hanson turns the key in the ignition. The engine rumbles and coughs, then suddenly roars to life. He steers the car back onto the highway and everyone cheers as they head towards the horizon.

Scooter climbs into the rear window shelf, taking the horse book with her. Hayley stretches out the full length of the seat below and closes her eyes, listening.

"Today, access to Sable Island is limited to just a few people a week to ensure the horses lives' remain undisturbed."

TWO

D awn on the prairies is a glory, raucous with bird song and electric with the energy of a new day. Hanson and Scooter are sequestered in a reed duck blind on a wide slough on a tributary of the South Saskatchewan. It is a universe of mallards and Canada geese, herons, king fishers and more.

"Scooter, are you awake?" He whispers harshly, wanting to be heard by his drowsy daughter but not every duck in the neighborhood.

Scooter rouses herself slightly. "Umm, un-huh, what's up?"

Hanson reaches over and pushes her leg with the toe of his rubber boot. "Very, very slowly I want you to lift one edge of the gunny sack and look out," he whispers.

Scooter sits up and gingerly lifts an edge of the burlap curtain and peers out into the dawn. The air around them is teeming with ducks in flight, ducks a-gabble, ducks feeding off the luxurious nutrients in the barely moving water.

A flock of birds as wide as Manhattan barrels past, turns and comes wheeling overhead. At the far end they turn and drop down to begin their approach to the tiny pond where Scooter and Hanson sit camouflaged. Scooter turns back to look at her father and nods vigorously.

"If you had a mind to shoot that thing, Dad, I'd do it now."

Hanson sticks out his bottom lip, contemplating the incalculable numbers of waterfowl raining down on them.

"I'm biding my time, Scoot." He beams at her. "This is the life though, hey? Just me and my best gal…"

"Yeah, yeah. Pull the damned trigger."

"Seriously, Scoot. It requires more than a bit of fore-thought. The minute I fire this baby, we lose 'em all."

Hanson raises the double barrel and sights along it as if it were a carbine. "Yep. I'm looking for the juiciest, the fattest lil' ducky your sweet mother ever saw and then."

"And then they'll be hauling you out of here on a stretcher, Daddy, if you fire a shotgun like that." Scooter reaches over and shoves the stock of the shotgun deeper into her father's shoulder. "Now really hold it in there when you pull that trigger."

Hanson smiles at his daughter over the double ham-mers of the shotgun as he pulls the trigger. He shouts over the roaring echo that follows.

"Here comes our dinner, Scooter."

Scooter throws both hands up over her ears as the duck blind explodes, followed by an explosion of light as the flimsy shelter disappears under the weight of a plummeting brace of ducks.

"Oow, goddammit, Daddy. I think your follow-through has given me a shiner. You damn well better have gotten us a duck."

"I got us TWO, Scooter. Two ducks, and I don't even have to wade anywhere to find them. How's that for shooting, girl?

THREE

A worn wooden screen door bangs again and again against the side of an old house. Slow and methodical it becomes the backbeat to the rising whine of wind. The paint on the house is peeling, the porch rail is bleached gray by the sun. In a corner of the dirt-packed yard the old sedan sits immobilized up on blocks. Its faded maroon paint is nearly identical to the rust that coats the fenders and hood. A skinny stray dog noses about looking for scraps that will never be found.

A tumble of dust and chaff blows past the porch on a hot summer wind as Hanson sits absorbed in a project in his lap. Beyond the green postage stamp of a garden a new-ish, double-wide trailer squats, surrounded by a perimeter of large river rocks that have been painted white.

Scooter steps outside onto the porch and shakes the chair Hanson is sitting on. She taps an empty beer can with her toe. "Can I play with some of these?"

Scooter stops to watch Hanson for a moment. "Whatcha making?"

"None of your beeswax, girl." Hanson is wielding a tiny pair of needle-nosed pliers, shaping lengths of stainless-steel wire around an empty beer can. He doesn't look up.

He stops and lays both hands over the project. "But yah, take as many empties as you want." He picks up the pliers again. "Leave me the full ones."

Scooter blasts past him and into the yard, a half-dozen empty cans in her arms. She runs out to the old wreck of a car and stops to drop all the cans on the ground.

Scooter rubs her hands together maniacally and tries an evil laugh on for size. "From

such small things...monsters may arise."

She stomps down with her one foot on an empty beer can and presto, monster shoes. Then she flattens a second can with her other foot.

Beer cans stuck to her shoes, Scooter takes a wild leap and lands upright on the river rock. The crashing noise of cans hitting rocks is deafening. She picks up her extra cans and clomps over to the rusting sedan, placing the cans on the front fender.

"Dad. Hey Dad! What do you bet I can hit both cans with just one rock?"

Hanson doesn't respond immediately; he's focused on his project and doesn't even look up. "Lemme see the rock first."

Scooter reaches down and plucks a good-sized rock from the ground. She holds it up over her head for Hanson to appraise.

"No dice. That's so big, I could do it from here—with my eyes closed."

Scooter drops it immediately and holds up another rock for inspection. This time Hanson actually looks up. "Okay, you're on. But back up three giant steps."

"D-a-d!"

When he doesn't give in, Scooter jumps back three giant steps. She winds up and throws the rock and hits both cans dead-on. Cans and rock careen into the engine compartment, from which a scrawny cat erupts in surprise. The cat leaps from the car fender onto the ground. A stray dog gives chase, baying as it runs. Scooter senses the game is on and grabs the fallen beer cans, beating them together like cymbals to add to the chaos.

From inside the house, Janie calls out, "Hanson? Are you watching Scooter?" There's a pause and then Janie adds. "Hayley, can you go outside and see what's going on. Please."

Hayley appears in the doorway and shades her eyes with one hand, looking out through the screen door. Hanson sees her out of the corner of one eye and tips forward, grabbing a beer can and tossing it towards the screen door. "Monsters are on the loose in the yard, Honey. Only you can stop 'em."

Hayley's face lights up. "It's okay, Daddy. I'll protect you!" She blasts through the door and quickly stoops to grab two beer cans. She quickly stomps them under her shoes and then rapidly clomps across the yard towards Scooter.

"Wait for me, Scooter. Wait for me."

The dog chases the cat up an old tree stump. Scooter and Hayley both clang beer cans together, making tin-stomping noises with their feet. The din is deafening.

Hanson sits unperturbed—grinning. He continues wrapping the wire into shape around the burnished beer can. Slowly the figure of a running horse is emerging.

A flash of sunlight on chrome catches Hanson's eye. A sleek, powder-blue 55 Fleetwood eases into the driveway next door. Its tires crunch on the gravel. High-pitched screams jerk Hanson's attention back to his own yard, as Scooter chases Hayley around their old car. "Scooter, be careful...Don't go too crazy now."

Hansen sets aside his work, stands and saunters across the yard to stand next to the Caddy, which has come to a stop. He grasps the rear door handle and swings the door open to pull a folded wheelchair from the back seat.

"Whoa, Oren, did you just get a new car?"

Oren Harris, their nearest neighbor, is broad-shouldered and once-upon-a-time handsome. Oren pulls the wheelchair close and slides himself into the seat. His spindly, lifeless legs follow.

"New to me, Hanson. Had some modifications made

after I bought it. Just picked it up. Drives like a dream."

Hanson uses his free hand to stroke the paint job as he closes the driver's door for Oren. The neighbor looks up from the wheelchair, nodding his head in thanks.

"One of the guys from the oil rig sold it to me." Oren wheels his chair forward a bit and Hanson steps up to walk with him. "God, oil riggin' was the life, Hanson. You should try it!"

Oren propels his chair up to the sidewalk that leads to his trailer. "More money than you can shake a stick at." Oren sighs. "And all the stuff that goes with it. High-stakes poker, high-stakes car racing. And unless you killed someone, the cops always looked the other way."

Oren turns his wheelchair back to Hanson for a moment. "I was going to add and lots of loose women, all of 'em ready to help you spend every penny." He pauses a moment. "I guess as a family man that's not much incentive though."

Hanson considers Oren thoughtfully as he reaches over to assist him up onto the ramp to his house.

"I was damn luckier than most, I guess," Oren continues. "Buggered my legs on the rig. But I found a good lawyer and the company shelled out handsomely rather than face a lawsuit."

At the top of the ramp, Oren looks down at Hanson thoughtfully. "I think my new Caddy will almost even the score. It's almost as good a magnet for the gals as two good legs."

Oren's smile is oily. "To be well-off in a poor town is no small advantage, Mr. Wells. I still have me some fun."

Hanson wipes his hands together to rid himself of the road dust from the car. "Hey Oren, how 'bout I pop over and hose down your new ride after dinner tonight? A pretty thing like this shouldn't be wearing a coat of dust, eh?"

Oren gives Hanson an appraising look. "That's downright neighborly of you, Mr. Wells."

Hanson grins his little boy grin. "Sure 'nuff. What are neighbors for? 'Course we could let the girls play in the hose too. Cool 'em down before bedtime, right?"

"Bring your girls over whenever you like then." Oren turns and opens the door to his trailer, whistling a little tune as he does.

Hanson returns to the porch and gathers up the leather apron and his work. He whistles to get his daughters' attention. "C'mon girls. Time to go inside and clean up for dinner."

Hanson steps over to the screen door and waves the girls inside, hurrying them along. He calls out loudly, "You wash your hands and your face, Scooter. Don't you just pretend."

Back in the kitchen, a heat-disheveled Janie places a tray of egg salad sandwiches in the center of the table before sitting down. Hayley brings over glasses of Kool-Aid and passes them around. Scooter jumps up and pulls a cold beer out of the fridge and hands it to Hanson.

They eat in silence for a long moment and then Hanson leans over and kisses Janie on the cheek. "These are great, Honey."

Janie smiles instantly. Hanson continues. "You know, I'll bet old Oren would love a couple for his dinner too."

Janie's smile loses some of its glow. "Hanson, I was housecleaning all morning at the Craigmiers' to earn these eggs!"

"C'mon, Honey, why not?" Hanson smiles his most winning smile. "He invited the girls over to play in his yard after dinner, to cool off with the hose."

Hanson pushes his chair back and takes his plate and empty beer can to the sink. "I thought maybe I'd run a rag over his car while the girls tear around a bit. A couple of sandwiches would be...neighborly. Give the guy a break. He lost his legs on the drilling rig and there ain't anyone to do for him nowadays."

Hanson turns to the girls. "You kids want to go, don't ya?"

• • •

In no time, the sun is sinking in the west. Hayley and Scooter are screaming around their yard and Oren's too, throwing cups of water at each other and creating a din. Hanson has a bucket at his feet and uses a rag to gently apply soapy water to the front grill of the Cadillac. He whistles a little tune as he does it.

The screen door opens and Oren rolls out onto his porch,

smiling at the chaos. Mavis, a chubby young girl about Scooter's age, slips out behind him and hovers nearby.

Oren is avidly watching the girls play. He's forgotten Mavis. "Evening, Hanson."

Hanson looks up, smiling. At the same time Scooter and Hayley stop mid-scream to register Oren on the porch and the silent Mavis waiting tentatively behind him. A long moment passes, and then Hanson replies with a bit too much gusto.

"Hey Oren, the girls are having a great time, thanks for having us over." He lifts the plate of sandwiches off the roof. "Scooter, come take these to Oren."

Scooter turns and scowls at Hanson. "Dad-dy... we're playing."

Hanson cocks his head meaningfully at Scooter. "Now, Scooter. "

Scooter stomps over to her father, grabs the plate from his hand and nearly loses a sandwich in the process.

"Scooter, mind yourself. You drop a single one of those and I'll tan your hide."

Scooter doesn't even glance at Hanson. She trudges up the ramp and thrusts the plate towards the grinning Oren.

As he takes it from her, Scooter locks eyes with Mavis for a moment before Mavis looks away. Scooter whispers, "You want to come play with us a while?"

Oren reaches over and pats Mavis on the upper thigh and shakes his head. "That's very sweet of you, Scooter, but Mavis was just heading back home to her mom. Weren't you, Mavis?"

Mavis sidesteps away from Oren and then turns and runs down the ramp towards home.

"You girls are welcome to play in the yard anytime you want, Scooter." Oren's smile makes Scooter squirm. "You know that, right?"

By now, Scooter is backing away. Oren watches every step she takes.

"That's mighty nice of you, Oren," Hanson says. "Scooter, don't you think that's nice?"

Scooter walks rapidly towards her own house. In answer to Hanson's question, she turns and spits on the ground between herself and Hanson. Then she quickly runs up the stairs and inside, away from Oren's gaze.

• • •

Later that night, Janie is lying on her side nearly asleep when Hanson rolls over towards her and snuggles against her back. He thrusts his hips against her provocatively.

When Janie doesn't respond, he whispers, "You can't possibly be asleep yet, Janie. Let's have a bit of fun."

"I *can* possibly be asleep. And NO, I don't want to have a bit of fun."

"Aww, c'mon Honey. Help a horny old man out."

Janie uses her free hand to slap at Hanson and then

push him away. "Go away. I have to be at Mrs. Craigmiers' again tomorrow right after breakfast."

"Now what're you doing over there?"

"She wants help emptying out her attic. They want to turn it into a spare room for the field hand they're gonna hire."

"Janie, I don't like that you're away from home so much."

Janie snorts. "Shit, somebody's gotta have steady work, Hanson." She pauses a minute. "Hey, do you want to apply for the job at the Criagmiers'?

"Hell no. I'd don't want to live anywhere else but with you and the girls."

"Don't be daft, Hanson, of course you'd still live here. I'm just thinking that it would be steady work for you."

There's a protracted silence. "Shoot, I got work, Janie. The beginning of next week with my brother Bob. I just forgot to tell ya."

Janie hoists herself up on one elbow and turns to scrutinize Hanson. "Really? That's great, Honey." She reaches out and cups Hanson's cheek with her hand. "Why didn't you say?"

"I wanted to be sure of it first." He flops on his back, resigned to employment. "The Mitchells are putting in another bathroom upstairs," Hanson sighs. "And the Stevens are finally getting rid of their outhouse." His voice is thick with remorse. "At this rate, I'll have work for decades."

Janie rolls over onto Hanson and kisses his chin, then his cheek and his mouth. "My man…" Janie hesitates and then continues, "I have something I've been meaning to tell you too." She rests her chin on Hanson's chest. "I think I'm pregnant again, Hanson."

"Whaaat!? Are you sure?"

Any further discussion is cut off by a protracted whimper from the living room where the girls sleep on the sofa bed. One of them is definitely troubled. Hanson sits up and peers through the dim moonlit interior of the house. He can see the two huddled forms on the sofa, and then the soft whimpering breath again.

Hanson throws his feet over the side of the bed and pads towards the living room silently, hitching up his boxer shorts as he goes. In the dim light he watches one of the girls roll over and sit up holding her head in her hands, moaning. As Hanson squats down beside the sofa he notices tears on Scooter's cheeks.

He leans over and kisses her bare knee. "Hey, hey Scooter-MacDooter. What's wrong?"

Scooter whimpers again as Hanson eases himself onto the sofa next to her. "You have a bad dream, Honey?" He pulls Scooter onto his lap and then awkwardly stands up again. "Must be pretty awful to make a big girl like you cry."

Scooter immediately slips her legs around Hanson's waist and lays her head on his shoulder. "It's my ear, Daddy. It hurts somethin' awful." She begins crying softly.

Hanson wraps his arms around Scooter and carries her to the kitchen. "Don't you worry, pussycat. Daddy can fix a silly ole earache." He paces around the kitchen. "Did you see where I left my smokes, Scoot?"

Scooter shakes her head 'no' and then cries out again in pain.

Hanson pats her back softly. "Sshh. Sshh, now we don't want to wake your sister."

After searching on all the counters, he discovers his cigarettes on top of the fridge. "First things first, Honey." Hanson pauses to light a cigarette, then takes a deep drag. "Ahh, that's the ticket." He begins slowly pacing the length of the kitchen.

He reaches up and turns Scooter's ear towards his mouth. "Is this the one?"

Scooter immediately covers her ear with her hand. "Don't touch it."

Hanson takes another drag on his cigarette, then places his lips over Scooter's fingers and blows smoke into it gently. He whispers, "Don't worry none, Honey. I won't touch it. You don't even have to move your hand for this medicine to work."

Hanson takes another puff and exhales into Scooter's ear. "Really, Daddy?"

"I promise." Hanson blows more smoke into Scooter's ear. "Ya know the Indians used tobacco as medicine all the time. It was them who taught the white man how important it was, so we started growing it for our-selves, eh."

Scooter moves her hand a tiny bit and Hanson blows more smoke into her ear. He begins to sing softly as he walks. *As I was out walkin' one morning for pleasure. I spied a young cowgirl, a ridin' along.*

Hanson circles the kitchen slowly. *Her hat was thrown back, and her spurs were a jinglin', and as she approached, she was singin' this song.*

Scooter lays her head on Hanson's shoulder, relaxing. Sounding very sleepy, she murmurs, "It doesn't go like that, Daddy. It's a cowboy in the song."

Hanson makes soothing noises. "Sshh, sshh, Honey. This is the *real* version, Scoot. Learned to me by an old cow-girl who said she taught every single cowboy how to ride."

Hanson continues rocking Scooter as he walks and sings more and more softly. *Yippi-yi, ki-yay, get along little doggies. You know that Wyoming will be your new home.*

Hanson enters the living room, carrying Scooter towards the sofa. "I grinned at that cowgirl as she was a passin', to ask if Wyoming is where she would stay?"

Hanson bends down slowly and lowers the sleeping Scooter to the bed. "Her eyes gleamed like campfires, her laughter like morning."

He finishes singing as he pulls a sheet up over Scooter's shoulder. *Ain't no place can hold me for more than a day.*

FOUR

The next morning, Hanson kisses Janie goodbye and then stands and waves as she trudges down the road to work. He's about to go indoors when he's brought up short by a comment from the deep shadows on the porch of the trailer. The tip of Oren's cigarette glows as he lifts it from his lips. "Why, she's almost a child herself, Wells."

Hanson turns and peers across the yard. He can just make out the pale gray smoke as Oren exhales in the shadows. The morning sun gilds the Fleetwood in Oren's driveway. "What's that you're sayin', Oren?"

"Nothing really. Just sayin' your Janie seems very young for a mother of two.

"Soon to be three, and she's not even thirty yet."

"Well, congratulations. I always say the more the merrier." Oren picks at something on his pants and then adds, as if an afterthought. "You're welcome to use my car to pick up the missus after work today." Oren stubs out his cigarette on the porch rail and tosses it into the river rock below. "I can keep an eye on the kiddies for you, if you like."

Hanson beams across at Oren. "Why thank you, Oren. I think a ride home would really tickle Janie pink." Hanson opens the screen door with a jaunty smile. "I'll drop by around four then."

Hanson stops at the bookshelf just inside the door and adjusts the silver-wire horse sculpture a fraction of an inch. He shouts, "Alright you dust bunnies…if you're not busy washing those mornin' dishes there'll be hell to pay, girls."

. . .

Promptly at four, Oren rolls his wheelchair through his screen door just as Hanson appears, herding his daughters across the dirt-packed yard towards the trailer. Long shadows stretch across the driveway.

Hanson deftly catches the keyset Oren tosses to him. "Alright girls, Oren is looking after you till I get back from picking up Mom."

Hanson tosses off a mock salute to Oren. "Thanks again, Oren. This is awfully neighborly of you."

Oren rolls his wheelchair into the shade. "It's nothing, Mr. Wells." He picks up a folding table and neatly flicks it open. "You know I actually like kids. I've got all kinds of games to entertain them here."

Hanson strides towards the car, clearly excited. Just before he opens the door he stops. "We'll see if you still like 'em by the time I get back." He turns and says, "Scooter, get over here. I wanna talk to you."

Scooter half turns, a scowl on her face. She marches across the yard to Hanson and stands facing him, hands on her hips. He opens the passenger door for her. "Get in a minute."

Scooter races around the car and dives inside.

Hanson gets in the driver's seat and turns to face Scooter. He slides his fingers along the walnut steering wheel, thinking. "This here is real walnut wood, ya know?" He looks her directly in the eyes. "Not plastic, or rubber. In fact, there's not a bit of cheesy, cheap stuff in this entire car."

Scooter angles her head at him. "Nothing cheesy, 'cept us, that is," she huffs. "Is this why you wanted to talk to me?"

"Scoot, your smart mouth will be your downfall someday." He lights a cigarette.

"What I'm trying to point out is the idea that there are good things in life that have passed us by, Scooter Wells."

Scooter is flipping switches, turning the radio on and off and trying out the electric windows. She starts poking the button on the glovebox.

"Scoot, stop yer damn fiddling around and pay attention." Hanson's voice rises in exasperation. "Opportunities for the likes of us don't come around very often. So, I'm warning you fair and square, Scooter, be nice while Oren's looking after you."

"Define nice, Daddy."

"This is exactly why I wanted to talk." Hanson stubs out his cigarette, irritated as hell. "Nice is…dammit, I don't know. Follow Hayley's lead. She always knows the polite thing to say or do."

Scooter is only partially listening as Hanson drones on. She pokes at the glovebox one more time and the lid pops open.

"We have the makings of a great opportunity here. I mean, this could be the little

springboard we've been looking for in life. So, don't piss him off, alright."

Scooter nods her head but slips her hand inside the glovebox to explore. She pulls out a map, a cigarette lighter. And then her eyes go wide as she turns to her dad.

Hanson's cracking his knuckles with tension as he talks. "With a bit of help from Oren, we could be on our way. He knows people, people who know other people." Hanson suddenly tunes into Scooter's expression. "Are you even listening, Scooter?"

"Jesus, Daddy, Oren's got a gun." Scooter indicates the interior of the glove box.

Hanson leans over and peers into the murky interior of the glovebox. He sees the snub-nosed revolver that Scooter's touching. "PUT THAT THING DOWN,

SCOOTER." Hanson leans over and snaps the lid to the glove box closed. "You best forget you ever saw that. I'll do my best to forget it too."

He reaches past her and pushes open the passenger door. "Okay, now go on and behave yourself." He pulls the door closed. "Just follow Hayley's lead. And not a word to Janie about that gun either. You hear?"

"I'm not an idiot, Daddy. And I'll let Hayley do ALL the talking." Scooter flounces away from the car. "I promise."

Hanson turns the key in the engine, and his face lights up as the engine roars to life. He carefully backs the car down the driveway and heads towards the highway.

Scooter tramps to the rocking chair on her own porch. She proceeds to seat herself where Oren can see her but turns the rocker so all he can see is her back. She begins rocking back and forth with a vengeance. She pulls a small ball out of her pocket and bounces it against the porch wall, focusing all her attention on the ball. She doesn't even glance at Oren.

Oren shoots a grim smile in her direction as he sets out a checkerboard on the little folding table for himself and Hayley. He watches Scooter rock and toss, rock and toss the ball to catch it and throw it over and over again.

• • •

Hanson has all the windows down, and his elbow rests on the driver's door, cigarette dangling between his fingers.

He guides the Fleetwood slowly beneath an archway over a farm gate that announces 'Craigmiers' Eggs.'

Janie is standing on the house porch. She raises her hand to shade her eyes as she peers at the car.

Hanson leans out the window. "Surprise, Honey!"

Janie comes down the steps and peers anxiously into the car. "Hanson, where are the girls?"

"Oren offered me the car to pick you up. Thought you might be tired. He said they could play in the yard and he'd keep an eye on 'em."

"He really just up and offered?"

"Ya, once I told him you were pregnant again. He said we'd have to take special care of you. That I should look for ways to give you a break from all the everyday stuff you do." Hanson was beaming. "Told me to drive you home in style."

"So, they're really just playing in his yard till we get home?"

"Yes ma'am. Oren is totally into it."

Janie suddenly turns and runs back towards the Craigmiers' house. "Great. Wait here a minute." She disappears inside and returns minutes later carrying two awkwardly stuffed pillowcases, one in each hand. She trudges back to the car and drops them on the rear seat. Then she lowers herself into the front seat with a deep sigh of exhaustion. As she closes the car door, she whips off the scarf that holds her hair back.

Hanson uses the rearview mirror to assess the two

pillowcases. "What gives? What is that stuff?" He puts the car in reverse and heads out to the road.

"Something for the girls. They're always looking for something to read and the Craigmiers had an old set of encyclopedias they didn't want." Janie sighs with pleasure as she tips her head back against the seat. "I grabbed them, thinking it would keep them busy for a while."

Hanson chews his lip a moment. "Janie, I don't like to be seen as being in need of people's castoffs."

Janie turns to examine Hanson's profile for a long moment, an expression of disbelief on her face. "You'll drive around in a borrowed car cuz we haven't the money to fix ours. But you draw the line at books for our kids?"

"Well, I'm just sayin' it looks bad. The car was just a favor for a favor, if you know what I mean." He turns and scowls at Janie. "It wasn't charity."

Janie studies Hanson for a long moment. "Okay, I'll tell the girls we just borrowed them. And we'll just forget to give them back." Janie moves to place her sweaty hair near the open window. She closes her eyes and relaxes into the breeze.

"I can't believe you told Oren I was pregnant again. I don't know if I'm comfortable with that, Hanson."

"Aw Hon, I was just being neighborly." Hanson chews his lip again. "I think he must get kind of lonely in that big old double-wide all by himself. Ya know, he used to be quite the lady's man, back in the day. Had all kinds of gals hanging off of him, he says."

"Oren? A lady's man?"

Hanson looks over at Janie and laughs. "Well, I could kinda see it. He was brawny and liked to have fun and had tons of money and didn't mind spending it on folks."

"Hanson, are you aware that most women do not consider the term *lady's man*

complimentary? At all…"

"Aw, come on, Honey, give a guy a break."

Janie sits up in the seat as Hanson slows down in anticipation of their turnoff. "I'll grant you Oren may deserve some slack. But you better mind your Ps and Qs, mister. We're gonna have another mouth to feed soon enough."

Hanson turns onto the dirt road and slides the Fleetwood into park in Oren's driveway. He leans over and pecks Janie on the cheek. "I'm all over it, Honey. Don't you worry."

Distracted, Janie looks around wildly, sees neither of the girls and leaps from the car.

Oren opens the trailer door and wheels out to the porch. "Don't you worry, Mrs. Wells. The girls are just fine, they just went to your house for a snack."

While Oren's attention is on Janie, the screen door behind him opens and Mavis slips quietly onto the porch beside him. Oren reaches out a hand and catches her wrist to hold her in place. "Mavis here just brought me over some dinner. Didn't you, Mavis? Here's the dollar I promised you, Honey."

Mavis' eyes are huge as she stares across the yard at Janie. She drops her eyes, unable to meet Janie's gaze. Mavis quickly slips the money into her shorts pocket.

Janie opens her mouth to say hello, but Hanson quickly tosses the car keys to Oren and preempts the moment. "Thanks again for the car, Oren. Janie really appreciated the lift home. Didn't you, Honey?"

Distracted, Janie turns her attention back to Oren. "What? Oh yes, thank you, Oren. Much appreciated."

Hanson grabs the pillowcases from the back seat and then loops Janie's arm through his and leads her towards their house. "Come along, Janie, dinner's already made. All you'll have to do is put your feet up."

Janie catches sight of Mavis disappearing around the corner of the trailer. Then sees Hanson shove the books behind their sofa.

He looks up, catching Janie watching. "Let's just tuck these away, for now. No sense getting the girls all excited before dinner." Janie frowns, but then lets the moment go.

FIVE

Next morning, Janie bustles into the bedroom, fully clothed. She approaches the bed where Hanson is still snoring fitfully and jiggles his feet at the end of the bed. "Hanson, rise and shine. It's only an hour until Bob gets here to pick you up."

"Wha…What Honey?"

"Work, Hanson. Bob. One hour. Coffee's on the stove, mister."

Hanson grudgingly sits up in bed and moans. "Aw shit. Why does work have to start so early?" He swings his legs over the bed and pulls on a pair of bib coveralls. Leaves the tops hanging down, he shuffles towards the kitchen.

Janie's at the stove frying eggs. The table is set for one. "I'm letting the kids sleep in. Thought it'd be easier for you to get out of the house without their nonsense," she whispers.

Hanson takes the cup of coffee she pours for him. "You are a princess, Honey."

She slips an arm around his waist and lays her head on his shoulder. "I don't remember the fairytale where the princess gets up at dawn to fry eggs for her man."

She grins up at him. "What was that one called again?"

Hanson huffs as he disentangles himself and pads to the table. "Any of 'em—the day after the happily ever after part."

Janie pours her own cup of coffee. "Too right."

Hanson shovels down the eggs and bacon. He turns to pinch Janie gently on the hip. "You just remember who your Prince Charming is, missus." He stands up and takes the coffee cup with him.

Janie and Hanson tiptoe past the sleeping girls and ease themselves out the porch door. They take a moment to simply stand together companionably. Hanson gives Janie a peck on the cheek. "Likely I'll be back by dinnertime, hungry and mean, Honey."

Moments later, a white panel van kicks up a cloud of dust as it trundles down the dirt driveway. Hanson's older brother Bob is a balding, slightly older version of him.

Bob leans out the driver's window and calls jovially, "Good Lord, baby brother, is that you all clean and shiny and ready for work? Early?"

Hanson ignores Bob and saunters around the front of the van and lets himself into the cab, placing his cup on the dashboard.

Janie calls from the porch. "Bob, you have my permission to work his tush off today. He went and got me pregnant again. I'm counting on you to make him pay for his sins."

Bob laughs out loud and punches Hanson on the shoulder. "You dirty old hound dog, Hanson. Congratulations."

Hanson takes a final sip of coffee and tosses the rest out the window. "C'mon, Bob, leave off. Get the lead out and let's get going." Hanson immediately slumps down in the seat as Bob starts the engine and drives away.

Oblivious to Hanson's reaction, Janie calls after them. "Have fun, guys. See you later."

After watching until the truck disappears in a cloud of dust, Janie goes back into the kitchen. She runs a finger along the windowsill, examines the track it leaves through the thick dust, and shakes her head. She finds the same fine residue atop the fridge. She crosses back to the sink and slams the window shut.

Hayley shuffles into the room rubbing her eyes. "Where's Daddy, Mama?"

Janie scowls as she fills a wash bucket from the faucet. "Off making our fortunes." She turns and notices Hayley's puzzled expression. "He's working with Uncle Bob for the next little bit. Remember?"

"He didn't say goodbye."

Janie turns towards Hayley, pure exasperation on her face. But when she notices Hayley's woebegone look, Janie softens. "He wanted to kiss you goodbye but I told him to let you sleep a bit longer."

Janie pushes to brighten her approach. "We'll see him tonight though. Want to help me plan a special dinner?"

Hayley merely shrugs.

Janie tries again. "C'mon. Let's surprise him. What should we make?"

Hayley's face brightens. "We could make cupcakes. We never make cupcakes, Mom. Please?"

Janie looks out at the unremitting sunshine, the dust devils in the distance and the dust covering the window-sill. She wipes her brow, already beading with sweat, and empties the bucket into the sink in surrender.

"Sure, why not, Honey." She puts the bucket back under the sink unused. "It's going to be hot as Hades again though. So, let's make them first and get a jump on the heat."

Hayley's answering smile is incandescent. "I'll help with breakfast. Should I put out the cornflakes?"

Janie turns to the cupboards and starts pulling out bowls and flour sifters and measuring cups. "Yes, Honey. And let's have toast and peanut butter too, I think."

Hayley opens the ancient fridge and reaches for the milk bottle and sets it on the table.

• • •

Andy is fiftyish and has been bartender at the Town Tavern since anyone can remember. He's paunchy and has a ready smile but also an electric cattle prod handy behind the bar. He grabs two beers from the fridge, snaps the caps off and sets them on the bar in front of two customers.

Nearby, Hanson is seated at a table, working through another beer. Empty glasses litter the tabletop. Bob strolls back into the room, zipping himself up.

"I'm heading home. You shouldn't stay much longer either, little brother."

Hanson sits back in the chair. "I'm just finishing up too. I'll roll along soon enough."

Bob stands a long moment, hoping Hanson will leave with him. Hanson doesn't move a muscle. Bob steps away from the table. "Right then. I'll pick you up again tomorrow at 6. On the dot."

"On the dot it is. I'll see your dot and raise you two dots, Bobbie." Hanson laughs at his own joke.

Bob heads for the door. "Right. See ya tomorrow."

Hanson swigs more beer, settling in.

• • •

Janie looks up at the wall clock, opens the oven and fans the heat away. She pokes the chicken with a fork and closes the heavy oven door again. She stands a long moment, hands on hips, considering.

"Scooter?" she calls. When there's no answer, she shouts. "Scooooo-TER!" Janie can hear the thunder of running feet, so she waits. Scooter skids to a stop in the kitchen doorway. "Yeah Mama?"

"Honey, I want you to trot into town and look for Bob's white van. It's likely outside Andy's Town Tavern.

Janie turns to start peeling potatoes at the cutting board. She turns back and skewers Scooter with a look. "You tell Hanson to get his skinny ass home, or this'll be the last dinner I make for him. Ever!"

Scooter turns and salutes. "Skinny ass...last dinner ever. Gottcha, Mom."

Scooter tears out of the kitchen and zips through the living room towards the front door. She comes to an abrupt stop and backtracks. She picks up a book and grabs a canvas bag off the coat hook. She hesitates a moment longer, eyeing the wire horse Hanson had created and placed on the bookshelf.

Scooter fiddles with the halter on the horse's head, slipping it on and off, on and off. She's very fast. Then, with the horse in hand and the bag over her shoulder, she blasts through the screen door.

She trots along the road, silver pony in hand. She holds it out, making it trot alongside her in the air. In the distance she spots Uncle Bob's white van coming towards her. It slows as it approaches, and Bob leans out the window.

"I was hoping Janie would send one of you. Otherwise, you know he'll sit there all night."

"I'm on it, Uncle Bob. Me and my pony will drag his skinny ass kicking and screaming back to the house."

Bob busts out a laugh and shakes his head. "He's at Andy's, of course. You go get him, Honey!"

Scooter watches the van for a moment, then turns her horse and trots it into town. The sign for the tavern looms ahead, and Scooter doesn't hesitate. She barges through the door. No one in the tavern even blinks an eye.

Scooter immediately spots Hanson at the back of the bar. She walks over and sits down in a chair on one side of him. She starts playing with the horse, slipping the bridle on and off, on and off.

Hanson opens his eyes and looks sidelong at Scooter. He raises his nearly empty glass, signaling Andy that he's ready for another round. Andy grabs a bar towel and bustles over, all business-like as he approaches the table.

"'Fraid you're gonna have to ante up before I can serve you another, Hanson."

Hanson's eyes rest on Scooter momentarily. She watches as he lifts his eyebrows at her and then drains his glass.

Hanson sets the empty glass down very deliberately. Scooter's eyes return to her horse puzzle, but there's a tension about her movements now that wasn't there before.

"Sure enough. What do I owe you, Andy?"

"Well, there's the beer and the pretzels."

Hanson raises one eyebrow, already questioning the tally.

"I said the FIRST bowl was on the house," Andy blusters. "You and Bob must've had three and now your kid's here."

Hanson scowls at Scooter. "She is a noted piggy."

Scooter just keeps working the toy.

"All told, I'd say you owe me ten bucks."

Hanson pushes the nearest glass away, trying to distance himself from the problem. "Holy smokes. You gotta be kiddin' me."

"C'mon buddy." Andy points to the evidence littering the table in front of them.

"No, no I'm not disputing what you're saying, Andy," Hanson mutters. "I'm just thinking I may as well go jump off a bridge now, as go home after this." He buries his head in his hands. "My wife, Janie, is going to kill me."

Scooter looks up briefly from her toy, giving Hanson an inscrutable look. Hanson notes it and uses it.

"See! Even my kid thinks I'm toast. Man, I am so busted if I go home broke."

Andy is not even close to being swayed. "The bill is what it is." Scooter's intensity of focus on the horse puzzle distracts Andy a minute. "Hey, what 'cha got there, kiddo?"

Scooter turns ever so slightly away, as if trying to hide the toy she's been playing with. The bartender bites. "Aw come on, lemme see that."

Scooter turns away just the tiniest bit more, hiding the toy with her body. Hanson makes a big show of pulling her back around to face Andy. "Oh that. It's just a little something I made for her to play with." Hanson takes the toy and offers it to Andy to inspect.

Andy wipes his hands on his bar towel before taking the object in hand. "You made this?"

"Yeah, from an old beer can. It's a kind of puzzle. To keep her busy and outa trouble."

"How's it work? Is it hard?"

"How hard can it be? My kid can do it. Go on, show him how, Scooter."

Scooter's eyes slide briefly from the tabletop up to her father's face—inscrutable. She lifts her eyes to the bartender's and grins a kind of goofy kid grin and holds out one hand. "It's easy. I'll show you." Scooter takes the puzzle back from the guy and sets it on the table. "See? Bridled." Then she slides the tiny silver slipknot, covering her motion with her other hand. "Voilà, unbridled."

The bartender reaches out to take the little horse. "Lemme try." Scooter quickly slips the bridle back in place. "Sure, try it. It's simple. Anyone could do it."

The bartender holds the toy directly beneath the overhead light near the table. "Yeah, I see how you did it now."

Scooter licks her lips a second time and half croaks, "Do ya wanna bet?"

Andy is deeply absorbed; he only half looks up from the toy.

"I dunno know. What d'ya wanna bet?"

Silence hangs in the nearly empty tavern. "How 'bout my daddy's bar tab? Solve it in the time it takes him to finish his beer."

The bartender swings his head around and skewers Scooter with a look only seconds before Hanson leaps in, cuffing Scooter on the head.

"Don't you pay her any mind, Andy. She's a mite over-protective of her daddy, is all."

"No, I'm not, Daddy."

Scooter shoots Hanson a quick look of apprehension, then folds her hands on the tabletop in front of her. "I just wanna see if this guy's actually smarter than a ten-year-old kid."

Long shadows precede Hanson and Scooter as they wend their way home. Hanson slips his arm around Scooter's shoulders. "I nearly had heart failure when you told Andy you wanted to see if he was smarter than a ten-year-old. You shoulda seen his face, Scoot."

"You shoulda seen yours! And then the two others who just had to try it too. Woo-hoo. Lucky they were all half cut."

Hanson pulls a wad of bills out of his pocket and fans one out for Scooter to take. "Go ahead, you earned it." They walk a couple of steps together. "Do NOT tell your mother where this cash came from, Scooter."

Scooter snorts in disbelief. "I am not stupid, Daddy."

"True enough." He pauses and then adds, "Just ugly as a new puppy." He bends and kisses the top of her head.

• • •

Scooter and Hanson walk together up the three wooden steps to the porch of their house. The smell of roast chicken and baking greets them through the screen door.

Hanson pushes the door open and they slip inside. He calls out loudly, "Someone's been busy making nice things for her man." He crosses the living room, lowering his voice. "Hey Janie, I'm home." He's met by silence.

Scooter lags behind in the living room as Hanson strides towards the kitchen. A silhouette appears in the kitchen doorway; it's Janie.

"Lordy woman, something smells good." Hanson reaches out, apparently oblivious to Janie's signals. He opens his arms for an embrace. "Ahh, there's my girl."

Janie crosses her arms over her chest and holds her ground a long minute, staring at Hanson. Then she backs away. Hayley joins her in the doorway.

Hanson smiles at the two of them. Still jovial, he gushes, "My girls, my very best girls. Come on. We got some dinner to eat." He rubs his hands together in anticipation. "It sure smells like you two have been busy."

Janie pushes at Hanson to get some distance from him. "Hanson, I am going crazy in this place." She takes another step away from him. "We boil all summer it's so damn hot, and then freeze all winter." Janie lets out a shaky breath. "The wind blows all the fuckin time." She turns away, starting to tear up. Her voice cracks. "I just can't stand this hellhole anymore. I have to get out of here."

Hanson is taken aback by the intensity of Janie's tirade. Again, he tries to take her in his arms. She bats him away again.

"Don't! It is too fucking hot. It's too fuckin hot to cook, too. But Hayley and I

spent the day cooking for you even though it was hot as blue blazes." She pokes him in the chest with her finger. "And now it's ruined cuz you were off pissin' around."

"Now Honey…"

Janie can't help herself; she starts to cry. Hanson approaches her and puts his hands on her shoulders, which are shaking with the intensity of her emotions.

"I've had enough. I can't stand this place any-more, Hanson."

"Sweetheart, I totally understand." Hanson continues to rub her back and as her stance softens, he wraps his arms around her from behind. "We're in a tough place right now and you're feeling especially sensitive to well… just about everything."

Janie pushes his hands away and turns to scowl at him. "Don't you dare start blaming everything on my *condition*—or I'll give you a condition of your own to complain about."

"No, no, Honey. I'm not saying that; but moving won't be easy." Hanson holds up his hands, signalling peace. "We're a growing family, and we don't own a car right now that is reliable." He shrugs theatrically. "What are we going to do, Janie? Walk?"

The girls' eyes swivel back to Janie, who seems at a loss for words. Tears well up in her eyes again, but this time do not fall. Clearly sensing their mother's distress, the girls' gaze swings back towards Hanson. He makes a face and shrugs again, as if to say, *What am I supposed to do?* He reaches deep into his pockets and pulls out all the cash he's won and offers it to Janie. "Look, I've already been saving up bits and bobs trying to get us ahead, Janie."

Janie takes the money from his hands, and Hanson puts his arms around her again. "Change is afoot, Honey. But we're going to have to work for it, all of us. Together." Hanson turns Janie slightly and looks at the girls. "Right girls?"

Hayley and Scooter nod their heads avidly—keen to avert more crying.

"With luck, we'll be gone before the first snow flies," Hanson continues. Janie clutches the money and wraps her arms around Hanson. He murmurs into her hair, "I promise Honey."

Janie wipes her face with her hands and stuffs the money into her apron pockets. "I didn't know you were saving for us, Hanson. Thank you."

Hanson levels a very pointed look at Scooter, then grins at Janie. "You bettcha. Now, who wants to eat?" Hanson escorts Janie to her chair and pulls it out for her. "It smells an awful lot like roast chicken. My own personal favorite."

Hayley dances in place next to her plate. "We know, we know. We've been cooking all day. We even have cupcakes too, Dad."

Hanson lifts the platter of chicken from the oven and places it in the middle of the table. "C'mon girls, let's eat our dinner before it gets cold." Everyone sits down and waits patiently while Hanson fills their plates and hands them out.

A homey silence reigns for a long moment as they eat. Hanson moans his appreciation after the first bite. "My god, woman, this is magic. It's so good, I may never eat again." He reaches a hand across the table. "Can I have some more gravy please?"

Hayley passes the gravy to Hanson, who puddles it on his chicken, takes a bite and chews a moment. His eyes dart across the table to Janie.

"Your mother and I have some news, girls." A tiny smile flickers on Janie's face. "Pretty soon you're going to have a baby brother or sister. Definitely by this time next year."

Hanson forks another bite into his mouth and continues. "It does mean we'll all have to work extra hard in the coming months." He swallows his mouthful of food and puts a big smile on his face. "But everyone will contribute to help Mom along, right?"

Hayley squeals with excitement. "Can we have a brother? Please, please? I want a brother, Mama."

Janie laughs out loud. "We can hope for a boy, Hayley. That's about all the control we have over it."

Scooter has stopped eating as she scrutinizes Hanson from across the table. "So, that's what you meant about Janie's condition?"

Hanson meets Scooter's gaze and nods obliquely. "Nothing gets by you, Scoot." He gazes out the kitchen window for a moment, watching as the setting sun haloes Oren's Fleetwood.

"Yup, isn't it great? We can all pitch in to help, right Scoot?"

Suddenly Hanson looks down at his dinner with renewed interest and scrapes up a final bite. He takes another quick look out the window, then pushes his chair back from the table.

"That was a terrific dinner, Honey. Thank you so much!" Hanson half turns, pointedly looking over at the pots of food still left on the stovetop. "It sure looks like there's lots left, eh girls?" Silence greets his statement. "It's kind of a shame, the thought of old Oren sitting over there all on his lonesome, while we have all this. Don'cha think?" Hanson lets his gaze circumnavigate the table. His eyes stop pointedly at Scooter.

Suddenly Hanson lifts his own plate and piles more food on it with a determined vigor. He slides the heaped plate across the table towards Scooter. "Scoot, do your old dad a favor. Run this over to Oren. Tell him we were worried for him, okay?" Hanson is smiling and genial, but his eyes have that *don't give me any shit* look.

Scooter bites her lower lip, thinking. Finally, she picks up the plate, rises from her chair and pads towards the door. Hanson calls to her as she pushes open the screen door. "And Scooter, can you just wait there for him to finish and bring the plate back with you?"

When Scooter doesn't respond, Hanson adds, "You hear what I'm sayin', Scooter Wells?"

The screen door to Oren's trailer is only steps away from their back door. The Fleetwood stands sentinel at the foot of the ramp. Dish in hand, Scooter hesitates a long moment and then steps off their porch.

SIX

Suddenly Scooter feels just as she did when her father threw her off the bluff of the South Saskatchewan river. Twooosh! Scooter plummets into the river feet first and drops with a rapidity that makes her stomach churn.

The sudden impact of hitting the water sends fish scattering as Scooter plummets into the depths. Gravity drags her down, down, down. Goosebumps rise on her arms and legs.

Helpless against the sheer velocity of her fall, Scooter waits, eyes wide open. One thin arm is flung up over her head, trailing through a halo of pale blond hair. She can barely resist the urge to throw up. The moment she reaches stasis, Scooter's arms and legs begin to flail.

• • •

At the top of the wheelchair ramp, Scooter pauses and knocks tentatively on the screen doorframe. Then she knocks more loudly. The night is so quiet she can hear the whir of the wheelchair wheels on the carpeting inside as it approaches the door.

Suddenly Oren is facing her with only the door screen between them. Scooter's voice is husky with trepidation. "My dad told me to bring you some dinner." She doesn't move a muscle as Oren slides the screen door open and reaches out for the dish.

"Did he now?" Oren takes the dish from Scooter and smiles his little smile. "Your father's a good man."

• • •

The next day, the living room is a disaster: dolls, sheets, blankets, pillows are everywhere as the girls do whatever they can think of to amuse themselves while it rains.

"Hey, you can't take that. I'm using it for my fort."

"Mom says you have to learn to share, Scooter."

Hayley grabs the pillow that is the perimeter wall to Scooter's fort. Scooter lunges for the corner of the pillow and grabs it. She tugs hard and pulls Hayley to her knees.

"M-O-M. Scooter's being nasty again."

Hayley tugs hard at her corner of the pillow and nearly hauls it free.

Janie shouts from the bedroom. "Scooter, you play nice."

Hayley cuts Scooter a *na-na, na-na-na* look. Scooter hauls hard on the pillow and the second Hayley is close enough, she doubles up her fist and clocks Hayley one in the stomach.

"Na, na, na to you too."

Hayley's mouth makes a little O of surprise and then she immediately begins bawling. When it becomes obvious no help is forthcoming from the bedroom, Hayley ups the ante and cries more loudly. Scooter plows ahead and finishes building her fort.

Hayley takes off her shoe and throws it at Scooter and misses. It's a near miss, though, and Scooter lets out a loud shout of her own.

A crash of thunder explodes from the storm outside and a burst of furious shouting echoes from the bedroom. "Girls, will you please just SHUT UP."

The bedroom door slams open, and Janie appears in the doorway, pastel blue taffeta draped over one arm and an array of straight pins in her mouth. "For chrissakes, both of you! I can't even hear myself think." The girls are shocked into immediate silence; even the rain seems to abate for an instant.

"I am trying to get these dresses made." Janie pulls the pins from her mouth. "Can't the two of you play together for fifteen minutes without my having to act as referee?"

"Scooter hit me."

"Mom. Really, you know me," Scooter pleads. "I don't just clobber people for no reason. She was stealing. She was in my face."

"She HIT ME, Mama!"

Janie sighs and looks from one girl to the other.

"Hayley tried hit me with her shoe. She coulda killed me, Mom."

Janie places her hands on her hips and studies them both for a long moment. "Are either of you actually hurt?" Both girls shrug in unison.

"Just what I thought." Janie suddenly remembers the drape of taffeta over her arm. As she turns back into the bedroom, the taffeta rustles behind her. "Scooter! Get your ass in here and let me measure you. That should keep you out of trouble. Both of you need time to cool off."

Scooter immediately shrinks back into the safety of the sofa. "Can't we do it later, Mom? After lunch maybe?"

Hayley is smirking. She's revelling in Scooter's discomfort. "Can't we do it later, Mommmie?" she mimics. Scooter raises a fist in warning.

Janie scowls at the tableau. "Get in here, Scoot." She turns back to the bedroom. "And Hayley, I expect more from you as the oldest. Next time I'll let her clock you."

Silence reigns for a long moment. Then Scooter shouts, "NO!"

Janie calls from the bedroom, "Don't make me come out there again, Scooter Wells. You're not so big I can't drape you over my lap and give you a good spanking."

Scooter hesitates in the doorway to the bedroom. Janie is seated at an old treadle sewing machine. Behind her, bits and pieces of the organza pinafore are draped over the lumpy double bed.

"Scooter, stop messing around and get your clothes off so I can pin this." Janie turns and points to the wooden crate in the middle of the crowded room. "We haven't got all day."

When Scooter still doesn't move, Janie marches over and grabs one arm and hauls her across the room onto the wooden crate. "Honestly, you'd think it physically hurts you to dress up occasionally."

"It does, Mama. It physically hurts me. I hate all that pinchy, scratchy, tight stuff you think is so nice on girls."

Janie forcibly turns Scooter, so they face each other. She takes Scooter's t-shirt by the hem and starts pulling it up over her torso. Scooter goes rigid, arms firmly at her sides.

"Help me, you big baby," Janie coaxes. Scooter doesn't budge. "Would it kill you to look nice every now and again?" Janie manages to get the t-shirt off and tosses it on the bed.

"Look nice for what, Mom? For who?"

"Whom. Look nice for whom, Scooter." Janie reaches for Scooter's shorts and starts to pull on them. Scooter grabs them and holds on tight.

"Stop it. Stop it, Mama. Why can't I just leave my shorts on this time?"

Janie tries to pull Scooter's hands away, but Scooter fights her with growing desperation. Exasperated, Janie throws up her hands and dumps the blue taffeta on the floor. "Fine then. Spend your whole life looking like you dressed out of a Goodwill bag." She picks up the taffeta at her feet and shoves it in Scooter's hands.

"Here. Take it. Merry Christmas. Use it to strain paint or some other stupid thing you do with your father. I'm sure between the two of you, you'll find a good use for it." She can't help herself; she starts to cry softly. Janie covers her face with her hands. "All I wanted was for my little babies to look nice for once. To have a photo of both of you in brand new dresses by the Christmas tree."

Scooter's lip trembles in shame and sympathy. She whispers, "Aw Mom. Please don't cry." She tries to hand the taffeta back to her mother.

"Here, take this stuff. It wouldn't be any good as a paint strainer anyway. You may as well finish the dress."

Janie's face brightens. "And you'll wear it?"

"Will you at least leave while I get dressed in it then?"

At that moment a loud boom shakes the house, as if the wind has thrown a brick against the living room wall. It diverts Janie's attention. She runs out of the bedroom, shouting. "Okay, take the shorts off while I'm not looking and put on that damned dress if we're ever going to finish it before Christmas."

Scooter looks to make sure her mother has gone and gingerly eases the shorts down off her hips. A long red scratch runs across the inside of her upper thigh. Her plain white cotton underwear is ripped across one leg opening.

Scooter hurries to cover the evidence with the dress before Janie returns and notices.

When Janie steps back into the room, Scooter is standing on the crate waiting for her. As she approaches, Janie puts the pins back in her mouth and mumbles, "Can you turn a quarter turn, Scooter?"

Scooter stands perfectly still while Janie pins the hem.

"Again, a quarter turn." Janie pins the final pins and then stands up and backs away from Scooter. She studies her a long moment. "It's a trifle long at the moment. But you do insist on growing, so, I think it will be fine for Christmas."

Scooter still stands perfectly still. "Am I done then?"

Janie nods, smiling. "See, it wasn't so bad. Be careful taking it off. I don't want one of the pins to poke you!" Scooter hops off the crate, grabbing her shorts from the bed.

Janie disappears into the living room, then reappears, holding a bulging pillowcase in each hand. "I've been saving these, Scoot. One bag is for you and the other is for Hayley." Janie smiles broadly. "But you get first pick, since I still have to pin Hayley's dress."

Scooter's eyes are glued to the bulging bags. "What's in them?"

"Choose one and find out. Which hand do you want?"

Scooter ponders a long moment. "Your right hand. Please."

Janie is nearly as excited as Scooter when she hands her the pillowcase.

Scooter immediately turns it upside down on the floor and a dozen volumes of an encyclopedia tumble out at her feet. She is instantly on the floor, turning them over and reading the titles.

En-cy-clo-pedia, F—H. Fantastic! We have these at school. Are they mine? For keeps?"

"They are yours *and* Hayley's. To *share*. Perfect for a rainy day, yes?" Janie hesitates a moment. "Maybe let's not tell your dad about them any time soon, okay?"

· · ·

The sun spreads fingers of light through the front windows of Andy's Town Tavern on its way to setting. Hanson is seated at the same table as before, having a beer. Empty beer mugs and whiskey shot glasses litter the tabletop in front of him.

Scooter is in a chair next to him, playing with the silver-wire horse. The two of them are surrounded by a gaggle of half-cut cowboys and farmers, intently watching Scooter perform her magic with the puzzle.

One cowboy, Seth Wickens, is tanked and cocky as a bantam rooster. He steps up to the table. "Shit. I kin do that, little missy." Right next to Scooter is the hot seat. Seth throws a leg over the back of the chair and holds out his hand for the toy.

Scooter's look, as she places it in the palm of his hand says it all: *Yeah, right. And I'm a Dalmatian.*

The cowboy takes a wooden match from behind his ear, sticks it in the corner of his mouth and turns his full attention to the puzzle.

Hanson holds up one hand over this head, gesturing to the bartender. "Okay, Andy, we got a live one."

Andy looks up briefly and begins to pour another mug of beer. The cowboy notices and stops fiddling with the toy. "Hey. What gives? I haven't even started yet."

Scooter huffs, "Yeah and five bucks says you can't FINISH before my dad finishes his beer."

The group gathered behind Hanson and Scooter reacts. Andy crosses the room and smacks the mug on the table. "Oooh. I'll put five on Seth."

Seth sets his wooden match between his teeth and mumbles. "Watch and learn, young'un."

Scooter shakes her head, picks three five-dollar bills off the stack in the center of the table and slides them over to a spot right in front of Seth. Hanson catches the movement out of the corner of his eye as he's lifting the mug of beer to his lips.

"A man with that kind of confidence shouldn't be afraid of a little double-or-nothin' bet," Scooter challenges.

Hanson chokes on his beer. The whole group bursts out laughing. Then more money hits the table at Scooter's dare. Hanson is bent double choking. Seth begins to fiddle with the puzzle. He doesn't look up as he speaks. "Yer on, sweetheart. And when I'm done, I'll teach yer old man a thing or two about drinkin."

Laughing, Scooter chortles, "There ain't no one can teach my dad a thing about drinkin'."

Hanson is still laughing and choking. Scooter reaches over and whacks him solidly between the shoulder blades to help control his coughing. "Shit, he's half cut already, but I'd still bet the rest of the cash on this table that he'd put you under it in a chug-a-lug."

The group lets loose with another roar of laughing. Someone shouts, "I'll put five on Hanson." Still more money hits the table.

"Gimme ten on Seth, Scooter."

"Yer on. Who else? C'mon you tightwads, fork over."

Moments later, Seth pounds the table in frustration. He pushes the horse puzzle back to Scooter, conceding the first bet, as he slams several five-dollar bills on the table. "Round two. Drinkin'. Now here's a bet I cannot lose." Seth twists in his chair. "Andy! Bring us some beers."

Scooter is tidying the pile of cash, counting as she goes. "Eighty-nine dollars on the table. AND the loser picks up the tab!"

Seth roars as Andy approaches with five beers for each man. "You're on young'un…Now, watch and learn."

The bartender sets a tray of frothy beers on the tabletop. Hanson picks one up and smiles in expectation. "Every man should have a child such as this at his side."

Half an hour later, Hanson and Scooter are wandering towards home, savoring their triumph. Hanson has his arm around Scooter's shoulders. They're just passing the front window of the General Store when Hanson pulls Scooter to a stop. "I want to buy you something, Scoot." His words are more than a little slurred, but heartfelt. Something nice—something you never thought you'd ever have."

Scooter looks around her as if mystified. "I thought you puked up all that booze back there in the bushes, Dad. But I'd swear you're still woozy."

"Aww, Give me a break. I don't have to be cold sober to appreciate you were brilliant back there, girl." He stops and peers into the glass window. "You deserve a reward. Janie will be over-the-moon when we hand all this cash over to her."

Scooter peers into the window too. "What she will be is instantly suspicious. What're you going to tell her?"

Hanson turns and looks at Scooter. "The truth, mostly, Scoot. A good lie has to be based on truth or it won't sell."

Scooter turns her attention away from the window of the General Store and raises her eyebrows at Hanson. "Anndd?"

"I'll tell her I murdered Seth Wickens on a quick run of 21. And he kept upping the ante to get his money back—and I kept winning." Hanson hesitates a moment, then adds, "But you made me stop and come home."

Scooter nods. "Nice. I almost believe it—and I was there. And what will you say about the work with Uncle Bob?"

"Ahh, I'm still working on that." Hanson scratches his jaw. "I did leave a message at the Mitchells' saying I was sick. And to let Bob know."

"Lame."

Hanson turns back to the window. "So what do you see that you like, Scooter?"

Scooter hesitates and then points her finger. "That blue cowboy hat."

"Aww, Scoot."

"You said *anything*, Dad!"

Hanson stops his grumbling and waits a moment to see if Scooter will change her mind. Finally, he strolls into the store, picks the hat out of the window and takes it to the counter.

Scooter watches through the plate glass window, grinning like a banshee. By the time he returns to her, she's hopping back and forth from one foot to the other, like she has to pee—she's so excited.

Hanson takes the hat in both hands and lifts it onto her head like a crown. Scooter looks up at him, beaming. The hat slips a bit towards the back of her head, but she doesn't care.

"At least I'll never lose you in a crowd, missy. Makes you look like a tiny poofter."

Scooter quickly checks her reflection in the window and beams. She grabs her dad's hand and starts him walking again towards home.

"You're just jealous, Dad."

"Poofter."

"Wrench monkey."

SEVEN

Early the next morning Scooter, noticeably without her hat, and Hayley have set up a checkerboard on the front porch. They lay out the pieces on the board with utter concentration—ignoring the shouting adult voices from within. They studiously begin moving the pieces around the board.

"Well, it's a damn good thing the Craigmiers asked for me again today. How long do you think this sore back of yours will persist, Hanson?"

The rumble of Hanson's voice drifts out to the porch and then gets louder. Hayley takes advantage of Scooter's inattention and jumps two of her pieces. She sets them aside with satisfaction.

"Look at it this way, Honey—the silver lining is now we have someone to look after the girls." Cupboard doors slam closed and pots bang onto the stove top.

"Yes. And we're reduced to one paycheck yet again."

Scooter grimaces and whispers, "You'll pay for that, Hayley."

Footsteps echo through the house, heading towards the front door. "Fair enough, Janie. Just leave the dishes, Honey. The girls and I can tidy up and make something to go with the chili."

His voice comes closer as he moves through the house. "And try not to worry so much, it's not good for you or the baby."

Janie blasts through the screen door and stalks onto the porch. She stoops and bestows kisses on Scooter and Hayley's heads, then barges down the stairs and out towards the road.

Hanson follows her out onto the porch and stands leaning on the doorframe, watching Janie power across the yard. "Marriage is not always an easy country to inhabit, girls." Hanson sighs a deep sigh. "But being single is worse, way worse." He turns reluctantly from watching Janie disappear in the distance and moves back into the house.

• • •

Half an hour later, Hanson sings out to the girls: "I'm making some muffins. Everyone can have just one, while they're warm. He's standing at the kitchen counter beating eggs in a bowl; wearing an apron. He stops to peek in the oven every so often to check the temperature. A pair of muffin tins sits empty by the sink, awaiting batter.

Scooter is now sitting backwards on a kitchen chair, tossing her blue cowboy hat at a chair frame post across the table from her. Hayley tries half-heartedly to catch the hat as it passes. But her eyes are mostly on her father, so her efforts aren't much rewarded.

"But I don't see why Scoot got a present. It's not fair, Daddy."

"It'll be your turn next time, Haley. Scooter was with me, and she'd helped me with a tricky problem, so I gave her a reward."

"But I help all the time, Daddy. Ask Mom. Scooter never helps. I help every single day."

Having retrieved the hat, Scooter tosses it again. This time Hayley snakes out a hand and grabs it mid-air.

"Hey. That's my hat. Give it back."

Hayley stands up, taking the hat with her.

"I'm warning you, Hayley, give me back my hat."

"Girls. Stop your bickering or I'll have to whack you both."

Scooter picks up a chair and lifts it over her head. "I'm way ahead of you, Daddy."

Hayley starts shrieking as Scooter raises the chair. Hanson turns from spooning batter into the muffin tins and shouts at both of them, slamming a nearby pot down on the stove with a crash. He stalks over to Scooter and wrenches the chair away from her in anger.

"Scooter, for chrissake, stop it before I seriously tan your hide." Hanson swats Scooter sharply.

"Give me the damned hat, Hayley. You're the oldest, I expect more from you."

Tears seep from Hayley's eyes, but she stands her ground. "That's what everyone always says. I'm sick of hearing it, Daddy." She sucks in a deep breath to keep from bawling. "Watch Scooter, you're the oldest. Be nice, you're the oldest." Hayley starts to leave the kitchen but turns back to add, "Pretty soon it'll be, mind the baby, you're the oldest."

Hanson takes a step towards Hayley and raises his hand as if to strike her. She immediately cowers and begins to wail. "Don't hit me, Daddy, please." Hayley throws the hat onto the floor. "Don't hit me, she can have it. It's ugly anyway." She runs from the kitchen in tears.

Hanson watches Hayley tear away, and slowly lowers his hand. He crosses the room to retrieve the hat. When he turns back to Scooter, he smacks her sharply across the top of her head and jams the hat back into place. "Leave the damn thing on your head, stupid."

Hanson returns to his muffin tins and places them in the oven. He twists the mechanical timer and sets it by the sink. Then he flips open the refrigerator door and lifts out a can of beer. "Fucking hell. You girls wear me out. I've a mind to not give you any muffins." He pulls out a chair and falls into it.

Scooter eyes Hanson dubiously as he takes a sip of beer. "I'll tidy while we wait for the muffins," she says. She runs water into the bowl, adds soap. and swirls the dishes around in the suds.

"These muffins are meant for your mom, Scoot. She works hard all day at the Criagmiers'—and here too. She deserves a treat sometimes too."

"I know, I know." Scooter swabs the mixing bowl. "You said we could each have just one." She rinses the bowl and sets it in the drainer. "That would still leave tons for Janie. You can't go back on your word, Dad."

"No, Scooter, dammit. Don't nag me. I hate nagging."

• • •

An hour later, Scooter and Hanson sit at the table, licking muffin crumbs off their plates. Hayley is just visible sitting in the rocking chair in the living room, still livid.

Hanson cranes around hoping to make eye contact. "Hayley don't be a spoilsport." He licks his fingers. "There's a muffin in here with your name on it."

Silence. Hanson waits a long moment and then turns to Scooter and shakes his finger at her in warning. He lifts a muffin from the tin and puts it on his own mostly clean plate and pushes back his chair.

He walks into the living room and approaches Hayley. He bends down on one knee and offers the plate to her in apology. "I know you do a lot around here without even being asked, Honey." He pushes the plate closer. "But none of us gets a reward every day we do something good."

Hanson's voice drops to a whisper. "But I'll get you something special, pumpkin. I will." Hanson wills Hayley to meet his eyes. "Way better than a stupid blue hat."

Hayley smiles slightly and takes the muffin plate from his hands. She whispers back, "Thank you, Daddy."

Gratified, Hanson stands and then looks down at Hayley as she takes a bite of muffin. "Hayley, you know I'd never actually hit you, right? You have to believe that." Hanson reaches down and strokes her hair, and she smiles up at him.

When Hanson returns to the kitchen, he stands for a moment and watches Scooter twirl her hat on her raised index finger. He steps closer to her, lowering his voice. "What-say we walk into town maybe and try to catch the afternoon crowd at Andy's, Scoot?"

Scooter stops twirling her hat. "Maybe we should avoid Andy's for a little bit, Daddy." She frowns up at him. "Seth was pretty friggin' choked at losing all that money. Might be some bad blood there."

Hanson blows out his breath and huffs. "The damned fool shouldn't have bet money he couldn't afford to lose." He rolls his eyes a moment later. "Okay, okay," he grumbles. "From the mouths of babies, Scooter."

"I ain't no baby, Daddy. Don't ever call me that again."

Hanson chuckles. "Lord girl, it's just a saying. I ain't callin' you no baby, partner!" He uses his finger to wipe up a stray muffin crumb from the table. "The after-work crowd could be a money mill for us though, Scoot."

There's a moment of silence between them; then Scooter nods. "Instead of Andy's...what about the tavern down on Route 6, by the truck stop?"

Hanson's eyes light up, and then his face falls again. "Too far to walk this afternoon and still get home in time to surprise Janie."

Hanson interrupts the moment of quiet and suddenly strolls back to the muffin tins still sitting on the counter. He reaches into a cupboard and pulls down a clean plate and places two muffins neatly onto it.

"What gives? I thought you were saving those for Janie," Scooter scowls.

"All the rest of them are for Janie." Hanson points to the plate. "These are for Oren." He turns and offers the plate to Scooter. "I want you to pop over and ask him if we could use his car for a bit this afternoon."

Scooter's face immediately goes blank. "What possible reason would we have to use his car?"

Hanson rolls his eyes heavenward, thinking. "Tell him I have to go see a man about some money." Scooter shakes her head adamantly: "No way."

Hanson gives her a look. But when it's clear she won't change her mind, he puts the plate on the table, then reaches over and lifts the blue cowboy hat off her head. He turns around and holds it under the kitchen water tap, his hand ready to turn it on.

"I've seen cowboys in movies water their horses this way. This hat holds a fair bit of water, I bet." He half turns back to Scooter. "'Course it ruins the hat."

Scooter skewers him with a glare, assessing him. Then she slowly slides the plate off the table and carries it out the back door.

Hanson grins at her back and carefully places the cowboy hat on the table. He turns to the kitchen window and watches as Scooter approaches Oren's door. He watches her knock, and Oren comes to the door and opens it. There's a pause as Scooter waits with the muffin plate in her hands.

As soon as the exchange is made and Scooter has turned to come home, Hanson leaps into action. He slicks back his hair with water and rinses his mouth, gargling away the residue of muffin. He's busy tucking in his shirt as Scooter pushes the door open and tosses him the car keys.

Scooter grabs her hat and stands watching him primp. "Let's get one thing clear, Daddy." She places the hat just so on her head. "My hat is off limits, understood? Or you'll be doing the rest of your gigs solo." She makes sure to make eye contact, then turns and marches out the kitchen door.

EIGHT

Hanson pulls off the highway and drives to the far end of the truck-stop parking lot. As Scooter gets out of the car, Hanson is already walking away, talking. "We don't want anyone to think it's us that owns this beast, Scoot."

"We don't?"

"No. It's all about optics, Honey." Hanson steps a bit closer to her and lowers his voice. "A shill relies on us looking as poor as paupers, but lucky. We can't appear richer than our *clientele*."

"Our clientele?" She throws a dubious look Hanson's way.

He wraps an arm around her shoulders. "Scoot, we're in business now. I'm not going to degrade the work we do by calling them marks. That's rude." Hanson turns and walks backwards, talking to her. "We're here to add some fun and excitement to their day. Like performers." Hanson turns and adroitly steps up to the front door as if he had eyes in the back of his head.

"So, they're kinda like our audience then?"

"Yeah. And we're the circus that's come to town" He opens the door with a flourish. "The curtain's going up, Scoot. Let's go see how things shake out."

Within minutes, there's a queue of curious farmers stretching back from Hanson's table to the big plate glass window. There's also a line-up of empty beer bottles nearly as long on the tabletop.

Hanson is pickled, but Scooter's not. She spots Andy from the Town Tavern as he saunters into the room and up to the bar.

"Wow, Dad, look what time it is. Mom's gonna be wondering where we are."

Andy stops to speak to Big Jim, the mid-forties paunchy but tough bartender. They shake hands, and Andy turns and leans casually against the bar a moment. His eyes roam the room and come to a dead stop when he spots Hanson and Scooter.

"What the hell are you going on about, Scoot?" Hanson sets down an empty beer bottle. "Your mom's still slaving away at the Craigmiers'."

Scooter gives Hanson a kick under the table. "Check your watch, Dad. I think it's time to head home." She jerks her head towards the bar, grimacing for emphasis.

Hanson's head jerks up and he spots Andy. He hastily

scoops the few dollars on the table into the canvas bag with Scooter's book. Scooter retrieves the silver horse from the hands of the latest loser and stuffs it into the bag too.

Within seconds, Andy appears at her elbow, smirking. "Funny, I just stopped by and was going to tell Big Jim about you two." He raises his voice and turns to the room. "But now I can show everyone who you are. Even better."

Andy makes a megaphone with his hands. "Listen up, everyone. C'mon you all, quiet down now."

Hanson scrapes back his chair and grabs the bag and Scooter's hand and pulls her away from the table. He marches them quick time to the nearest exit.

"Just leaving are two flimflam artists." Andy points to be sure everyone sees them. "These two bilked Seth Wickens out of a month's pay over at Town Tavern yesterday."

Voices are raised in response to Andy's announcement. "What? They bilked Seth Wickens...those two just leaving?"

"I'm offering a free beer right now to all of you if you'll do me a favor." Andy knows free beer is guaranteed to get them listening. "If any of you see these two shysters in any tavern within fifty miles, you tell the owner. Tell your friends too. Help me spread the word, and a FREE cold beer is all yours."

The crowd's murmurings have turned to an affirmative shout. And then they start lining up at the bar for their beer. Andy smirks, watching as Hanson and Scooter scurry past the plate glass window in retreat, the satisfying thunk of beer glasses hitting the bar top behind him.

Hanson opens the driver's door to the car and folds himself inside. Scooter climbs in the passenger side. "Don't get too comfortable, Scoot." Hanson quickly gooses the car forward and then pulls out onto the highway. Fifty feet beyond the tavern parking lot, he pulls off onto the shoulder of the highway. "Get out, Scoot, and come over here."

Scooter throws him a doubting look.

"You heard me. Get out."

Still dubious, Scooter gets out of the car and comes around to the driver's side.

Hanson pushes the door open and then slides across the seat to the passenger window. "Get in, yer driving." He pats the driver's seat. "C'mon, we haven't got all day."

Scooter gets into the car and closes the door. She can barely see over the steering wheel.

Hanson reaches into her canvas bag and pulls out her book. He uses his thumb to indicate she should lift herself up and he slides the book under her bum. "Okay, first thing you need to know is, this is not hard. Any idiot can drive."

"Case in point."

"Don't sass me. Listen." He shades his face with his raised hand, pointing down the road. "It's a straight shot to home. Stay on the right-hand side of the road, and only go as fast as you're comfortable doing. And don't be flashy."

"This is illegal, Dad, even I know that."

"It isn't if it's a life-threatening situation and you're the only one available to drive me to safety."

Deeply skeptical, Scooter sits tapping the top of the steering wheel awaiting further explanation.

"Well, it clearly would have been life-threatening if we had stayed any longer," Hanson mutters. He suddenly opens the door and pukes. He sits back up and closes the door. "And clearly I am in no condition to drive—to keep us out of the life-threatening situation of being caught in that parking lot."

He reaches over and turns on the left turn signal. "So, you're going to drive us to within a mile of home." Hanson puts the car into gear. "Okay, turn the wheel towards the asphalt and ease your foot down on the gas petal…Softly, gently." Scooter does as he says and soon the car is puttering along the highway.

"Stop at the turnoff to the house and wake me up. I'll take it from there."

Scooter is shocked into taking her eyes off the road and the car snakes sideways a bit. Hanson reaches over and corrects her steering. Once she's back on the straight and narrow he lays his head to rest on the door. "You heard me! And if you are stopped by the RCMP tell them I have fainted, and you couldn't revive me—so you had to drive me to safety."

"Dad!"

"Scooter! You absolutely cannot get into trouble for driving for me in a medical situation." He closes his eyes and sighs. "Whereas I can get into a world of shit for driving this drunk." Hanson lifts the book bag to use as a pillow against the car door. "Ergo, you're driving".

"I hate you, Hanson P. Wells."

"C'mon, you've seen me do this a zillion-billion times. Don't be such a baby."

With one final exasperated look, Scooter pushes a little harder on the gas pedal. "You will pay for this, Hanson."

Hanson doesn't hear her. He was asleep the instant his head hit the book bag.

An agonizing amount of time later, Scooter eases the Fleetwood off the tarmac. The crunch of gravel beneath the tires awakens Hanson. He sits up slowly, and then closes his eyes instantly.

"Oooh, Mary-mother-of-god. Maybe I should let you drive the final mile too, Scoot. You've done a great job, Honey. I swear my friggin eyes are fried."

Scooter rests her forehead on the steering wheel. "Oh, shut up, Daddy. Shape up and drive." She takes a deep breath and then sits up again. "That was horrible. I kept thinking I was gonna get stopped every second of the way. People kept passing me and giving me the hairy eyeball and honking as they passed." She opens the driver's door and slides out.

"Really? I heard nothing." Hanson slides across the seat behind the steering wheel.

As Scooter climbs in again he reaches over and tips her cowboy hat over her eyes. "Aw, Hon, you have to learn to relax a little. Imagine if Bonnie and Clyde had been wired so tight."

Scooter slumps in her seat and pulls her cowboy hat down low over her face. "Just drive, Daddy. We are not Ma Barker or Dutch Anderson or Bonnie and Clyde." She takes the hat off and hits him with it. "I don't want to be any of those stupid people. I just want to go home and be me."

Hanson puts the car into gear and carefully moves it onto the highway. Moments later he pulls into the drive by Oren's trailer and parks the car. Oren is seated on his porch in his wheelchair. Hanson hands Scooter the keys to return to Oren.

Oren calls out as Hanson struggles to stand. "Profitable trip, Mr. Wells? I hope so—your wife is already home." Scooter trudges up the ramp and puts the keys on the railing in front of Oren. "Will I see you later with dinner, Miss Wells?"

Scooter is already turned away and marching across to her own house. She whispers to herself, *not if I can help it, asshole.* She stomps up the porch steps and slams the door as she careens into the living room.

Janie is indeed already home, and on a tear. Cardboard

boxes are scattered throughout the living room and the kitchen. She stops taping together one of the flattened boxes when Hanson arrives.

"Where the hell have you been, Hanson Wells?"

Scooter stops just outside the kitchen door, listening and watching.

"Janie, what the hell is going on here? What are you doing?" Hanson barks.

"What does it look like? I'm packing—we're leaving Summit, Hanson—tonight, tomorrow. As soon as humanly possible."

She returns to packing, not noticing Scooter in the doorway. Scooter's eyes are alight at the mention of leaving.

"I suppose I should be grateful. I wanted to leave," her voice cracks. "But not like this…"

"What? What are you talking about? And where'd you get these boxes?"

"I had some flattened underneath our bed. Insurance against your next fuck-up, Hanson."

He lifts his hands palms up, shrugging his shoulders. "Whaaat?"

"Jesus, will I never learn." Janie starts crying softly. "I'm talking about you fleecing the Criagmiers' nephew, Seth Wickens." She picks the wet dishrag off the kitchen faucet and throws it at Hanson. "They fired me today, you son-of-a-bitch, and then implied they'd be doing a count of their silverware to make sure none was missing."

Janie returns to packing, but it's lethargic and unfocused. "Hanson, I haven't got a hope of getting work in this town now. Because of you, we have to move!"

Hanson studies her a long moment and then crosses the room and tries to put his arms around her. She hits him on the chest and shoulders and then slaps him on the face. "Why? Why Hanson?" She continues to pummel him. "We moved here because you had such great hopes of working with Bob."

"Oh, to hell with Bob, Janie." Hanson's face brightens. "But he will help us out of this mess. I know it. I mean blood is thicker than water, right?"

"Apparently not, Hanson. He's washed his hands of you too." Janie runs her hands through her hair. "He's had to, in order to stay in the good graces of the whole town. His business depends on it."

At this point Janie breaks down and really starts to cry. She hides her face in her hands and simply bawls. Hanson wraps his arms around her and rocks her gently. "That's right, Honey, cry it out. Get it all out and then we can put our heads together and come up with a plan."

After a long while, Janie's tears start slowing down, and she wraps her arms around Hanson and leans her head on his shoulder.

"You know what a whiz I am at getting us out of tight places, right?" Hanson pleads. "Remember you used to call me Mr. Magic? Remember?"

Janie wipes her face with her hands and sighs heavily. "First we should eat something." She grabs the potholders and moves towards the stove. "I made some chili. Everything looks better on a full stomach." Hanson crosses the kitchen and smiles down at Janie and then squeezes her tight against him.

Scooter's face falls and she turns and walks quietly away down the hall. She lets herself into the bathroom and shuts and locks the door. Then she climbs in the tub with all her clothes on and brings her knees up to her chin, wrapping her arms around herself. She rocks herself slowly back and forth, back and forth.

NINE

In the kitchen Janie has finished setting the table. Hanson is leaning against the cabinets drinking a beer. Janie calls out loudly, "Dinner's ready, girls. Dinner." A gust of wind rattles the kitchen windowpane, and she turns, an anxious look on her face. Beyond the glass the trees outside are bending against a rising wind.

She turns back to Hanson. "Storm's coming up again, dammit. Hayley, Scooter—come eat." She starts filling the bowls with chili and setting on the table as Hayley sits down beside Hanson. "Where the hell is Scooter?"

Hayley looks up from her bowl of chili. "I think Scooter's sick, Mommy. She's locked herself in the bathroom and said she can't eat no dinner."

Hanson cocks his head and looks at Janie quizzically. "She didn't look sick an hour ago."

Janie continues to dole out the chili. "Will one of you close the damn screen door! That wind is going to blow dirt all over the kitchen." She stops to let Hayley hurtle past her to the door. She places another bowl and spoon on the table.

"Scooter, if you don't eat now you can just go hungry tonight."

Hayley joins in with a shout of her own. "Scoot, if you don't eat, I get your DESSERT!"

Scooter's retort from the bathroom is barely audible. "I don't care a rat's ass. It's only stupid Jello."

Hanson pushes his bowl of chili away and stands up to shout, his voice more than a little menacing: "Scooter, get the hell out here right now."

He whispers an aside to Janie. "Don't fret none, Janie. Let's just get the kids fed."

"Scooter, don't make me come get you!" Hanson threatens. Silence. A long moment follows, punctuated by the sound of a door slamming. Scooter appears in the doorway, lounging sullenly. She refuses to enter the kitchen. Hanson scowls at her from the dinner table.

Hanson scrapes remnants of chili from the bottom of his bowl. "You didn't seem sick an hour ago. In fact, you don't look that sick right now. Just pissy." He reaches across the table and grasps Scooter's bowl of chili. "Last time! You gonna eat this?"

Scooter shakes her head adamantly 'no'. Hanson eyes her a long moment and then thrusts out the bowl to her. "Okay then, take it across the yard to poor Oren.

I'm sure he'll be real grateful for a home-cooked meal."

A variety of expressions flit across Scooter's face. Her eyes meet her father's. Suddenly, a tear slides down her cheek. She shakes her head slowly back and forth.

• • •

Suddenly Scooter is back in the river, falling, falling, falling. The sudden impact of hitting the water sends fish scattering as she plummets into the depths. Gravity drags her down, down, down.

Helpless against the sheer velocity of her fall, Scooter waits, eyes wide. One thin arm is flung up over her head, trailing through a halo of pale blond hair. The moment she reaches stasis, Scooter's arms and legs begin to flail.

• • •

"Nuh-uh, Daddy I don't want to. I don't want to visit Oren anymore."

Janie looks up at the tone in Scooter's voice. She half turns in her chair. "Hanson, maybe Hayley can do it tonight?"

The banging of the shutters against the side of the house distracts Janie for a moment. The howl of the wind rises. "Jesus. When are you going to fix the damn shutters, Hanson?"

Janie leans across the table, her attention back on Scooter. She lays her hand on Scooter's forehead and cheeks. "Hanson, there's a storm coming up. Oren Harris can wait another night for dinner from us."

Hanson's fist slams down on the tabletop, effectively silencing any further debate. "Goddammit, Scooter, get over here and take this bowl to Mr. Harris or I'll have your hide."

"I can't, Daddy." Scooter starts to shake. "I just can't."

Hanson doesn't notice her shaking. In a blind fury, he picks up the bowl and crosses the room to Scooter's side. Janie is half out of her chair, but Hanson throws her a threatening look and she sits back down.

"If you know what's good for you, Janie, you'll stay the hell out of this." There's an edge to Hanson's voice as he grabs Scooter by the arm and forcibly hauls her to the kitchen door and roughly shoves her out onto the step. He thrusts the bowl of chili into her hands. "You best do as I say, Scooter Wells."

Scooter's hair is whipped around by the growing force of the gale outdoors. Her shivering grows more violent once she's thrust out onto the porch. Hanson slams the screen door behind her.

Then Hanson abruptly slams the kitchen door closed too as he returns to the room. Hayley sits, spoon raised, a shocked expression on her face. The top of Scooter's head is visible through the door window.

Beyond, the wind is picking up, buckling the nearby trees. Scooter takes one step off the porch, cradling the bowl of chili in her cupped hands. She inches towards Oren's house. The wail of the wind seems to grow louder with each step she takes.

Scooter passes in front of the Fleetwood and hesitates at the lip of the wheelchair ramp. Inexorably she walks forward. At the top, she raises one hand to tap on Oren's kitchen door. She gazes longingly at the reflection of her own home behind her in the glass.

Scooter raps again on the doorframe and is just about to leave when a light blinks on in the interior of the trailer. The door opens and Oren is silhouetted in his wheelchair.

"I got some chili for you, Mr. Harris."

Whispering, Oren smiles at Scooter. "I've told ya little lady, call me Oren." He backs his massive bulk away from the doorway so that Scooter can step inside. She stays rooted to the spot. "Why some of my little friends even call me Orie. Or Uncle Orie. You could try that. Go ahead, let me hear you say it."

"Or-rie," Scooter whispers, remaining stock still in the doorway.

Janie is at the kitchen sink looking out. She sees the light appear in Oren's house. As she does the dishes by rote—washing, rinsing—she can't help but hear the rise in the whine of the wind outside. She can't take her eyes from the window. Behind Janie, Hanson is playing checkers with Hayley at the kitchen table. Hanson has cut pieces of the lime Jello into circles which he moves carefully about the board.

"Should we save Scooter some Jello, Dad?" Hayley asks.

Janie turns, wiping her hands and watches Hanson and Hayley a moment. Hanson takes a swallow of beer. "Never you mind about Scooter."

Janie dries her hands on a tea towel. "There really is a storm brewing, Hanson."

Hanson pushes the checkerboard across the table, scrapes back his chair and begins to pace. Anywhere except near the window, where he might actually look out and see Oren's house.

"Don't you worry about our Scoot. No one knows how to handle herself better than she does."

"What do you mean by that, Hanson?" Janie suddenly looks out the window again, this time with a new intensity.

Hanson stops his pacing to focus on Janie. "It's just an expression, Janie." He runs one hand through his hair. "You worry too much."

Janie immediately sets down the tea towel on the countertop, turns towards the kitchen door as if in some kind of dream time. "And you don't worry enough, Hanson. This is the third or fourth time that Scooter's felt sick around dinnertime."

As she reaches for the kitchen doorknob, she's intercepted by Hanson. He puts his hand on her shoulder and stops her before she can slip outside. "I'll go. I think it's best if I do the checking on her." As Hanson steps outside, the wind wrenches the door from his hands and slams it repeatedly against the side of the house. Janie shrinks against the doorframe.

Oren wheels into the living room, with Scooter following, carrying the bowl. He pivots his wheelchair and studies Scooter. "C'mere little pony...bring me my dinner. That's what your daddy sent you over for, right?"

Scooter holds out the bowl as far as she can reach. Oren stretches out a hand, reaching for the bowl, but uses his other hand to capture Scooter's wrist. Oren calmly sets the chili on a nearby TV tray. But while Oren is focused on the chili, Scooter twists away and leaps onto the sofa.

"You're cornered, little pony, it's only a matter of time." The position of Oren's chair has Scooter trapped in the living room. She crouches on the sofa, looking for a way out.

"I'm nobody's fuckin' pony."

The storm smashes something against the roof of the trailer. Oren is momentarily distracted by the crashing sound, and seeing her chance, Scooter jumps.

Oren moves fast. He reaches out and snatches Scooter out of mid-air and hauls her kicking and punching into his lap. He laughs with delight when several of Scooter's punches land on his face. He pulls her into a sitting position and twists one arm behind her back. "There, there little gal."

Breathless, Scooter shouts, "You may as well break it, Oren. I won't do what you want."

Oren chuckles so softly it's almost inaudible. Scooter flinches from the inherent malice in the sound. Holding her tightly, Oren uses his free hand to lift a piece of rope off the frame of his wheelchair. He lifts it towards Scooter's head. Scooter sees the rope coming and begins to struggle anew.

Oren's laughter is melodic and so childlike it's chilling as he squeezes Scooter in the vise of his massive arms. "Oh, I'd willingly break both your arms darlin'…if only we had the time."

In the kitchen, with all the sound and fury of the storm about them, Hanson's nonchalance is stripped away. He leaps in long, loping steps down the porch stairs and crosses to Oren's house in a matter of seconds.

A massive branch from a cottonwood tree is snapped off and echoes like thunder overhead and sails into Hanson's path. He picks it up and tosses it aside as he wades up the steps to Oren's kitchen door.

Janie watches him a moment from the window and then turns and begins to pace restlessly back and forth. She spots a half-full cardboard box and sets to packing things with a fury; but her eyes are constantly drawn back to the kitchen window.

Oren Harris leans forward precariously in his wheelchair, looming over Scooter, who has been turned to face him. He has the end of the rope wrapped tightly around his fist and has pulled the noose around Scooter's neck. His gaping mouth covers nearly half her face.

As Oren's free hand begins to slide into the waistband

of her shorts, Scooter struggles with renewed fury. She cocks back her head and then smashes her forehead on Oren's nose. He howls in pain.

Neither of them hears Hanson come through the front door. What they do hear is his strangled shout as he enters the room and absorbs the sight that greets him.

There is real anguish in his voice as he howls her name. "SCOOO-TER!" He stalks past the TV tray, scoops up the bowl of chili and smashes it across the side of Oren's head. The blow forces Oren to release the rope holding Scooter in place.

Chili covers the front of Oren's undershirt and neck. Bits of it splatters across Scooter's face. With his other hand Hanson reaches down and grabs the man by the hair as he catches a wheel spoke with his foot and upends the wheelchair.

Quickly Hanson drops one knee into Oren's chest and wraps the end of the rope around his neck and tightens it. "How does it feel, Oren? You LIKE?"

Scooter drops her hands to the floor, panting from the sudden inrush of air to her lungs. She loosens the noose and pulls it off. Across from her, Hanson tightens the rope until Oren's face reddens and his mouth gapes, fighting for air. "Does this make your little pecker hard, Oren? Does it turn you on?"

Suddenly Oren smiles up into Hanson's eyes. Oren's eyes go dreamy, and he gasps. "Ahhh god. You bet,

Hanson. Tighten the noose some more."

Hanson leaps off the man's chest in disgust and backs away from him. He reaches down and scoops Scooter off the floor and settles her on one hip. With his free hand he grabs Oren's wheelchair and pivots, throwing it through the living room window out onto the lawn. Hanson strides towards the door, wrenching the wall phone off its mounting and pulling out the wires.

Janie looks up at the crash of window glass. She shrieks as the wheelchair lands on the ground outside Oren's trailer.

"Holy Christ. . . Oh my god, my Scooter." Janie turns and races to the front of the house as she sees Hanson carrying Scooter towards the Fleetwood.

The overturned wheelchair's wheels are spinning, the spokes winking in and out of a pool of light from the living room. Shards of glass litter the grass around it. The scream of the wind is rising. Debris from nearby buildings swirls through the front yard.

Hanson strides down the wheelchair ramp, holding Scooter tightly. He crosses Oren's yard and wrenches open the rear door of the Fleetwood. He sets Scooter gently on the bench seat in back of the car and takes a moment to gently brush a bit of chilli out of her hair. Then he slams the door closed and heads to the driver's side of the car.

The roar of the engine catching is louder than the wind.

Behind the steering wheel, Hanson twists to see behind him as he wheels the car away from the trailer, and into the front yard of his own house. He positions it near the porch, exits, but leaves the engine running.

Janie comes flying into view on the front porch, Hayley just behind her.

Hanson jumps up to the porch and shouts. "We have to leave right now, Janie. Get some things together and get your ass moving."

Hanson pulls Janie and Hayley into the house and starts throwing clothing and dolls and pillows into a blanket. Then he races back out to the car. Janie watches as Hanson throws it all into the trunk of the Caddy. Then suddenly, Hanson is back on the porch shouting again.

"DID you HEAR me? We're leaving, Janie. We have to go, now!" Hanson disappears into the kitchen.

Screaming, Janie watches him pass her. "Hanson, what is going on?" She looks down, bewildered. She picks up the pillowcases of books from behind the sofa, but she seems at a loss to know what to do.

Hanson races back to the living room carrying a box of stuff from the fridge. He uses his free arm to herd Janie and Hayley out of the house. The storm buffets the trees around them. Hanson tosses the box into the trunk and then leaps into the driver's seat, gunning the engine on the Fleetwood. Janie and Hayley have only moments to close the car doors before the car lurches into gear.

TEN

Hanson presses the accelerator to the floor. Rocks and turf spew out from the rear tires of the Caddy as it catapults onto the narrow dirt road. The interior is filled with the sound of rubber tires trouncing the gravel as the car gains traction.

In the distance the funnel of a tornado drops down into a nearby field and advances towards the old house. Hanson spots it and turns the Caddy in the opposite direction.

The girls cower in the back seat, holding on to each other. Hanson sends the car hurtling down the highway, weaving between large chunks of debris.

Janie's voice is tense and shaky. "For pity's sake, Hanson, talk to me!"

"Light me a cigarette, Janie."

Janie finds his cigarettes and hands him one. When Hanson reaches for it, his hands are shaking. "Just let's get us some distance from this storm. Then we can talk."

Scooter huddles in the back seat, clinging to Hayley. The whine of the wind outside turns into the whine of the tires on the road as the car hurtles through the night. In her dreams she's mesmerized by the thought of the spinning of the white-side walls against the black of the tarmac.

Muted music plays from the radio as Scooter, clad in shorts and her chili splattered t-shirt, awakens. She's lying on the shelf along the back window of the Fleetwood. Stars wheel and turn in the velvet sky overhead.

Janie and Hayley sleep. The only light is the faint glow from the speedometer and Hanson's cigarette. Whispering, Hanson exhales Scooter's name along with his cigarette smoke. Silence. Scooter never takes her eyes from the sky.

"You can't stay mad at me the whole rest of our lives, Scooter." Hanson takes a long drag on the cigarette. "After all, I did save you." Scooter doesn't answer, just keeps looking at the stars in the sky.

Hanson lets the moment rest. "I could tell you their names—the stars you're looking at." Hanson tosses his cigarette out the open window. "I spent a lot of nights as a kid looking up at a sky just like this one."

Hanson pauses to give Scooter a chance to say something. "That bright one down close to the horizon is probably Venus." He looks again in the rear-view mirror. He can see the whites of Scooter's eyes glowing in the half light. "And those four stars that look like you could draw a big X if you connected the dots—that's Orion."

Scooter rolls over as far away from Hanson as the slant-ing rear window of the sedan will allow. Hanson notices. "You probably think I shoulda killed him. Right, Scooter? Don't think for a minute I didn't want to, Scoot." Hanson's eyes flicker back to the mirror to gauge Scooter's reaction to his confession.

Hanson lights another cigarette and takes a noisy drag, his eyes sliding back to the roadway before him. Silently Hanson smokes and watches the road.

In the darkness, Scooter reaches out and traces the stars' path on the back window, whispering to herself as the miles unravel. "Orion. Cassiopeia. Sirius, the dog star—Venus, Mercury and Mars.

The headlights of the Fleetwood flash on a road sign as it hurtles past it. The sign reads: Mona's Roadside Diner—2 Miles—Gassup 'N Go.

"Ya hungry, Scoot? Why don't we stop and get us a burger and a brew?"

Hanson reaches over to gently jostle Janie awake. "Honey, we could all use a break, don'cha think? Scoot needs to make a little pit stop, so let's stop at Mona's."

Janie opens her eyes reluctantly and sits up. "Hanson, we don't have money to waste on anything but gas. So, bathroom break only."

Hanson turns the big car off the highway and sets his sights on Mona's gas pumps. He swings the Caddy alongside and cuts the engine. He searches the rear-view mirror for Scooter's eyes. He grins into the mirror. "Sometimes you don't need money, Janie. Do you, Scoot?"

Scooter studiously avoids his eyes as she rolls over.

"You leave Scooter out of this, Hanson Wells," Janie warns.

Hanson reaches over and stuffs a wad of bills into the glovebox. "Hang onto this for me, Janie. For safekeeping. We'll be right back." Hanson opens the driver's door and rolls out of the car and stretches. He's already pumping gas into the beast, when he cheerily calls to the girls still rubbing sleep from their eyes.

"Who's hungry? Who wants to go have a burger with Daddy?"

Hayley and Scooter sidle out of the back seat and drift warily over to Hanson as he replaces the gas pump nozzle. From the car, Janie calls to him one more time. "Hanson, this isn't a good idea." He affects a jaunty air and leads his kids towards the tavern side of Mona's dining establishment.

The inside of Mona's Tavern gives tawdry new meaning. Everything was built to stand the test of time, and beer, and urine and brawls. Six pairs of eyes, including the bartender's mean-looking walleye, study Hanson as he stops to survey the room. He picks a table and leads the girls to it. Hayley clings to his legs like a toddler.

Scooter hangs back, sizing up the situation, and finally

in a low-pitched whisper, calls to him. "D-A-D! Let's get out of here."

Hanson waves her blithely away and finds a seat at a table near the bar. "Bartender, some of Mona's famous burgers for me and my daughters." He waves one arm to indicate the girls. "And I'll have a beer. No, make it two."

"Grill's closed, buddy. We got ham sandwiches though."

Scooter still has not joined them. She's rooted at the entry to the tavern.

"Sure, that'll do. Give us two sandwiches each here at the table—and a couple more for the road." Hanson cocks his head, indicating Scooter behind him. "My Scooter can eat like a truck driver. Doesn't look it though, does she, fellas?"

Hanson seems oblivious that his attempt at barroom banter is falling on deaf ears. Scooter slinks to his side and sits. Hanson takes this as his cue to start their con.

"Scoot, I've got a little something I've been saving for just the right moment. Made it for you this afternoon at that rest stop back along the highway."

Hanson pulls the little silver horse out of his jacket pocket.

"Stop it, Dad."

The bartender sets Hanson's two beers on the table and serves up a platter of ham sandwiches and chips. He's about to turn away when Hanson plucks at his sleeve.

"Bet you've never seen anything like this, eh buddy?"

Hanson lifts up the wire horse for the guy to see. "It's kind of a puzzle… I made it for the whiz kid here. She's so smart, my Scooter, she solves it in a minute flat." As if only just inspired, he continues. "Why I'd be willing to bet you that you can't figure out how to get the halter off this horse." Hanson beams across the table at Scooter, inviting her into the old game.

"I don't give a shit about yer kids or yer puzzle, mister," the bartender glowers. "But I'm thinking I'd like to see the color of your money."

Hanson pales noticeably but pulls a thin slip of folding bills from his front pocket and makes a great show of thumbing it. "Oh, it's green, mister. Just like everybody else's."

As the bartender turns back towards the bar, Hanson casts a pleading look at Scooter. She refuses to meet his eyes. Hanson takes a long swallow of beer and searches the faces of the other patrons in the tavern, praying for a likely mark. But without Scooter's help, Hanson has run out of luck. And he knows it.

He lifts his half-finished beer in salute to Scooter's choice and finishes it. "C'mon girls. We don't want to keep your mama waiting any longer than we have to. Do we?"

He bundles up a couple of sandwiches in a paper napkin and passes them and the money from his pocket across the table to Hayley. "Go ahead, get yourselves out to the car."

Hanson flips Scooter a coin. "And Scooter, put something loud and rockin on the jukebox on your way past."

Nervous, he runs a hand through his hair. "I'll just finish this last beer and be right out."

Grim-faced, Scooter catches the coin in mid-air and then takes Hayley's hand and leads her towards the door. Scooter stops and drops the coin in the slot of the jukebox and punches in a number. Moments later BTO's *Takin Care of Business* blasts across the bar from every speaker. Scooter glances over her shoulder at her father, watching as he drains the second beer mug. She stops for a moment, frozen in place, as Hayley proceeds out the bar door.

"Buddy, you must be a fortune teller," Hanson says to the bartender. "Cuz I can barely pay for my beers, let alone the food and gas." Hanson sets the silver horse on the table and stands up, pulling the lining of his pockets out to indicate he's broke. The bartender rounds the corner of the bar and strides purposefully towards him.

"The rest? Well, I'm hoping we can come to some kind of arrangement," Hanson continues.

The bartender scoops up the silver horse and crunches it into a ball with one hand. A second later, his fist smashes into Hanson's face. The sound of fist hitting flesh carries across the room to where Scooter is rooted in the doorway.

"Son-of-a-bitch, that's a mean hook you got," Hanson mumbles. Then he is silenced by a flurry of blows to his face and body. The thud of fists is quickly followed by the sound of retching as Hanson gives up his beer. It all carries clearly over the driving rock music.

Scooter watches silently for a moment and then turns away. She pushes through the café door into the night, refusing to look back. The jukebox music, the sound of fists landing against flesh and chairs breaking echos behind her.

Scooter only just makes it back to the car when Janie's attention is caught by the sight of Hanson stumbling from the tavern. He careens towards the car, barely making it to the sedan as he falls against the driver's door.

"For god sakes, Hanson, what happened?"

Hanson folds himself into the car and starts the engine with a roar. "Later, Janie. We gotta get out of here." He wipes blood away from his eyes. "We gotta get out of here before that barkeep decides he wants more than blood and bruises for his beer."

Hanson carefully pulls out onto the highway. "I'll just get us a ways down the road and then we can switch drivers."

"Are you out of your mind? I can't drive this thing. I've only ever had one driving lesson, Hanson, and that was on Dad's tractor."

"Well, yer gettin yer second lesson tonight." Hanson wipes his eye again. "I can't drive much longer—my eyes are swelling shut too fast."

He stomps the gas and the car surges ahead, screaming down the highway oblivious to Janie and the girls' terror as they clutch each other for comfort. Hanson sways in the front seat, struggling to remain upright.

. . .

The sun is just peeking over the horizon, and Janie is in the driver's seat exhausted from driving all night; but she's coping. The kids in the back seat have finally succumbed and are sleeping.

Hanson has a torn bit of t-shirt tied over one eye; he peers through the puffy lid of the other. "There, on your right. Aim for that driveway, Janie."

Janie turns where Hanson has pointed. A hundred feet down the rutted track lie the remnants of an abandoned farmhouse. "What is this place, Hanson?"

"Abandoned, obviously. And home for the rest of the day while we both get some sleep." Hanson's head drops back against the seat. "Pull around behind, so the car's not visible from the road."

Janie slows down as she approaches, guiding the car carefully behind the shack. "I don't like this, Hanson. It looks like it could fall over at any minute." Janie purses her lips, "And I bet it's filthy."

"Yes, it is all those things, Janie. Which is why it is the perfect place to rest up for a bit."

"Hanson, I don't…"

"Shut the fuck up, Janie. I really don't care what you think. I need some goddamn sleep."

The girls are now wide awake and cowering together as Hanson's voice rises in volume.

"My fuckin head feels like it's breaking in two. I can't

see jack shit and you're whining about a bit of dirt."

Janie moves as far away from Hanson as possible in the front seat of the car. She shuts the engine off and squeezes against the driver's door.

Scooter leans over and wraps an arm around Janie's shoulder. "Daddy, you should shut up! It's your stupid fault your damn head hurts. It's your fault we're sitting in a stolen car, in front of some dump hiding out for the day."

Scooter opens the back door of the Caddy. "C'mon Hayley, Mom—let's go see just how bad it is." Scooter rolls out of the back seat and holds the door for Hayley to get out too. Then she helps Janie out the front door. They walk to the door of the shack and try the handle. Its doorknob falls off in Scooter's hand. She pushes and the door swings open.

She turns and shouts to Hanson. "You comin?" Hanson doesn't reply. Instead, he slides down farther in the front seat and stretches out to sleep.

The back entrance opens onto a kitchen area with a cracked linoleum floor and a window with filthy glass. Scooter reaches over the sink and shoves on the window; it slides open. Hayley presses close to her sister, never leaving her side.

Janie follows the girls into the house, looking around them with distaste. "First off, let's try the pump, see if it works, girls."

Scooter struggles to lift the heavy iron pump handle at the edge of the kitchen sink. She nods for Hayley to help. With both of them working it they slowly get it moving. They pump it up and down a few times. Nothing. "Shit."

Janie frowns at Scooter's language. "It likely needs to be primed. See the little hole? If we pour water down that, and then pump, we might get water."

Near tears, Hayley wraps her arms around her own torso. "But we got no water, Mama."

"That would appear to be true. We have to think, girls." Janie pivots on one foot surveying the kitchen and the living room beyond. "Hayley, can you look around and see if there's a broom somewhere?"

Both girls edge away cautiously. Janie notices and chuckles. "It's okay, really there's nothing here but dust and cobwebs. If you think this is bad you should have seen the root cellar at our old farm."

Slowly Hayley edges away and begins to search the house by herself.

Scooter watches her sister disappear. "What're you gonna do with a broom? You gonna dowse for water?"

Janie laughs out loud. "Lord, the stuff you know, Scoot. No, we're not dousing for water."

Hayley pokes her head back around the corner. "Mom? Do you think if there's water in the radiator bag we could use it for the pump?"

Janie and Scooter's eyes meet. Scooter jumps into the air, fist raised. "Hayley, you are a fuckin' genius."

Janie smiling broadly, shakes her head in dismay at Scooter. "Please do watch your language, Scoot. That's not at all ladylike."

Scooter races off laughing. "'K, Mom. Hayley, you're a lady genius, unlike myself, who is no kind of lady at all."

Janie watches as Scooter runs out the front door and grabs the canvas bag that hangs off the radiator cap of the Caddy. It's full to bursting, but she walk-runs it back into the kitchen.

Janie reaches for it and twists off the cap. "Okay, Scooter. You and Hayley work the pump handle." Janie lifts the bag over the sink. "I'll pour in a bit and then you both pump like crazy."

Janie tips the bag over the priming slot and pours. She nods to Scooter and the girls begin to pump. Nothing happens. They stop to rest a moment, discouraged.

"Okay, rest a minute—but don't give up. Let's give it one more try, okay?" Janie readies herself. "But we don't want to waste our water either."

Scooter and Hayley begin pumping again, and this time a couple of drops dribble out of the spout. "It's working, it's working!"

"Don't stop, girls. Keep pumping."

As they continue pumping, a gassy sound of air hisses out of the pump and then more water coughs out of the spout. It's rusty and smelly, but it's wet. And then suddenly it runs clear.

Scooter stops and grabs Janie's and Hayley's hands and they swing each other around in a circle, laughing and screaming for joy. Finally, they all wind down and stand winded, but smiling. Hayley grins, "I'll go look for that broom. And a bucket too!"

Janie is genuinely smiling at both her children. "YAY for my girls!" She slaps the dust off her skirt. "Now we can clean up."

Hayley's voice echoes from some vacant room. "Now, we can bathe."

Scooter shakes her head. "No, no, no. Forget that. Now we can have a water fight!" At Janie's look of disapproval. Scooter whispers, still grinning, "And then read books?"

Suddenly her smile disappears as she realizes she never thought to pack her books from the house. "My books, Mom. I never got to…"

Janie reaches out to put a hand to Scooter's shoulder. "It's okay, sweetheart, I packed your books. I wouldn't forget." A smile blossoms on Scooter's face and she throws her arms around Janie's waist.

• • •

As the sun slides towards the horizon, Janie and the girls file out of the house—clean, rested and tidy. All three stop to bang loudly on the roof of the Fleetwood.

The most Hanson has moved all day is from the front seat to the back seat. At some point, they gave him a damp rag to cover his eyes. He now has two days of stubble on his face. Hanson groans and waves them away. "Leave me alone."

"Hanson, it's getting late. You should get up." Janie gingerly opens the back door of the car. "There's water, you can have a splash bath before we set out." She reaches out a tentative hand to shake Hanson awake. Her eyes drift to the floor of the car and she notices multiple empty beer cans and vomit.

Janie shakes Hanson quite roughly. "Shit. Hanson wake up! Hanson! Where did you even get beer?"

Hanson struggles to sit up and smiles weakly at the faces crowded around the open door. Hayley takes a horrified step away from him. "Eww, Daddy. You stink."

"Christ, Dad. Did you barf in the car? The whole car stinks."

Hanson rubs his face with his hands. "Uh, sorry girls. I guess I did." He offers up a lame smile. "Good thing I had a couple of beers stashed away…That's what settled my stomach, I think."

"God Almighty, you were out here getting drunk again while we were all worried sick about how you were doing. For Chrissake, Hanson."

"Okay, he's been sick." Hayley grimaces, "Won't do any good to whine about it." She grabs one of Hanson's arms and pulls on it. "Let's just help him do a quick wash-up so we can stand to be in the same car with him."

"That's my girl, Hayley. Someone kindly show me this miracle of plumbing you've discovered."

Hanson levers himself from the car and uses the door to get upright. He sways a bit, but Hayley grabs his hand and steadies him. "Hey Scoot, do your old man a favor and tidy up the back seat and maybe air out the car a bit." Hanson leans on Janie and Hayley as he starts to stagger towards the shack. "We'll be on our way faster than you can blink, Scoot."

Scooter and Janie exchange a look, then Janie shrugs acceptance. "Hayley, can you manage him? C'mon, Scoot. I'll help you. The sooner we start, the sooner it's done."

Scooter watches Hanson stagger away. "Mom, he is not a child. We should not be cleaning up after him. I won't do it! Make him do it himself. The pig."

Her voice trembling, Janie begs. "Oh please don't start, Scooter, please. I just want to get out of here and get you guys something to eat."

"Me too. But this has to stop. We're always picking up the pieces of his disasters, Mama."

"I know, you're right. I've known for some time it isn't fair to you girls to live with such chaos." Janie puts her hands over her face. "He wasn't always like this, Scooter. When we met, he was clean-cut and handsome. He had a good job as a bus driver and he seemed so ...so reliable."

"Well, he's not now. His only reliable skill is getting reliably drunk." Scooter softens her tone, "This isn't fair to you either, you know."

Janie wraps her arms around Scooter and tears fall. Scooter slips her arms around her mom's waist.

"I just don't know what to do, Scoot. How do we get out of this, now that we're in it?"

Scooter hugs Janie tightly. "I don't know either, Mom. Let's start by cleaning the goddamned car so we can get out of here."

Janie leans back and looks Scooter in the eyes. She wipes her tears with the back of one hand. "I love you so much, Stephanie Jane Wells."

"Scooter, Mom. I will never be anyone's Stephanie Jane." Scooter lets her eyes meet her mother's. "Well, the Jane part, I don't mind. Okay?"

They separate and in tandem, open all the car doors and thoroughly clean out the inside.

ELEVEN

It's nearly dark, and a far cleaner and more attentive Hanson is at the wheel as they pull away from the old homestead. Everyone is jubilant to be setting out again. Scooter is again lying on the shelf beneath the back window with an encyclopedia open.

Hanson pulls out onto the highway and lets the car gather speed. Soon they're hurtling down the highway towards the horizon. "Oh man, I feel like I got a hole in my stomach the size of Idaho, I'm so hungry. My eye still works well enough to spot a hamburger stand from a mile away," Hanson announces.

Hayley chimes in, "Mine is as big as the CN tower in Toronto, Dad."

"How 'bout you, Janie? How big is the hole in your tummy?" Janie takes a breath and is about to describe how hungry she is when the car begins to sputter and jerk. Soon the Fleetwood begins to lose speed, moving more and more slowly until it stops by the side of the road.

Hanson hits the steering wheel with his hand. "Damn it all to hell." He attempts to start the car again. The engine grinds and groans, but nothing catches. He tries again. Nothing. "I cannot get a break."

He rapidly turns to face Janie. "We're out of fucking gas, Janie. Didn't you think to check it even once last night! How stupid do you have to be to let a car run out of gas?"

Janie doesn't answer—she cowers against the door.

"Huh, Janie? How stupid are you?" Janie understands that no answer will satisfy Hanson's growing fury. But she tries. "I thought you filled it up, Hanson. You did, I saw you at Mona's."

Livid now, Hanson's voice drops low and menacing. "So, yer saying this is my fault, eh Janie?"

"No, Hanson, that's not what I'm sayin."

"That's sure what it sounds like to me. Doesn't it sound like it to you, girls? Mommy thinks Daddy is to blame. He's to blame for everything."

In the back seat Hayley starts to cry. Scooter is stiff with apprehension.

"Hanson, you're scaring the girls. Stop it!"

Hanson uses his free hand to slap Janie hard across the face. "Don't you dare tell me nuthin', Janie Wells."

Before Janie can draw a shocked breath, Scooter has launched herself from the back seat and torpedoed Hanson where he sits. While he's off balance, Scooter reaches over and twists the door handle and shoves it open. Then she pushes Hanson out of the car and onto the shoulder of the highway.

A speeding trailer truck swings wide to avoid him, blaring its horn as it passes.

Scooter leans over Janie, fumbling with the glovebox catch. "Where is it? WHERE IS IT?"

"Scooter, what are you looking for?"

Scooter answers Janie's question when she pulls out Oren's revolver from the glovebox, turns and levitates herself out the driver's door after Hanson, who is now on his hands and knees by the highway.

While Hanson is still trying to right himself, Scooter takes a stance ten feet away and lifts the gun and aims it directly at his chest.

Scooter cocks the trigger. The quite audible click is unmistakable; it focuses Hanson's attention like nothing else in the world could. He looks up and all he sees is the sunset refracting off the barrel of a Smith & Wesson pointed right at him. He rises to his knees and shouts, "What the fuck! What are you doing, Scooter? Give me that damn gun."

"Daddy, if you move an inch in any direction but away from me and Mama, I will shoot you, as god is my witness."

"Scooter…"

"Don't temp me, Daddy." She takes the gun off safety. "You can be sure I will not miss at this distance. So, the farther away you are from me, the better your chances of living."

Hanson's face is wreathed in panic. "Janie, get out here. Come talk some sense into your child."

In the distance, oncoming headlights become visible. Hanson raises his eyes from Scooter's face, watching a pickup truck slow down as it approaches from behind Scooter.

"Someone's coming, Scoot. Put the gun down right now before it causes a scene."

The crunch of wheels on gravel announces the arrival of a vehicle some distance behind Scooter. A cowgirl, lithe and androgynous, gets out and starts walking towards the Fleetwood.

"Best be careful—my young'un has a gun and it's loaded," Hanson shouts.

Scooter can hear the bite of boots on gravel as the person approaches. And then all sound stops except the purr of the truck's idling engine.

Scooter calls out over her shoulder. "Whoever you are, I'm warning you. If you try to take this gun, I'll shoot this one dead."

"Duly noted, sister. It might be worth sayin that it's a rare event to see a woman pointing a gun at a man where there isn't just cause."

"Aw c'mon, lady. She's a ten-year-old kid. I'm her father."

"Hmm. Is that true, girl?"

"Yes'm. He is my daddy. But now he's hit my mama for no good cause. Plus, he slept the day away in a drunken stupor while his family had to scrounge for survival and go hungry."

Scooter dares a look over her shoulder. "This was the only way I could think of to serve notice to him that I've had enough."

"Well, you certainly have his attention now. Anything in particular either of you want to say?"

"Stop humoring her; this is not funny. Help me get that gun."

"So that's it? You just want my help getting the gun back, mister?"

At this point Janie pulls herself out of the car. Her hand covers her nose, but blood seeps between her fingers as she walks around the car. The cowgirl spots her and nods a greeting.

Turning back to the girl with the gun, she asks, "What's your name, child?"

"Name's Scooter, ma'am. And that there's my mama, Janie. And this useless piece of shit is Hanson."

The cowgirl nods again to Janie. "Evening, ma'am. I can surely see you've had some trouble. But can you help me out a little bit here?" The cowgirl nods towards Scooter. "I think we need to assure Scooter that she will be heard— even without a gun in her hand."

Janie nods in agreement and moves closer to Scooter.

"Scooter, she's right. Can you put the gun down so we can talk?"

"No, Mama, he'll just weasel his way out of this mess too. You know he's not to be trusted."

Janie reaches out her hand and places it gently on Scooter's shoulder so as not to startle her. "Then let me have the gun, Scooter."

"Mama, NO!"

"It's okay now, Scooter. You can trust me. I won't let him weasel out of this one."

Slowly Scooter leans into Janie's touch and then offers her the gun, still keeping it pointed directly at Hanson.

Once Janie has firm control of the weapon, Hanson begins to get up. "Thank god, Janie. I was startin' to worry."

"You should still be plenty worried, Hanson." She fires off a shot into the dirt next to him. "I'm not very good at this. I might kill you. Accidentally, of course. Maybe it's better to stay the way you were."

"I don't believe this. Have you both gone crazy?" He returns to kneeling in the dirt by the side of the road.

Scooter turns to face the cowgirl. "You see how he is! I want to be quit of him. I don't want to help him fleece innocent people anymore. I don't want him to sell me to creepy old men for favors." Tears begin to trickle down Scooter's cheeks.

"He did that to you, young'un?"

"Now wait just a minute…" Hanson stutters.

Janie waves the gun at him. "Don't tempt me, Hanson. Shut up. Yes, he did that. And if he can do that to my precious child…what won't he try next? Can you help us, ma'am? Please?"

The cowgirl releases a low whistle of dismay. "I can, Missus, and happy to. Who's that left in the car then?"

"Hayley, can you get out of the car please? Janie calls.

Hayley gingerly levers herself out of the car and walks around to join Scooter and Janie. Hanson looks up as she approaches and tries to smile at her. "Aw Honey, I know this looks bad, but this nice lady is going to help us work it all out."

Hayley steps up beside Scooter and slips an arm around her sister's waist. She says nothing.

The cowgirl tips back her hat and huffs out a breath. "Okay, so where were you headed? You got family in town, or somewhere to go?"

"No ma'am, we got nothing. Only what we could grab and run with when Hanson stole this car. He completely blew away any chances I had of paid work back in Summit with his stupid, stupid con games."

"And you weren't aware of this con game?" The cowgirl searches their faces. Scooter hangs her head. "No one was in on it but me. He made me help him.

And I did, thinking we could get enough money to move on and start over."

"Aw Scoot, don't lie to the nice lady. You loved being the center of attention…just like me."

Scooter begins to shake. She reaches down to grab Hayley's hand and holds it tight. She can think of nothing to say.

"You son of a bitch," Janie yells. "Unlike you, Hanson, Scooter is sorry. I doubt she will ever fall for a con game again." She takes a deep breath. "You were her father. She trusted you. We all trusted you, Hanson."

"I can do better now, Honey. Honest, I can. Girls?"

Scooter openly scoffs. "Daddy, I'm not sure you even know what the word better means." Scooter turns back to Janie. "Mama, I wouldn't trust him any farther than I could throw him."

The cowgirl seems to come to a decision. She turns to Janie. "I was just headin' into town to post a job notice at the general store. If you want, I can take you all into town and help you get sorted out."

Janie and Scooter look at each other and nod agreement.

Janie looks to her other daughter. "Hayley? Shall we catch a ride into town?"

Hanson is grinning now in relief. "Thanks, miss. We can get into town and have something to eat and then sort this all out as a family."

Janie turns the gun back towards Hanson. "I don't think so, Hanson. I'd prefer the girls and I ride into town together, as a family." Janie's face is rigid with anger. "You can stay right here with your beloved car."

"Janie, are you crazy leaving me here? You can't raise a family alone." Hanson turns pleading eyes on Hayley. "Hayley, talk to your mama."

Hayley's face contorts in anguish and sadness. "I'm sorry, Daddy. But I think maybe Mama's right."

Janie looks directly at Hanson and cocks her head as she sights down the barrel of the gun. "Girls, get what's important to you outta the car and pile it in the bed of her truck." The girls jump to it and grab books and dolls and blankets and race to the pickup truck.

The cowgirl moves to turn away to head back to the truck too. "I'd say you got lucky, mister. If it'd been my child, I woulda shot ya dead without a second thought."

The cowgirl swings by Janie and slips her arm around her shoulders. She offers to take the gun and Janie hands it over to her as they walk to the truck. Hanson is left on his knees as Hayley, Janie and the cowgirl climb into the cab of the truck.

Scooter hesitates a long moment, and then taps on the cab window frame. "Pardon me, miss, but my mama's gonna be looking for a job soon. If you're looking to hire help—maybe she could help you? She's awfully smart and a hard worker too."

Scooter ducks her head and climbs into the bed of the truck, facing backwards, so her eyes meet Hanson's.

Without taking her eyes off him, Scooter jambs her

blue cowboy hat on her head and gazes across the tarmac at him. Her face is impassive.

The truck pulls slowly out onto the highway. Scooter's eyes never leave Hanson's face. As the truck gathers speed, her father is still kneeling by the side of the road, growing smaller and smaller with each passing moment.

Once he's no longer visible, Scooter pulls the brim of the hat down over her eyes, so no one can see. She sobs until she cannot find her breath.

*the
kingdom
of
heaven…*

ONE

The room is small and dimly lit except for a spotlight in the middle that illuminates an old wooden desk with a water bottle and a stool. A teenaged boy stands stiffly beside the wooden stool. Dressed in summer shorts and a striped t-shirt, he affects nonchalance.

"Go ahead, Connor, tell me your story." A man's deep baritone is soft and not unkind in his request. He's invisible to Connor Lowry, fourteen, who stands alone in the halo of a single spotlight. The remainder of the room is lost in dusky twilight.

• • •

Connor clutches a small Bible to his heart. After a long moment, he begins to sing softly.

"What a friend we have in Jesus, all our sins and grief to bear. What a privilege to carry everything to God in prayer." He stops to take a shallow breath and continues. *"Oh,*

what peace we often forfeit. Oh, what needless pain we bear. All because we did not carry everything to God in prayer.'

Connor pauses and then begins. "You know, at first I thought when I got to camp, I'd just lip-sync the words while everybody else sang the hymns. But then I started watching *Billy Barnes' Gospel Hour* on TV and realized a man of the Lord can spot a fake a mile away.

"So, I figured I'd better do some homework if the game plan to finally discover my one and only true best friend was going to have a hope-in-hell of success." Connor laughs ruefully at his *faux pas*. "Sorry about the swearing."

"I found this cool website on the internet where you can look up nearly any church song ever written and actually hear how it's sung. And I kind of knew what titles to query from watching the *Gospel Hour*."

Connor creates quotation marks with his hands and deepens his voice: '*Technology can be a cool tool for the Lord; just don't let it steal your soul.*'

"That's what Revered Billy Barnes always said. So, I spent a few nights practicing singing, just me and my iMac, turned way down low so my parents wouldn't hear me. After a couple of nights, I could actually sing along with some of the stuff on the *Gospel Hour*. And after a couple of weeks of that, I figured what harm would it do for me to drop to my knees a couple a times and actually ask God to help me a tiny, tiny bit with this quest.

"At camp, once we all finished singing the opening

hymn, those that had chairs sat down. I usually had to stand 'cuz I often got to assembly late. But I didn't mind; it meant I could move around a bit so I could see everyone. At *Jesus Is Lord Bible Camp for Boys* everyone sounded a tiny bit like Reverend Billy Barnes—the campers, the counselors and of course Reverend Skinner. Especially Reverend Skinner."

Connor adopts a typical southern accent. '*And the Savior Jesus said, "Suffer the little children to come unto me," and he spread his arms wide and welcomed children of every color into his arms, just as we here at Bible Camp welcome all you boys to a full month of love in the name of Lord Jesus.*' Connor mimics the pacing and delivery of Reverend Skinner quite well. He even makes his voice deeper when quoting him.

'*My name is Reverend Skinner and I promise you the time of your lives here, boys. You're going to learn the Bible like you never knew it before. You'll make friends and you'll make memories that will last your whole lifetime. And the rules are simple—anyone can follow them—'cuz there's only one: Do unto others, as you would have them do unto you. Who can tell me what that rule is called? The Golden Rule, that's right. And it's golden because if you follow it completely, boys, every minute of every day, your life will be golden too. Now we're going to start our first day at Bible school with a Bible reading. Who wants to start? All right, Counselor Paul, what verses will you share with us tonight?*'

"Then Counselor Paul opened the big Bible on the podium and started reading.

'And God spoke to David and said, Be not afraid. For you are the chosen of God and no harm shall ever come to you… And much heartened, David took up a small handful of stones, washed smooth by a brook, and settled them in his pouch and went into his tent and slept untroubled for the remainder of the night.

'The next morning David stood on the battlefield and called forth the Giant Goliath. And when the giant lumbered onto the field and swept his eyes over the plain and they finally came to rest on the lowly shepherd boy, the giant laughed as if someone had played the greatest joke in all the world on him.

'Anger colored David's face, and he placed a stone into his sling and began to turn it round and round over his head. Before Goliath's laughter had finished echoing across the plain, David smote the giant with the stone and the giant fell dead at his feet. And then the Israelites cheered as if to raise the heavens.'

"Then Counselor Paul reverently closed the Bible. It was clear he knew that passage by heart, but he thumbed through the pages again, almost as if he'd like to do the reading all over again.

"Ya know, I keep thinking I'll find a best friend like David. Someone, you know…not a rock star, or a lead singer in a band—but just an everyday someone. That would be enough for me. Someone who liked me—and that I liked too.

"So even though I didn't ever go to church much as a kid, I signed up for Bible Camp thinking I might finally meet my best friend. And then, after I signed up, I freaked and began staying up late at night studying like crazy! 'Cuz, I was thinking that my new best friend would know the Bible backwards and forwards—and would never talk to me twice if I was as dumb about it as I was when I signed up.

"I started drilling myself on the Good Book on the school bus, all the way to school: Genesis, Exodus, Leviticus, Numbers, Deuteronomy. Reciting the chapters of the Bible under my breath so no one would hear me. I wanted to know them by heart.

"And on that long stretch of highway, before we picked up the Marshall twins, the sound of the bus tires rolling along, made a kind of singsong of the titles. After a few days it got easier to remember most of them if I kept up that rhythm."

Connor starts tapping his foot on the floor and then starts chanting in time to it.

"First and Second Samuel, First and Second Kings, Joshua, Judges, Ruth. It could almost be a rap song, except I'm not Black and I wonder if Reverend Skinner would have kittens over the idea of Bible rap. Although it could become a thing, ya know?

"And then, there were the stories. I had to know some of them in addition to the hymns. So, I went to the public library and looked through all the children's books on Bible stories. I figured it would be way easier to read *those* than search through the whole Bible to find the most famous ones.

"'Course, I told the librarian that I was looking for just the right book for my baby brother. She kind of looked like she didn't quite believe me, but since I wasn't picking on anyone while I was there, she left me alone in the toddler section. It turns out, some of the stories were really cool, like the David and Goliath thing.

"I have to say, I would've been David's friend in a minute. He was kind of like me, ya know? Kind of. Like he mostly was by himself a lot and he had all these older brothers that thought he was useless 'cuz he was smaller than them. I don't have any older brothers, but both my parents mostly act like they couldn't wait till I grew up so they could serve me drinks and talk about the stock market and real estate deals. When really, I think I'm more like David. But it's not something I can say out loud to them. They'd ask too many questions. *'David who? Where'd you meet this David?'*

"I had the most time to think at camp when I was getting ready for bed." Connor sets the Bible down on the desk and mimes washing his face, brushing his teeth, making faces in the pretend mirror in front of him.

"I think it was pretty cool that David got to hang out outdoors all the time and play with the little sheep. At Bible Camp we all slept in log cabins with rickety old bunk beds—ten boys to a dorm. I'll bet David always slept under the stars. And he probably knew all the names of the constellations. I gotta say it took me a while to get used to sleeping with nine other people in the room.

"Changing clothes was the hardest part. In gym class there are alcoves with curtains. At camp, trying to be sure no one was looking when I got undressed for bed was always tricky." Connor mimes looking around to make sure no one is looking, and then pretends to drop his shorts and pull up pajama bottoms.

"I bet David had a dog, too. The Bible doesn't say that, but all the stories you read about shepherds, they have dogs named Shep, or Blue, or something like that. And they're really well-trained dogs 'cuz you spend so much time alone with them out there with your sheep.

"And they do all kinds of tricks that are almost like magic—like you whistle in some special way and the dog works the sheep without even appearing to think about it. Bedtime was the hardest part really." Connor mimes climbing into the lower bunk on a set of bunk beds and pulls the covers up to his chin.

"Dogs love you no matter what. You hear stories all the time of kids being separated from their dogs, like by accident. They're vacationing or something and the dog gets left behind in Osoyoos and suddenly driving through Burnaby someone finally notices.

"Weeks go by, and then, one day when the kid's nearly given up all hope of ever seeing his dog again, there's a scratching at the door. And when the kid goes to open it, his lost dog bounds into the room and knocks him down he's so anxious to lick his face."

Connor falls to his knees and pretends to embrace the dog. "And the kid wraps his arms around that dog and hugs him so hard he's afraid he might actually hurt the dog. And he says to the dog, *I'll never let you out of my sight again boy!*' And the dog whimpers 'cuz he just wants to please the kid and chase a ball."

Connor sniffles in sympathy with this imaginary boy and then climbs to his feet.

"And the kid can't help it—he does this little crying thing, scaring himself, thinking *Oh my God, he's the best thing in my life and I almost lost him forever.*" Now Connor is actually crying too, with a hiccup or two thrown in for good measure.

"At camp, whenever any new kids cried at night, someone always shouted '*Oh, fer Chrissakes, shut up and go to sleep, crybaby.*' Even though you're supposed to 'do unto others'—ya know?"

Connor looks up and wipes his eyes with the back of his hands. "And so, I tried to just go to sleep. But the thought of that dog can get me going again so easy. I guess, I shouldn't think about it."

Connor begins singing again: *'Jesus loves me! this I know for the Bible tells me so. Little ones to him belong; they are weak, but He is strong.'* I learned this from *Billy Barnes' Gospel Hour* too.

"It turns out, my favorite place in summer camp was the barns. I went there as often as I could, even if it was dusty." Connor brushes himself off as if he had been covered in hay. "For one thing, it smelled so good. Even the horse poop smelled okay. Not at all like human poo, or even dog poo, which stink to high heaven."

He giggles self-consciously at his choice of words. "Sorry, that's a funny saying, eh—'stink to high heaven'. You'd think anything close to heaven would smell, well—heavenly.

"So anyway, I'd stand and feed the horses hay, which was everywhere. And sometimes if I could find oats that they'd dropped, I'd feed them that too. They flocked around me like angels."

Connor mimes petting a horse's head, holding his hand out flat as if it had oats in it. "Come here, boy. Don't be afraid, I won't hurt you. Here boy. Here." Connor lowers his voice again, becoming one of the older counselors. *'You do know the horse barn is off limits except during your riding hour each week.'*

"Oh, ah…I'm sorry. I forgot. I was just looking for a place to…"

'Couldn't sleep, huh?'

"Yes sir, er, no sir, I mean."

'Homesick?'

"Not really, sir. I just like horses...and sheep. Like David."

'David?'

"And Goliath, you know. The shepherd that killed the giant. The Bible story you read to us the first night."

'Ahh well, horses will have to do this morning. Bible Camp doesn't include any shepherding classes. You're new this year, aren't you? I'm Counselor Paul and I'm the camp riding instructor.'

"I know. My name's Connor, sir. Can I look at the horses while I'm here?"

'Sure, you can help me feed them if you like. The first thing we do is fill all the buckets with feed.'

Connor goes through the motions of putting oats into buckets. "Paul showed me how to weigh each bucket, so we didn't give them too many oats. Then we took the buckets and put them through the bars into each of the eight horse stalls. The last stall was the biggest and the horse in it was the most beautiful animal I had ever seen." Connor nods his head avidly.

"Paul—Counselor Paul—told me the horse was a Palomino stallion and that his name was Cisco."

'Ya know, not just anyone can climb into the paddock with Cisco,' Counselor Paul said. *'This horse doesn't suffer fools*

gladly. I understand that attitude, because I don't suffer fools easily either. You don't seem to be too much of a fool, Connor. So maybe I'll let you stick around.'

"Then we went into the horse stalls one-by-one, and Paul showed me how to brush them and even pick up their feet and clean out all the guck that gets caught in them."

Connor mimes bending over and leaning against the horse's shoulder, then gingerly picking up a hoof and squeezing his knees together to wedge the horse's hoof tightly to scrape out the mud.

"You have to hold their feet firmly between your knees like this. It's interesting. Horses' feet are kind of delicate, in some ways. They look all tough and hard—you can actually drive nails into the edges of the hooves, to hold their iron shoes in place. That's pretty tough!

"But horses' hooves aren't happy being wet for long periods of time. So, if your horse is plodding through a really mucky trail or he's left in a stall where he's treading on his own piss and shit"—Connor grimaces and shrugs an apology—"well, ya gotta clean it out or it makes the horse's feet go soft. Wouldn't be any different than you running around all day in soaking wet sneakers, which is bad for your feet—and smells about as bad too.

"So, we cleaned their feet and fed them, then let them go to the outdoor paddock. And then we would just stand and watch them a while." Connor puts one foot up on the stool rung, as if on the bottom rail of the paddock fence and leans forward as if watching the horses.

"I have to say, when the sun finally came up over the tops of the trees and hit Cisco's coat it was as if someone had set a mirror in amongst the herd of horses. He just gleamed. I couldn't take my eyes off of him. I remember Counselor Paul laughing and saying, '*You sure got eyes for that horse, Connor-boy.*'"

"And I said, 'I know this is going to sound stupid, but do you believe in love at first sight? That's how I feel about Cisco. I've never seen anything so beautiful in my whole life.'

"And Paul laughed again in a really nice, kind of growly way, and said, '*Let's see if Cisco feels the same way about you.*'

"The horse must have heard his name, 'cuz he turned his head and looked right at us, and then after a little pause, he ambled straight over to the fence where we were leaning. And he stretched out his nose and took this big sniff of me. All that time he was chewing on a bit of grass that he'd picked up somewhere and just looked me dead in the eye.

"And then, he took a step closer to me and he just breathed out—and don't think this is too weird—but it was the most beautiful smell in the world—all dried grass and warm horse breath. And then, he put his big horse head next to mine and nibbled at the bits of my hair that hung down over my ears and his breath just streamed down my neck and his whiskers tickled my cheek.

"And then—I don't know, it was really stupid. But I

started to cry. Tears just rolled down my cheeks and I couldn't stop it."

Connor heaves a big sigh. "It was like that horse was the first time anyone ever truly loved me, just as I am, no questions asked. Cisco just stepped right up and said he loved me by breathing me in. And Counselor Paul said that was all the proof he needed. *'Do you want to come by first thing tomorrow morning and start to learn how to ride, Connor-boy?'*

"I reached out and put my hand on Cisco's cheek and his hair was so incredibly soft. I couldn't imagine that he would actually ever allow me to ride him. But I told Counselor Paul that I would be happy the rest of my life if I could ride Cisco even once before I left camp that summer.

"Counselor Paul laughed again in that low, growly way of his and clapped me on the back like he was kind of embarrassed for me and said, *'Oh I'm pretty sure Cisco will let you ride him more than once. With enough practice, you'll probably be a really good rider by the time you leave summer camp. But you have to promise to come back next year—if I'm going to put all this work into you this year.'*

"I laughed, too, like he was insane. *Of course* I said I'd be back both sessions every year for the rest of my life."

Connor starts singing again, pretending to walk out of the barn in utter joy.

'This is my Father's world, and to my listening ears. All nature sings and around me rings the music of the spheres.

This is my Father's world, the birds their carols raise, the morning light, the lily white, declare their maker's praise.'

"That day goes down in history as the best moment of my whole life. My very best day at camp that summer. I was filled with joy, so much joy that I had to sing it out on the way back to breakfast—or I'd burst.

"I was still so full of joy at breakfast in the meeting hall that I did something I had never done before. And truly never imagined I would do, ever. I volunteered to read a passage from the Bible for the morning Blessing. I didn't even really think about it. But the minute Reverend Skinner opened his mouth, my hand shot into the air like it had been ordained to happen. I didn't have to think a minute about what passage to read, either.

"I practically ran up to the podium and flipped to the middle of the book—Psalms, of course. King David. You know, he was a poet and musician and shepherd and then after he killed that giant, Goliath, they made him a king.

"I didn't have to read from the book; I had this passage memorized. For a moment I became my hero, David, in the act of reciting the poem for the very first time—enthralled by the inner joy that filled his soul.

'Make a joyful noise unto the Lord, all ye, all ye lands. Serve the Lord with gladness: Come before His presence with singing. Know ye that the Lord He is God. It is He that hath made us, and not we ourselves. We are his people and the sheep

of his pasture. Enter into His gates with praise, be thankful unto Him and bless His name.

For the Lord God is good; His mercy is everlasting, and His truth endureth to all generations.'

"When I finished reading, the room was incredibly quiet. I got embarrassed and hurried back to the table where I had left my food and bowed my head for Reverend Skinner's blessing.

'Dear Lord in heaven, to thee we pray, blessed are the hungry for they shall be fed, blessed are the thirsty for they shall find drink and blessed are they that come to know your name.

'Thank you, Lord, for that rousing hallelujah from our newest Bible camper, Connor Lowry. Only a man who was well and truly 'on the path' could have read that passage with such passion. We know you will keep young Connor under your ever-watchful eye, dear Lord, and lead him gently home to salvation with the help and loving kindness of all his fellow campers.'

"Reverend Skinner went on at some length after that too, but that's all I heard. My ears were burning—I'd never had such praise in my whole life. I had to stop listening; it was just too much.

"It was weird, the rest of the day went by too fast and too slow. I could feel the eyes of the other boys on me. Especially when one or another of them ran up to link arms with me and walk with me a bit, bending our heads close to consult on a passage from the Good Book.

"It was both the most exciting thing that had ever happened to me—and the most excruciating. 'Cuz deep down I was a fraud—I knew it, and they were bound to find out. If this is what being popular was like, mostly it was horrible. Being singled out by Reverend Skinner suddenly made me the most sought-after boy at camp. Everyone seemed to want a part of my glorious salvation.

"And now, all I wanted was to turn off the spotlight that I'd spent my whole life scheming to get turned on. Any number of campers and counselors seemed ready to do battle for the privilege of being the one to lead me gently home to Jesus. There was just no way to argue. But by the time we had bedtime prayer circle, Randy Atkins and Ben Kershaw both insisted on walking me to my bunk and praying together yet again while I tried to shinny into my pajamas.

"I was already fretting that sneaking out in the morning to the horse barn might be a problem. Just as my bunkmate Simon was warming up to offer to pray with me first thing when we woke up, suddenly sweet inspiration came to my rescue. 'Wow, today has been so…ah, heavenly. I'm beginning to think I really need to be alone for a bit, to pray. Are you guys okay with that?'

"Really, that's all I had to say. The circle of Bible campers surrounding me immediately started offering their own excuses for me—and Simon conveniently uttered the opinion that all the greatest prophets actively sought time apart from their brethren to commune with God."

Conner mimes placing his head on a pillow and closing his eyes for a mere moment, a serene smile on his face.

"The next morning, I jumped out of bed and threw on my shorts. I tiptoed out of the cabin and then, looking both ways, I raced across to the horse barn. I easily beat Counselor Paul to the barn again. I already knew what to do, so I started filling the buckets with oats. I knew I shouldn't feed the horses yet though. That's totally a Counselor Paul thing. It turns out, if you overfeed horses on oats or corn—any of the grains that you normally feed them—their feet can just turn to mush. They kind of melt away from beneath them.

"Weird, hey? So, Counselor Paul said one of the first things he tells his 'wranglers'—that's what he calls me, his wrangler—'Never, ever feed the horses grain without my permission. Period. You'll never get another riding lesson at Bible Camp if you do.'

"So, I figured I could get everything ready before he arrived, and we'd have more time for the lesson. I had everything set up when he walked in. At first, I could tell he was a little pissed off that someone had been mucking about in his barn. But then, when I said we'd have more time for riding, he laughed and said, 'Connor-boy, I think we're going to get along just fine.'

"Whew. For a minute, I thought maybe I'd really blown it." Connor wipes his brow. "So we fed the horses, brushed them, turned them out and cleaned the stalls. Then just as I was finishing up the last stall, Counselor Paul hauled over a couple of hay bales into the middle of the aisle between the stalls. He stacked one on the other and laid a bareback pad on top.

"He must have seen my face drop when I noticed the hay bales, because he kind of winked and then patted the middle of the bareback pad. *'You thought I was just going to throw you up on the back of the only stallion for miles around without a bit of instruction prior to it?'"*

Connor stands and rests his hands on his hips, as if in thought.

"Counselor Paul did have a point. I mean, I hadn't really thought it through. I had just imagined me bareback on Cisco—racing along a seaside beach somewhere as fast as he would go.

"Bible Camp is set on 1,000 acres of scrub pine forest. Even the lake we swim in is man-made, for God's sake, so I really couldn't see us galloping along in the deep surf any time soon, ya know!

'It's clear as the nose on my face that Cisco likes you, Connor,' Counselor Paul said. *'And he's mostly one of the sweetest tempered stallions I've ever met—but look at him. He's full of ginger and cussedness when he wants to be, and I'd be taking your life in my hands to put you up on his back without some kind of warm-up for the real thing.'*

"My disappointment melted into a grin as I gazed at

Cisco playing among the other horses. Counselor Paul encouraged me. *'C'mon, Connor. If you're half the kid I think you are, you'll breeze through this lesson and be on Cisco's back in no time.'*

Connor smiles fondly as he recalls Paul's words. *'Okay, Connor. If this were a real horse, you'd be approaching him from the left-hand side. Correct?'*

"I knew this, I'd been reading about riding. So, I spoke up and added that I should be standing facing the rear of the horse, reins in hand.

"But before I knew what was happening, Counselor Paul grabbed me around the hips and tossed me up onto the bareback pad. Then he laughed that low-down growly laugh of his when I hiccupped from surprise.

"I caught the middle of that hay bale with my legs as tight as I could to keep from sliding off the other side, nearly squeezing it in half. More laughter from Counselor Paul.

'Now son, if you do that on any horse worth his salt, he'll be galloping away with you before you know it. To any well-trained horse, squeezing your legs tightly means let's get going!'

"Then Counselor Paul just slipped his hand in between my legs so matter of fact, and he ran it all the way up the inside of my thigh, real slow.

'When you're up on Cisco out there in the paddock, you've got to leave some airspace here, and here.'

"He kind of cupped the part of my leg he was referring to, squeezing it as his hand slipped along between my legs.

I felt like a deer caught in the headlights of an oncoming car. I was *hypnotized* by the thought of getting to ride Cisco and I confess, by Counselor Paul's hands. Honestly, things were happening so fast I didn't know how to react.

"So, I did nothing. Counselor Paul continued on with tips about using your weight to signal the horse. Mesmerized, I could feel myself settling into the rhythm of his voice almost—but not quite—against my will.

'Cisco's going to try to deek you out, 'cuz he's exactly the type of horse that just has to try to outfox his rider at least once a ride.'

"I couldn't help myself, at the mention of Cisco's name, my eyes strayed out the door. Just outside the doorway, he was prancing around the paddock as if pantomiming for me what a grand time we were going to have together—if only I could get through this little bit of weirdness.

"Cisco loved me. Out there in the sunshine, frisking about with all the other horses, he waited. I guess each of us knew at that moment that I'd do anything for Cisco.

'Now squeeze for me again, like you did before.' Counselor Paul's hand had come to rest along the inside of my thigh. I hesitated; I didn't quite know what to do. If I did as I was told, squeezed my legs tightly, it was going to push Counselor Paul's hand right up against my...you know—thing.

"While I was trying to figure out how to act, there was this kind of deafening silence, where all I could hear was my own breath. I could feel my eyes blinking—like a computer warning light, or something—while I madly tried to figure what the hell I was supposed to do.

"And then, Counselor Paul decided for me. He just kind of vaulted up behind me on the hay bale and reached out and put his hands on top of both my thighs and pressed down and pulled me close. Not hard, or mean, but insistent in a way that I couldn't have resisted.

'You don't squeeze, son, you simply sit deep. You open up and let the horse enter between your legs'.

"There I was, pressed in between Paul's legs. And suddenly I could feel the heat of his…um—thing, pressing into my bum.

"Counselor Paul continued to give me tips on how to ride as he ran his palms slowly up and down the tops of my thighs. Then his hands flowed back up the inside of my legs, each time stopping so close to my crotch I could feel the warmth of his hands radiating towards me.

"He did this several times—a slow pathway down the tops of my legs and then back up the inside. Talking in his growly voice right behind my ear all the while.

"I could feel his breath along the side of my neck as he talked, and I realized I had stopped breathing altogether. At some point I had started to hold my breath and I couldn't remember when.

"I could feel his heart hammering against my shoulder blades as his arms enfolded me. And I remember thinking to myself, 'how long can I not breathe and still continue to live? Thirty seconds, a hundred and thirty?' I could feel my throat constrict inside me, cutting off any possibility of breath.

"And when he finally made the last long stroke up the inside of my thigh and slipped his big hand inside the leg of my shorts, he was hard as a board behind me."

"And so was I."

· · ·

After a long moment of silence, the dim lights beyond Connor are ratcheted up a bit and he can see a man listening in the shadows. The man's voice asks softly, "School starts soon, Connor—what grade will you be? And do you know what age Counselor Paul is?"

Connor swallows and takes a breath, then sighs. "I'll be in ninth grade this year. I think Counselor Paul will be in eleventh grade."

"And can you tell us why you never told Reverend Skinner or the other camp counselors about this, Connor?"

Connor doesn't answer for a long, long moment. Then he shrugs and adds, "They would've made us stop."

Another long silence follows Connor's statement.

"And why did you come forward today then, Connor?"

"I feel like all the blame will fall on Paul, and I don't think that's fair." He pauses a moment, swallowing with difficulty. "It was two people's decision to do what we did, so it should be two people who share the responsibility for what happened."

"So, you're telling me you weren't coerced in any way?"

"That's correct."

"At barely fourteen? I find that a little hard to believe, son."

Connor meets the man's eyes directly, "I don't think you remember fourteen extremely well then, sir."

river
of
no
return

ONE

August 4, 1962. A radio sits high up on a shelf, tuned low, broadcasting a lush, symphonic version of an old Italian song. The quiet of the night, the room, the person sleeping—head on his arm stretched out along the ticket counter—all add to the ambiance of the music. In the distance a heavy door slams closed, and the sound of booted feet thumps along the wooden floor, coming ever closer.

Just as the door to the hall opens, the final notes of the song fade from the airwaves. The radio announcer closes out the hour with a hushed caption to the song. "That was 'Cara Mia', by the Montovani Orchestra, taking us to the hour at two a.m. Mountain Standard Time."

Calvin Two-Knives, the sleeping station master, stretches and yawns. "Gawd, I may murder Tommy if I have to work another double shift because of him."

Adam Heber hangs in the doorway smirking. "Uh-huh. And I'd help you get away with it too. I'd simply tell the police Tommy caught the last freight out of Jasper heading to fame and fortune on the coast. That'd teach him."

The radio switches to a newscast. "And now, the news at the hour on the Canadian Broadcasting Corporation." Out of long habit, both Adam and Calvin tilt their heads to hear the broadcast more clearly. "In a bid to appease prairie farmers, Ottawa has offered to buy up surplus grain from what appears to be a record-breaking wheat harvest."

Calvin lets out a slow breath. "Sounds like it's gonna be a super busy autumn for grain heading to Vancouver." He tips a coffee cup and uses his index finger to wipe out the final drops of java.

Adam laughs out loud. "Oh my gawd, you have the constitution of a horse, Calvin." He turns to cuff Calvin on the shoulder. "If we're going to replace Tommy, we better do it quick then, eh?"

The radio interrupts further conversation. "And tonight, a sad note from Tinseltown. Authorities have confirmed that movie star Marilyn Monroe has been found dead in her home tonight."

Adam takes a sharp intake of breath, followed by a guttural, "No way."

Calvin steps closer and carefully holds up both hands, instinctively limiting Adam's movement. "Hey, let's hear this out, okay? Don't go overreacting, Adam."

The newscaster continues: "An apparent suicide, Miss Monroe's body was discovered in her bungalow on the outskirts of the film capitol. Sources close to the star say that…"

Adam's shout drowns out the announcer. "Horseshit, Calvin. She wouldn't do that." His face is a mask of fury and pain.

"Miss Monroe had been depressed of late, relying heavily on drugs and alcohol. Reports from the star's latest film shoot alluded to problems beyond those usually associated with Tinseltown's sometimes petulant film stars."

Now Calvin reaches out with both hands and grips Adam's arms. "Adam, steady on, man. Don't do something crazy."

Adam turns his face away from his friend and shakes his head. "I can't stay here, Calvin. I can't stay." He takes a step away. "I have to go see what happened."

His step turns into a run as he barrels down the long hallway.

"Adam!" Calvin immediately tears down the hall after him, shouting. "Stop it, Adam, come back."

Outside the CN railway station, the great shadowed wings of the Rocky Mountains embrace the small town of Jasper and the entire Athabasca River valley. Every night Adam Heber has walked the train tracks to ensure they're clear within a kilometer either side of the station.

As he runs, Adam sheds the jangly variety of work tools that hang off his belt. He jumps off the loading platform and tears down the center of the tracks, quickly passing from the halo of the loading platform light, through the yard lights—one, two, three—and into the bowl of the black night beyond.

Adam's feet find the railway ties, creating a rat-a-tat-tat-tat rhythm that pumps him towards a distant star on the horizon. Behind him, Calvin calls his name in vain. All Adam can hear is his own labored breathing. All he can see is that great shining star directly in front of him. Its fierce light streams from horizon to horizon, bracketed by the black primordial forest on either side. His breath comes in heavy sobs now.

The wail of a fast-approaching locomotive shatters the night. It screams for Adam to vacate its path. Adam's eyes are seared by the engine's lamp as he throws his arms wide in a furious embrace and disappears into the blinding light.

TWO

July, 1953. The height of summer in Jasper, Alberta, and hot as blue blazes on the best days. Other days it snows, or hails, or a chill wind blows off the Rocky Mountains that would freeze you solid if you gave it a minute.

Blond, lank-haired young Adam Heber and porcupine-haired Calvin Two-Knives materialize from the blaze of the noonday sun. They stand at opposite ends of a stolen railway pump car. The car is mostly used for hauling gear out to any spot on the track that needs attention. More often it's stolen by local youth. The pump car is vintage even in 1953. The boys are already pumping as fast as two skinny, thirteen-year-olds can work the handle to power it down the track.

"Holy crud, Calvin, get the lead out. We're gonna be late. We gotta work harder."

"I am working hard, but this was your dumb idea, Adam. I just wanted to…"

They continue their slow glide past the train station on their way to town. The old pump car squeaks and groans as it sidles past the station. The boys work harder, trying to move fast enough that the station master won't spot them. But there's no one even there to watch them slide slowly past.

It's mostly desperation that's keeping the creaky cart in motion. Adam is desperate to get into town. Calvin is equally desperate not to disappoint his best friend. The shining metal track beneath them leads straight ahead, through the town and for a million miles farther west. The old railway station is draped with red, white and blue bunting. A crooked, hand-lettered "WELCOME" sign hangs from the eaves. More bunting is draped along the baggage carts lined up on the platform. Confetti is spread along the train tracks for at least a mile. It's clear they have missed one hell-of-a party.

Adam scowls at the abandoned station and blurts, "Jee-hos-a-phat. We should get off here and run. It'd be faster." He tries slowing the cart's hard-won momentum, with little effect. "Calvin, stop pumping."

They reverse their rhythm and finally get the cart to slow down.

"Dammit, Calvin, I told ya not to stop earlier," Adam yells. "You coulda used the washroom here and we woulda been on time."

A slight breeze lifts a handful of confetti and swirls it around the boys and down the track, practically begging them to follow. Calvin drops a solicitous hand on his friend's shoulder. "Should we jump and just let the brakemen find it afterwards?"

The afternoon breeze brings the sound of a very distant band playing. The boys both cock their heads to listen. "D'ya hear that?" Adam says. Without a second thought, he leaps off the now barely moving cart and begins to run straight down the tracks. "C'mon goof. They must be at the square."

Calvin doesn't hesitate. He leaps off the cart and races after Adam. After running for a few minutes, they skid to a stop. "I think it's getting louder," Calvin says. "Let's go this way."

An hour later, Adam and Calvin dawdle despondently down the centerline of the main highway. There is no traffic, and as far as the eye can see there is no one else on the road. The two boys slouch towards the apron of a driveway, slowing further.

"Sorry. Guess we shouda turned the other way." Calvin shrugs his remorse.

Adam shrugs in response: "My mom says everything happens for a reason."

A huff of disbelief bursts from Calvin's mouth. "You know, Adam, everyone thinks your mom's a bit of a nutbar."

Taken aback, Adam replies, "Ya know, Calvin, I don't think you can get away with calling my mom a kook. Even if she kinda is."

Calvin walks backwards, keeping Adam in his sights. "I didn't say she was; other people say kook. I say, Oracle of divine wisdom. Sayer of sooths." He grins across the asphalt at Adam. "Frog gigging tomorrow?"

Adam sighs in frustration. "My mom told my dad to hide my gigs. She thinks frogs are cool. Too cool to kill." He takes a couple of steps farther down the road. "Maybe I'll come over after chores, okay?"

"What'd I tell ya. She's at least a bit kookie." Calvin snaps off a salute to Adam. "So, I'll look for you after your chores, which I take it means pee-an-o practice? Ride your bike over, eh? We'll do something."

Adam turns towards home. He passes the time hopping from one segment of painted centerline to the next. Fifteen minutes later he hasn't taken more than two steps onto his front porch when he hears his mother's voice call through the screen door. "Adam, is that you, *lib eyner*?"

He stops and touches his fingers to his lips before placing them on the mezuzah attached to the doorframe. Before he can reach the handle on the screen door to let himself inside, the shadow of his mother, Emma, appears silhouetted against the light from the interior of the house.

She wipes her hands on a dish towel as she walks towards him, brushing a stray hank of dark hair from her face. "Did you and Calvin get to see the film stars?"

Adam slumps to the floor and simply shakes his head "no" in response. "Calvin had to go to the bathroom, which seemed to take forever." He looks dejectedly at his mom: "We were late getting to the station and then ran all over town but never found them."

His mother opens the door and bends down, gently smoothing the sweat off his tanned forehead. His cheeks are pink from being in the sun, his hair bleached to pale straw. "Papa's working in the kitchen at the lodge tonight. There's a big dinner happening for all the film folk, *ja*?"

Adam visibly perks up at this. He scrambles to his feet as his mom turns to go back into the house. She stops a moment with the screen door ajar. "Papa said, if you get there before it starts, you can help Minnie with the coat check."

Adam peers through the screen door, grinning. "Thanks, Mom. You're the best." He hurtles off the steps of the porch and grabs the mongrel bicycle leaning against the wall. Adam pushes it ahead of him and leaps aboard like a rodeo cowboy aboard a bronco.

His mother calls out after him, "Be back home before dark, Adam." But Adam is already cycling down the driveway, a maniac on wheels.

• • •

The sun is slinking towards the peaks of the closest mountains as Adam speeds along on his bike that looks as if it were scrounged from about ninety other bicycles. His skinny little legs shake; he's driving himself hard to get maximum efficiency.

He turns off the tarmac and coasts his bicycle around the rear of the hotel to the kitchen door. He tentatively pokes his head into the wide-open back door. When he doesn't see any of the bigwigs around, Adam silently slips into the kitchen. There is barely controlled mayhem inside as sous chefs chop, braise, blend, roll, dust, ice, spread and fry mountains of edibles, all the while keeping up a din of questions, answers, invective and other assorted commentary.

The Head Chef, Henri Lavoie, paces from counter to stove, to sink, to pastry board and back again, tasting, testing and then tasting some more. The prothesis on his left arm in no way hampers his speed of movement, nor his razor-sharp critiques.

Adam carefully makes his way to the far side of the room to stand next to the pastry board where his papa, Heinrich, reigns over his flour dust kingdom.

Adam is nearly as tall as Heinrich already, and about a third as wide. Heinrich's shoulders are stooped and rounded from years at the pastry board. He efficiently rolls out a huge slab of pastry dough with an enormous rolling pin. As he catches sight of Adam, he quickly pinches a tiny corner off the dough and places it in the palm of Adam's hand.

Solemnly Adam places it on his tongue. He nods approval, slowly savoring the flavor and texture. Adam raises his eyes questioningly to his father's. "You didn't use butter, Papa?"

Heinrich smiles his approval. "Very good, Adam." Heinrich returns to rolling out the pastry.

"No, I've been testing a new product. Mar-gar-INE, it's called." Heinrich pauses and frowns. "It's supposed to be more healthy and not so expensive, neh?"

Adam snitches another small corner, tastes it again, then shrugs, "But the flavor, Papa?"

Chef Lavoie spies Adam standing across the kitchen from him. He frowns very pointedly at Adam's father and bellows across the room in a heavy Québécois accent: "Herr Heber, this is not a nursery school."

Adam's father continues rolling out the dough in front of him but leans over and whispers to Adam, "Promise me you'll leave for home before dark." Adam avidly nods agreement.

"Try helping at the coat check," his father says as he shoos Adam away. "Minnie will appreciate it, and you won't look too out of place. Go. And *behave* yourself."

Adam smiles in response and scuttles from the room, keeping to the edges and out of Chef Lavoie's way. He deeks down a long hallway and can hear the brash summons of a phone ringing and then the bellhop paging someone in the lobby. He makes a sharp turn and scuttles towards the large ballroom that is spilling light into the hall.

THREE

The dining room is flooded with light from candelabras, discreetly placed table lamps, and multiple fireplaces. The light glints off the flatware on the tables, the silver serving trays, the cufflinks on men's shirts and the gems nestled against women's wrists and collarbones.

Adam's attention is glued to white linen tablecloths, the susurrus of chiffon sheaths and wraps as women move about the room and the quiet buzz of many voices talking at the same time. At a piano near one of the fireplaces a sophisticated man sits, readjusts his tails minutely, then brushes the key cover in a caress before opening it to reveal the keyboard.

The man leans over, turns an ear attentively to the keyboard and begins to gently, oh so gently, coax snippets of melodies from the keys. Women take turns leaning across the corner of the open lid and whispering things in his ear. He smiles benignly, but nothing intrudes on his attention to his fingertips.

Adam stops, caught up in momentary admiration for the man. Then suddenly he scoots along the perimeter of the room and arrives at the coat check. Breathless with excitement, he nods to Minnie and slips inside and peers up over the countertop.

The ice chimes against the guests' crystal highball glasses. The understated laughter of men's and women's voices is interwoven with the bell-tone of the ice. Near the fire, a group of well-dressed men surround a female figure. The circle opens just enough to let a waiter collect empty tumblers and replace them with new drinks. Another waiter mingles in the throng, bringing tidbits from the laden buffet table.

The circle opens again, this time wide enough to permit Adam's first sight of Marilyn: platinum curls, long line of thigh encased in form-fitting red silk sheath, one bare arm casually looped through some lucky fellow's arm. She laughs—a melody to Adam's ears—and then laughs again as she hands the waiter her glass and accepts a new drink.

Her face glows with a kind of divine illumination. As soon as the waiter's task is complete he exits, looking back over his shoulder at her, and the circle closes again. Men's faces surround her, all turned towards her as flowers towards the sun. Marilyn's laughter is full throated and inviting. Adam's eyes are riveted; he cannot look away.

Across the room, Robert Mitchum is levered away from

the group in which he is tangled by the promise in that laugh—as is every man in the room. They circle restlessly, posing only long enough with one cluster of people to give themselves permission to move on, closer to where they really want to be.

Marilyn knows it, she feels it all and exults in the glory.

Who is Adam to resist that blazing allure? He watches everything with avid attention.

Minnie gathers a coat handed off to her and passes the splendidly dressed gentleman on the other side a token with a number on it. She hangs up the coat and joins Adam at the counter.

"That must be Robert Mitchum, eh Minnie?" Adam says, pointing. "And that MUST be Marilyn Monroe."

Mitchum forces his way into the group, shouldering others aside. A softer, less determined fellow holds his ground a moment, then turns away, ceding his space with regret. He stops a waiter and places his empty glass on the tray and leaves.

Mitchum nods a greeting to the other men, snaps his fingers at the nearby waiter, who immediately glides within reach, proffering drinks. Mitchum lifts a fresh whiskey to his lips, nods his head across the diameter of the group acknowledging the fellow with Marilyn—but pointedly refuses eye contact with her.

Adam's eyes slide back to Marilyn. "Holy cow, she's beautiful, Minnie."

The actress notices Mitchum's silent rebuke and a shadow of a doubt flickers across her face. Her voice is that trademark baby-doll voice: "Bob. I didn't think you were ever going to join us."

Mitchum's eyes follow the flow of red silk along the long curve of Marilyn's thigh, but it's her escort's eyes that he meets.

"My apologies, Miss Monroe, I hadn't realized my absence had been noted."

Marilyn emphasizes her grip on her escort's bicep but continues her banter. "Ooh, noted and remarked upon, Bob."

Mitchum takes a deep swallow of his whiskey. "Remarked upon. Well, I guess I was later arriving than I had thought."

With a mischievous glint in her eyes, the starlet counters, "But not too late. My friend Natasha's still here. Waiting."

She nods to indicate the corner where Natasha Lytess, her acting coach and best friend, is seated. Natasha, a thin, tweedy woman, is deeply involved in conversation with an older-looking, bookish gentleman.

Now Marilyn is outright mocking. "And still looking for the man of her dreams, it appears." She's indulged by chuckles from her circle of admirers.

Mitchum raises his whiskey glass in Marilyn's direction. "Clearly. But alas, I'm afraid I'm a married man." Polite laughter follows his remark.

Marilyn turns away, tossing a final comment over her shoulder. "And suddenly that matters, Bob?"

• • •

The room is even more crowded than before, but the shine has gone off the party. Every flat surface in the room has a garland of abandoned highball and champagne glasses. It's clear most guests have passed the crest of the hill and are on that slow downward slump to a morning hangover. Adam still hangs over the sill of the cloakroom door, eyes watching every detail.

Marilyn takes a moment to extract herself from her coterie of men and glides to the side of the concert grand. The pianist pauses ever so briefly and looks up, but his fingers continue to move effortlessly. Marilyn whispers, "Play me something."

He nods, a slight smile accompanying his response. "I thought you'd never ask." He allows himself a moment to think, then segues into a melody. He turns to Marilyn, "I'm pretty sure you know this…"

Adam is close enough to hear the whole conversation and he holds his breath. Has the piano man guessed right? Will she know it?

Marilyn hums along with the first few notes and then begins to sing. "You made me love you, I didn't want to do it. I didn't want to do it."

As her sultry voice gains assurance, the stragglers of

the party drift towards the piano. Marilyn forgets they exist. Seated beside the pianist, she plays with the hair at the nape of the man's neck as she continues to sing. "You made me want you. And all the time you knew, I guess you always knew it."

Adam lets himself be carried away as he watches her.

Natasha and the bookish man excuse themselves from the small group at the table where they have been sitting. She tries in vain to catch Marilyn's eye, then waves good-bye in her general direction.

Minnie has stopped gawking, returning to reading a dime store novel. Noticing that Adam is still swooning over the door sill, she leans over his shoulder and whispers, "Don't spoil the night by making your mama worry, son." Minnie points to her wristwatch. "You should hop on your pony and ride, Adam."

"Awww, not yet, please?" Adam whispers back. "Five more minutes, Minnie."

He turns an irresistible hound dog look at her. "Pleease."

Minnie looks out over the room, shakes her finger at Adam and mouths, "Five minutes."

Adam's face lights up and he quickly turns back to the party. Marilyn finishes the song to a soft patter of applause. She leans down and kisses the top of the piano player's head; he grins up at her.

A cluster of men swoop in as a group to surround her once again. Marilyn resignedly reconnects with a token physical contact with her date, but he has turned his attention to the man to the right of them. They are deep in conversation.

Mitchum merely observes them all from over his whiskey glass. A younger man approaches Marilyn, whispering, "I saw you in 'Millionaire'. You were simply fabulous."

Marilyn winks at him. "Me? Or the clothes?"

"Well, both, *darling*." They laugh companionably.

"Is this new role in 'River' much of a stretch for you?"

Marilyn studies her drink for a moment. 'It's not intended to be...

"But?"

Marilyn meets his eyes, "It could be... it could be meaty." She absently squeezes the bicep of the man she's with.

"Are you sure we're talking about your part *dear*, or his?" They all laugh softly, enjoying the shared joke.

Mitchum's mind appears to be elsewhere, but his eyes never leave the star.

Serious for a moment, Marilyn shrugs. "I mean, both the male and female leads are quite *complex* characters." She lifts her voice to carry over to Mitchum, who she knows has been listening. "Don't you think so, Bob?"

"Whatever you say, Stanislavski." Good-natured laughter follows his comment.

Undeterred, Marilyn continues, "No, really. I feel my character is willing to risk so much. I kind of want to play her as a chanteuse on the outside—but with a Stanwyck core."

Marilyn takes a step away from her date's side, towards Mitchem, warming to her topic.

"For instance, the scene with the young kid where I'm dealing with the loss of all my worldly possessions. In that scene, my character Kay gets to be so many things… mother, teacher, older sister."

Mitchum's reptilian eyes slide over the enthralled group of men surrounding Marilyn. He motions to a waiter, grabs a fresh glass.

Marilyn continues, "I want to play each facet of the woman, as she moves from archetype to archetype." The men have totally gotten into the discussion of the scene. One prompts Marilyn.

"For instance? Give us an example. C'mon."

Marilyn turns and slides into a typical Barbara Stanwyck pose. Minnie chooses that moment to break from her novel and cross over to Adam, who stands enthralled. Minnie grasps his shoulders gently but firmly and turns him towards the door.

"Okay, this is the set-up. Kay's a dancer who is just hitching a ride to another town with a guy and his son. While crossing a river with their wagon, it tips and most of her stage outfits are carried away by the current. She only manages to rescue one fabulous set of shoes from the entire collection."

"Go on, then what happens?" one of her fans asks.

Marilyn picks a used glass from a nearby tray. She bends over it. "This is the scene. She's trying to salvage this single pair of shoes when the boy comes up to check in with her." Marilyn strikes a pose and continues in character.

"Hey friend." She mimes cleaning the shoes. "Elegant, aren't they?" She wipes a stray tear away. "Got to take care of them now, they're all I have left."

Across the room a plump, bald-headed fellow only now arriving at the party receives a curt nod from Mitchum. Otto Preminger, the film director, spots Mitchum's nod and immediately nods in return.

Elevating his voice to interject into Marilyn's monologue, Mitchum grumbles, "Finally, I was beginning to think Otto wasn't going to grace us with his presence tonight."

Marilyn stops and looks quickly across the room at the director. It's clear he's headed in their direction, and uncertainty now splays across her face.

"That was great, do more," urges one of her male chums. A chorus of voices agrees.

Mitchum takes a long swallow of his drink, his eyes minutely watching Marilyn's impromptu performance.

Rattled, Marilyn brings her attention back to her group. "Okay, so let me think. The kid asks, 'Why do people get married?' And then I say, 'Oh, if they're lucky, because they fall in love'." Marilyn looks up and sees Preminger slowly moving their way.

Another of her fans whispers, "Go on. What happens next?"

. . .

Adam tears himself away, knowing he absolutely cannot stay any longer. He slips out the back door of the ballroom and, still star-struck, wanders listlessly into the lobby and out the front door.

Dusk is edging towards true night. Adam stands a moment in the entryway and blinks. The first stars are scattered across the indigo sky. He notices and hisses to himself, *Criminy, Mom's gonna roast me alive!* He darts from the doorway and races around the corner in search of his bicycle, oblivious to anything around him. He runs directly into a very large boy, and before Adam can react, the bully, Gordie Rogers, shoves into him.

"Watch where you're goin', Kraut. You are a Kraut, right? I'd hate to get it wrong."

Adam barely stays on his feet. As he recovers, he quickly shifts into a defensive position, crouching but with one fist raised. It's clear he's been down this street before.

"What?" Gordie feigns surprise. "Oh, that's terrifying." He cups one ear, "Did I hear you say, 'pardon me, sir, sorry I bumped into you'?"

Ignoring Adam's raised fist, Gordie reaches out and pokes

at Adam's chest. Peering closely at Adam in the growing darkness, he says, "No, I don't think I did hear you say it."

He pushes Adam again. "You still hangin' out with that stinky injun boy? 'Course, you are, who else would have you? A Pollack half-breed and a Jerry. Perfect."

• • •

Marilyn is back in character and fearless. "The kid says to Kay, 'What is love?' And Kay's line is, 'It's like an ache in your heart when you're near someone special that only grows worse when you're apart'. The kid's young, so he gives Kay a puzzled look."

Still in character, Marilyn reaches out a hand and gently cups the cheek of the man next to her. 'You'll understand when you're older, son. At least I hope you do."

The group around Marilyn spontaneously applauds softly.

"And then what happens?" one of the men blurts.

Before Marilyn can respond, Mitchum steps forward, grinning. "What happens next is," he reaches over and soundly *slaps* Marilyn's ass quite loudly.

Of course, Marilyn falters, her focus completely shattered. "Ah, line please." She shakes her head in confusion. "Oh sorry, I've lost my lines." She's uncertain how to continue.

All the attention is now on Mitchum, who winks broadly to the men in the small circle, ensnaring them in the joke. Many are uneasy but remain silent. A few men laugh nervously as Mitchum drains his drink.

"See? Works every time you want to remind a woman what her place is in life."

More nervous laughter ensues, just as Otto arrives and joins the group. "Bob, you've told a joke that I didn't get to hear." He smiles at all the men. "Now, you're going to have to start all over again."

Mitchum shrugs nonchalantly, "Always willing to oblige a director, Otto." He pulls back his hand, miming a new slap. "Am I right, Marilyn?"

Marilyn looks about hastily as if seeking escape, but there's nowhere to go.

· · ·

Adam looks about nervously, trying to find some means of escape from Gordie. Suddenly a glowing tip of a cigarette appears behind them. Chef Lavoie stands leaning against the back wall of the lodge. His voice booms across the darkness: "Little children should be home by now, don't you think, boys?"

Gordie stops cold, his fist still gripping one corner of Adam's t-shirt. He lets go for a moment and Adam uses the opportunity to slide away from him.

Adam whispers to the chef, never taking his eyes off Gordie. "Yes, sir, I'm going right now."

"Good." Turning to Gordie, Chef Lavoie says, "And

you, little man, shouldn't you be going home to mama too? You do have a mama, don't you?" The chef pauses. "Oh, I remember now. One of the chambermaids has actually claimed you as her son. Am I correct, little man?"

Scared now, Gordie turns and bolts away down the path.

Adam sidles past the chef, about to turn the corner when the huge man reaches out and plucks the sleeve of his t-shirt and stops him in his tracks.

Chef Lavoie takes the cigarette from his mouth and whispers, "Be careful, son; be very careful with this one and his friends." Then he releases Adam into the night.

FOUR

Through a screen of evergreen boughs, the faded red siding of a Canadian National Railway caboose flickers in and out of view as the morning breeze sets the trees' limbs in motion. Inside, the caboose is fitted out as a makeshift dressing room/cum bedroom for Marilyn.

Natasha Lytess, slightly graying and in her forties, is at a dropleaf table making notes on an open script. The morning breeze neatly gathers the smoke from her ever-present cigarette and wafts it towards the bunk bed in the corner. Natasha exhales audibly and lifts her voice to be heard at the other end of the caboose. "So, we can play this scene a number of different ways. What's your gut feeling on it?"

Wrapped in a sleeping bag, the script propped up on her knees, Marilyn sits huddled against the far wall. "Um, I have some ideas." She takes a drag on the cigarette in her hand. "So, Kay, the saloon singer, thinks she's in love with the card shark who wins a gold mine in a shady hand of poker. Right?"

Natasha nods.

Marilyn yawns prodigiously. "Hell, does it never get warm in this country?"

Natasha shakes her head, "Stay focused, Mimsie."

Marilyn scowls at her. "Nastie, I hate that nickname. It reminds me of some stray cat."

Natasha raises one eyebrow and merely cocks her head in response. "Fine. So anyway, she meets Matt—Mitchum's character—who she thinks she hates at first."

"*Quel suprizio.* Another unexpected plot twist."

"Nastie, spare me the film critique. We're working here."

Marilyn shakes her head and continues. "But then as they get to know each other, Kay's feelings turn to love.

"Yeah right," Natasha mumbles.

"Don't. You're screwing up my concentration." Marilyn takes another drag on her cigarette and continues. "Bob says his character Matt doesn't want to get close to anyone since his wife died. Besides, he's trying to reconnect with his kid, and even that's too much for him emotionally."

"Bob Mitchum said that?" Natasha's look of surprise seems quite genuine.

Marilyn smiles sweetly across the room at her. "He's not an asshole all the time, Nastie. Anyway, Kay is way ahead of Matt on that score. Both she and the kid are struggling emotionally too and have discovered each other."

Marilyn hauls herself off the bed, keeping the sleeping bag tightly wrapped around her. She tosses the script down on the table and helps herself to a sip from Natasha's coffee cup.

"Would you actually like some of your own? I can ask our production assistant to fetch you some."

Marilyn smiles, "'Course not."

They chorus together from long habit: "I only want a sip of yours."

Marilyn begins pacing the length of the tiny caboose, the sleeping bag trailing on the floor behind her. "Anyway, Kay's outside the cabin talking to the kid. But she knows the dad is inside listening."

Natasha throws up her hands and moans, "God, this is such dreck, Mimsie. What the hell are we doing here?"

Marilyn turns to look at Natasha and then just deflates completely. A long unhappy silence ensues. She locks eyes with Natasha. "We are working with the hottest director in Hollywood. It doesn't matter that I am along as the tits and ass on a third-rate script set in the boonies."

"Third-rate would be elevating this script, Mimsie."

Marilyn brushes away Natasha's comment with one hand. "Don't you think I know Otto cares more about the light on the goddamned mountains than he does about his female lead?" She raises one finger in the air to mark her next point. "Your job, your *only* job, is to help me lever this material up a notch. If you can't do that, then I need to find a new coach."

Natasha visibly deflates and nods a reluctant yes.

"So, Kay's talking to the kid, knowing his dad is listening and she wants to use the moment… use the moment to say, 'Hey, I'm more than you think'."

"Okay. Such as…"

"Well, we all know what Mitchum's character thinks of Kay. I think she uses the moment to say, 'Hey this is not all I am. Sure I perform in bars and dancehalls, but I do other things too.'" Marilyn stops a moment, thinking. Then she inhales deeply and blurts out, "Maybe she writes poetry."

Natasha openly scoffs. "Honey, she probably can't even read! Most people on the frontier in those days couldn't. Try again."

Stymied for a moment, Marilyn turns and looks out the caboose window. The film crew is busy setting up for the day's shoot. The tiny cabin that's the focal point of the scene has a backdrop of a fabulous blue-green river and towering mountains.

She turns back to Natasha. "God, Natasha, can you even imagine what being a woman was like in those times? You'd be dirty all of the time, and cold as billy-hell most of the time, and always, always tired from just trying to scrape by."

Marilyn wraps the sleeping bag more tightly about her shoulders. "And you'd dream of moments when you could just sit, maybe next to a fire in a rocking chair and relax for a single minute. And Kay thinks this guy, Matt, can give her that."

Marilyn throws a look at Natasha, daring her to challenge her assumptions about the character.

Instead, Natasha laughs. "Okay, okay we can work with that. Maybe she makes up her owns songs, though. Not poetry." She rubs her hands together to warm them. "Are you telling me that Kay's desperate for a man, then?"

Marilyn grins a response. "No, not at all. She's with men all the time. Surrounded by them." She pauses, "But Kay's lonely. And this is where she and Matt can intersect, because he is essentially lonely too, but doesn't know how to say it."

Natasha nods her head in agreement. "This is good, Mimsie, really good." She stands up and grabs the script from the table. "We can definitely use this."

A knock on the door interrupts any further collaboration. "Hair and make-up in five minutes, Miss Monroe."

• • •

The afternoon is ablaze with sunlight when Adam is trotting casually along behind a battered pickup truck. The truck's tailgate is missing, and the bed is rusting and dinged. In the back of the truck, Calvin and several younger brothers are sprawled, chatting to Adam as he trots alongside it.

"You sure you can't come?"

One of the younger kids leans over and offers his grimy little hand to Adam to haul him onto the truck bed. Adam's face is bereft. It's clear he soooo wants to join them, but he shakes his head 'no'.

"Calvin, you know I can't. My mom always wants the family together for Friday dinner. It's special at our house."

"You could just leave her a note. And then say later you totally forget it was Friday. It's easy to forget what day it is with no school."

Adam hesitates at the hope in Calvin's face. Then, he stops abruptly in the center of the highway and shakes his head with bitter resignation. "I can't, Calvin. I just can't."

The pickup truck gathers speed as it pulls farther away from Adam and finally disappears around a bend in the distance. For a long moment Adam simply stands and watches the empty horizon. If he wasn't nearly thirteen, his face says, he'd break down and cry. Instead, he turns and begins walking homeward. His hands are shoved deep into his pockets, his shoulders rounded forward and his head hangs against his chest as he tussles with his own disappointment.

• • •

Marilyn is seated on an old tree stump in the shade behind the movie set cabin. Behind her, the mountains glow with the Honey-colored sunlight that saturates the afternoon.

A battered red high-heeled shoe sits in her lap. She holds the matching red shoe in her hands, very carefully cleaning it and examining it for flaws.

The film's director calls sotto voice, "And AC-tion."

A young boy about eleven enters the frame and stands watching Marilyn clean the shoe. "Hi," he says shyly.

"Hey friend," Marilyn whispers, but continues cleaning the shoe. The boy lifts the shoe from Marilyn's hands and examines it thoughtfully.

"Cut, cut, cut," Preminger growls. Both actors freeze in place. Their faces mirror guilt, along with a bit of puzzlement.

"Camera." Preminger holds up one hand, to stop the action. "The light has shifted slightly on us. Joe, double-check our perspective before we go again."

Both Marilyn and the boy relax; it wasn't their acting that stopped the filming. The young boy returns the shoe to Marilyn and walks off camera.

"Sure, Otto." A moment later the cinematographer nods his head and calls, "We're good to go."

Preminger drops his hand, and a cameraman calls out, "Camera rolling."

Marilyn meets Natasha's eyes, standing just off camera, nodding and making a fist. "Be strong," she mouths. Marilyn smiles ever so slightly in response.

A second crewman steps in front of the camera with a slate and snaps the clapper closed. "Scene 9, take 2."

"Alright, let's try it again everyone," Preminger calls. "Miss Monroe, sometime today while we have the *light*. And AC-tion."

. . .

Later, Marilyn is slumped in the rear seat of the limo, pounding the back of the seat with a red high-heeled shoe. Her mascara is slightly smeared and her lower lip trembles as she throws the shoe.

The chauffeur who drives her to and from set peers at her in the rearview mirror, not unsympathetically.

FIVE

Adam is still idling his way home, walking the center-line of the highway like a tightrope. He jumps from one yellow strip to the next, aiming not to fall off on either side. He's pretty good at it. An automobile is gaining on him from behind, but he keeps whistling, concentrating on that yellow centerline.

As the limousine draws even with him, the rear window nearest to Adam slowly descends. Marilyn's head and shoulders appear, framed by the car window. The wind gently ruffles her platinum curls. Adam pretends not to notice.

"Hey stranger…" Her voice is a little shaky.

Adam continues playing his game, still not looking up. "My mom always told me to be careful talking to strangers," he mutters, belatedly adding, "ma'am."

Marilyn finishes rolling down the window. Adam glances out of the corner of his eye. She looks a little tired, a little unhappy.

"What did she tell you about playing in the middle of the highway?" Marilyn counters.

"I don't think she's had cause to pronounce on that yet," Adam replies dryly.

Marilyn laughs out loud. "She hasn't?" Turning to her driver, she says, "Sammy, can you stop the car please."

As the limousine halts, Marilyn opens the rear door and puts one nylon-clad leg out. She joins Adam in the middle of the road. "Can anyone play? Or does your mother have a pronouncement on that too?"

Like a true gentleman, Adam steps aside and sweeps his hand forward to indicate it's Marilyn's turn. "No Ma'am, she hasn't gotten around to the issue of *playing* with strangers yet."

Sammy hides a chuckle in the palm of his hand as he allows the limo to glide alongside the two. Marilyn balances along a yellow line, one step at a time, then leaps to the next one. Perfectly, of course.

Adam deadpans, "You should maybe have to jump two lines cuz your feet are bigger than mine. Unfair advantage."

Marilyn stops, hands on hips, scowling at Adam. "They are NOT bigger than yours."

"You're Marilyn Monroe, right?" Adam peers at her out of the corner of his eye. "I was searching all over for you yesterday. Me and Calvin."

This acknowledgement of her fame cheers Marilyn considerably. "You looked ALL day?" She is obviously begging for more details.

Adam notices and plays down their misadventures. "Well, part of the day. Me and Calvin, my best friend. He's part Pollack and part Cree." He bends down and picks up a stray pebble off the roadbed. "We looked for a little bit."

He tosses the pebble and hits a tree trunk off to the side of the road. "Bet *you* can't hit that pine tree." He points at the tree his rock has just barely nicked. Then he picks up another stone and tosses it again, hitting the tree solidly this time.

"Looks like you can barely hit it yourself, bub."

Adam shrugs and walks away. "It's okay with me if you don't want to play."

Immediately contrite, Marilyn quickly picks up a couple of small rocks and races after Adam. "I do. Really." She offers up one of the pebbles. "Here. Take this. We'll take turns."

Adam grudgingly turns and takes the stone from her hand. "Okay, I'll take one more shot. Then you get your three." He turns to see if she's in agreement. When Marilyn nods her head eagerly, he continues, "Whoever has the most hits *wins*... and the loser has to buy them an ice-cream soda!"

Adam aims oh so carefully, cocks back his arm and

throws. CLUNK. His rock hits with a certain authority. Triumphant, he turns to Marilyn and motions for her to take her turn.

Marilyn steps up to the line, stones in hand. She holds one carefully, feeling its weight. Sammy allows the limo to creep as close to the movie star as he dares, not wishing to miss a thing.

Marilyn takes her stance, winds up and throws. The stone goes miles and miles but drops like a bomb and cracks the tree knot. Without a minute's hesitation,

Marilyn tightens her lips and winds up and throws again. Clunk. The stone creams the pine knot and ricochets away. She immediately leaps into the air in excitement. "Me, me, me!"

Adam watches skeptically. "May I remind you… I have two hits to your two. We are officially tied, ma'am."

Marilyn stops and stares him down. "Oh, you'll be sorry for that 'ma'am'… *little* boy." Adam snorts in derision.

Marilyn begins her wind-up, then whips her arm forward. The rock whistles towards the pine knot, landing with a solid clunk. She immediately begins jumping up and down in triumph. "I won, I won."

Adam shakes his head and folds his arms over his chest. "No way a girl could have made that shot. No way."

Marilyn is jaunty as she leads the way back to the limo. She opens the door for Adam before Sammy can even get out.

As Adam folds himself into the back seat, Marilyn whispers. "News flash, Adam, *I'm really a man...*"

• • •

Sitting in the limo, Marilyn and Adam are contentedly sipping sodas. Out the window, the sun is nearly setting, creating a stunning glow against the mountains. The first night star has appeared on the horizon. Adam leans forward and taps Sammy on the shoulder.

"You can let me off at the top of the driveway. No need to take me all the way to the house. I really appreciate you getting me home on time, Miss Munroe."

Sammy glances into the rearview mirror for Marilyn's approval. She smiles and nods permission.

"Ashamed to take me home to meet your parents, Adam?" She pokes Adam in the ribs and laughs.

Adam blushes furiously. The car turns off the highway and slows, then stops.

"Heck no, Miss Monroe." Adam extends his hand to Marilyn to shake goodbye. "It's just that Papa, my dad, is at work still. And my mom will be busy making supper. We always eat as soon as he gets home on Friday nights." Suddenly self-conscious that he is babbling, Adam stops. "But this was swell. Really swell."

Marilyn ignores his hand and says, "It was the BEST. And please stop with that ma'am and Miss Monroe stuff." She winks. "We're friends, aren't we?"

As Adam climbs out of the car. Marilyn calls to him, "Come by the set tomorrow…if you want to, that is."

"You mean it? I'll check with Papa. Maybe in the afternoon, okay?"

Marilyn smiles and leans over to open the door for him. "That would be perfect, Adam. See you then."

SIX

The only sound is the metronome. Adam's fingers fumble with the slow, careful first movement of 'The Moonlight Sonata'. Its cadence of repeating three notes is astonishingly demanding when done well.

He reaches up, stops the metronome and gets ready again. This time he rises slightly and pretends to doff tails from beneath his seat, just as the pianist did at the Hollywood gala. He rubs his fingertips lightly together and then begins, using the barest whisper of touch to sound the notes.

From the kitchen his mother calls, "That was pretty good, *liebkin*. The tempo was perfect. But you're hunching over the keys, aren't you?"

Adam looks at the huge clock clearly visible on the kitchen wall from his vantage point at the piano. The large black minute hand passes twelve and starts its way through another minute.

"Sweetheart, all the time you spend looking at the clock doesn't count as actual practice time. Try it again *with* the metronome this time, the same touch and straight spine," his mother admonishes.

Caught in the act, Adam sighs heavily, then bends to his task, head inches from the keyboard.

Unnoticed, his papa has ambled down the hallway and stops to watch his son struggle at the keyboard. Heinrich pauses to lean against the door jamb. Sunlight from the kitchen dapples Adam's hair.

His father can't resist. He lifts one hand, using two fingers to create a bunny shadow on the sheet music in front of Adam. Adam jumps, then laughs. His father joins him on the piano bench, ruffling Adam's hair with affection.

"Please don't tell me we need to buy you eyeglasses, son.

Adam bolts upright in horror at the thought. "Heck no, Papa." He frowns again at

the sheet music in front of him.

"I'm lost here…I just don't have the delicacy to master this." He looks again

at the kitchen clock and then at his father's face. "It's summer… and *everyone's*

outside playing, but me. Please, Papa?"

His father's brown eyes soften. He reaches over and gently closes the book of sheet music. "So… go play then, son. Next time I want you to play this piece like a marching band; pound it like sledgehammers. Maybe delicacy will follow after that, eh?" Heinrich smiles as he notices the delight in Adam's blue eyes.

"It takes time, Adam, for every good thing to become itself. You just practice the best you can every day."

His father drops his eyes to the keyboard and begins softly playing the opening notes to the piece Adam has been struggling with. He looks at Adam, who is eager to leave. "A friend mentioned that the lodge might not be the safest place for you these days, son. I want you to stay away from there for the rest of the summer."

But Adam is already out the door and doesn't hear him.

• • •

Adam is barreling along on his motley bicycle, looking for the movie set. At the intersection of a gravel road and the highway he slows and turns sharply, skittering around the turn in the loose gravel. It only takes a second to right himself and he's speeding down the access road.

Moments later he is standing next to Marilyn's acting coach, Natasha, off to one side of the set. It's the same cabin as in the previous scene, from the inside this time. The camera captures Robert Mitchum looking through a window watching Marilyn and the young actor replaying their scene. This could be the final take, if all goes well, and that fact is on everyone's faces. The circle of crew surrounding them are all holding their breath.

The boy hands back the red shoe to Marilyn. "Why'd you get married?" he asks.

"I fell in love, I guess." There's a wistfulness to her response.

"How'd you know you were in love?"

"It's so hard to know, son." She shakes her head in puzzlement. "It's like standing over a deep river, wanting to swim but afraid to jump. And then you do. It's the only way to really know in the end. You have to make the jump."

Marilyn has doctored her lines. She holds her breath. Otto remains steadfastly silent. The actors continue.

"How old are you?" The boy's delivery is all innocence.

Marilyn reacts just as Kay would have. "That's no question to ask a lady." She begins tidying her blouse and tucking it in. "But then I'm no lady, really."

"What?" The kid is mystified. "Why aren't you?"

Marilyn continues to dress, laughing softly. "See me in a couple of years and I'll

try to explain it to you then."

A moment of silence descends on the set and then the crew erupts into cheers.

Preminger bellows, "Cut. That's a print." Applause follows from all around. "The play of light and shadow across Matt's face inside was genius, Joe. Nice work."

Marilyn lets out a sigh of relief. "Well, that went better than I hoped." She makes eye contact with Natasha and smiles. Marilyn turns to the young boy in the scene and gushes, "Nice work, Tommy."

Tommy is briskly being bundled into a heavy coat and hat by his mother and hauled off the set. He casts a wan look over his shoulder. His mother casts a scathing look in Marilyn's direction and rushes him away. Marilyn's face registers confusion, and surprised hurt.

The set A.D. shouts, "Okay everyone. Break for lunch. Crew back in one hour. Cast in two, please."

As the crew strides away from the shoot, Adam appears, grinning. Marilyn spots him and smiles. A wardrobe P.A. returns Marilyn's sleeping bag to her in exchange for the red high-heeled shoes.

Marilyn puts an arm around Adam's shoulders and pulls him with her as she begins to stroll away from the scene. "We'll be back on time, Natasha, I promise."

Natasha waves her away. "Go. Enjoy."

Marilyn squeezes Adam's shoulder briefly. "So. What'd you think?"

Adam steps away to look into her face and gauge the question. "Really?

"Yes. Really."

"Your acting is cool. I mean you explained some of it the other night at the party."

"You were there?" Marilyn asks, surprised.

"Yeah, in the coat check with Millie." Adam grimaces, suddenly self-conscious.

"Anyway, it's neat what you were trying to do. And it worked." He steps back close to her again. "But the kid's a dope. I mean, what's with that…"—here he shifts to a whiny voice laden with feigned innocence—'why did you get married?' malarkey."

"You think it's malarkey? Getting married, I mean."

Adam turns and starts walking backwards to continue the conversation. "No, no. That wasn't my meaning. I just thought the kid's delivery was so fake." He shrugs, "No kid ever, ever asks adults about love and stuff. Especially not to a girl, and most especially not to someone who is like a mom."

Adam turns forward just in time to avoid running smack into a reflector tripod. He looks askance at Marilyn. *"You woulda let me run smack into that!"*

"Whaaaat? You were miles from it yet. I woulda saved yuh!"

"Yeah, right."

They cross from behind the cabin and Marilyn leads him towards the solitary caboose near the main track. She quickly takes the three short steps up to the doorway.

"Mi casa, su casa," she says, waving her arm expansively to motion Adam inside. "That's Spanish for my house is your house. My housekeeper in L.A. is teaching me some phrases." Her smile of accomplishment is huge.

Adam peers inside, hesitating. "Neat." The interior is a dimly lit mess: bed clothes, scripts, an ailing potted plant, a baseball and bat along with a million other items cluttering the small interior. "The Spanish, I mean. Obviously."

A picnic basket sits on the fold-down table where Marilyn and Natasha had been working. Next to it is a very large thermos. Marilyn grins and tosses the thermos to Adam, who bobbles it but hangs on. She blithely picks up the basket and heads back out through the door.

"Nice catch. Maybe you should consider a career in sports. Baseball maybe?"

Just beyond the railway siding, the limousine sits across the tracks from the little red caboose. Adam is a little slower off the draw and joins her just as she begins her march across the tracks to the car. "Gotta hurry if we're going to find a nice spot for lunch and still get back for our call time."

Adam shakes his head in dismay but obligingly trots after her.

Sammy spies them from the driver's seat of the Caddy and leaps out to open the back door for the film star. He nods his head to Adam as the boy appears moments later and climbs into the back, beside her.

Sammy closes the back door, walks briskly to the front of the car and slides behind the wheel. Adam leans forward saying, "Good afternoon, Sammy. How are ya?"

Sammy touches the brim of his hat and flashes a tiny smile at Adam as he adjusts his position. Adam leans back against the seat and props the huge thermos on one thigh. After a moment's silence he whispers, "He's not very nice to you."

Marilyn looks at him quizzically.

"The old bald guy who shouts all the time."

Marilyn giggles. "Do you mean Otto? The director?"

Adam shrugs. "I guess. Is that what a director does is shout everything and pick on people who are trying their best?" He pauses. "Some job."

Marilyn squeezes Adam's arm. "My hero."

"It doesn't take a hero to notice when people aren't nice, Miss Monroe. The same kind of junk happens all the time at school too—like to my best friend, Calvin. Guys will stand around in a gang and say stupid stuff about him being an injun and a Pollack. And they go on and on until one of us breaks down and..." Whoops. Adam realizes he's maybe said too much.

After a long moment, he finishes lamely. "Well anyway. They always end up saying 'Criminy, can't you guys take a joke or nuthin. You're such babies'. They make it out that's it's our fault that what they say hurts. How stupid is that?"

Marilyn turns a sympathetic look his way. But her tone is teasing: "Wow, you're almost smarter than you look, kiddo."

Adam looks abashed for a moment and then counters her comment. "Yeah, well according to my mom that wouldn't be hard."

Marilyn leans forward and points through the windshield. "Sammy, can you just turn in here and pull up as close to the river as you can?"

Sammy pulls the car off the road and cruises along a bumpy dirt track next to the river. He finds a lovely spot beneath a cluster of birches that grow right down to the riverbank and lets the limo roll to a stop.

Marilyn opens the door and scoots off the back seat of the car, hauling the picnic basket along with her. "C'mon, slow poke."

Adam scrambles out, dragging the abandoned sleeping bag with him. Marilyn notices he's struggling with the thermos and the bag.

"We can have Sammy carry that you know." Marilyn suddenly swoops back and scoops up the bag over her free arm. "Or I could do it!"

Sammy gently lifts the hamper of food from Marilyn's arm and follows them down to the river. Using the sleeping bag for a picnic tablecloth, Marilyn eagerly starts unpacking lunch and handing out napkins and paper cups.

Adam watches as Sammy returns to the car, pulls out a rag and begins to polish the fender of the limo. He leans over and whispers to Marilyn, "What about Sammy?"

Marilyn stops and turns, considering her driver for a long moment. She turns to Adam, whispering seriously, "What do you think we should do about him?"

"Well, we can't just leave him there. It's not right."

Marilyn contemplates her driver a moment longer, then

puts her fingers to her mouth and whistles an astonishingly loud blast. When Sammy immediately looks up from the car, Marilyn motions for him to join them.

"Leave off, Sammy. Come eat with us." Marilyn waves to the spread of edibles before them. "C'mon, we haven't got all day."

Sammy hesitates, then drops his rag and comes to join them. Grinning now, Marilyn sets out a new napkin and paper cup.

Adam nudges her. "Miss Monroe, can you teach me to whistle like that?"

Marilyn laughs with delight. "What? You do know how to whistle, don'cha? You just put your lips together." Grinning, she says, "Sure I can teach you."

"Hey, I know that line. It's a line from a movie, isn't it?" He looks at Sammy for verification; Sammy's grin says it all. "Okay, don't tell me. I know it—I swear I do."

• • •

Adam is back in the circle of crew surrounding Marilyn and her young co-star, Tommy, for the afternoon shoot. Make-up does a final touch-up on Marilyn's nose, fluffs her hair and retreats.

The character Kay has a guitar and is preparing to sing to her young friend. The camera crew have a measuring tape out and are making the final adjustments for what begins as a close two shot and then dollies back and out as the star stands and walks towards the cabin, playing guitar and singing.

The assistant director shouts, "Quiet on the set. And roll camera."

The sound crew scrutinize their dials and shout, "Speed." Preminger points a

 finger at the actors and calls, "Annnd, Action."

Marilyn begins to strum the guitar, chording quite proficiently. She gazes down at the boy next to her and smiles, then begins to sing. Halfway through the first bar, she slips on the chord and the song goes amiss.

Marilyn stops immediately, "Sorry." She resets herself, and murmurs. "Let's go again, can we?"

"Miss Mon-roe." Preminger draws out her name, like a swear word, but says nothing more.

Concerned, Marilyn looks up; then readies herself to begin again. "It won't happen again. I'm ready." She squares her shoulders and runs her fingers through a few quick chord sequences to limber up her fingers.

"Spare us the overture, Stravinsky."

Marilyn's face tightens visibly at the jibe, but she doesn't respond.

Preminger is on a tear now. "Wardrobe," he shouts, "Can someone from wardrobe get their asses over here and make sure our audience gets to see what they'll be paying big bucks to see."

There is a ripple of movement at the far edge of the

crowd, but not fast enough to please the director. He yells, "Wardrobe, give us some cleavage on this shot if she's going to put us all to sleep singing."

Marilyn's first reaction is a shocked intake of breath. A harried woman from wardrobe hustles onto set and reaches out to adjust the neckline of Marilyn's blouse, pulling it lower. Then, surprise on Marilyn's face is replaced almost instantly by smoldering anger. She looks over at Adam and Natasha for a moment.

As the woman from wardrobe reaches forward to adjust the blouse farther, Marilyn drops her hand from the throat of the guitar and grabs the woman's wrist. She holds it fast.

"I'm singing to a child, for chrissakes, Otto." Marilyn tosses the woman's hand away and readjusts her neckline. "You want cleavage in this scene, Otto, show us yours."

After a tense moment of silence, a sudden shrill whistle of appreciation erupts. Adam's hand quickly moves to cover his mouth, while heads swivel around searching for the source.

"Oops, sorry, Miss Monroe. I guess I learned how to whistle." Raucous laughter erupts from the cast and crew on scene.

SEVEN

Calvin is busy whittling a stick, sitting on the edge of Adam's front porch. He has a pouty look on his face when he looks up at Adam. Adam is pumping air into the tire of his bicycle and lifts his head briefly, catching Calvin's look of frustration. "What?"

"I'm just wonderin' if you're pissed at me or something." Calvin stops whittling and looks at Adam frankly. "I could understand that you have your piano lessons. That's your parents' thing. I get it." Calvin tosses the stick aside brusquely. "But hanging out all the time with this lady." Calvin looks a bit uncomfortable. "It's weird…kinda. Don'cha think?"

Adam sets the tire pump aside and flops on the porch next to Calvin. "It is…And it isn't, really." Adam continues, "*It is*, because she's like, in the movies and American too. I don't always get exactly what she's sayin…it's like she talks in code or something." Adam sighs heavily. "But it *isn't* weird, cause she's so familiar, almost like my Aunt Sadie. I feel like she knows stuff almost before I say it."

Calvin folds his pocketknife and shoves it into his pocket as he clambers to his feet. "Well, you know she's not going to stick around, Adam."

Adam stands up and punches Calvin awkwardly on the arm. "I know. Aunt Sadie never does either. But at least she writes now and again from Montreal."

Adam steps off the porch and picks up his bike. "C'mon, walk with me to the highway. I'm gonna be late."

As they reach the road, Calvin stops and watches Adam get on his bike. "I wouldn't get my hopes up about any letters from this one, Adam."

Adam looks at his feet a moment and shrugs. "I know. I'm not stupid, ya know."

• • •

Adam cycles up to the turnoff to the lodge and slows, hesitating. Everyone, even Papa, said 'stay away'—yet it's clear he's got an important mission here. He peddles a short distance towards the lodge until he can see the Canadian flag on the lodge roof fluttering in the ever-present Alberta breeze. Adam stops his bicycle and gets off.

Knowing that his bike will give him away, he shoves it into the underbrush at the side of the roadway. He dusts off his hands, squares his shoulders and starts walking, looking for ambushes right and left. When it becomes clear that no one's looking for him, he relaxes somewhat and strides on. A slow smile spreads across his face and seems to grow bigger with every step. Bird song is carried on the breeze and the sun is shining. It's a perfect day.

Adam jauntily salutes the Canadian Mounted Police officer, all spruced up in his dress red serge, who's standing at the lodge door. When their eyes meet, Adam winks. "Adam Heber. I have a luncheon appointment with Miss Monroe."

Without missing a beat, the Mountie consults a clipboard in his hand and then opens the door for Adam. Adam scuttles by him and enters the lobby. Inside there is mayhem. Marilyn is perched on one of the big old leather chairs, surrounded by a gaggle of photographers and reporters scribbling notes. She's in form fitting pants, cowboy boots, a fabulous skin-tight angora sweater. Adam stands and watches.

"Miss Monroe, Miss Monroe…is it true?" one reporter shouts. He's cut off when a flashbulb pops right in front of his face. More flashbulbs pop as a second reporter jumps into the opening.

"About Dimaggio. Is it true?"

Adam sidles along the edge of the room, keeping to the shadows to not draw attention to himself. He watches Marilyn preen a bit and then switch out her pose.

He grabs the opportunity to climb over one of the over-stuffed chairs, putting it between him and the reporter scrum so he can see the action without being noticed.

"What about Dimaggio?" Marilyn coos and pouts prettily. "Really, we're just good friends."

The first reporter jumps in again. "Really, Miss Monroe? How good friends are you?"

Silence falls. The star milks it for all it's worth. She pouts her beautiful lips and tries to look guileless, as she switches her pose again. "Well, we haven't talked baseball yet."

This brings a chorus of appreciative guffaws from the covey of male reporters. Adam merely looks mystified.

Marilyn yawns, somehow managing to make it photogenic. As she stretches a bit, the bandage around one ankle become visible. Flash bulbs pop in a delirium of photographic frenzy.

"Miss Monroe, what happened to your ankle?"

Before Marilyn has time to frame a response, the bookish man from the party ambles in and begins showing the reporters to the door. He's methodical, insistent—and yet shouted questions still filter back to the star.

"Is it true you may be looking for a summer home here, Miss Monroe?" shouts a reporter being hustled from the lobby. Marilyn leans back into the deep leather chair, ignoring him.

"You can come out now," she gaily waves a hand over at Adam. She pats the chair next to hers, motioning him to sit down.

"You know when I found out we were going to shoot in Canada, I thought for sure there'd be igloos everywhere. But I haven't seen one yet! I don't get it," she says shivering slightly. "It certainly feels like winter every day since I arrived." She tosses her legs over the arm of the overstuffed chair.

A lodge maid brings a lap robe and places it over the star's shoulders. As Marilyn settles into the chair, she smiles at Adam and finishes her sentence. "What would be the point in buying a summer home? I'd never get to use it. It's never summer this far north."

Marilyn eyes Adam's bony knees and bare legs sticking straight out from the seat of the chair. "Look at you in shorts, no less. Why aren't you blue?"

Adam blurts, "Cuz I'm happy to see you." He laughs self-consciously and blushes furiously.

Marilyn laughs with him. "That's awful. You're a poet, and didn't know it," She taps one of his sneakered feet with her foot. "But your feet show it—they're long fellows.

Seeing Adam's blank expression, she adds, "*Longfellow*, the poet—and long fellows, you have big feet. Get it?" There's a significant pause and then Marilyn says, "You've never heard of Longfellow?"

Startled at her assertion, he sputters. "Sure, I have. Everyone knows '*By the shores of Gitche Gumme, by the shining big-sea-water*'. That's Hiawatha."

Marilyn throws her hands up over her ears and loudly

babbles nonsense in response. Thunderstruck, Adam stops immediately. He has never known an adult to act so screwy.

Marilyn motions for the maid and says, "When you get a chance, could you go back to my cabin and bring me the small book on my bedside table, please?" Marilyn presses a dollar into the woman's hand. "We'll be in the dining room."

Turning to Adam, she claps her hands together. "Well, I invited you here to lunch. Shall we dine then, kind sir?"

"I say, we shall." Adam squirms off the big chair and approaches Marilyn, his elbow extended so that she can take his arm. "May I escort you, madam?" He stands ramrod straight and smiles gleefully.

Marilyn slides off the chair and onto her feet. Both feet. She takes Adam's arm and stops him from stepping out. "Okay, we got to do something about this 'ma'am reflex' you got going, Adam." She wears a mock frown as she faces him down. "You can ma'am your teacher, the librarian or your neighbor…but don't ma'am me. And especially don't call me madam."

Adam ducks his head with embarrassment and whispers, "Yes, ma—" he twists it at the last minute and it comes out "Marilyn."

"See that wasn't so hard, was it?" She laughs, grabs his arm and turns him to march towards the dining room. They step out together with a spring in their step. Marilyn never lets go of his arm.

Adam looks down at the star's bandaged ankle as they walk. There is absolutely no sign of a limp in her walk. He consciously lifts his eyes back straight ahead, swallowing the question on the tip of his tongue.

Marilyn has watched him out of the corner of her eye. An impish smile washes over her face. "Fast healer," she deadpans.

Adam merely nods as he leads her to the table reserved for them by the maître d'. "I never thought nuthin' else. Honest."

• • •

An hour later, Adam and Marilyn have the dining room to themselves. The remnants of a splendid lunch litter the tabletop. They are both half-heartedly spooning the remains of a banana split into their mouths. They have eaten more than they ever thought possible. Finally, Marilyn pushes away the half-eaten ice cream dish. "I feel sick."

Relieved to be given permission to stop, Adam copies her immediately. "I have to admit, I have felt better in my life."

Marilyn pushes back her chair and stands up, pulling at the waistband of her jeans. "Tasted so good going down, didn't it?"

Adam drapes his napkin like a teepee over the remnants of the confection. "I don't even want to think about what it might taste like coming back up!"

"Oeww. Okay, that's disgusting."

She uses one manicured finger to point to an old coffee table set right in front of the fireplace. Sitting on top is a game board, some playing cards and dice. "Do you think you could drag yourself over there?" Marilyn says.

Adam looks where she's pointing. "And play checkers— my specialty?" He stops suddenly, remembering his manners. "Sorry. Maybe you have to get going, Miss Monroe?"

Marilyn lifts the bandaged foot for Adam. "Injured, remember?" Guess they'll just have to shoot around me." She abandons the chair and shouts, "First one there gets to choose." She's already racing ahead.

Adam scrambles to get free of the chair, but he's no match for an adult's larger stride and Marilyn's head start.

Marilyn grabs the chair nearest the fireplace and chortles. "Beat ya." This time Adam doesn't say a word as Marilyn holds up the cards in triumph. "You're not even going to protest."

He looks at her, patience personified, and shrugs. "My dad says a real lady could never cheat and a real gentleman would never suggest it."

Marilyn bursts out laughing. "In another ten years you are going to be brushing the gals off like flies, my boy." She starts shuffling the deck as Adam sits down across from her.

As the cards riffle through her fingers, Marilyn's attention becomes absolutely riveted on them. "You know actors often are intensely superstitious, right?"

Adam watches the transformation from playful companion to intensely focused croupier with fascination. Marilyn deals out the cards.

"How so?" he says.

She picks up her seven cards and begins to spread them out in her hand, viewing them. She is pleased with what she's been dealt. "Little weird things. Like

you buy a new hat, and *that* night you give the performance of your life. After that, the two become linked in your consciousness." She looks up from her cards at Adam, who is simply staring at her. "You can look at your cards, kiddo."

Adam slowly picks up his cards and fans them out in his hand the way he's seen Marilyn do it. "Perceived cause and effect," Adam offers. "There's no real connection between the two."

Across from him, Marilyn takes a deep breath. "It's your belief system that powers your choices, Adam." She places her cards face down on the tabletop in front of Adam. "For me, playing Gin Rummy is a bit like having my fortune told."

She taps the king visible on the tabletop between them. "The king, he's authority and power and it's all out there. I'll have to work to grab any of it." She shrugs, self-conscious, and quickly begins to gather up the cards and end the game. She starts to put them back in the box, certain she's made a fool of herself.

A long moment passes. Adam reaches out and takes the cards from her hands and adds his to them. He begins to shuffle them, not as expertly, but quickly. "I never mentioned the really old *Canadian* superstition, eh?"

He starts dealing, alternating one to her, one to him. "In Canada, once you start a game of Gin Rummy, it's totally *bad luck* not to finish." He continues dealing. "I mean people have reported their sugar maples going dry, hockey sticks breaking—and I even heard of a curling stone that cracked right in two all because someone didn't finish their game of Rummy."

He places the remaining deck of cards between them on the tabletop. "It's just superstition, but…" Adam motions for Marilyn to lift the top card for them to see. She turns the card up and places it on the tabletop in front of them. She frowns and looks at Adam curiously. "The women here use stones to curl their hair?"

Adam shakes his head in confusion. "Whaaat?"

Marilyn puts a threesome of five-cards on the table. "You said a woman cracked her curling stone. For her hair?"

Adam bursts out laughing and can't stop. After a moment he's bent over holding his stomach, still laughing. "It's a game we play, with big, polished rocks."

Marilyn openly scoffs. "You do not…You're shitting me!"

This makes Adam laugh ever harder.

EIGHT

As Marilyn limps out the front door with Adam, a commotion behind her in the lobby grabs her attention. She turns, shading her eyes for a moment against the afternoon glare of the sun.

Natasha turns from the front desk in the lobby, sees Marilyn in the doorway and hurries over to her. She has a small tan book in her hand.

"The maid asked me to give this to you. I've been looking all over for you," she growls.

Marilyn shushes her, turns and motions to Adam to wait. She slides the book into the back pocket of her jeans. "You remember Adam, Natasha?"

"Hey kid."

"Miss Lytess, nice to see you."

Marilyn approaches Adam, book in hand, and motions for Natasha to wait for her.

"Let me walk my guest out, Natasha." She shrugs, "I'll be right with you. Promise."

As she and Adam begin to walk down the walkway together, Marilyn calls back over her shoulder. "By the way, Nastie, is there a flight coming in tonight?"

Natasha folds her arms over her chest and scowls, tapping her toe in annoyance. "Umm, much as I hate to be the bearer of bad news, yes, there is."

Marilyn's face lights up, and she turns back to Adam, a new lightness in her step. Natasha calls after her, "Don't forget, that ankle's still 'sposed to be sore. Maybe a wheelchair would help you get into the part."

Marilyn immediately limps dramatically. "Oooh, that hurt."

"Miss Monroe, you don't have to walk out with me if you're still injured," Adam admonishes.

Natasha throws up her hands and walks back inside.

Marilyn limps along beside Adam in silence. The wind ruffles the leaves of the nearby trees, birds still sing, and the sun is streaming down.

"You really are a lucky kid to grow up here," Marilyn says.

Adam stops too and looks around, trying to see what she sees. "I thought you said it was too cold."

Marilyn plucks at his short-sleeved t-shirt. "It doesn't seem to be *for you.*" She sighs. "Today, right now, it feels *just perfect.* Don't you think?"

Adam nods his head, understanding.

Marilyn puts her arm around Adam's shoulder and pulls the small book from her back pocket. "Here, I want you to have this. I marked a special page just for you. Do me a favor. Read me the last five lines of that poem."

Adam squints at the print, his lips move, but he takes a moment to speak. "I shall be telling this with a sigh, somewhere ages and ages hence."

Marilyn joins him, reciting the lines from memory. "Two roads diverged in a wood and I... I took the one less traveled by. And that has made all the difference."

They stand together in silence for a moment, then Marilyn reaches over and opens the book to the front page. She pulls up a pen, signs with a flourish and tucks the book into Adam's shirt pocket. Then she reaches down and places a very gentle kiss on his cheek.

As Marilyn turns and walks away, she shouts after him. "You and your friend should come by the airport tonight at eight, if you can."

"Okay. Why?"

Marilyn throws up her arms in excitement. "You'll see. Just be there."

Natasha watches Marilyn walk up to her, the wistful expression still on her face. "You really should have kids, Mimsie."

Marilyn smiles her most dazzling movie star smile. "Maybe I will... and move here and *bring them up right.*"

"Oh, please Lord, not with that Dago, good-for-nothing baseball player."

Marilyn's face falls. She chides Natasha: "That is so rude, Nastie. Don't call him a Dago."

Natasha shakes her head and says, "C'mon, we got work to do."

Marilyn hobbles along after Natasha. "But my sprain. Ow, ow, ow."

Heartless, Natasha propels Marilyn through the lobby and down a hall. "I had 'em park a piano in your cabin. You sprained your ankle, not your voice. We'll give your lungs a workout and let you rest that terrible, terrible injury."

"But Nastie, I have a date tonight," Marilyn pleads.

Natasha replies with a wicked smile. "Then you better get on it. If you're a good girl, you'll still have time for a beauty nap and massage before dinner."

• • •

Adam is powering along on his bicycle, hell-bent-for-leather. He spies an abandoned bicycle up ahead and pedals faster. As he closes in on the bike, he recognizes it as Calvin's. He yells into the low-growing shrubs that blanket the riverside.

"Calvin… CAL - vin, it's me, Adam. Where are you? I saw your bike.…"

He slowly fights his way through the bushes. In a

clearing by the river, he spots several boys. "Are you okay, Calvin?"

Just then he sees that Gordie has Calvin's right arm trussed up behind him like a WWF wrestler. Pain is evident on Calvin's face.

"Go ahead, answer him," Gordie says as he wrenches Calvin's arm up another notch. Calvin grimaces in renewed pain but remains silent. "Go on. Or I'll be using this arm for fish bait after I rip it off, *keem-o-sabe*," Gordie taunts.

Adam rushes towards them, yelling. The bully laughs.

"Sure, he's okay. Why wouldn't he be okay?" Gordie lets go of Calvin's arm, telling his buddies, "Watch him, guys." He heads towards Adam, looking for an excuse to lay into him. Adam uses his eyes to signal to Calvin, '*Go.*'

Calvin looks to the bush, then locks eyes with Adam. He shakes his head minutely. Gordie is scrutinizing Adam. His eyes land on the tip of the little tan book peeking out of Adam's shirt pocket. He pounces on the book and rips it from Adam's pocket before Adam fully realizes what is happening.

"Hey, stop it. That's mine," Adam growls.

Gordie briefly examines the book and looks up from it, smirking, "Not anymore."

Completely forgetting himself, Adam leaps at the brute. Unfortunately, the bully's twin companions move at the same time and pin Adam's arms behind him.

Gordie flips through the pages. "Oooh, poetry, boys. Our little Jerry loves poetry." He studies a page, then rips it from the book and throws it away. Flipping through more pages, he nonchalantly rips out more.

Calvin maneuvers closer to a branch at the edge of the bushes. Adam struggles valiantly but is held tightly by the bullies. "Stop it, STOP IT," he yells. He tries to squirm out of the grip of the two boys. "Do you have any idea what...."

Gordie cuts him off when he sees the book's title page with the handwritten inscription. He croons, "To a fellow poet, in spirit if not in fact." Suddenly recognizing the signature, he freezes for a moment. The two boys shout, "What does it say? What does it say?"

For a moment they are distracted, and Calvin grabs the branch and swings with all his might. C-R-A-C-K. He whips it solidly across the backs of Gordie's knees and topples him with one blow. Stunned, Gordie knocks down his two buddies as he struggles against the blow.

Calvin and Adam sprint for their lives towards their bicycles in the bushes. Adam manages to scoop up a single fluttering page from the book as they race away.

NINE

That same evening, none the worse for wear, Adam and Calvin race on their bikes as fast as their skinny legs can pump the pedals. They're both stoked, even if the afternoon was so sketchy. They've been invited by Marilyn Monroe to meet whoever is flying in to see her!

Overhead, the sound of a single-prop fixed wing aircraft is strumming the early evening air. Both boys look up instantly. Adam looks back over his shoulder and sees the tiny white blip that is the plane glowing in the sun against the purple-shadowed mountains.

"Hurry up."

Calvin looks over his shoulder, too, sees the plane, then points left across the road and to the runway. "Cut over, it's faster."

"No way…"

The sound of the Cessna's engine growing louder prompts Calvin to action. "C'mon, chickin." He jerks his handlebars and heads cross-country through the grass and gravel. Adam has no choice but to follow. They hit the edge of the small runway and bump up onto the tarmac. Then it's smooooooth sailing. Calvin looks back at Adam and flashes him a big 'I told you' grin.

The tiny plane is just making its approach to the end of the runway. It trims its flaps and descends, engine still roaring. As its wheels touch down it slows considerably. The boys and the plane reach the apron in front of the small flight shack at almost the same instant.

Adam and Calvin look across the airstrip and spot the sleek black limo parked there. Sammy leaps from the driver's seat and races around to open the rear door.

"Hey, that's Sammy, Miss Monroe's driver." Adam cuffs Calvin's shoulder. "You'd like him; he's great."

A final ray of the setting sun envelopes Marilyn as she emerges from the back of the car.

"Oh *man*. She is so pretty." Calvin can't take his eyes off Marilyn. She is stunning: blond hair, tousled by the wind. Mink coat, tiny strapless shoes on her feet. She runs lightly towards the now silent airplane.

At the sight of her running, Calvin turns and looks at Adam accusingly. "I thought you said she sprained her ankle?"

Adam nods knowingly. "Fast healer."

"Oh, like my Aunt Trudie!"

The passenger door of the plane opens and a casually

dressed lanky fellow drops down. The rear door opens too and a couple of burly guys exit. They pull several bags from the passenger compartment.

The first fellow is hardly out of the plane before he's grabbed and wrapped in a bear hug by the star. After the first hug, he makes her open her mink coat so he can slip his arms inside and hug her again.

Calvin frowns across the tarmac, trying to place the fellow. "Who'd ya say he was again?"

Adam shakes his head. "The reporters at the lodge were asking her about someone named…" He scratches his head, trying to remember. "Guy, Jean, or Joe maybe…"

"Jean? You think it's actually Jean Béliveau? Marilyn Monroe's hanging out with Jean Béliveau. *Oh man.* Let's go get an autograph for my pop, eh?"

Adam reaches out a hand and stops Calvin. "I don't think it was a Jean. No, it was definitely Joe somebody." He's silent a moment. "Dimaggio, I think they said." Adam looks at Calvin, and they both shrug, not recognizing the name.

From across the tarmac, Marilyn spots them as she, Joe and the two goons walk towards the Cadillac. She waves them over. The boys obligingly trot over with their bikes in tow. The star spins Dimaggio around so he can't fail to see the boys coming.

"Awww, gee Honey. I thought this was a vacation."

The two goons break ranks and take a step towards

the boys. "Want me to get rid of them, boss?" one of them mutters.

Marilyn looks up into Dimaggio's face, pleading. "C'mon Joe. Just say hi. Do it for me; they're both sweet kids."

Dimaggio sighs but puts on his happy face as the boys come closer. "Okay, this little favor for you." He squeezes Marilyn's arm tightly. "And you can do a really big favor for me later."

Marilyn giggles and pulls the mink coat more tightly around herself.

Adam and Calvin stop several paces from the adults. They can feel being scrutinized. Marilyn motions them closer. Adam drops his bike on the tarmac, wiping his hand on the leg of his newly clean shorts. Calvin imitates him exactly.

"Adam, I'd like you to meet a very good friend of mine," she says, putting her hand on his shoulder. One of the goons sniggers into his hand. Marilyn ignores the stupidity. "Joe Dimaggio, this is Adam Heber."

Adam extends his hand to shake. "Welcome to Canada, Mr. Dimaggio."

The great Dimaggio takes Adam's hand and shakes it very formally. He smiles. "Polite little bugger, isn't he?" he whispers to Marilyn

Marilyn beams approval at Adam. "Will you introduce your friend, Adam?"

Adam nods. "Yes ma'am. Happy to."

Another snicker from the goons. Adam blinks self-consciously. "Oh sorry, I meant to say Miss Monroe." Adam places his hand on Calvin's shoulder and says very formally, "Mr. Dimaggio, I'd like you to meet my best friend, Calvin Two-Knives."

As Calvin steps forward offering his hand to Dimaggio, one of the goons whispers, "Whoa boss, he's a genuine..." Marilyn turns and throws the lout a deadly look. She covers for his stupidity, saying, "CREE. Calvin, is a genuine Cree Indian."

Dimaggio rises to the moment, stepping forward to shake Calvin's hand.

"This is quite a day for me, young man. I mean, I've played a few Braves, but I've never actually met one."

Calvin smiles at him. "And Pollack, sir."

"Pardon, kid. Wadya say?"

Very dignified, Calvin repeats, "I'm Polish too, sir. On my mother's side."

Dimaggio nods grudging approval. "A switch-hitter. You gotta admire that, hey boys?" Dimaggio turns back towards the limo, dismissing the kids. He wraps one arm possessively around Marilyn's shoulders and leads her towards the car.

Over his shoulder he calls back: "Hey Adam, thanks for minding the fort while I wasn't here to keep Miss Monroe company. Much appreciated." Dimaggio pivots, pointing his finger at Adam like a loaded gun, then fires. The two goons laugh as if it's the funniest thing they've ever seen.

Sudden comprehension washes over Adam's face. He's just lost Marilyn, perhaps for good, to that adult world of guys and dolls where he can't even reach the doorknob yet, let alone pry the door open. He was only a plaything, a toy while Marilyn waited on the real thing to come sweep her off her feet.

Adam bolts across the tarmac, pelting towards the Caddy. Too late; Sammy has put the car into gear and is throttling up, gathering speed. The distance between Adam and the Caddy grows exponentially.

Finally, Adam stops running, breathing as if his lungs might break. His expression says his heart's already broken. Calvin trots up to his pal and throws an arm around Adam's shoulders, patting his back. He can tell something is amiss but he's not sure why.

The sun finally drops behind the mountains, leaving the boys standing in the sudden evening quiet as the limo passes from sight around a distant bend.

• • •

The next morning, Marilyn is lying in a heap on the bottom bed. in the tacky old caboose. All that's visible is her platinum curls and mounds and mounds of blankets bunched in the very center of the bed.

Gray morning light is visible through the small window over the table. As usual, Natasha is pouring over the script, cigarette dangling from the corner of her mouth.

A solid knock on the door precedes a voice. "Ten min-utes, hair and make-up,

Miss Monroe."

Natasha stubs out her cigarette into a nearby ashtray. "So, you gonna go out there cold?"

Marilyn pulls the blankets more tightly over her head. Her voice is muffled.

"I've been cold for weeks, Nastie. I'm sick of it."

"Ha, ha. Very funny." Natasha stands up and pushes back her chair. "Right then. Let me know when you decide to try acting again." She crosses to the door of the little caboose, opens it in a fury and then slams it again, LOUDLY.

Seconds later, Marilyn erupts from the tangle of bed clothes and calls out, alarmed. "N-a-s-t-i-e, wait!"

As she spots Natasha leaning against the wall in the shadows by the side of the door, she grumbles, "You are such a rat, woman."

Natasha returns to her seat at the table and opens the script. "Now, where were we?"

"We were out in the middle of God-KNOWS-where Canada, working on a worthless piece of crap script, freez-ing our very famous titties off when I could be cozy and warm all snuggled up to a very famous ball player."

Natasha deadpans. "Plays with his balls, does he? I knew it; I can spot the type a mile away."

Marilyn shakes her head in dismay and throws her feet over the side of the bed. "C'mon. Let's go do this thing."

Putting on her shoes, she walks to the doorway and grabs the script off the table. "God, I hate this film."

Natasha throws her a sour look. "It's better than planting beets."

"I'm not so sure about that, Natasha." The two women leave the caboose, stepping into a crisp morning.

The P.A. who knocked is waiting, somewhat nervously, at the bottom of the steps. He holds out a piece of paper to Natasha. "Miss Lytess, the producers asked me to remind you of company memo 1359A."

Natasha takes the proffered piece of paper and scans it. Then she begins to read more carefully. She glances up at the now very nervous P.A.

"Young man, you can't possibly feel this memo refers to me, can you?" Natasha's voice is as icy as the banks of the river.

The production assistant clears his throat. "All cast and crew were provided a copy of this memo Friday last... ma'am."

Natasha holds it out for Marilyn to read. CLOSED SET. She crumples the paper into a ball and tosses it back to the unfortunate P.A.

Marilyn reaches for Natasha's hand. "C'mon, they wouldn't dare."

The P.A. calls out after them, "I'm sorry, Miss Monroe. I was only doing my job."

• • •

In the bushes near the river's edge the director holds court, explaining his vision to the actors. "All right, now in this scene I want the audience to be able to see Bob fishing." Preminger gestures wildly as he speaks. "Bob! Bob, I want you to go stand by that pool of water for a moment."

Mitchum steps into camera view, dressed in frontier attire, carrying a long, pointed stick instead of a fishing pole. The camera crew obligingly push the big camera on the specially laid down rails for the shot.

Preminger shouts, "And voilà, you roll into view for the audience and we never lose the picturesque backdrop of the Rockies."

The director steps to the side and swings wide with his arm, pointing. "Here we find our saloon singer." But where Preminger's arm is pointing is only a patch of bare bush. "*Gott verschone mich. Ich bin umgeben von Schwachsinnigen.*" He pivots on his heels, searching. "Where is that cow?"

Moments later a flustered Marilyn arrives, searching for her marker. The camera pans two degrees farther and encounters Natasha Lytess just out of range.

The sight of Lytess in the wings sets Preminger off for real. "*Nun sprechen Sie schon! Ich bin nicht den ganzen Weg in dieses gottverlassene Land gekommen, bloss um zu warten!*"

He stops for breath and switches to sarcastic English. "Miss Monroe, *thank you so much* for joining us today.

I'm assuming you have not received the new company memo reminding all cast and crew that 'River' is now a closed set."

Marilyn casts a glance back over her shoulder at Natasha, who lifts her shoulders in defeat and begins to turn back to the caboose.

"See ya back at the ranch."

Preminger launches one final verbal volley. "Finally, shall we get some work done today?"

As Marilyn is physically rehearsing her gestures, bending and plucking berries, she mutters, "What a pity they closed the set. I had hoped to invite Joe Dimaggio out to set tomorrow."

TEN

Natasha is sitting in the sun on the bottom step of the caboose, smoking and reading a novel. She doesn't notice Adam trudging up the short hill pushing his bicycle. He stops, cradling his bike by the handlebars, not sure of his welcome.

"Hi, Miss Lytess."

Natasha looks up and grins. "Well, look what the cat dragged in…"

Adam dutifully looks around to see if she's really speaking to him.

Natasha continues. "It's a *saying*, it doesn't mean there's really a cat."

"I *knew* that," Adam shrugs. "What're you doing here?" He fiddles with his handlebar grips. "I mean, why aren't you on set? Um, I hope that's not rude."

Natasha stubs out her cigarette and flicks it away. "It is rude. That I'm not on set, I mean." She stands up slowly and puts her finger in the book to mark her page. "That rude bastard closed the set."

Adam's eyes narrow. "Preminger, you mean? That's bad isn't it, that the set's closed?"

Natasha coughs out a laugh. "You have a way with words, kiddo." She walks down the three short steps to join Adam. "C'mon, I'll walk you to the road." Adam obligingly turns his bicycle around and Natasha falls in beside him.

"It means the old turd won this round."

Adam raises his eyebrows but says nothing.

"It also means, until further notice the likes of you and me are not allowed to watch Miss Monroe while she works." Natasha lights another cigarette. "It means no one's there to give her moral support."

Incensed, Adam interrupts. "That's not fair. You're her best friend. Isn't there anything we can do?"

As they reach the turnoff for the highway, Natasha puts her hand on Adam's shoulder and looks him in the eyes. She whispers, "We can hold our breath and pray like hell to every god we know…" Natasha looks towards the horizon. "That she somehow survives this tyrant of a director, survives her current *man and the next, and the next…*"

Suddenly self-conscious, Natasha laughs again. She pats Adam on the back and motions for him to head off. "Don't mind me, kiddo. I have a flare for melodrama." Natasha shrugs, "I'll try to keep you posted if we get an all clear, okay?"

"Thank you, Miss Lytess. That's very kind of you." He sets his bike in motion and heads down the road.

• • •

Marilyn is seated in a warming tent set along the river. She's wrapped snugly in a wool blanket, sipping a hot drink and reading a book. The P.A. can be seen just across the way, handing out another memo to all the cast and crew. Marilyn takes a sip of her drink and turns a page in the book.

The P.A. makes a point to seek her out and hands her the latest production memo. It reads: SET TO REMAIN OPEN THROUGH NEXT WEEK.

An hour later, Marilyn is back at the riverbank location. Robert Mitchum is at the river, trying to spear fish. She is crouched down in the bush gathering berries. In the storyline of the film, neither knows the other is there.

Preminger calls out curtly. "All right now, Bob, you hear a noise in the bushes."

Robert Mitchum looks up, then leaves his fishing spot to investigate. He raises the spear he's been using, leading with the heavy end of the stick. When he sees the bushes move, he sneaks up on the unsuspecting Marilyn. The camera dollies back, following him.

Mitchum's character is all set to conk who or whatever he finds, but then he discovers it's the saloon singer. Marilyn, backing up a step, puts a hand over her heart in shock. "Gee-whillickers, you could have warned me you were coming."

Mitchum picks a couple of berries out of the tin she's collected them in and pops them in his mouth. "You could have warned me you were out here in the bushes. I could have killed you."

"You're lucky it was me," Marilyn retorts. "A bear would have gulped you down without blinking twice."

Preminger interjects. "Cut, cut, cut. Miss Monroe, please stick to the dialogue as it is written. Let's wrap this shoot sometime today, if you don't mind."

• • •

Marilyn spots Dimaggio, wearing a starched sport shirt, sport coat and spotless slacks, sitting in his canvas folding chair. She smiles and strolls over to stand in front of him. "My man. Well, what did you think, Hon?"

Dimaggio's face is impassive; he could be thinking anything…or nothing. He slides out of the chair, brushes at make-believe dust on his slacks and walks off set. "Is it always so…filthy?"

Marilyn hesitates a moment and then follows him. All around them crew are bustling to stow away the equipment and all the paraphernalia that goes with a film shoot.

"Well, soundstages are cleaner…but not by much," Marilyn says. "I meant, what did ya think of your first film shoot?" Her face is a beacon, turned up to the ball player. She can't bring herself to ask, 'What did you think of my acting?' but her face certainly implies it.

The A.D. marches past shouting, "Wrap party tonight at the lodge, eight o'clock sharp. "You're welcome to come too, Mr. Dimaggio."

Dimaggio smiles acknowledgment and keeps walking beside Marilyn. "I don't know. In some ways it's kind of a silly way to make a living. I mean, you dress up in costumes and play make-believe?"

Marilyn is crestfallen. It's been a tough day and a tough shoot. She's fought for her dignity nearly every day, and now her lover tells her the whole exercise is silly. This from a man who makes his living hitting a ball with a stick.

Then Joe puts his arm around her shoulders and draws her in for the final blow. "I mean, really doll, how long do you think this bubble can last?"

He smiles down at Marilyn and pulls her along towards her limousine. "But at least we're going to get one hell of a dinner out of it.

"Oh Joe, can't we just skip the wrap party. Say we forgot?"

"Babe, c'mon. All those film folks are gonna want autographs from America's favorite slugger." He rubs his hands together in anticipation.

ELEVEN

The lodge has pulled out all the stops for the cast farewell party. Marilyn, Dimaggio, Preminger and the script recorder are all seated at a table discreetly removed from the other diners. It's clear that everyone is a good distance into their cups. Otto has had a great deal to drink.

Marilyn looks exhausted and bored as Preminger drones on about life on the set. Dimaggio appears completely fascinated by the director's tales. He elbows Marilyn and grins. "Ain't this guy a hoot?" Marilyn smiles gamely, wishing she could leave.

• • •

Adam is lying on the brakeman's cart on a siding, just outside the train station. He's on his back, looking up at the sky overhead. Glittering stars flicker down at him. In the distance he can hear the faint whistle of an inbound train.

Suddenly he sits up and turns in the direction of the oncoming train. *Ya know, stupid, you really don't have to stay here.*

The whistle sounds again, coming closer. He repeats to himself: *I can go away with her when she leaves.* Galvanized by this new and sudden inspiration, Adam leaps to his feet and jumps off the brakeman's car. He screams for joy at the sudden solution to his problem. *I don't have to stay here.*

• • •

Toying with her food, Marilyn chooses a lull in the frivolity to change the direction of the conversation. She nudges Dimaggio. "Speaking of the Bible, I hear 20th Century is considering a new story concept."

Film talk brings everyone's attention back to focus—especially talk of projects pending. "I hear it's something with Heston again…" She looks up. "Maybe he'll play Jesus this time."

Dimaggio brightens and nudges Marilyn in return. "Hey, maybe you could be in it too, Honey."

The table titters. Dimaggio scowls and gets defensive on her behalf. "Why not? It'd be a cast of thousands."

Marilyn smiles indulgently and pats his arm to placate him. "Maybe I could, Joe. I'll ask around." She smiles at him warmly. "I'm sure there's several parts worth considering."

Dimaggio preens at her and responds. "Yeah, like Mary."

Preminger interrupts, "Ahh, the whore."

This time the laughter at the table has an uncertain edge to it. Marilyn colors visibly at the gibe.

Preminger looks around the table innocently. "Well, you couldn't have meant the virgin, Joe. Even Miss Monroe is not that gifted an actor."

It's been a long day. Marilyn has drunk too much and a director she hates is holding her up to ridicule. She whispers, "Excuse me. I have a splitting headache. I should go." Without waiting for a response or permission, she leaves.

• • •

Adam lopes up to the main entrance of the lodge and stops to consider the front door. After a moment he deeks around the side and trots down one of the walkways towards the guest cabins. Little dimples of light are scattered along the path by the garden lighting.

As he races past the nearest cabin and its porch light, he fails to notice a shadow moving across the path ahead of him. Before it can register, Adam's loose t-shirt is snared in Gordie's ham-sized fist.

"Ah, we meet again. It must be a sign from the mystic stars. Weren't you running the last time we saw each other too?"

Adam struggles to no avail. Gordie has him fast. "Let me go."

Gordie tightens his grip. "Say pleease."

Adam hesitates, looks over the bully's shoulder and sees Marilyn's cabin—so close. If he can just get loose for a minute, he'll be there. He hangs his head and pushes down his anger. "Please. Please let me go, Gordie."

In reply, Gordie shoves Adam roughly to the ground. Adam falls. Hard. He lies there a moment, stunned, trying to catch his breath.

"Oh, sorry. Did I let go too fast?" Gordie takes a step closer to Adam, exuding menace. "I guess you want me to return your little book-wookie, too." Gordie pulls the small book out of his back pocket and holds it out towards Adam.

Seeing the book, Adam sits up but remains silent. His eyes move from the book in the boy's hand and then back to Gordie's face. For a moment their eyes meet and then POW, Gordie clocks him right in the face.

Adam collapses back onto the pathway. He manages a rough whisper. "Go ahead, keep the book. You can have it."

Gordie reaches down and grabs Adam's t-shirt and pulls him back up to a half sitting position. "Chicken… What's wrong— afraid to ask for what's yours?"

Adam's eyes skitter back to Gordie's face. He hesitates, "That's not it at all, Gordie." He sighs; this will not end well no matter what he says. "The book will always be mine. It was a gift from someone who valued me enough to give it." He shrugs, resigned to the truth. "You could steal it, but it will never actually be yours."

"What do you know, you stupid Kraut." Gordie tosses the book aside and grabs Adam's shirt collar, punching him again and knocking him to the ground. Gordie leaps to his feet and starts kicking Adam hard, shouting, "What do you know, you stupid Jerry?"

Adam curls in on himself, groaning. Desperate to stop Gordie somehow, he shouts, hoarse with pain. "I know that *if I die*, Gordie, Miss Monroe will tell the sheriff everything I've told her about you. You should probably start praying I live, right now. 'Cuz everyone will believe Marilyn Monroe, the movie star, over a dumb fuck like you."

• • •

Most of the cast and crew have moved to the lodge lounge and the bar. But no one at Preminger's table has shifted an inch. He's in full swing now blasting off on a payload of Vodka-Collins.

Preminger leans back in his chair, an evil smile playing about his mouth. "Such an amusing story in the local paper. The reporter wrote that young Retig, who played your foster son with such conviction, Miss Monroe, had to get special dispensation from his priest in order to join the cast."

"Whaaat?" Dimaggio interjects. The others listening at various tables chuckle at the thought.

Preminger is glowing in triumph now. "Ah yes. In fact, he had to beg the priest to let him join the cast in order to even appear in a scene with our own redoubtable *virgin*, Miss Monroe." Preminger laughs out loud and of course the others follow.

Dimaggio seems to get a big kick out of the story. "Well, I'll be go to hell. Really?"

Marilyn's face crumples; she's near tears. The men don't notice; their laughter continues to echo around her.

Satisfied, Preminger holds up his empty glass to the waiter. "He had to ask the priest. Can you believe it?"

• • •

When a nearby cabin door slams, echoing in the silence, Gordie instantly turns away from Adam. He steps off the path and cuts across the lawn, running for his life.

Adam lies still for a long moment, oblivious that Gordie has gone. His head feels as if he's on the school merry-go-round, churning in circles of ever-increasing pain. He can't breathe, and his eyes are so swollen he's not sure if they are open or closed.

Maybe he passes out. What wakes him is a light that switches on somewhere to his right. He urges himself to move but can't remember why it's important. And then he remembers. Marilyn Monroe is leaving in the morning. Going away, far away from this place...and he must go with her. But first, he must tell her about Gordie.

This is what moves him. He rolls, and he thinks the pain will kill him as he pushes himself to his knees. He begins to crawl in the direction of the light. His hand touches something softer than gravel, something thicker than the abraded skin on his knees. It is his book, ripped and torn, but still recognizable. It is this that makes him start crying softly as he continues to head for the light.

Inside Marilyn's cabin, Natasha has opened a bottle of champagne and lit a fire in both fireplaces. Candles flicker in the darkened corners of the room. As Marilyn opens the cabin door and steps inside, Natasha whispers, "Congratulations." She raises a coupe glass of bubbly and offers a glass to the star.

Marilyn's face is a mixture of emotions. Finally, she offers a pitiful half smile as she tosses her stole on a chair. "Oh Jesus, Joseph and Mary, let's get out of this place." She reaches for the glass of champagne. "Please, Nastie, knock me senseless and revive me when we get back to L.A."

Natasha chuffs a laugh and they clink glasses. "Amen to that." She knocks back the entire shallow glass of bubbly and is reaching for the bottle when an audible thud resonates through the cabin door.

Marilyn is closest, so sets her glass down and throws Natasha a quizzical look. As she opens the door to investigate, Adam collapses against her and slides to the floor. Marilyn squeaks out a gasp of shock, then instantly bends down as she recognizes Adam.

"Jesus, Natasha, it's Adam." She rolls him over and jerks back from what she finds. Illuminated by the porch light, all of Adam's injuries appear in full technicolor. Natasha is at Marilyn's side instantly. She takes one look at Adam and reaches over and snaps off the porch light.

"Natasha, we've got to call the front desk. He needs a doctor."

"Yes, he does. I'll take care of it, Mimsy." Natasha strides back to the table and deposits her glass. She lifts Marilyn's stole off the chair and returns to the door. "You, however, are going for a walk. *Your nightly constitutional*, which you take every night." She holds the coat out to Marilyn.

"Are you out of your mind? This boy needs help right now."

"He does. And I will be the one to make sure he gets it." She drapes the stole over Marilyn's shoulders. "You will be nowhere in sight when that doctor appears with a covey of reporters in tow. You are not going to jeopardize your whole career for an underage hayseed, no matter how sweet a boy he is. Do you hear me?"

She pushes Marilyn out the door. "GO. And take your time. Walk back around to the front of the lodge. Be sure to walk through the lobby. Stop and chat to people on the way." Natasha grips Marilyn's arm firmly. "Go. Protect yourself...I will take care of him. The sooner you leave, the sooner I can call for help."

Marilyn looks uncertain, and then Adam moans. She crouches down and watches as one eye flickers open. She cradles his cheek in her palm. "Adam? Adam, can you hear me? My God, Adam, please don't die. You cannot die." A tear rolls down Marilyn's cheek.

Adam's mouth moves, his voice a harsh croak as he reaches out towards her. "Gor, Gord" is all he can utter.

Marilyn throws Natasha a look of horror. Natasha mouths the word 'GO' silently. Bending over Adam, Marilyn whispers, "I have to go right now…but Adam, I will come back. Do you hear me? I will come back."

Natasha lifts her up and sets her moving. "Don't worry. Leave everything to me. Now go!"

Natasha stands a long moment and watches Marilyn leave. Then she turns to survey the setting. She crosses the room and lights a couple of discreet lamps. Then she strides to the table and finishes off Marilyn's glass of champagne and lifts her own shirt tail to wipe the glass clean. She upends it on the serving tray as if it had never been used.

Finally, she crosses back to Adam and stops to really examine him on the threshold of the door. Natasha notes the regular rise and fall of his chest, the blood splattered on his shirt front. The abrasions on his elbows and fore-arms from crawling away from his attacker. She does not miss the small book clutched in Adam's hand. She bends down to retrieve it and recognizes it, of course. Thumbing through it, she notes Marilyn's signature on the flyleaf. Without hesitation, Natasha strides across the room and tosses it in the fireplace. She watches long enough to make sure that it catches fire and is burning.

Only then does she pick up phone and dial the lobby desk. "Hello, this is Miss Monroe's suite. I'd like to report an intruder. Can you be sure to alert the doctor that he is needed immediately? And please, let's just keep this between us!"

Natasha listens a moment. "Yes, this is Miss Lytess. I was in the suite waiting for Miss Monroe to return from dinner. My guess is she decided to go walk for a bit. Then this injured boy fell through the door." Natasha returns to the doorway, again visually checking Adam's breathing.

Moments later the doctor appears, black bag in hand. "Miss Lytess, what have we here?"

"Bizarrely, this young man seemed to fall through the door as I opened it. I was checking for Miss Monroe to return from her dinner."

"My goodness, he appears to have been beaten quite badly." The doctor snaps open his case and pulls out a pen light. He flips it on and bends over Adam, gently lifting the eyelid on the less swollen eye. "This will help me decide if he's suffered a concussion from the beating."

The instant the light hits Adam's eye, his arms flail outwards weakly, as if struggling to protect himself. The flare of light on his retina is like a solar eruption and then he passes out again.

• • •

Years later, Adam steps off the railbed as the freight train swooshes past mere moments later. The din of its passing is mind-blowing. He's buffeted by an erratic wind that kicks up dirt and debris from the railbed and spatters him with it as if in anger.

He stands, chest heaving, face still wet with tears. He finally admits he doesn't actually want to die. It would be pointless. Really the best gift he might offer Marilyn in farewell is to live…and live well. To find a place where he could fully be himself—whoever that is—a place where she might have become herself too.

The train is still lumbering past Adam when he begins to run again, this time alongside it. Once he's up to speed he looks over his shoulder for the fast-approaching caboose with its ladder. He grabs hold as it passes. The momentum of the train swings him out and then back around until his feet can find a footing on the caboose's platform.

Adam grips the ladder rung like life itself, and then he climbs aboard. The moon shines down on him as he stands, chest heaving, watching his town spool out behind him. The train spirits him away, the whistle blowing, clearing the track ahead to where he should have gone years and years ago.

the
tenant

ONE

A ripped and torn piece of newsprint rattles down a city street. The early morning light is blue and cold. Ice and filthy snow are mounded at the street curbs and along the sidewalks.

The grimy piece of paper catches momentarily against a light pole, flutters helplessly and then is ripped away by the wind. It scuttles past a street person huddled, fetus-like, beneath a tattered blanket in an alcove between two doorways. Other bits of ragged newsprint peek from beneath the frayed edges of the blanket.

Down the side street there is an old-style schoolyard with a crumbling brick schoolhouse. The sound of a throng of kids at recess pierces the air. They have built a snow person of indeterminate sex: three lumpy heaps of snow, a scarf and a scruffy baseball cap, beer caps for eyes and a good-sized carrot for a nose.

Carly Sampson is in her mid-thirties, but she looks old from living on the streets. She might have been pretty once; it's impossible to tell because she has been worn thin. Hunched against the cold, the wind and the noise from the schoolyard, she shuffles along the ice-encrusted sidewalk, trying to miss the piles of dog shit.

"Cold today as a witch's tit, a witch's tit, a witch's tit. Weatherman's a son-of-a-bitch, son-of-a-bitch." Carly sings in a kind of jump-rope rhythm beneath the scarf wrapped around her face.

The scrap of newsprint catches against one of Carly's legs and the incessant wind holds it there. She reaches down, exposing one dirty hand, the back of which is covered with ink scribbles. Seemingly random words and phrases are scattered across the backs and fronts of Carly's hands, her wrists and on up her arms. While she's down, bent over freeing her leg, she examines the scrap of paper.

Pictured is a modern, clean, art-filled apartment. As Carly straightens, she smooths out the edges of the picture, folds it carefully into a neat square and shoves it into her coat pocket.

The noise of the schoolchildren reaches a fever pitch as the clock inches towards a return to class. Carly places both hands over her ears and makes a horrible face at the kids tearing around the dilapidated play area. Her eyes scan the haphazard basketball court and other signs of a school that has been severely underfunded this year, last year and probably several decades before.

And then Carly spots the snow person with the *massive carrot*. She's so hungry, just the sight of anything edible generates hunger pangs. She twines her arms around her torso in pain, but her eyes never leave the beacon of that carrot.

The class bell rings, alarmingly loud, and Carly claps her hands over her ears. All-the-while she carefully watches the kids straggle up the three short stairs and back to class. "Th-a-t's all, folks." She uses one hand to wipe the invisible TV screen in front of her eyes.

She gingerly takes a step to straddle the falling down school fence and trots the couple of steps to the snow person. She r-e-a-c-h-e-s up and twists the carrot nose, wrenching it off. Carly pivots to make a hasty retreat with her prize.

Not soon enough, though; a snot-nosed kid on the school steps has spotted her and alerts the others still filing past him. "Hey you! That's not yours. Give it back. You guys, that old lady's messing with our snowman."

Panicked, Carly snaps a big bite off the carrot and gathers speed to create some distance between herself and the hellions.

Oblivious to the bell, the kids hurtle down the stairs again, intent on pursuit. But the snow isn't being any kinder to them—they're half sliding, half running in place.

Carly may be encumbered by cold and hunger but she's beginning to lengthen her lead.

The teacher appears in the doorway and the whole pursuit immediately fizzles.

Carly is halfway down the block, but she can hear the kids' shouted protestations.

"Teach, it's not fair. Who asked that old bag to mess with our stuff?"

Carly turns and looks over her shoulder. The kids are being ushered in through the school doors. She's safe. She snaps another great whack off the end of the carrot and chews it energetically.

As the last kid is shepherded inside, the lady teacher turns and meets Carly's eyes. From a distance, no one could accurately say what that woman is thinking, but the look makes Carly stop a moment. She yells back at the teacher: "Not fair, who cares, no one ever wants to share." The teacher just shakes her head as she closes the school door.

The sounds of the city and the schoolyard fade as Carly clumps further into the crappy neighborhood. She pulls her ratty toque down over her ears and turns her overcoat collar up as far as it will go as she steps gingerly off the curb and crosses the street.

She passes an old boarded-up grocery store, windows knocked out, posters covering every square inch of available space, maybe two or three layers deep. Carly stops suddenly and studies a poster for a baroque string quartet.

Pulling a sharpie from her pocket, she inscribes the word 'baroque' on the back of her left hand. Finished, she examines the poster a moment longer, then wipes her runny nose on her sleeve.

More snow begins to fall, rendering Carly's world utterly silent. She detours through an empty city lot. Rusted car skeletons are made almost beautiful by the blanket of snow.

A smoking garbage can midway through the lot promises some warmth. Carly's eyes scan the rubble-strewn lot, which appears empty. Only then does she approach the smoking can. She shoves the carrot deep into her coat pocket, then lifts her hands to warm them over the bit of heat that smolders in the bottom of the barrel.

She stamps her feet to warm them and opens her coat to the heat, capturing what she can and then wrapping the garment tightly about her again. Carly's eyes are ever restless, watching, assessing the neighborhood around her. Her gaze seems continuously drawn back to the backside of an old tumble-down brick building just on the other side of the empty lot.

When she's as warm as she's going to get without climbing into the barrel, Carly tucks her hands under her armpits and trudges to the far side of the lot. The snow isn't deep, but it's been trod into muck and splashes her shoe tops and pant legs. Still she persists.

• • •

By midday Carly is leaning against a wall in a packed and fetid hallway. The odors of cooking food are wafting down through the crowd from the dining hall, blending with the high aroma of old sweat, dirty socks and pissed-in pants. Carly leans against the wall for comfort, weak from hunger, trying to create some space in the melee of flesh. She whispers continually to herself: "Move over, stand back, back off, me first, first-come first served."

Squeezing in and out between the crowds is a 'sister of mercy' from the NEW DAY! Gospel Mission in Abbotsford. The woman has her Bible open and is reading aloud chapter and verse the words guaranteed to feed their souls. All the folks from New Day do everything with capital letters and exclamation marks, it seems to Carly. She just keeps mumbling her mantra to herself, not giving the sister's words the power she craves. Carly has enough exclamation marks in her life already.

As the Bible-thumper nears her, Carly pulls the bit of newsprint from her pocket and pretends to use it as a hankie, turning her back to the sister. The sister rapidly passes, her sights perhaps on a less infectious soul down the line. Once she passes, Carly smooths the newsprint back into a neat square and tucks it back into her pocket.

The woman next to her in line laughs. "Y'er not as dumb as you look." She smiles at Carly. "I hate that, doan you?

Hate that dash of brimstone as the appetizer for every meal you get here."

Intensely blue-haired, with one wild eye, the woman leans over and shouts in Carly's ear. "Gospel food kinda puts a dent in yer appetite, if ya know what I mean."

The line around them surges ahead and Carly slides along the wall, then quickly lurches into a seat in the dining hall along with her new-found friend. A bowl of steaming *something*, with bread as a side dish, is already parked on the table.

The Blue Lady crashes down into the chair next to Carly and begins shoveling the food down before she's even managed to scoot her chair to the table.

Carly's slower. She actually looks at the food, spoons it into her mouth and chews it slowly. The Blue Lady notices Carly's restraint and pauses a moment, watching. Then she nods her head in agreement. "I get what yer up to. Ya eat *it slow*, so it lasts longer… and ya actually get to sit long enough to get warm." She adopts Carly's manner and pretends to savor each mouthful, taking her time. "Yer a cagey one, doll."

Carly merely grins a quick response and continues to eat. She tucks the slab of bread into her pocket for later. Blue Lady sees this too, and mimics it as well.

Moments later, she nudges Carly with her elbow as the sister-of-mercy wades into the dining room from the hallway. Her book's still open and she's still preaching, laying on her hands and praying over anyone who will sit still for it.

Blue Lady tilts her head, indicating the upcoming Bible Hour. "We stay much longer we're risking eternal salvation, girl."

Carly and Blue Lady scrape back their chairs and begin threading their way along the crowded dining room table. Carly notices an abandoned rump of bread left alongside an empty bowl and scoops it up, shoving it deep into her other coat pocket.

Outside, the sun is struggling to make an appearance. Spring seems more certain than it has in months. On this afternoon, it feels like a distinct possibility. Blue Lady waits patiently for Carly to join her as she waddles away from the soup kitchen door. But Carly has other ideas. She picks the opposite direction and slips and slides as quickly as she can away from her new-found friend. Blue Lady blinks her eyes, absorbing the rejection and then turns back to her own itinerary.

Stomach now quiet, Carly putters determinedly along the sidewalk looking for treasure. As she approaches a bus stop, she spots a woman just exiting a coffee shop. Carly can hear the bus approaching. She begins to genteelly search the trash container near the bus stop.

A queue of commuters begins shuffling aboard. Mrs. Coffee Cup is holding her still-steaming, delicious-smelling coffee, which the bus driver spots and smacks the door closed in the woman's face. She looks up to pro-test and he simply points to the trash can nearby. The woman hesitates, takes one more quick sip and sets the coffee cup on the bus stop bench. The bus doors magi-cally open, the driver smiles a despotic little smile, and the woman gets on.

Carly has watched the whole performance and doesn't hesitate a second after the doors close. She scoops up the hot coffee, smells it lavishly and then takes a sip. A smile wreathes her face. Carly samples a second taste and closes her eyes in ecstasy. She makes a great show of seating herself at the bus stop, gathering her garments around her for warmth, and takes a long satisfying drink.

Behind Carly a cab pulls to a halt into the now-empty bus bay. On the other side of the trash bin, a well-dressed, middle-aged executive couple have just exited a brown-stone and are hurrying towards the cab. An argument is in progress as they both hurtle towards the street.

The woman pulls the man to an abrupt stop. "I don't care. Do you hear me, David? Do you even comprehend how tired I am of this topic?"

David plucks at her sleeve, wanting to talk, but she brushes his hand away roughly.

"Fuck it, David. You'll never understand." She pulls a house key out of the front pocket of her purse and throws it wildly across the expanse of snow. It disap-pears instantly. "Keep your goddamned key…and your stupid-ass excuses about why work always trumps time with me."

She brushes past David and sweeps by Carly at the bus stop on her way to the cab. She stops a moment and faces David one more time. "You are just not worth the energy any longer, David." She rips open the cab door, climbs in and orders the driver away.

Carly stares at the woman, and then back at David, who is rooted in place. A loud honk shakes him from his stupor as a second cab pulls up. David sends one more bewildered look at the disappearing cab that holds his ex-girlfriend and then crosses to the one at the curb. Seconds later, the waiting cab squeals away from the curb and executes a quick U-turn in the middle of the avenue.

Carly picks up her still warm coffee and takes another big gulp as if washing down the scenario she just witnessed. She whispers, "Wow, tough day, David. Tough luck, big bucks, life sucks, eh?"

The coffee finished, Carly attempts to toss the cup into the trash bin but misses. As she reaches down to retrieve the litter, she notices a small depression in the gritty snow. A heavy, solitary key is cupped in the snow, naked with promise.

TWO

Reflected in the cracked and foggy mirror of a well-used gas station washroom is the key, now snug on a piece of string looped around Carly's neck. Her neck is filthy, her hair disheveled and ratty—but there is a look in her eyes that definitely was not there before.

Carly tucks the key deep within her layers of clothes and gathers up her bag of scavenged pop cans. She rattles and clanks her way out of the washroom and into the convenience store. At the checkout counter she deposits her bag of valuables. The clerk is not impressed—but by law he cannot refuse to refund the pop bottles. He counts up the turgid mess, slides the bottles into a handy recycle bin and immediately reaches for the glass cleaner and paper towel. Finally he punches a key on the cash register and counts out the money due to Carly. He slides it over to her with obvious distaste.

Carly raises her eyes to meet his and holds eye contact while she scoops the money and shoves it deep into her coat pockets. She brazenly slides a coin back across the counter towards him. "For your service." The clerk is the first to look away. Carly purses her lips, clearly about to say something.

At that moment, the door chimes and another customer holds it open.

"Hey, so where'd you hide the 30-weight oil?"

The clerk bolts from behind the counter, forestalling any further business with Carly, pocketing the coin as he leaves.

After a moment's consideration, Carly turns and pushes through the door out into the deepening evening gloom. More snow has begun to fall. She pats her chest in the place where the key now resides and smiles the tiniest smile.

Well past midnight, Carly dozes in a far corner of an empty coffee shop. She wilts over a half-cup of cold coffee. At the front of the café, the night shift busboy is stacking chairs on the tables, bussing the last of the dirty dishes, preparing to close for what's left of the night.

A bang startles Carly awake. She watches the busboy a moment, then her eyes slowly close again and her head sags on her chest. Moments later the shop owner approaches on light, silent feet. "Excuse me... *por favor.*" He bends over and gently touches Carly's forearm where it rests on the table. This time she is startled completely awake and instantly alarmed. Her eyes dart about the place trying to assimilate where she is, what's going on and where the closest exit is.

"Sorry, *Señorina*, excuse…" His voice is soft, soothing; his eyes are brown, kind and wreathed with concern as he watches Carly waken. "It's okay. My name is Jorge Ruiz."

Carly's face settles, she nods and begins to gather her raggedy coat, her shawl that she winds over her head and ears. She has the look of the eternally sleep- deprived— agelessly tired.

Jorge's eyes flicker to the snow still falling outside the window and he succumbs to a weak moment. He picks up Carly's cup and shrugs. "I will have to lock up and go home, *soon.*"

He crosses to the coffee pot on the warmer and refills Carly's cup and brings it back to her. "But sit here. Stay warm. And help me finish off my terrible coffee until then. *Si?*"

Carly blinks at the sudden reprieve. She lifts the cup to her lips as the busboy appears at Jorge's elbow. He's ready to depart, dressed in his ball cap and heavy coat.

Jorge winks at Carly, then turns and crosses to the front door. He pulls his keys from his trouser pocket and lets the busboy out into the night.

Carly sips the hot liquid and watches as Jorge relocks the door. "How DO you stay in business?" she asks. "This coffee *is terrible.*"

Jorge turns a crestfallen expression on Carly, shaking his head in dismay. "You have a saying in English, '*That something is so bad, you cannot give it away*'?"

Carly nods and takes another sip. "Well, it appears you just did … to me. But my question is, who would PAY for it?"

Jorge laughs. "No one. This blend is free to a very select clientele. My friends." He crosses back over to Carly and reaches for her cup and takes a sip. "Ahh, nectar of the gods, don't you think?"

She is incredulous that the man would drink from her cup. Who knows what kinds of diseases and infections she might harbor?

"You, *Señorina*, are the sole recipient of coffee the way it was meant to be drunk." Jorge turns and points to the array of coffee urns on the countertop. "The undeserving masses drink that." Jorge retreats to the hotplate and pours himself a cup of 'special' java and swoops up a tin of cookies. He returns to the table where Carly is seated and bows gracefully.

"May I join you?"

Carly studies Jorge's face for any hint of danger or artifice but sees only genial humor in his brown eyes. She lets herself be caught up in the game. "*Uno momento, Señor.*"

Carly sips delicately from her cup. "I am en route to a very important appointment and really shouldn't tarry."

She smiles over the rim of her cup. "But coffee like this doesn't come along every day."

They both laugh and then Jorge pushes the cookie tin towards her.

Outside, the night sky is absolutely crystal clear and it's bitterly cold. To Carly it feels like twenty below. For the city, this early morning quiet is as about as good as it ever gets. An intermittent car or two passes, shushing through the intersection whose light has switched to a blinking yellow caution. A much-muted siren wails in the distance.

Carly steps gingerly onto the sidewalk; broken ice crackles beneath her step. She peers back through the window of the coffee shop. All the lights are off, and it appears Jorge has finally gone home. There's a neon sign glowing in the dark a couple of blocks away and Carly begins to trudge in that direction. Nothing else moves.

Once underway, she passes a box of free newspapers, stops, opens it and helps herself to handfuls of the papers. She wads them up and stuffs them inside her ratty coat. She tightens the scarf around her ears and moves on. With every step the low whine of a country-western tune strengthens. She finds her pace unconsciously matching the rhythm of the music blasting from the bar ahead.

Soon Carly's close enough to see inside the bar windows—and knows immediately that this is not an establishment she is going to want to enter. A shotgun hangs on the wall behind the bar and a half dozen biker guys are left nursing their drinks at this hour of the morning. They seem like the kind of guys that practice *mean* as a religion.

Instinct pulls Carly into the shadows the moment the bar door opens and two thugs stumble into the cold, locked in an embrace that will surely see one of them die. They reel past Carly, who is pressed against the wall of the building. A knife flashes as the biker nearest her flicks it open.

The second biker howls, "You son-of-a-bitch, you sliced me." His knife flashes open too. "You've been asking for this all night, you asshole."

The men circle and swear and take turns lunging at each other, inches from the niche in which Carly has imbedded herself. Trapped, she can only cringe deeper into the shadows, trying to make herself as small as possible. She panics as she realizes the newsprint in her coat rustles every time she moves. She freezes instantly, eyes riveted on the bullies before her.

Oblivious, they continue their drunken lunges and circles. Finally, two other bikers exit the bar and come over to view the fight's progress. One chooses to lean against the building dangerously close to Carly's position.

"Aw, either kill each other or let's go. It's fuckin freezing out here." He flaps his hands against his arms, then rubs his palms together. He pushes away from the wall and grabs the arm of the nearest fighter and hauls him some distance down the sidewalk. The remaining fighter weaves and calls out after them, brandishing his knife. "I'll fuckin kill you next time I see you. Don't think I won't."

The crunch of their boots fades into the distance. In her alcove, using the wall for support, Carly slowly pushes herself to her feet, crunching newsprint announcing her change of position. She smooths it down beneath her coat and her fingers find the key against her chest. For a moment, she clutches it in her fist.

Then, barely daring to lean out of the alcove, she checks the street in both directions. Completely deserted. Hesitant, Carly ventures forth once again.

• • •

Inside the last city bus of the night, Carly is sitting half asleep on the bench seat directly across from the driver. He steers the bus over to the curb, stops and opens the folding doors. He reaches up and switches on all the lights in the interior of the bus, then switches off the light which illuminates the bus name and number directly over his head.

"Sorry, end of the line, lady."

Carly's eyes flutter open and she reflexively lifts one hand to shield her eyes from the sudden light.

"The A train don't stop here anymore, darlin." He grins at his own joke. "Well, it does actually—but not until later this morning." He pulls some change out of his pocket and presses it into the palm of Carly's hand.

"Go on. Go buy yourself a cup of morning java. On me."

Carly sighs from the bottom of her soul. Her hand closes on the change the driver has given her, and she gathers her stuff around her and rises from her seat. Her free hand grasps the chrome pole and she hauls herself upright. As she descends the bus steps, she meets the driver's eyes and nods solemnly. "Thanks That was very nice of you."

The driver delivers a mock salute, then closes the door in Carly's wake and guns the bus back into the center of the road.

A few stray snowflakes begin to fall in the glow of the bus shelter light. Carly stands a moment, rubbing her palms together for warmth, trying to get her bearings.

On the corner of the intersection, directly across from the bus stop is the grimy suburban gas station and quickmart. She spots a recycling bin overflowing with old newspapers in the alley beside the gas station. Crammed into a narrow space between the bin and the back wall of the market is Carly's cardboard box, big enough to hold a standard size refrigerator—or a very tired street person.

Later, Carly uses both palms to rub the sleep from her bleary eyes and squints into the too bright quick-mart lights. She steps out into the street, not even checking for traffic. A taxi careens around her, narrowly missing her as it pulls across the line of traffic and slides to a halt at the curb before the brownstones. The driver turns around in the front seat to open the rear passenger door without having to leave the comfort of the cab.

Carly pauses on the threshold of the convenience store, spying. Businessman David is unfolding himself from the back seat of the cab. He shouts at the cab driver as he begins his sprint to the front door of his brownstone. "I only need two minutes to grab my passport. Wait right here!"

Carly is startled from her reverie by the quick-mart clerk, who shouts at her from behind the till: "Get in or get out, lady." She steps inside; a tiny smile plays upon her face. "The key to the washroom, please."

Superclerk picks up the key, then leans forward onto the counter, dangling it from one finger. "Our washroom's for customers only."

Carly hesitates. Through the plate glass window behind the clerk she sees David, briefcase in hand, racing back out to the curb and levitating into the cab. Bolstered by the sight, Carly lifts her head and meets the clerk's eyes fearlessly. She extends a fist towards him, palm up; her fingers uncurl to reveal the handful of coins the bus driver donated. "I guess good service is optional, eh?"

She walks over to the counter and briskly extracts the key to the washroom from the speechless clerk's hand. As she turns her back and walks towards the rear of the store, the clerk grabs a doorstop off a shelf and raises it to throw.

Carly spots him in the reflection of a circular security mirror overhead. A similarly placed camera records all it sees. Her smile widens as she raises her eyes to the mirror.

"Throw it! Go on, I dare you. There isn't a judge or jury in the country that wouldn't convict you of assault after watching that tape."

The clerk hesitates and Carly lets herself into the bathroom and closes the door. The clerk shouts, "Just be quick about it, lady. I'm closing in five minutes."

Outside the glass window of the door, the clerk spots a mixed group of late-night revelers weaving their way down the ice-encrusted sidewalk. He watches them veer in his direction. He immediately crosses to the desk and flips a couple of light switches. The outdoor floodlights surrounding the pump and exterior of the building snap off. Moments later, multiple fists thud against the door.

Superclerk shouts, "I'm closed. Come back tomorrow."

Five young men and a woman—all in their mid to late twenties—cluster about the glass doorway. They're all in various stages of inebriation, pounding on the door again.

"Go away. I can't help you," the clerk yells.

Carly chooses this unfortunate moment to emerge from the washroom. The drunks at the entryway spot her as she makes her way to the front of the market.

"If she can pee, why can't we?"

The clerk is getting pissed off. All he wants is to pack up and go home. He takes two giant strides to the register, leans over the counter to haul up a baseball bat and brandishes it at the boys. "She's my mother. Now clear the fuck outta here, or I'm gonna call the cops." He swings the bat threateningly.

The oldest guy is incensed by the threat and flips the clerk off. He smacks the glass hard again with the heel of his hand. "Just try it, asshole…we'll see how long you last."

Carly is appalled by the whole scene. She tells the clerk, "Look … forget my coffee—keep the change." She looks around nervously. "Is there another way outta this place?"

He shrugs. "Yeah, sure. I can let you out the delivery entrance. I go out that way myself at night."

Superclerk leads Carly to the back of the store and through a pair of swinging doors. In the stockroom a heavy metal bar is in place across the midsection of a set of metal double doors. The clerk reaches up and flips a light switch off.

"This is 'sposed to be on 24 hours a day, but I'll shut it off for ten minutes so you can ditch the Brady bunch out front."

He checks outside the back of the store, then motions for Carly to exit. "Okay. Go on… get outta here."

Carly doesn't move quite fast enough to suit him, so he gives her a little push as incentive. As soon as she's clear, he slams the door closed and rams the bar to lock it.

THREE

Carly hesitates a moment, getting her bearings. With the floodlights off at the back of the store the loading dock is murky with possibilities. She sees the stairs to the parking lot to the left and shuffles towards them. The din of trash cans being upended out front by the gang of drunks sounds frighteningly close.

At the bottom of the steps, she nervously checks around the corner of the building towards the front of the lot. Mere yards away are the newsprint recycling bin and her cardboard home.

The dull thud, thud, thud of fists on glass echoing from the front of the gas station spurs Carly into action. She takes one final look and then races across the wide-open stretch of ice-covered tarmac between her and the recycling bin. When she reaches the edge of the cardboard container, she launches herself into the open end.

Inside, Carly draws her knees up against her chest to sit upright. She closes the end flaps on the box and dives down into the newsprint. Her head surfaces near the front of the box and she peeks out of one of the tiny portholes she's poked into it.

The wail of a police siren coming closer pulls a smile onto Carly's face. She peers intently as the gang outside the front of the market scatters in all directions. The strobe of the police searchlights fractures the inky blackness of the darkened parking lot. Suddenly, the lights come back on. Carly guesses Superclerk finally remembered they were off.

The gravelly murmur of men's voices drifts to Carly's box. She chooses a different porthole and watches just long enough to see Superclerk meet the police in front of the store.

Carly is lying on her side, her back turned to the strobing police lights. She faces a picture ripped from a glossy magazine that is taped to her cardboard wall. The police searchlights splay across the photograph of an upscale apartment filled with artwork. She gazes at it and doses off to sleep.

Untold minutes later, Carly is suddenly awakened by the sound of male voices that have definitely had too much to drink. The voices are eerily familiar; two of the drunks from earlier have returned.

"Looks like the cops have gone, Billy. Let's do this thing, quick."

"Hold on a sec, Matt." This is followed by the sound of a zipper.

From inside the box, Carly listens intently and then grimaces at the sound of piss hitting the sidewall of her box. She eases carefully to the farthest corner, trying to get as far away from the urine as possible.

"Ahhh, oh my god, I needed that."

For Carly, the peeing seems to go on forever.

"Shit, Billy, now I gotta go again." The sound of another fly being opened is deafening to Carly. She raises her hands over her ears, trying to block out what's coming next.

"Never start, that's what I say. You'll piss the night away if you do." Both the guys laugh at the witticism.

Carly is horrified to see a steady stream of urine streaming down the inside wall of her box, all over her magazine pictures. For a moment she is rigid with fury; then she simply lifts herself to her heels and headbutts the side of the box where the piss is coming from.

"MY HOUSE. GO AWAY!" she screams.

"What the hell." Both guys, the box and Carly fall into a jumble of thrashing arms, legs, cardboard and dirty rags.

Carly crawls out of the box and leaps on the nearest kid, Billy. That leaves Matthew, alias Mr. Furious, time to come to his senses and figure out it's the old gal from the quick-mart.

Carly is doing what damage she can, considering the boys both outweigh her by fifty or sixty pounds. She's pummeling Billy about the head and shoulders. Suddenly Matthew grabs Carly by the hair on the back of her head. He makes a fist and socks her in the face, hard.

Billy sits up and shakes his head to clear it. He notices that Matthew is winding up to punch the daylights out of an old woman. He grabs Matt by the arm, "Jesus-murphy, Matt, stop it. Are you crazy?"

Matt struggles to free his arm but Billy tackles him and they both roll off Carly and do a couple more drunken turns before they stop.

"Jesus, Joseph and Mary! Matt, have you lost your mind? You could've killed her." Matt finally stops struggling and pouts instead. "So what!"

Billy is suddenly very, very sober. He stands a moment and stares down at Matt. "What has gotten into you? I ain't going to prison for life because of your stupidity, Matt. We gotta help her, man. If she dies, we are so toast." He turns back towards where Carly had been lying. "Shit. She's gone."

Matthew rolls over and struggles to his feet. "Good. She's not dead then, see.

Problem solved." He bends down, picking up bits of the newsprint and packing material from the packing crate. He pulls a packet of matches from his hip pocket and holds the lit match to a bit of packing material. It catches and then greedily speeds along, gobbling the newsprint in its path. A whoosh of flame erupts as the whole box goes up.

Billy turns and runs from the parking lot, calling over his shoulder, "Run, you stupid asshole." Matthew watches the fire another moment; then he hears the sound of sirens again and he, too, turns and races from the parking lot.

The packing crate fire blossoms—burning intently for an instant longer and then begins to subside. For a brief moment it lights up the runnels of snow where Carly has dragged herself from the parking lot towards the low-growing hedgerow that separates the quick-mart from a row of tidy brownstones.

With a trembling hand, Carly reaches out, gathers snow and carefully packs it on her upraised cheek and eye. She moans quietly as she touches the wound. The bruising is already beginning, radiating out like a starburst. A tear trickles down her other cheek; snot runs from her nose. She is not a pretty sight.

Shivering in her sleep as morning takes hold, Carly is barely disturbed by the increasing din of the city surrounding her. As she awakens, her hand reaches for the key still hanging around her neck. She turns to gaze longingly at the front door of the brownstone.

Her attention is suddenly diverted by a sound in the parking lot next door. Someone is kicking the cardboard remnants of her home. Defensively, Carly ducks her head, making herself less visible. She gets a squirrel's-eye view of Matthew, who has returned to the scene of the fire.

He is kicking through the charred remnants, apparently looking for something. He upends a bit of the charred cardboard and even climbs the rungs of the recycle bin to have a peek inside. From this vantage point, he scours the neighborhood.

Carly's certain that he can see her. As soon as he begins to descend the ladder, she begins a slow crawl towards the deepest part of the hedgerow. Behind her she can distinctly hear the crunch of his footsteps in the snow, drawing nearer.

She crawls faster, pushing herself to her limit while remaining silent. At the end of the hedgerow, Carly is confronted by brighter daylight. She looks desperately up from beneath the hedgerow at the cubicle of darkness formed by the little alcove to David's house. Carly gathers herself, takes one panicked look over her shoulder and runs awkwardly the short distance to the door. She cringes back against the doorframe, willing herself invisible in the shadows. She can still hear Matthew crunching around in the snow. Her heart feels like it might explode.

Her hand leaps to the hidden key for comfort. Suddenly, she stiffens with an outrageous idea. With trembling hands, she jerks on the string that holds the key and pulls it from around her neck. She cowers lower and fits the key into the door lock.

Carly swears Matthew's footsteps are only inches away now. She turns the key, very gently slides the door open and steps inside. She quickly closes the door behind her and turns to look out the peephole.

Nothing. Everyday city traffic and pedestrians stream past the tiny portal. Still Carly watches. Finally, a meter reader in uniform strides past, clipboard in hand, mind on the next meter. Carly heaves a sigh of relief and allows herself the luxury of relaxing against the door.

Slowly, she turns and slumps to the floor. Exhausted, she closes her eyes, her breathing becomes slower and finally she sleeps.

FOUR

It's a sunny morning. The entryway where Carly is slumped is magnificent in the golden light that pours down on her from a transom window. Carly stirs awake, stiff and awkward from her sleeping position and the beating. She opens her one good eye and immediately closes it in defense against the brightness. She lifts one hand to shield the eye and looks again.

Before her, the apartment glows white and clean. Fresh flowers sit in an elegant vase on the small table in the entryway. Tasteful prints line the wall of the long hallway. Carly wraps her fetid overcoat more tightly about her body and uses the doorknob to haul herself upright. She blinks several times as if testing her vision. At first she cannot move, only stand and gawk.

A tiny, perfect bathroom with scented soap lies just off the entry. Carly swears she has never smelled a room so very clean. As if approaching a holy shrine, she takes her first step towards the altar of the living room. The artwork on the wall distracts her a moment, but the lure of the double French doors pulls her onward.

David's living room is like her treasured magazine photos come to life—and more. A halo of light pours onto the leather sofa from an overhead skylight. Graceful long-limbed palms create a natural arch in which a free-form sculpture sits. Carly's face hurts from smiling so extravagantly.

She takes a tentative step into the room and looks around. No alarm goes off; no one calls the cops. She takes another step, and another. Starting in one corner, she carefully walks around scrutinizing every square foot of space, every book title, every piece of art. Mesmerized by the sheer extravagance of the place, she examines items from every conceivable angle but is careful not to touch a thing. Finally satisfied, she lets her gaze wander to the kitchen and immediately follows where her eyes lead.

David's house is a mansion to Carly. Polished granite counters bounce the natural light onto a set of crystal water pitcher and glasses. Clear glass cabinet doors let her peek at what's inside without having to open the doors. Again, she inspects everything minutely.

She ends up in front of a gleaming, darkly paneled two-door refrigerator in which she can see her own reflection. The face of a harridan looks back at her. Carly is startled; the spell that she has been under since entering the living room is obliterated.

Moments later the sound of a key turning in the lock shatters the silence of the place. It's quickly followed by the sound of muted voices. Carly looks about wildly, trying to conjure a place to hide. The open spaciousness of the apartment now becomes a trap. She'll be spotted the moment someone enters the living room.

Two women carrying mop and pail, a light vacuum, dust rags and other cleaning supplies push their way into David's apartment. They chatter away, oblivious to any clues that someone else might have preceded them.

"What time is it, Marie?" the younger woman asks. "You do upstairs, I can do downstairs this time."

"And watch your TV show, eh Lucinda?" Marie mutters. Lucinda shrugs, she doesn't care. She's divided up the work the way she wants it and hauls her stuff into the living room. "I'll do upstairs next week."

There's a small white envelope on the hall entry table. Marie's name is written on the outside in beautiful flowing script.

"Ya right. Is Oprah on vacation or something next week?" Marie scoops up the note as she walks by, heading for the stairs. "I *love* this man, always pays cash and cleans before his cleaners arrive every week."

Lucinda plops herself onto the leather sofa and picks up the remote-control unit. "Yeah, you can't tell me that's natural in a man." She raises her eyebrows meaningfully and flicks on the TV.

Oprah is holding forth on some subject near and dear to women's hearts: wife beating, gang rape, whatever. Marie's voice filters back to Lucinda from the stairway. "He could give my Tito some lessons."

Lucinda's already deep into Oprah and doesn't hear her.

Carly is scrunched up like a sardine in a tin can, next to a stacking washer and dryer and assorted cleaning implements. She cracks the door the barest bit and peers out into the living room just in time to witness Lucinda pull the coffee table closer with one foot and stretch out both legs on top of it. An exquisite piece of statuary teeters precariously. Carly instinctively draws in a sharp breath of alarm, then instantly cringes. She scrutinizes Lucinda to see if she noticed.

Unaware, Lucinda calmly sandwiches the artwork between both feet and moves it farther along the table to make room for her feet. Disaster is neatly averted. In the closet, Carly slowly lets out her breath. She spends cramped, stuffy moments in the broom closet. Feeling beneath her for something to sit on, she locates a trash can and pulls it close enough to rest her bum on. As she does so, she dislodges a dust mop that falls, clonking her on the head. Startled, Carly very gingerly closes the broom closet door and sets the dust mop upright again.

Loud voices echo in the living room. Marie is shouting over Oprah. "Turn that damn thing down! I've been yelling my head off upstairs, Lucinda." She moves towards the kitchen, while Lucinda stays seated on the sofa. "I want you to sweep through the kitchen and then let's get out of here."

Lucinda calls out after Marie, "Way ahead of you. I already did it."

"You *did it*? While you were watching Oprah?" Disbelief weights Marie's response.

Lucinda gathers up her stuff from exactly where she set it down fifteen minutes before. "Yeah, I did it during the commercials. You can practically do this guy's whole house in one of Oprah's commercial breaks."

Marie scrutinizes the kitchen, the living room and finally the whole apartment. She bends down and straightens the coffee table on which Lucinda has rested her feet. Not entirely satisfied, but not wanting to create a scene either, Marie picks up her work tools and heads towards the door.

"Fine then. Let's go. But next week we are blitzing the place before David gets back from his trip. You hear me, Lucinda?" There's a warning tone in Marie's voice, like that of an exasperated mother scolding a perpetually stubborn child. The two cleaning women shoulder their tools and disappear from Carly's sightlines.

Inside the closet, she relaxes a bit but continues to listen intently. She can hear the murmur of their voices and then the click of the door opening and its abrupt clunk as it closes behind them.

Still Carly sits in the silence. The sound of a pendulum clock keeps her company. After several moments she opens the broom closet door as far as it will go. Her hair and face are sprinkled with debris from the dust mop. She wipes at it absently, still listening intently. Silence.

Finally, she allows herself to step out from the closet. Fine grains of sand and grit fall to the floor as she pats herself clean. Carly bends down and gathers the dirt neatly into a pile with her bare hands, then carefully scoops it up and into the garbage can. She crosses to the living room sofa, plumps the cushions and repositions the sculpture a centimeter to the left on the coffee table. As she passes from the living room into the hallway, she checks that everything is perfect.

Carly spies a slip of white paper on the hallway table and moves to examine it—the bill for the maid service. At the bottom is Marie's signature and a happy face. Carly's eyes widen at the total. Fifty dollars—for twenty minutes of Oprah. Astounding.

She stands, holding the bill for a long moment and scrutinizes the apartment. A tiny smile pulls at the corner of her mouth. Placing the bill back on the hall table, she shuffles towards the front door and takes the key from around her neck. She steps forward solemnly and inserts the key in its lock. She sighs luxuriously at the solid clunk as the deadbolt slides home.

• • •

Several days later, Carly again joins the afternoon line-up that stretches along the soup kitchen wall and down the sidewalk. Her face is still clearly sporting the scrapes and bruises of a serious encounter, but thanks to her magic key, she's cleaner and happier, and her abrasions are on the mend.

The line inches towards the open double doors of the kitchen. Blue-Haired woman whips into the dining room minutes ahead of Carly, her hair a mélange of hair-color product samplers. Carly tucks her chin in low, pulls a pen out of her pocket and very studiously inks a new word on the back of her immaculately clean hand. Doing so provides a focus so Carly won't inadvertently meet the woman's eyes. She gulps her food and scuttles away from the food kitchen as soon as possible.

She wanders the city for the remainder of the afternoon, visiting old haunts and discovering new ones. She sits at a bus stop, admiring the small buds on a tree. She's tempted to return to David's house just for the thrill of using the key, accessing a portal to a space she used to know but had almost forgotten. She wraps a hand around the key on the string around her neck. David's away, so she could simply hunker down at his suite for the duration, but she has made a pact with herself to not change her habits at all.

She already feels a disorientation that she's never felt before on the streets. It's as if she now straddles two very different worlds and her balance is precarious in each of them. Being on the street suddenly feels hard, harder than she ever remembers before she found the key. This new dissonance has tempted her to throw the key away, but she finds she just can't do that—yet. In frustration, Carly gets up and walks in the opposite direction from David's house. She does not allow herself to look back.

By nighttime Carly finds herself on the sidewalk outside the coffeeshop. She looks in at the small knot of people gathered on one side of the roomy interior. A fire is roaring in the fireplace and Jorge is busy wiping down vacated tables. He happens to look up and sees Carly's pensive face in the window. A smile spreads across his face and he waves her inside.

Carly hesitates, then shakes her head 'no' and turns away. Jorge tosses his damp rag on the table and scoots across the room and out the door after her. It only takes him moments to catch up to her. He reaches out and gently touches Carly's shoulder, so she turns to face him beneath a streetlight. The sight of her still-bruised face wipes the smile off his face. "Mother Mary, what happened, *Señorina*?"

Carly reaches up to touch her cheek, almost as if she'd forgotten. She shrugs.

"Life. It's a cabaret, old chum. But I did find a safe place to wash and clean up. So, I win in some, lose some!"

Jorge shakes his head sadly, then wraps Carly's arm

up in his own and tows her back towards the coffeeshop. "Welcome to my bistro and let me make you one of my special coffees. Your timing is perfect." He waves his hand to indicate the empty café. "We have the place to ourselves."

As they pass a nearby table, Jorge swoops up a Reserved sign and leads Carly to a corner near the back of the restaurant. It provides a pleasing view of the fireplace and the few passersby through the window. He places the Reserved sign carefully on the leading edge of the table.

"Your table, madam. Though madness swirl about us … this corner will be your refuge."

Carly looks about, a trifle self-conscious. Against the rise of tears in her eyes, she cocks her head gamely, trying to match Jorge's playful tone. "Oh, dear sir, you *really are* too kind." She pats the tabletop. "Will you join me?"

"Ah, madam, nothing would give me more pleasure." Jorge looks around somewhat sheepishly. "But I tell you, of all nights for you to appear…I fear tonight you will see me at my worst."

Jorge reaches over to the next table, grabs a flyer and hands it to Carly. "Tonight, I become a huckster, a self-promoter…a shill. All simply to sell a bit more coffee." His grin belies his words. "I have been…how do you say… roped into hosting a performance series here. Sadly, as the owner, I must announce the acts." Jorge finishes his soliloquy on a high, shaky note, making Carly laugh outright.

"Jorge, it can't be that bad."

"It can be and it will. I am hopeless on the stage." Jorge's voice has gone quite high with anxiety.

"Stop. Stop, I'm going to wet myself if you keep making me laugh," Carly spouts.

This draws a surprised retort from Jorge. "Ah, we will be even then. By the end of the night, I suspect that will be my own fate the minute I step foot into that spotlight."

Carly continues to titter helplessly as she motions Jorge away from her. He bows gallantly and heads back to the coffee bar, where he busies himself. He puts together a small teapot and cup with a saucer laden with a few cookies. He hands the tray off to his young waiter, motioning the fellow to carry it to Carly's table.

Carly meanwhile is surveying the room from her reserved table. She notices sparkling multi-colored bunting has been draped around the room, looping down from the rafters. A glitter ball turns slowly, bouncing bits of street lighting from its surface.

The young waiter serves Carly, carefully laying out flatware and a paper napkin as if she were royalty. Carly looks across the room to Jorge and does the only thing she can think of—she blows a kiss to him, indicating the tea and cookies. Jorge grins, shrugs, then pantomimes checking his wristwatch and biting his nails. He waves goodbye and hurries from behind the bar towards a nearby washroom door.

The sound of the rain outside the window has allowed

Carly to lapse into a light sleep as she leans against the wall. The tea in her cup is cold; the cookie plate is empty. The coffeehouse is deserted. The young waiter is tidying and organizing clean glasses and cups along the back of the bar. Jorge is counting the cash from the day's earnings and moving it into envelopes for banking the next day. He organizes the float for the evening event.

Carly stirs herself awake, rubs her face and gathers her used dishes. She eases her way out of the booth and crosses to the busboy's station and deposits the china. She disappears into the washroom and reappears moments later.

Jorge looks up from his counting and smiles briefly. "Good, you had a rest. The night will just be getting started soon."

"I'm worried I've overstayed my welcome, Jorge." Carly eases towards the door.   "Never, *Señorina*. Please do stay. I may need a second pair of hands, if you wouldn't mind leaping into the fray if called?"

Carly stops a moment and scrutinizes the empty café. Then she looks outside at the steady drizzle, hesitating. "Seriously? A second pair of hands?"

Jorge grins as he continues to count cash. "Wait for it. You'll see."

Only moments later the café door springs open and a tall slim man walks in and waves gaily to Jorge. "Am I the first one here, Sweetheart?"

"You are, Conchita."

"Thank Jesus. I'll get hot water."

Jorge nods, indicating Carly. "Carly will be assisting tonight. Carly, this is Conchita."

"Umm, and who do you want to be when you grow up little girl?" he jokes. When Carly draws a blank look, Conchita throws his hands in the air. "Okay, okay it sounds way better on stage."

As Conchita strolls towards the back of the café, he scoops Carly up with one arm. "Don't worry, love, I'll show you the ropes. You'll be a pro by the time the others arrive."

Carly blinks rapidly as Conchita finds light switches and begins illuminating what might have been a large storage room. In fact, it's a large dressing room with rolling racks and hangers and three large dressing tables, each with surround lights.

Conchita hands Carly the drycleaner bags he's been carrying and points to a rolling rack. "Bring that closer, please, and can you unpack my outfits while I start my makeup?"

Carly's eyes have adjusted to the brighter lights, but she's still adjusting to the world she's just been parachuted into. Without further pause, she grabs a rack and rolls it closer to the makeup station. Conchita sits down and immediately opens a large makeup case and begins placing her tools on the vanity. As Carly positions the rack, Conchita says, "That's perfect, doll. Now, once you defrock my outfits, put the black one first for the first song and then the red and finally the baby-doll pajamas."

Carly is left breathless at the new world she's discovered, but she hides it well. Conchita takes note and smiles. "Once you've got it all unpacked, can you take the pitcher into the kitchen and fill it with really hot water? Jorge's old heater will give out just about the time I need a *dib-and-dab* to freshen up."

Again, Carly rushes to comply. In the kitchen she nearly runs into Jorge, who is now wearing a 1930's style coat and tails; a top hat rests on the countertop. He's also pasted on a pencil-thin mustache above his upper lip. Surprised, Carly takes a step back as she approaches the sink.

"Ah, Conchita's famous *dib-and-dab;* she hates it when there's only cold water left," Jorge jokes. Carly can honestly think of nothing to say.

Jorge notices and laughs out loud. "You are going to have so much fun tonight, Carly. Hang tight until the performances start and you will find yourself amazed."

FIVE

Inside the open-faced bus shelter early the next morning, Carly sits rigidly bundled against the cold and damp as she watches the rain pelt down all around her. Her eyes are alert for the first time in months and a smile plays about her lips.

Directly across from her is the gas station quick-mart and next to that, David's brownstone. Carly watches as a light snaps on in an upstairs window of the row house. A shadow moves across the backlit window shade.

A second light appears on the first floor of the brownstone. A car pulls into the quick-mart parking lot and the day clerk gets out and unlocks the front door. Moments later, the lights in the interior of the gas station blink on.

Carly relaxes somewhat, hopeful that she will have a warm, dry place to sleep out the day, if she's patient. And the musical chaos of the past night still pulses in her mind.

Jorge was right…joy was born out of that avalanche of chaos. How could that be?

Traffic on the roadway in front of Carly is picking up. Near the corner, a doughnut shop's neon lights flicker into action. Seconds later, a cab cruises down the street and pulls up in front of David's apartment. The blush of dawn has barely streaked the sky.

The cab bleats one sharp blast on its horn. David appears, as usual, briefcase in hand, hurrying along the walkway to the cab. He throws himself inside the back seat and leans forward to urge the driver onwards. The taxi pulls away from the curb and launches into the thickening stream of traffic on the way to downtown. Still Carly does not move. She forces herself to sit and watch the house, the street, the neighborhood.

Down the sidewalk, a paperboy cuts across the tiny lawn of the brownstones and haphazardly places newspapers on a few of the doorsteps. Carly watches until he has safely passed, then jumps off the bench and crosses the street. She trots up the walk to David's doorstep. She stops and listens a moment, hand on the doorknob, key at the ready.

Next door to David's apartment, a downstairs light pops on, and the click of the deadbolt being drawn echoes in the morning. In tandem, Carly turns the lock in David's door.

The neighbor cracks open the door of his home and reaches down for his newspaper. At the same time, Carly quickly slips inside David's apartment. She rattles home the deadbolt on the door and freezes in the entryway. Her rapid breathing is audible in the silence. On the hallway table a white envelope gleams in the morning light. Marie's name is penned in elegantly flowing script.

Carly snaps to attention at the sight of the envelope. She looks down and notices the puddle on the floor beneath her tired sneakers. She touches her hair, only now realizing she's soaked and is soaking the floor at her feet. Too late, she remembers today is cleaning day. David would have left the apartment immaculate.

Carly turns and peers out the peephole to the bus shelter across the way. Morning is in full swing; commuters are jammed into the shelter and a bus cruises into sight. "Damn it. I just can't go back out there like this."

Carly eases out of her overcoat and uses the lining to towel dry her hair. She bends over and runs the coat over the splattered hallway, stepping out of her sneakers as she does so. A new puddle forms instantly and she retrieves the sneakers and mops up again. Frustrated, she shoves each sneaker into a coat pocket.

As Carly makes her way down the hallway, she notices a slip of paper that has fallen to the floor. She retrieves it and reads: "Marie, I noticed a god-awful smell in the house last week. Figure out where it's coming from and take care of it. Maybe my take-out in the fridge has gone bad." Signed, David.

This stops Carly in her tracks. *Damn and double-damn.* Slowly, ever so slowly, she raises her free arm over her head and sniffs in the direction of her armpit. From her expression, it's clear what she encounters is not good. Next, she lifts the overcoat to her nose and sniffs. Eww! *Clearly sink-bathing is not enough.*

Carly looks around the entryway, as if searching for answers. Her eyes fall once again on the white envelope addressed to Marie. A long, silent moment ensues and then Carly tosses the envelope back onto the table and crosses to the front door and chains it.

She immediately begins stripping off all her clothing and piling it in the hallway to the small downstairs bathroom. She enters, stark naked, and flips on the light. The pristine, all white bath tiles, bath towels and bathrobe are instantly illuminated with soft, glowing light. How grimy she has gotten becomes apparent the moment her skin is contrasted against the stark white tiles.

Twin showerheads send cascades of steaming hot water in jets of bliss into the very center of the shower stall. Carly steps in and groans with pleasure. She turns her head and soaks her hair. A necklace of grime forms around both biceps and in the hollow of her throat. The skin from her fingertips to past her elbows is riddled with ink scratchings: words cadged off posters, magazines and bits of newsprint.

Carly turns and turns, letting the steamy water cascade

over her face. She looks out into the bathroom where everything sparkles and gleams. She reaches up and turns up the intensity of the water flow. As she does so, she catches sight of her own reflection in the full-length mirror.

As Carly steps out of the pummeling stream of water, a skinny scarecrow of a woman looks back at her. Hair wet and bedraggled, skin void of luster or tone, hollow eyes look across the room at her. She can't tear her eyes away from that other woman's eyes.

Carly turns the water on even harder. The rising steam finally obliterates the image in the mirror as she steps back into the shower. She reaches for a small, perfect bar of French milled soap that smells of lavender and vanilla. "Aaahhhh," another sigh of deepest pleasure escapes her lips as she turns her face up to lather it.

The simple luxury of the touch of well-made soap, the beautiful aroma of *cleanliness* suddenly brings Carly fully in touch with how far she has fallen. The first sob is torn from deep inside her. Face half buried in the torrent of water, Carly reaches for the shower wall to support herself. Another surge of grief grips her and squeezes tight. She slides down in the corner of the shower, wraps her arms around her knees and gives herself over to mourning her loss.

Only now, in the steamy safety of a meticulously clean bathroom and behind a solid locked door does Carly finally let herself cry deeply, for the first time in years.

The water continues to beat on her bowed head and shoulders, completely unnoticed. Rivulets of blue ink course down her arms and over her hands, pooling at her feet and then into the drain as her old life washes away.

Half an hour later Carly steps from the bathroom, glowing and ruddy. She has wrapped a towel around her hair and borrowed a pure white bathrobe. As she exits the bathroom, she runs smack into her filthy pile of discarded clothing. Carly can't help herself; she takes a step back at the sight of their sheer dinginess.

But the mass of soppy sodden clothing will not be denied. Steeling herself, Carly bends over and bundles the whole pile into her arms and turns towards the kitchen. There, gleaming on the entry table, is Marie's cleaning money in its pristine envelope. That stops Carly in her tracks. She turns once again and checks that the chain is still on the door. She snaps up the envelope with a free hand and shoves it into the pocket of the robe and continues to the laundry room. She piles the soaked clothing into the washer, adds some detergent and flicks the dial to start. The machine immediately hums to life. What power, what satisfaction. Carly stands there a moment, hands on her hips and relishing her ability to make things clean! The chiming of the pendulum clock spurs her into action again. *Think! Carly, think.*

Carly enters the kitchen and pivots towards the refrigerator. Flinging the door open, she instantly spies the take-out containers David's note mentioned. She pulls them out, sniffs, makes a face and sets them on the countertop. She continues to search the interior of the fridge, which is packed with more food than a family of five could consume in a week. It's hard for Carly to stay on track; she's constantly compelled to reach out and examine the labels on mysterious jars and tins. *Focus*, she tells herself; Marie could arrive soon.

Finally, inspiration strikes when she spots a container of guacamole dip. Carly grabs it and slams the fridge door closed as she races back down the hall to the bathroom. With the container of dip in her hand she stares in the mirror. The bruising from the beating is definitely starting to lose its glory, but it still colors the high arch of her cheekbone and around her eye.

The pendulum clock marks the hour once again with its sonorous tone.

Carly lifts the lid on the container, reaches in with two fingers and lifts a slab of guacamole to her cheek. She spreads it around, really layering it on. *Smells nice. And no jalapeños in it.* She stops to survey her work, risking a slight smile. *As camouflage, it will definitely hide the obvious.* Soon, all that's visible is her lips and her eyes—now large and luminous in a pea-green face.

• • •

Carly's eyes widen at the sound of a key rattling in the front door lock. She snaps the lid back onto the container and shoves it deep into her bathrobe pocket. She can hear the door open and then thunk as it hits the safety chain.

"Heeelllo," Maire calls out.

Taking a deep breath to center herself, Carly replies as nonchalantly as possible. "Oh, just a moment … I completely forgot today was cleaning day."

Lucinda and Marie halt in their tracks at the entrance. They set down their equipment and exchange looks of puzzled amusement. "Looks like David got lucky last night."

They see a hand reach up and disengage the safety chain and swing the front door open. A woman wearing what is obviously David's terry-towel bathrobe and a towel wrapped around her still damp hair appears in the open doorway. Her face is covered in a heavy-duty cleansing cream.

"Good morning," she says. "I'm so sorry, David warned me you might be by today."

Carly reaches into her pocket and pulls out the envelope with Marie's name on it. She extends it towards Marie. "He asked me to pass this along to you, Marie. Now that I've moved in, he won't be needing your services any longer."

Marie adopts a semi-smile of understanding. "Thank you, Miss ah… *Miss*?" She leaves a blank space, hoping Carly will fill in her name.

Carly doesn't. "You'll notice there's only half of your fee there."

Marie's sucky face immediately disappears.

"We felt that was fair since it was clear you only cleaned half the apartment last week."

Lucinda's mouth drops open and Marie turns a wrathful expression on her.

"Marie, it's no direct reflection on you, for sure. We simply won't be needing your services any longer."

Marie knows when to cut her losses. She bends down and picks up her cleaning utensils and nods acknowledgment.

"Thank you, though, for being so consistent, Marie."

The washer buzzer announcing the load completed echoes from the laundry room. "Oh, that will be the laundry. I really should be going, ladies." Carly smiles brightly from beneath her guacamole facial and briskly closes the door on the two cleaners.

When she has ensured that Marie and Lucinda are down the steps, she allows herself an agonized moan as she races back to the washroom. The dip might not have jalapeños, but something in it is sure cooking Carly's face. She splashes water on her face, rinsing the creamy goo down the drain. More water, more soap, scrubbing her face clean. When she looks in the mirror, a gleaming and burnished Carly Sampson peers back at her. "Facial and exfoliant all in one handy container," she mutters. "And nutritious too. What more could a girl want?"

She finishes toweling off and ties her hair back with a piece of twine and then begins to scour the bathroom. Lost in a flurry of activity, she almost misses the sound of the dryer announcing that her clothes are dry. Carly stands in front of the dryer and pulls on her old but immaculately clean clothes. They still retain the warmth from the dryer, and she hugs herself to keep it against her skin a moment longer.

As she tosses stuff from the fridge and starts David's laundry, she begins to sing. At first to herself, but then louder and louder. It's one of the gospel mission songs that has stuck with her, and it feels so perfect for the moment. '*I got that joy, joy, joy, joy / Down in my heart, down in my heart / I got that joy, joy, joy, joy down in my, down in my heart to stay.*' Carly keeps singing while she dusts and mops and irons. It's as if her lungs don't know how to stop.

SIX

For the next few days Carly's life is almost routine. She window-shops, checking out the bargains at the local discount shoe store. She knows the shoes are not well made, but they are cheap and practical. *But honestly,* she tells herself, *anything would be better than the ratty high-top sneakers she currently wears.* She notes what time the store closes and decides to come back the next day to purchase a pair. If they'd let her, she'd buy one shoe at a time; but she knows that won't fly.

Carly makes a point to swing by Jorge's café several times a week. She still can't quite believe his kindness to her is real …but every visit brings her closer and closer to believing. She, Jorge and the young waiter, Arnold, share laughs and exchange gossip over cups of black steaming java. For long moments now, Carly actually feels happy. And then she wakes up alone at some isolated bus stop in the middle of the night panicked as if this new sliver of life is only a dream that evaporates at dawn.

• • •

Almost daily she continues to clean the house. It gives her days structure and purpose. She takes the risk of leaving David a note on the hall table to explain the new frequency of her cleaning visits. His only response is a poorly drawn thumbs-up. Carly finds joy in the work, making certain everything remains just so. It reminds her of what normal used to be like. Her appearance is subtly shifting—her clothes are now routinely cleaner and her person is definitely tidier. She trims her hair herself one morning fresh from the shower.

Early one afternoon, a small hardcover book on the coffee table catches Carly's attention. The cover shows a bus stop with a homeless person slumped against the backrest, surrounded by dirty shopping bags. A close-up of the cover in Carly's hand reveals the title: *HOMELESS* (inner city photography and poems) by Wade Stone. She stops what she's doing and picks it up, thumbs through it and instantly becomes engrossed. The book feels like someone had a porthole into her own life.

Still thinking about the book, Carly climbs up on the counter to wash the cloister windows. She is down to her last rag, so she slips off the countertop and crosses to the broom closet. Next to the washer/dryer she finds a large paper bag stuffed with cast-off clothing from David. A large note is pinned to the top item: "Marie, please toss these out."

Carly reads the note, then carefully folds it and tucks it away for safekeeping. She hauls the large bag out of the closet and carries it to the living room and plops it in the middle of the area rug. She drops down beside it and begins to sort through it all. A couple of well-made but very large men's dress shirts. She holds one up to her shoulders. "Not exactly junk ... I mean, I've seen junk. Heck I've even worn junk." She sets the dress shirt aside. Next is a man's suit; very nice material but has a small hole in the lapel, like a cigarette burn. Carly turns out the inside label and her eyes widen. *ARMANI.* "Oooh, I really like this." She strokes the sleeve and sets the jacket aside. "Very special."

Next come a handful of ties, horrible and flashy, definitely *not* David. Carly holds them up and examines them with a critical eye. One tie is a silk homage to Labrador Retrievers—panting, playing, dewy eyes staring soulfully into hers.

"Five will get you ten, these are office Christmas presents. I can shop better than this with no money at all." Still, she sets the ties aside thoughtfully and continues to rummage.

• • •

Days later, Carly is clutching a large shopping bag as she hops off the bus and drops onto the bus stop bench. She rummages through the shopping bag and hauls out the Armani jacket. She's intentionally punched a few more holes in the jacket's lapels to camouflage the original ciga-rette burn. Now she's embroidering a mystical 'eye' around each of the holes in various intense colors. She doesn't even hear the man who strolls up the sidewalk and leans against the frame of the shelter.

"Hey, good morning."

Carly looks up and immediately pricks herself with the needle. A parade of emotion—fear, surprise and pain—flits across her face. She hesitates, recognizing Matthew. Clearly he does not recognize the old street woman he had beaten to a pulp a month ago.

"Hey, yourself." Carly forces a smile onto her face.

"Sorry, didn't mean to startle you." His grin would be considered disarming if Carly didn't know him so well. "I just wondered if you knew when the uptown bus starts to run?"

Blinking fast, trying to remain calm, Carly watches as the doughnut shop sign flickers to life. She could run there, if needed. "You didn't really scare me."

She wills herself to take a breath. She starts again, cor-rects herself, keeping track of the conversation. "I think it's another twenty minutes or so." She pointedly looks past Matthew's shoulder. "Usually not until the first tray of doughnuts appears in the window."

Matthew turns, following her gaze, and nods approval.

"Cool. That means there's time for coffee and dough-nuts then." He turns without another glance and begins to cross the street. Clearly, to Matthew, the assault never happened.

Carly watches as he saunters across the street towards the doughnut shop. How does a person acquire that amount of self-importance or pure egocentricity? She picks up her sewing again but can't stop her hands from shaking.

Wasn't scared, wasn't scared—just surprised. But her eyes keep wandering back across the street to where Matthew is opening the shop door. *Surprise isn't scared. Doesn't count, doesn't count.*

Carly has to set aside her sewing because her hands are shaking so violently. She stuffs it into her bag, punching it down. She starts crying. *You can't scare me, scare me, scare me!* She grabs the sewing bag and hurries from the bus shelter, nervously looking back over her shoulder towards the doughnut shop.

• • •

That evening at the café, Jorge is in a tizzy, flitting from table to table as he wipes and then returns to the coffee bar. Carly has a new look as she nods hello to the young waiter and slips across the room to her table. She's created a dress shirt out of one of David's cast-offs, and with her new shoes, she's definitely looking more arty than home-less. But oddly enough, there are still ink words scribbled on the backs of her hands.

As usual, the Reserved sign is placed prominently in the middle of her table. Across the room, Arnold holds up a mug and shrugs, *Does Carly want some?*

Carly nods yes. He pours a steaming cup of joe, puts it on a tray with cookies and flatware and crosses the room. As he places her refreshments on the table, Carly smiles. "Does Jorge have a gig here again tonight? Does he need help again in the dressing room?" Really, she's not *asking.* The young guy nods assent. He slips a flyer onto the table next to Carly's coffee cup and turns away to bus a nearby table. Carly picks up the flyer and smiles, then calls out, "Hey, tell Jorge I know this guy. He's great." The author of the book that was on David's coffee table, Wade Stone, is grinning up at Carly from the flyer.

Over at the coffee bar Jorge's head pops up from Wade's book, which he's been scanning, trying to make sense of it. "You *know* him?" Book in hand, Jorge crosses to Carly's table.

"Well, I know *of* him. I just finished reading his book." Jorge sits down opposite her. "Actually, I read some of it several times. It's quite compelling."

Jorge pulls a pencil from behind his ear and scribbles the word on a napkin snatched from his breast pocket. "Compelling ... that's good. What else?"

Carly reaches over and takes the book from Jorge's hands. She smooths her hands over the cover while she talks. "Some of it's really sensuous, and gritty … and real."

Jorge keeps scribbling like crazy. "This is fantastic. What else, what else?" Carly closes the book and quietly hands it back to Jorge. She looks him directly in the eyes.

"Did you even read this?"

"Three times. It was like being dyslexic and being handed a crossword puzzle." Jorge thumbs through the book again. "It may as well be written in Greek."

Carly sighs heavily and shakes her head.

Jorge sighs, "The guy's going to be here in an hour and I haven't got a clue how to introduce him." A sudden light goes on in Jorge's eyes, but he hesitates. Then he whispers, "You could do it!"

Carly practically chokes on her coffee. "Jorge, this muck has finally corroded your brain."

"Seriously, Carly. Just say what you just said to me. Please?" Jorge smiles his most charming smile. "You loved his book, just tell him that. I mean, you know it's only going to be him and his girlfriend that show up for a poetry reading anyway."

Jorge hands Carly another freshly baked cookie from the plate in front of her. "Please, please, please."

Carly takes the small volume back from Jorge and slowly looks through it again. She shakes her head, as if she will say no. When she looks up and sees the pleading in Jorge's eyes, she shakes her head more adamantly, no. "Honestly, I won't be any better at this than you, Jorge Ruiz."

A huge, beautiful smile illuminates Jorge's face. "You are so very, very wrong. You will be fantastic, and I will be able to stop hyperventilating enough to serve my customers."

A brief glimmer of fear flickers across Carly's face. "Easy for you to say, you're off the hook." She knocks the tiny book against her forehead over and over again. "I have finally lost my mind."

Jorge is practically dancing back to the coffee bar. "You'll be brilliant, Conchita, I know you will."

• • •

A young couple hesitates in the doorway of the coffee-house. Jorge spots them and waves them inside with a grandiose gesture. "Here for the poetry reading? *Excellent*. Let me show you a table."

He grins across the room at Carly as he seats the couple. "You'll be brilliant," he mouths. Carly buries her head in the open volume of poetry. "I think I'm going to throw up, Jorge."

Half an hour later, the coffee bistro is actually close to full. It's all college kids and writers so everyone is nursing their single cup of coffee and killing time waiting for the reading. Jorge is buzzing around waiting tables, fussing here and there. He's happy.

Carly is sitting at her reserved table, nervously tap, tap, tapping her forefinger on the tabletop. Through the window, she's keeping an eye on a guy pacing up and down the sidewalk. Poor slob, must be the writer.

"That's Wade Stone and his girlfriend and publisher, Myra Daniels," Jorge whispers to Carly. Then he reaches up and turns the dimmer switch on the lights. Still outside, Wade catches the change in lighting. If the expression on his face is any indication, you'd think he was facing execution.

Carly slowly lets her breath out and rises from the table. She crosses the café to where Jorge has created a faux stage: a stool, a glass of water and a floodlight turned straight down on where the speaker will stand.

Carly steps into that spotlight, holding on Wade's book as if it were the hand of the savior. "Good evening … whoa, that sounds way too formal doesn't it?"

Some people in the café chuckle and turn to give Carly their attention. She continues, "Anyway, welcome and thank you for coming."

Carly holds up Wade's book for the audience to see. "Tonight is something special. For me, anyway. Wade Stone is an author that I've read and really liked." Carly ducks her head a minute. "Earlier I had all these big words when I was talking to Jorge about Wade, which I've now completely forgotten."

The crowd titters good-naturedly, which gives Carly a boost. "Anyway, tonight Wade is going to read from his book of poetry, *Homeless.* I like to think of it as Wade giving us a personalized tour of a palace on the skids that he built for us." Wade smiles, seeming to like this analogy.

Carly continues: "In a lot of ways, it's like the Pharaohs coming back and taking you on a tour of the pyramids. The pyramids have been there forever, everyone can see them but there's so much you can't possibly know or *see* until you actually speak to the fellows that created them."

Wade is beaming. Carly can see she's had an impact, and that's good for her self-confidence too.

"A reading can be like that, like a guided tour of an unknown world. So, here's Wade Stone to share his monument, *Homeless*, with us tonight."

Carly flees the limelight and Wade steps up, bolstered by the introduction. He half sits on the stool, dangling one lanky limb over the seat while his other foot remains firmly on the floor. He opens the volume of poetry but doesn't really consult the page in front of him. He's got the whole thing memorized.

"I had kingdoms in mind when I met you," he begins, eyeing Myra.

Carly skirts the perimeter of the coffeehouse, making her way back to her usual spot. Jorge is already there to welcome her. He whispers, "That was terrific, Carly." He pats her hand and silently mouths 'thank you'. Carly leans closer and whispers back, "Are all these people here just for Wade?"

Jorge shrugs non-committedly. "Well, we do have a show planned for the Second Act. If we get swamped, can you help out with the girls?"

Myra is beaming adulation across the room to her man. Wade pretends oblivion but harnesses every mote of energy she sends. He's reading from his book to a sell-out crowd because of Myra.

Respectful applause follows Wade's final verse. He closes his book, savors the moment and then reluctantly slips off the stool and leaves the spotlight. More polite applause follows.

He searches the room, spots Myra sitting with Jorge and Carly, and crosses over to them. Wade pulls out a chair, uncertain whether to sit or stand. It seems anti-climactic to simply blend back into the huddled masses.

Myra pats the seat of the chair next to her. When Wade sits, she leans over and kisses his cheek fondly. "You were just brilliant tonight, Sweetheart." Carly nods enthusiastically.

Wade allows himself a proud grin. "Way easier than I expected." He nods to Carly. "Of course, your introduction really set me up. Thank you."

Carly drops her eyes. Jorge beams. Wade continues to ramble through the play-by-play for himself. "Granted, my first piece was a little rough ... and I think I want to rework that passage about the breakup." He pauses, "I dunno. What do you think, Sweetheart?"

"I think I could use someone like you, Carly" Myra says unexpectedly. Carly's eyes pop up at the sound of Myra's voice.

"Really. I don't know if Jorge told you, but I actually publish books—mostly art, theatre and poetry." Myra smiles a winning smile. "I could sure use someone in the office to help arrange a series of show openings and book launches this summer and fall."

When Carly doesn't immediately respond, Myra continues, pushing a little harder. "Really. Someone just to phone a few places, set up a few things." Wade turns pouty, unhappy at business taking precedence over his poetry.

"And of course, to book a few more gigs for Wade's book, for sure. What do you say?"

Jorge leaps in where Carly fears to tread. "She'd love to. Wouldn't you, Carly?"

Carly looks from Myra to Wade and finally at Jorge, who grins encouragement.

"But I don't really know anything about art, Myra."

Myra scoffs. "No one does, *really*. We all just make it up as we go along. And honestly, all you have to know about are the books I publish, and I'll give you copies of those."

Jorge nudges Carly, waiting for her to accept the offer. Glancing at him, she finally say, "Well. Okay, then. I guess."

Wade bursts in on the conversation. "Fantastic. I'll see you at every reading." He reaches out and rubs the top of Carly's head. "My new good luck charm."

Myra rises to leave, gathering her purse. She hands Carly a business card. "Come by tomorrow afternoon, and we can sort out the details." She steps away and then turns back a moment. "You can do afternoons and evenings routinely, right? Like tonight's event?"

Carly offers a less than eager nod. Myra strides towards the door, waving her hand gaily in farewell. "See you tomorrow then, any time after two."

"You stay longer and enjoy yourself," she says to Wade.

SEVEN

As Myra exits, Conchita slips through the front door. She spots Carly and winks, nodding her head to indicate the dressing room beyond the bar. A smile leaps onto Carly's face and she immediately pushes back her chair. Jorge just catches a glimpse of the long line of Conchita's thigh and the flash of her stole as she disappears into the gloom of the back room.

Wade is caught off guard by Carly's sudden decampment. "Hey, what gives?"

Jorge titters slightly. "The second wave of tonight's event has arrived." He leans forward and whispers conspiratorially. "I fear our Carly may be star-struck."

Wade watches Carly disappear into the back room behind the bar. He turns his attention back to Jorge. "Second act?" He looks vaguely disgruntled. "What second act?"

Jorge picks up on Wade's irritation and downplays the forthcoming show. "Oh, it's just a little something we throw together for the tourists, so to speak." He shrugs, "No point in wasting the crowd we drew for your poetry reading, Wade."

Backstage Carly has leapt into unpacking Conchita's gear. She disappears for a moment and brings back a pitcher of steaming water and places it on the makeup table. She's even found a tight-fitting lid for it.

Conchita smiles at Carly through the mirror while applying her foundation. She looks at Carly a long moment in the mirror, then grabs Carly's arm as she passes. "You look good tonight, girl."

Carly can't help but smile and blush a bit too. "I had some spare time and thought this old jacket I found could use some sauce."

Conchita rubs the material between her forefinger and thumb. "That's an Armani or I'm a straight white man in glasses."

Carly giggles and struts a little for Conchita. Conchita draws her closer and fixes her shirt collar, then rolls up one of the sleeves on the jacket.

Carly backs away, but too late. Conchita notices the florid ink marks—words and drawings—that snake up Carly's arms.

Carly instantly deflates in embarrassment. Conchita stands up, takes Carly's other arm and raises that jacket sleeve too. More sinuous tracery slithers up the arm.

"You should show this off, Carly, not hide it. This plays really nicely into the embroidery you've sewn onto the jacket. You see that, right?"

Conchita pulls Carly over and seats her in front of the mirror. Conchita stands behind her and uses her fingertips to trace the ink lines up Carly's arms and then follows the embroidery threads up the remaining jacket sleeve. "See, it's all of a piece. It's fabulous." Conchita lets her fingers slide back down Carly's arms again.

Carly shivers and their eyes meet in the mirror.

"This is you, baby," Conchita says. "Embrace it."

Conchita turns Carly around and puts her hands on her shoulders. "People always tell you, 'just go out and be yourself'. That's just bullshit. What I tell all my babies is to go out and *find* yourself, darlin'."

Conchita turns Carly around to face the mirror and pushes her down onto the makeup chair. "You are soooo close to becoming your very own self, girlfriend." She bends down and looks over Carly's shoulder at her face in the mirror. "Now, will you give me fifteen minutes and let me make you up in a way that says 'this is who I want to be'?"

A tentative smile flits across Carly's face as she looks up at Conchita. She nods once, very seriously. "Can you?"

Conchita claps her hands in excitement. "We'll have to hurry. I want you finished before the other girls get here. Agreed?"

Carly's smile lights her eyes, fills her chest with heat and threatens tears. Conchita laughs at her and growls, "You go crying once I get your makeup on, darlin', and my powderpuff will never grace your cheeks again." She swirls a plastic cape over Carly's shoulders and cackles. "You trust me?"

Carly smiles back in the mirror. "For ever."

"Okay then. Who do you want to be when you grow up?

Carly stops and looks at herself in the big mirror. She remembers Matthew's swaggering disregard for her fright. Wade and his assumption that of course she would prune her life to fit into his. And David, who felt every minute of his girlfriends' lives should be tailored to his own.

She looks up at Conchita tentatively and whispers, "I want to be a man. I want their self-assurance, their conceit, their sense that the world revolves around them, and should always do so. I want that, Conchita. If only for a minute, I want to know what that's like."

"Drag king, then." Conchita bursts out laughing and throws her arms around Carly's shoulders. "Okay girl. Close your eyes and let me work my magic. When I'm done, I'll clap my hands and the door will be open. But It will be up to you to step up and seize the moment. *Carpe diem*, baby doll. *Carpe diem*."

by our
hands
be
we
whole

ONE

Rain sluices down off the metal overhang that's supposed to protect the arriving passengers as they grab their luggage from the driver. It almost works.

"SCOOTER!" A female voice lifts over the sound of the thundering rain like a soprano's voice rises over the male voices in a choir.

Scooter Wells quickly lifts her head and her luggage. The suitcase stays dry, the back of her head and peacoat get a dousing from runoff she won't forget for a while. Regardless, she's smiling like she has just won the lottery. Her older sister, Hayley, runs to Scooter, wrapping her in a crushing embrace. She, too, is grinning like Scooter won the lotto.

"Damn, Hayley." Scooter is forced to take a step back. "You weigh a ton at fifty miles an hour."

Hayley jumps up and down waiting for Scooter to drop her bag and return the hug. "Yeah, but for a nano-second while I'm jumping, I'm weightless," Hayley quips.

Scooter laughs, "Your logic is somewhat flawed. But I'm really jazzed to see you too." They have a proper hug. Scooter looks surreptitiously over her shoulder. "Did you bring a car?" She struggles not to sound too hopeful.

Hayley takes a step back and grabs Scooter's backpack and starts walking towards the terminal. "C'mon. goof. Grab your bag, there are real live taxicabs just out front."

"Cabs? Damn. You've gone all uptown on me, Hayley." Scooter picks up her suitcase and hustles after her sister.

From the cab window, Scooter is immersed in the sights and sounds of the city. Vancouver is not large, but it's a damn sight busier than any prairie city, even Regina ... *and wetter.*

"Okay, I should just blurt this out. Get it out in the open from the get-go, eh sis?"

Hayley inspects Scooter from over the top of her severe black glasses. "I can't wait."

"So, ahh, does it *always* rain like this here?"

"*This?* This isn't rain, Scooter. This is merely the beginning of the rainy season. We may see sunshine any minute, or any week, or sometime before the end of the month. Wait for January. December is rain and cold and d-a-r-k; unrelenting. Sometimes in January we Google SUN just to remind ourselves of what we're missing."

"Gawd, Hayley, you are so full of shit today."

Hayley leans over and kisses Scooter on the cheek.

"I know, I can't believe I actually missed you." Hayley snorts a laugh at Scooter's discomfort. "How's Janie? and baby Lana?"

Scooter's face drops into a frown. "Don't start. Lana is great. And a really good kid. I was never half so nice at ten." Scooter takes another peek out the window. "She would be so excited and delirious to get to see Vancouver."

Hayley sighs. "I know. I wish you all could have come. Even the baby-brat."

The cab slows and pulls to the curb in front of a large blue three-storey house set towards the back of a lot with a sketchy bit of swamp grass out front. Hayley pays the cabbie and he pops the lid of the trunk. Clearly, he's not getting wet for a skimpy two-dollar tip.

"Right. Okay, Scoot, ready. Blast out, grab your bag and run for the front porch. I'll be right behind you."

Both girls erupt from the cab and execute the game plan perfectly. Scooter improvises a scary slip and then slides in the muddy grass but makes it to the porch steps mere seconds after Hayley does.

Hayley is laughing while she unlocks the door. "Good thing we have the house to ourselves for a bit. You can jump into the shower and then change into dry clothes. Better to grab it now, while there's hot water available."

The door swings wide and Hayley lets Scooter go first. The living room is chock-a-block with La-Z-Boy chairs, a sofa, various bookcases laden with vast quantities of textbooks and reference works. An old dog stretches lazily on the sofa and yawns. He spots Hayley and his tail begins a slow wag back and forth. He oozes off the sofa edge like molasses. His departure reveals a discarded pair of jockeys and a t-shirt.

"Holy cow. Exactly how many people live here, Hay?"

Hayley reaches down and scratches the old dog's ear. "It varies. This month we have four paying rent, one away in St. John's and a visitor couch-surfing for the week. Hence the sleeping apparel left behind, and the dog. It's supposed to go between the seat cushions. Not the dog, the underwear."

Hayley moves towards the stairs, still toting Scooter's backpack. "C'mon, let's get this stuff upstairs. If we leave it until people start trickling in from class, we may never find it again."

Scooter obligingly follows Hayley up the stairs, muttering, "Whoa, have you ever loosened up, Hay."

Hayley snorts a reply. "Welcome to Vancouver, dear sister."

• • •

Hours later the two sisters are seated at a large kitchen table that's mostly covered in textbooks. They clear two spots by moving books aside, then help themselves to spaghetti from a large pot on the stove. Soon after, the first roommate, Maggie, returns from class and joins them. She pushes the books farther down the table. When Jacob and

Joey saunter into the room, they begin stacking books on the floor beneath the window.

Scooter has been silently watching the household coalesce around her. Jacob pulls up a chair and immediately starts picking food off the girls' plates.

"Jake, there is more spaghetti in the pot," Hayley prompts.

"Salad too," Scooter offers sotto voice, keeping her eyes on her plate.

Jacob reaches over and pats Scooter's hand. "Don't worry, your plate is safe. You're still officially a guest."

As Joey wanders towards the kitchen, Jacob calls after him, "I'll give you fifty cents if you bring me a plate of spaghetti, Joe."

"Don't call me JOE, Jake."

"He's very *sensitive*," Jacob explains. "I know he only calls me Jake to needle me, so I'm immune."

Maggie and Hayley titter. Jacob smiles at them appreciatively. He turns to Scooter, who merely scowls. "Ah, I see you're not impressed," he quips.

Scooter carefully swallows her forkful of spaghetti and drawls, "So far you come across as a bit of a dick, *Jake*." She intentionally meets his eyes as she emphasizes his name.

Jacob holds her stare for a long moment, then slams his palm on the tabletop, smiling. "Fuck, busted in only thirty seconds. Hayley, did you prep our Miss Scooter? What is your real name anyway?"

Hayley and Maggie look from one to the other and back again as the barbs fly across the table.

Scooter stands and slides her chair back from the table. "My friends call me Scooter." Scooter nods her head to Hayley, indicating they should go. "I'd prefer if you called me Ms. Wells…but really don't call me at all unless my sister's hair is on fire, Jacob."

Scooter ducks into the kitchen and leans against the door jamb. "Joey, nice to have met you. We're headin' out for a walk on the beach, now that the rain has stopped for a while. I'm dying to see the ocean!" Scooter beams with enthusiasm. "Catch you later, eh?"

Joey looks up from ladling food onto a dish. "Ah sure. Thanks, Scooter. Nice to have met you, too." Joey is hiding his smirk, but his eyes shift sideways to glance at Scooter in the doorway. "Nice parrying Jake's stupidity. We're going to get along fine, I think!"

Scooter grabs her coat from a hook near the front door and thunders down the steps where Maggie and Hayley are waiting. Both carry furled umbrellas. Scooter tweaks her sister's cheek as she passes, nearly running down the street towards the bay. "C'mon, Hayley, it's not gonna rain. Let's go swimming."

Maggie casts a disbelieving look at Hayley. "Really. You two are related?"

"I've been sceptical since Janie introduced us, but it's apparently true. I think mom was going for the yin and yang of daughters with us two."

Maggie snorts. "Where does that leave your little sister, Lana, then?"

Hayley shakes her head, "Oh fuck, poor kid—bewildered, I think. Maybe it's a good thing she's ten years younger. Scooter can't influence her too much!"

Hayley takes off down the hill after her sister, yelling "C'mon, we'd better catch Scooter or she really will shuck down to her skivvies and go swimming." Maggie trails behind.

• • •

Later, the three girls are seated on the beach with their backs against an ancient beach log. Scooter is barefoot, with her trousers rolled up and sand clinging to her feet and pant legs.

"I am coming down here every single day that I am here, Hayley. Maybe even twice on the days the sun comes out." She leans over and scoops the sand between her legs into a small hill. "How often do you guys come down and just hang?"

Maggie and Hayley turn looks of long-suffering on each other. Maggie breathes out a long sigh. "I've lived here my whole life, Scooter, so really October isn't a month that I spend much time at the beach. Or November or December. Winter can be a little sketchy. Usually by July it's nice enough to hang out here a bit."

Hayley shrugs. "I don't really like sand, Scoot. It gets in your shoes…

"Take 'em off."

"And your socks…"

"Take them off too."

"If you're wearing shorts, it lodges in places you can only imagine." Before Scooter can interject, Hayley hurries to add, "And NO, I will not take 'em off."

Scooter falls on her stomach in the sand and places her chin on her hands and looks out at the ocean. "It's mesmerizing, don't you think?" She rolls over on her back and bolts upright, facing the two girls. "I can't stand it. I want to lie here and listen to the waves all night long, and at the same time I want to jump up and run in circles like a Spaniel. It's just so damned neat."

Hayley stands up and reaches down for Maggie's hand to help pull her up. "We should be heading back, Scooter. Both Maggie and I have classes tomorrow. And I still have homework to do."

Scooter grabs her shoes and socks and walks with them across the sand, then back up the hill. By the time they arrive at the house, Scooter is yawning to beat the band. The house is dark and silent as Maggie unlocks the door. "The boys must've gone out."

Scooter stops halfway up the stairs. "I might wake up way early tomorrow, cuz of the time difference. If I go out, how will I get back in?"

"There's always a spare key beneath the big rock outside, by the stairs," Hayley replies. "Just be sure you put it back if you use it, Scoot."

"Great! Nighty-night."

Maggie watches Scooter disappear up the stairs. "Yin and yang just about says it all, I think, Hayley."

Very early the next morning, halfway down the hill to the beach, Scooter runs into Joey, walking up it. She waves and he crosses the street to join her.

"You never saw me walking up this hill."

Scooter scrutinizes him. "Say what?"

Joey laughs. "I'm 'sposed to be *running* up the damn thing. Conditioning."

"Walk back down with me and then run back up it then, you idiot. It will give you a fresh perspective." Scooter grabs his arm and turns him around before he can answer. "Everyone in Saskatchewan told me you guys out here are all freaks. Running everywhere, munching on granola and sitting around chanting *Om, shanti Om*."

Joey grins in response and falls into step beside Scooter. "God, that's what you hayseeds think of us, is it?"

"Yup. The rest of the country wonders if it's the water." She punches his shoulder. "Or all that, you know, marijuana."

"Okay, just cuz it's you, I'm going to be honest. I run as a cardio workout for my badminton game. I'm on a scholarship and can't afford to lose it. And two, marijuana or any kind of smoking is super, super bad for heart and lungs."

After several steps in silence, Joey leans closer and whispers, "But secret lab tests at UBC have confirmed there is something freaky about the water here."

"Aw shit." Scooter looks panicked. "How much does it take to turn me into a granola-munching tree-hugger? I honestly could not show my face at home again if that happened."

Joey puts an arm around Scooter's shoulders and hangs his head. "The longer you stay the worse it will get, Scooter. You're likely already contaminated, what with the rain, your swim, the shower and all the water you guzzled because it was so darn good last night."

"Aw hell, so I may as well just commit to living here now, eh?"

Joey dances a few steps in front of Scooter, laughing. "Yes, yes, yes. You can have Sophie's old room."

"The girl who went to St. John's for Thanksgiving?"

"Yeah, she called to say her boyfriend proposed the minute she got home, and she said yes." Joey raises his eyebrows questioningly. "So, are you in?"

Scooter grabs him before he can dance right in front of a car. "It's not that simple. I should check in with Hayley about how she'd feel if I moved in with you all."

"Why do I feel like there's an 'and' coming?" Joey says.

"And I don't know if you noticed, but Jacob is a major

dick-head." They cross the street with the light and the beach waits enticingly just beyond a fringe of trees. "I don't know how much of him I could take."

Joey walks with Scooter to the beach. "Think about it. I'll go for a little run and swing back around and pick you up. I've known Jacob, or JP as we called him in middle-school, a long time. He is a dick right now—but he wasn't always. I kind of hope he's working his way back to being dickless again." Joey snorts out a laugh. "Well not dickless...oh hell, you know what I meant." He takes off running.

TWO

Around the dinner table that night, Joey pours sparkling grape juice in all their glasses. Hayley passes around a large bowl of macaroni and cheese and Maggie sends the tossed salad in the other direction. Scooter heaps food on her plate and passes the macaroni to Jacob. "Wow, this looks great. Do you guys eat together every night like this?"

Jacob looks perplexed as he ladles out a portion of pasta. "Naw, usually only when someone has gotten engaged or cracked some major milestone in life." He looks across the table at Joey. "Which is it, maestro? Why have you called us forth?"

Joey raises his glass. "Both, kind of. Sophie called today to say she's gotten engaged to her old boyfriend in St. John's." Joey lifts his glass in a toast. "To Sophie." Everyone follows suit.

Jacob immediately pretends to gag on the juice. "Gah, this is just juice, Joey!"

Joey laughs, "Of course it is, I can't break training. Bottoms up, everyone."

Maggie holds out her glass for more. "Okay, I'll bite. What's the second occasion?"

Joey stands, pushing his chair back, and adds a dribble more juice to all the glasses. "A toast to welcome our new roommate."

"What? Who…?" They all look perplexed.

"Ladies and gentlemen, I give you SCOOO-TER Wells."

Scooter chokes on her juice, wipes the dribble off her chin and onto the back of Joey's t-shirt. "Joey, I never said I would. I just said I'd think about it."

Hayley immediately pops up and runs around the table to hug her sister. "Yes, yes, yes. You have to, it would be perfect."

Maggie's face lights up. "Oh, that would be so super, Scooter. Please say yes."

"You guys, I can't just abandon my mother and baby sister. I mean, they think I only came out here for a holiday." Scooter is mostly speaking to Hayley, who tries valiantly to wipe the smile off her face.

Hayley jumps in, "Oh Scooter, you know Janie will understand."

"But I never really said goodbye to either of them. Not a permanent, I'm leaving home goodbye. It was just a see you in a couple of weeks goodbye."

Joey sits back down at the table and shovels up a forkful of macaroni. "What if they came out here to visit, and then you could do the proper goodbye thingy then?"

Scooter looks more perplexed than upset. "Janie can't afford to just fly both of them out here, is the problem."

Maggie downs her juice, and offers, "Could she afford one ticket, do you think?"

Hayley leaps in before Scooter can answer. "Let's ask her, Scooter. You know, Janie always has money squirreled away for emergencies."

Scooter shrugs. "I'm not sure this qualifies as an emergency, Hay."

Joey's face lights up. "Okay, so you guys know my dad's an airline pilot, right?"

All eyes turn to Joey. "Oh. You didn't? Well, he is—and he often gets a chance to fly family from back east out here to visit. What if I tell him the story and see if he can finagle a seat for one—if Janie can pay for the other?"

Hayley and Scooter both fling themselves at Joey, lifting him out of his chair and dancing him around the table. After a few seconds, all three are out of breath and have to stop.

Joey deadpans, "I'll take that as a yes then, ladies."

• • •

The next morning, Scooter is seated in the kitchen, drinking coffee and reading through a sheaf of neatly typed papers. She scans the final page and places it back on the pile with the others, neatening the stack. She inserts the pages in a manila file folder and takes another sip of coffee. Moments later, she stands and rinses her cup in the sink, then picks up the file folder and walks to the front door. There is a sense of impending doom on her face. The lag in her step speaks volumes about her errand.

As she stands on the front porch and locks the door, Joey bounces up the stairs towards her. "Hey, I never saw you at the beach this morning." He waits while Scooter unlocks the door for him. "Uh, you okay? You look a little panicked, maybe?"

Scooter turns a forced smile in his direction. "Today I find a job."

Joey grimaces a response. "'K...you go, girl. Go bring us all home some bacon, Honey!"

As Scooter marches soberly down the front steps, Joey waves theatrically at her departing back. "Be sure to hit all the bookstores on 4th Avenue—they always need people."

Scooter waves a hand in acknowledgment without looking back. At the corner she turns and marches up the hill, a lonely soldier headed to the front lines for duty. At the top of the hill, she turns and proceeds down the sunlit side of 4th Avenue. At every store doorway, no matter the welcome or lack of it, Scooter offers a neatly typed résumé from her file folder.

"Good Morning, how are you today?" She proffers the

résumé. "My name is Samantha Wells and I'm looking for a job. My friends call me Scooter, and that's because I've always had so much energy. I'd like to offer to put that energy to work for you, helping you in any way I can."

"You're looking for a job?"

"Yes, sir, I am."

"Why not just say so?"

"I'm looking for a job. Are you hiring?"

"No. But the résumé's nice."

In a few places, Scooter manages to relay the whole spiel. But most often, the appearance of the résumé negates the remainder of her introduction and elicits a wave of dismissal. By noon, she has walked the entire sunny side of 4th Avenue from Alma to MacDonald. At MacDonald she stops at a bakery to buy a coffee and knish, but only after handing out a résumé and chatting up the baker.

After a washroom break to tidy her appearance, Scooter crosses the street and heads back down the hill, her cowboy boots thunking on the sidewalk. The meat market only wants her if she is already trained. The next bakery wonders if she knows how to make bread. At the leather store she is seriously tempted by the black leather belt with the shiny stainless-steel rivets, which sadly she cannot afford. The gem shop is cool, but a little airy-fairy. The Naam restaurant is tempting, and they accept her résumé gladly. Scooter thinks they are perhaps a little too eager for help. It's a tad discomforting.

It is now mid-afternoon. Scooter's feet are swollen and hot inside her boots. She is borderline cranky and should probably quit for the day. She checks her folder: five more résumés. Scooter looks up at the plate glass window and into the store beyond. The glass is decorated with the likeness of a woman, clad in a toga, with a large sword slung across her back. *ATHENA's BOOKS—"the thinking woman's bookstore"* is emblazoned underneath.

As Scooter steps through the doorway, her eyes fall immediately to the round antique display table. By habit, she begins circling the table, reading the book titles: *Manmade Language; The Female Eunuch; Surfacing; Beyond God the Father; Against Our Will; Halfbreed; Of Woman Born; Fat Is a Feminist Issue; Our Bodies, Our Selves; Not Vanishing; The Color Purple; Outrageous Acts and Everyday Rebellion; The Young in One Another's Arms; Disappearing Moon Cafe."*

Scooter shakes her head in disbelief. "I've never heard of any of these books," she turns and says to the woman seated at the nearby cash desk. "What the hell—I mean heck—kind of store is this, ma'am?"

The woman's laugh starts in her substantial belly and spirals rapidly up her torso until it encircles her face with a wry smile. Her face has the most beautiful skin Scooter has ever seen. And the most outlandish hair—spiking and curling in a corona around her head, tips colored red, navy blue and silver without any thought to uniformity.

The woman smiles, a twinkle in her eyes. "This is a store dedicated to women writers, readers and thinkers." She raises one beautifully articulated eyebrow in question. "Of which I believe you may be one—or even all three?"

Scooter cannot hide the huge smile that erupts unbidden. "I never thought so until now, ma'am, but I swear I would pay you to let me stay and read every book on that table."

"You want to pay *me*?"

Suddenly Scooter remembers her task and steps forward to offer a résumé. "Well, if I were rich and not desperately in search of paid employment at the moment—yes, I would. Gladly."

The woman reaches for Scooter's hand and forces her fingers to relinquish the résumé. She scans the neatly typed page and looks up. "You typed this yourself?"

"Yes, ma'am." Scooter is aware that hope layers her response, but she can't help herself. She must have this job.

"Do you have any bookselling experience?"

"I've read a lot of books and spent way more money on them than I probably should have." She belatedly adds a "ma'am" to the sentence.

"Well, that counts for something." The woman points back at the table that Scooter had examined. "Go ahead, pick out one book to take home tonight and read it. Be back here tomorrow by ten a.m. with a book report and a can-do attitude and we'll see how you work out."

Scooter's face erupts with joy. "You're hiring me? And I get to read too, Miss ...Ms..." Scooter stutters to a halt, not knowing what to call her new employer. "Ma'am?"

"Well, I do have you at an advantage—I've seen your résumé, Samantha. Please call me Delphine, *never Del*—or your employment will be a very short story indeed. I am the owner of Athena Books and yes, you have been hired."

Delphine turns back to the computer on her desktop and grumbles, "Now get out of here. I have to order some books before the distributor closes for the weekend."

Scooter marches back to the table and swoops up a book and pulls it to her chest as if it might fly away. At the doorway she stops a moment to look back and calls. "Thank-you, Delphine. I will be the best employee you ever had."

"Well, you'll be the first one, that's for sure. Which book did you pick?"

"*Outrageous Acts and Everyday Rebellions.*"

"Be sure to read the essay, 'If Men could Menstruate'."

Scooter exits the store but immediately stops outside and looks back in the window. Every corner of the room is filled with books: the shelves, the tables, boxes waiting to be unpacked. Scooter can't imagine where those unpacked books will fit; the store looks stuffed to the rafters already.

Delphine spots her outside and makes shooing motions with her hands. Scooter backs away and heads down the street. Suddenly she views the street in a completely different way. *I live here now. This is my neighborhood.* Fourth Avenue: a vegetarian restaurant, a record store called Zulu, a shop featuring exotic hookahs in the window and an assortment of pin-on roach clips. A mundane gas station on the corner features two pressurized air stations—one for bicycles, the other for cars. Never in her wildest dreams had Scooter ever thought this would be her grown-up world. She had always assumed she would be in Regina for the rest of her life. But now she lives in Vancouver, near the ocean, on a hippie street in a communal house. How wonderfully un-Saskatchewan that is!

• • •

After she returns home, Scooter flops on the sofa and reads for hours. Finally, she levers herself off the divan to shower before the others start to trickle home. Hair still damp and dressed anew, she pads down the stairs in her stocking feet to find Jacob lying on the sofa, apparently absorbed in her book.

"Hey, don't get too engrossed. I still have a lot of reading to do tonight."

Looking vaguely guilty, Jacob sits up and rushes to set the book aside. "Is this for a class you're taking?"

Before Scooter can respond, the door opens and Maggie shoves her way inside with an armful of books and binders. Scooter steps over to take some of the load and sets it on the coffee table.

"No, no. Homework for my new job." Scooter beams as she says this.

"You got a job!" Maggie gives her a one-arm hug as she dumps the remaining texts on the table alongside the binders. "Wow, that was quick! Where?"

"That *was* quick." Jacob looks baffled. "And they gave you homework?"

Scooter laughs. "Well, my boss might have been kidding about giving her a book report tomorrow when I report to work. But I don't want to chance it, eh!" She leans over and picks up the book and pulls it close to her chest again. "I'm working at Athena Books starting tomorrow morning."

"Not Athena!" Jacob looks honestly alarmed. "It's a den of iniquity and sin, Scooter."

"Athena's fabulous," Maggie leaps in before he can say more. "They have tons of events and everyone who's anyone shops there. You'll meet so many interesting people, Scooter."

"You mean she'll meet every feminist, man-hating bull dyke in Vancouver."

"Oh, shut up, Jacob." Maggie takes Scooter by the arm and pulls her towards the kitchen. "C'mon, let's have tea while you tell me how you scored a job there."

Scooter lets herself be towed into the kitchen but casts a look back at Jacob. He's making the two thumbs down sign, shaking his head vigorously.

• • •

Dusk is clouding the windows in the kitchen when Maggie turns from the sink and puts a plate of sandwiches on the table between Scooter and herself. "It's too bad Hayley won't be back till late. You know, she works at the library two nights a week shelving books. Right?" Maggie gestures for Scooter to eat. "I do think she would want you to be open-minded about the job at Athena. But I also think she wouldn't want you to go to work tomorrow without any sense of just what you were getting into." Maggie takes a bite of her sandwich.

Scooter swallows her first bite and asks, "So, it's mostly professors and politicos who frequent the store …and feminists?"

"Yeah, and believe me, you'll meet some incredible people."

"But what about, you know—Jacob's concern about the lesbians?"

Maggie locks eyes with Scooter across the table. "Scooter, if you can tell me which one is which after three months there, I'll drop dead with surprise." Maggie rolls her eyes heavenward. "It's not like they jump you from behind the bookshelves, and they don't wear identification badges. They're not all bull dykes at all. You won't know who's a lesbian unless they tell you."

Maggie continues: "They are people, Scooter— people who are picked on, gossiped about and maligned constantly by people who never even realize they're gossiping *with* a lesbian."

"So, you've met someone who is?"

Maggie nods, smiling. "And lived to tell the tale!" She reaches out and puts her hand on Scooter's arm. "You can't be in the Women's Studies Department without knowing lesbians. We're allies, we want the same thing—liberation for women. All women, Scooter."

Scooter huffs out a withheld breath. "Okay. I'm glad we talked, Maggie. Thank you." Scooter stands up and takes the dishes to the sink. "I'll do these in the morning if you'll leave them for me, okay?" She turns to retrieve the book, "But right now I've got some serious reading to get through."

"You're going to love your job, Scooter. Don't let Jacob influence you."

THREE

Scooter waits patiently at the front door of Athena Books. Periodically she peers through the plate glass window to see if the lights have been turned on. She looks at her watch, knowing she had arrived early. But now, according to her calculations, her boss is actually late.

Just as she thinks of walking over to the Naam to see if they know Delphine's phone number, a light blinks on at the back of the store. Scooter waits a moment longer and the front-of-store lights flick on too.

Moments later Delphine eases her way out of the back room and into the store proper. She immediately sees Scooter at the window and raises one finger, indicating she will be a minute longer. Delphine unloads her briefcase off her shoulder, stacks her armload of books on the desk and very carefully positions a large travel mug where it won't tip or spill. She stands a moment longer, catching her breath.

Scooter watches her sidle towards the door, turning her bulk first this way and then that to avoid the boxes of books stacked helter-skelter around the store. Delphine is not a tiny woman, and the chaos of the store challenges her footwork just to get from the back of the store to the front. She unlocks the front door, clearly out of breath.

"Morning, Delphine. You okay?"

"Good Morning, Samantha. Did you enjoy the book?"

"Yes ma'am." Scooter hesitates. "Um, Delphine…You know how you said I should never call you Del?"

"Umm?" Delphine is now mincing her way back through the maze of boxes.

"Well, I'm hopin' you'll forget you ever heard the name Samantha. All my friends and family call me Scooter."

Delphine stops and turns a quizzical eye on Scooter. "Okay. Consider it done." She turns back to the cash desk and grabs her coffee. Once she finds a stool, she takes the first sip and sighs extravagantly. "Sooo good. Now the shit can hit the fan. I won't care."

"So, do you want my book report first?"

"No, not yet." Delphine sneaks another sip of coffee. "Frist, I want you to go out back and unload the trunk of my car. I stopped at the distributor's warehouse to pick up some special orders coming due for a class at the university." Delphine blithely tosses a bulky set of car keys at Scooter.

Slightly caught off guard, Scooter uses her book as a backstop and the keys fall into her hands. She makes an I-don't-know face as she surveys the store. "Ah, just where do you want me to put them, Delphine?"

"Three open boxes can sit right here at the cash desk. I'll log them into the computer while you start sorting this place out. Deal?" Delphine doesn't wait for an answer. She raises her coffee to her lips again, sees Scooter still standing there and says, "Go!" As she swallows another mouthful of coffee, Delphine calls after Scooter: "The other boxes can stay in the trunk of the car."

Scooter makes quick work of hauling the three boxes to the cash desk. When she's delivered the third heavy box, she takes a moment and huffs out a big breath.

Delphine beams at Scooter. "I knew I liked you!"

A sharp bark of a laugh erupts before Scooter can squelch it. "So, essentially you hired me to be the muscle?" She's smirking as she says it.

"Pretty much." Delphine cocks her head, questioning. "Well, as you can see, I DO need the help. And really most bookstores can only support one *princess* at a time." She dusts her hands as if they were soiled. "I hate getting dirty."

"That's where I come in then?"

"Strong and clairvoyant. We are going to get along like pancakes and syrup." Delphine sobers and indicates the boxes at the front of the store. "Let's start unpacking those first. I think there is a cardboard display stand inside one of them that you can put together and place right about where the boxes are now."

Scooter nods understanding and strides towards the tower of boxes. Without a moment's hesitation she pulls a folding knife out of her back pocket and slices into the first box. "It looks like there's two or three different logos on these boxes—which one do we want?"

Delphine looks up from the computer. "I think Harcourt Brace has the display unit in it."

"Okay." Scooter's already looking for the logo.

Delphine watches her a long moment, a smile tweaking the corners of her mouth. "Okay, so what made you pick the book you chose from the table last night?"

Scooter looks up at Delphine. "It was the only author I'd actually heard of in the whole display." She pulls the display case materials out of the box. "And I liked the cover."

"Two points for you, Scooter. Most buyers want an author they recognize. And cover art pays a crucial role in convincing them to pick up the book of an author they never heard of before."

"Really?" Scooter studies two pieces of the cardboard display stand, bending one to fit into the other's notches.

"Really," Delphine confirms. She appraises the size of the stand from the pieces Scooter's holding. "Move it farther from the door before you add the books to it or the door won't open all the way." Scooter nods agreement.

"Did you read the book from front cover to back?" Delphine asks. "Or did you dip in and out because a chapter title caught your attention?"

"I read it from front cover to back. I thought you were going to quiz me, so I was careful."

Delphine laughs. "Well, I wanted to be sure you took it seriously. But you are going to have to do a shitload of reading to get up to speed, Scooter. Fall is our busiest time of year."

"Delphine, I promise you I will be ready!"

• • •

"When were you going to tell *me* you got a job?" Hayley's expression is a mixture of irritation and pride. "My God, you are the only person in the world who could start a job search in the morning and have bagged one by dinnertime."

Scooter sticks her thumbs in her armpits and struts like a bantam rooster. "Who rocks?"

"More like rock head. So, Maggie said you're at a bookstore."

"Yeah, right up on 4th Avenue, Athena's." Scooter watches Hayley's face fall. "What?"

"That's the store Jacob says sells pornography and other smut, Scooter."

Scooter's scowl is instantaneous. "If they do, you must have to ask for it—which is how Jacob would know, I guess.

Seriously, I haven't seen anything like that, Hayley. And I was unpacking and shelving books all day." When Hayley still doesn't stop glaring, Scooter raises both hands in surrender. "Okay, I promise if I see any hint of it, I'll quit."

"Immediately!" Hayley adds.

Scooter hesitates. "No, after giving Delphine fair notice. It's only right since she's stuck out her neck and offered me a job."

"Okay, agreed. We totally should figure out a way to get Mom and Lana out here. Do you think they'd come for Christmas?"

Scooter blows out a slow breath. "Pretty short notice, Hay. And a really bad time of year to travel. What's the weather like here in December?"

"Rainy, cold...awful, really."

"Aww, better suggest spring. They'd have a way better time, and it would give Janie time to save up a bit too."

Hayley leans over and throws her arms around Scooter. "Well, I was thinking of a family Christmas. But at least I'll have you—that's half a family for Thanksgiving and Christmas, eh? Oh Scoot, this is going to be so much fun. You and me, just like old times."

"Fuck, Hayley, saying old times is not an inducement to stay put," Scooter shoots back. "Do you even remember old times? It was horrible."

"Oh Scoot. I just meant me and you...together again. It'll be great, you wait and see."

• • •

The next afternoon Delphine is standing with her hands on her ample hips, surveying the new spaciousness of Athena Books. "Alright, Scooter, this is starting to look pretty damn good. If I can navigate from front to back without tipping anything over, we are definitely making progress, girl."

From the top of a stepladder Scooter looks out over her new domain and smiles. The books are mostly shelved, but lots have been relegated to the back room as overstock. Delphine has said sorting the back room will be the next big task, which will make tidying the store look easy by comparison.

"I think I'd like to buy you a soda or coffee or whatever it is cowgirls from the prairies drink in the afternoon," Delphine says. She takes some money from her tiny back-pack and hands the bills to Scooter. "Pop over to the Naam and get us a couple of deeply delicious brownies. Coffee for me, of course, and something to whet your whistle too."

Scooter carefully descends the ladder. Earlier, the toe of one of her cowgirl boots had caught in the rungs, so now she is being uber careful how she steps. "You don't have to do this, Delphine. I mean, you are paying me."

"Oh shit. I totally forgot about that. Give me back that money." As Scooter extends the wad of cash towards her, Delphine bursts out laughing. "My gawd, girl, do you not know sarcasm when you hear it?"

Scooter rolls her eyes and shoves the money in her back pocket. "No, never heard of it—must be a Vancouver invention. Guess I'll have to add that to my homework for tonight, Del." Scooter races out the door before Delphine can throw something at her.

Ten minutes later Scooter is backing into the store, trying to keep the door from slamming closed as she juggles two overly full cups and a small bag of brownies. She nearly backs into the first customer she's encountered in the three days she's been working. "Aw, excuse me, ma'am. I'm awful sorry. I didn't see you there."

And then she recognizes Maggie and can't stop the blush that sweeps over her face. "Maggie..." She can't think of a single word to say. Finally, she mumbles, "Darn...you're in my store." Scooter rushes towards the desk, fumbling the coffee as she tries to extract herself from an increasingly ridiculous situation.

Delphine can't help but notice Scooter's discomfort. A smile ghosts across her face. "Thanks, Scooter," she says as she picks up her coffee. "So, you and Maggie know each other?"

Maggie pretends to examine the books on the antique display table. "Scooter's become one of my new roommates. She only recently arrived from Saskatchewan but decided to stay and has moved in with her sister Hayley."

"Well, not just my sister," Scooter interjects. "There are five of us at the house." She doesn't know why she feels suddenly so uncomfortable. She and Delphine had been getting along so naturally until now.

Delphine lets the moment stretch out a bit longer between the three of them. When it's clear no one is going to offer anything further, she takes the lead. "Well, your timing couldn't be better, Maggie. I just finished entering the Women's Studies texts into the computer. Do you want to pick up your books today or when we deliver to campus on Monday?"

Maggie suddenly seems as agitated as Scooter had been, as if the question caught her off guard. She certainly takes her time in replying. "Ah, I was just stopping by to see if they had arrived. I can go ahead and take delivery on Monday along with everyone else." She drifts towards the display racks. "Any exciting new books in today that I should know about?"

"Scooter unpacked them all and shelved them too," Delphine boasts. "Scooter, anything you might recommend to Maggie?"

Scooter freezes for a moment, then steps gingerly forward and asks, "Are you thinking of fiction or non-fiction, Maggie?"

Maggie turns her disarming smile on Scooter. "I read way too much non-fiction for school, Scooter. Have you got any fiction you think would interest me?"

Panicked, Scooter turns and looks quickly at Delphine for guidance. Delphine mouths the word '*AUTHOR*' back at her.

Relieved, Scooter responds. "Well, do you have a favorite author or genre you prefer? We just got in some new editions of a couple of old classics and some great new poetry by Marg Piercy."

"Oh, she's one of my favorites." Maggie offers Scooter another kilowatt smile. "What are you reading right now, Scooter?"

Delphine watches the two young women disappear into one of the book aisles and allows a tiny smile to light up her eyes. She shrugs and returns to stickering price tags on the books in front of her.

FOUR

Joey sits at the kitchen table with a friend, C, up to their eyebrows in glue guns, photographs and magic markers.

"No, no don't even attempt landscape layout." C advises. If we put these on telephone poles the wrap-around will make them lose all context. Stick with portrait mode, okay?"

Joey holds up a half-finished poster. "See, not too bad, eh? How many do you think we can turn out?"

"How long can we work tonight?" C asks hopefully.

"We can work until we drop, but not here. Everyone will be getting home soon; we should relocate pronto to avoid unseemly questions, especially from JP."

The guys begin to gather up their materials. Joey unplugs the glue gun and piles it on top of the poster materials. "Let's take it all into my room." They trudge up the stairs only moments before the front door opens and Maggie and Scooter let themselves in.

"Hi Joey, we're home." Maggie watches him troop up the stairs, preceded by the mysterious friend whose arms are laden with craft materials.

Scooter only catches the barest glimpse of the boys. She closes the door and nods, indicating the stairs, the boys, the poster project. "What's afoot, Maggie?"

Maggie huffs, pulling off her shoes at the door. "It looks as if Joey and friends are making posters for one of Joey's extravaganzas."

"A badminton thing?"

"Well, not exactly." Maggie flees the living room and heads to the kitchen. "You should really ask Joey for clarification, Scooter. I never know what all he's up to."

"Okay." Scooter pokes her head through the kitchen door and holds up her newest homework reading. "I'm going to crash on my bed and get some reading in before I totally crap out."

Maggie turns a disappointed face towards her. "Okay. Don't let Delphine push you too hard though, Scooter. She's not paying you for this, you know."

Scooter shrugs. "I know. But did you know that bookstores in particular, and retailers in general, make nearly half their revenue for the entire year in the three months before Christmas?"

"Ah, no. I didn't know that."

"It's important that I not hold Delphine back just because I'm green as grass at bookselling." She smiles a wan smile but to her credit she starts the long trudge up the stairs to the room she shares with Hayley.

Several hours later Hayley returns home and bounds up the stairs to unload her books and schoolwork. She turns on her desk lamp and encounters Scooter sound asleep on her side of the room, book opened on her chest. Hayley tiptoes over and peers at the book title. She lifts the loose blanket at the foot of the bed and spreads it over Scooter, then tiptoes out the door and down the stairs again.

Maggie stands in the open doorway of her ground-floor room and lifts one eyebrow at Hayley slipping back down the stairs. "You forget something?"

"No. But Scooter's conked out from her day. Fell asleep reading a book called *Halfbreed*."

"Ah. Maria Campbell. That'll break her heart—but open her eyes, for sure."

"You know it then?"

"Yeah! I think it's the first book published in Canada by a Métis woman."

"Do you know this Delphine? Is she trustworthy, do you think?" Hayley looks perturbed and then glances back up the stairs. "I hope she's not taking advantage of Scooter… with all this homework stuff."

"Scooter is going to receive one hell-of-a feminist education working for Delphine. And for free!"

Hayley shakes her head dubiously. "JP says her store is a hotbed of lesbian intrigue and sex."

Maggie bursts out laughing softly. "If that were so, Delphine would be rolling in the dough, Hayley. Sex sells, as they say."

"That may be so. But I don't want my little sister doing any of the selling."

"She'll be fine. Honest." Maggie sighs. "JP should learn to mind his own business."

Hayley starts for the living room, but then turns back. "I think he's got a soft spot for Scooter, actually. He strikes me as being kind of protective towards her."

Maggie throws her hands over her face and shakes her head 'no'. She looks through her fingers at Hayley. "Scooter does not need any protection, Hayley. Especially not the sort JP might offer her."

"Maybe you're right. Scooter has always been incredibly independent," Hayley admits. "Tea?"

"Yes, please. I'll be out in a minute."

• • •

Delphine has left Scooter at the store on her own. She stands behind the cash desk watching every single pass-erby through the window. Every time someone glances inside, Scooter immediately plasters a smile on her face and stands a little straighter. No one comes in.

Thirty minutes pass with nary a soul entering her domain. Scooter crosses the front of the store and opens the door and wedges a bit of cardboard beneath it. The breeze is fresh and invigorating. Clouds scud across the slash of blue sky visible from the sidewalk. Scooter ambles back to the desk and takes up her post again.

Ten minutes later, she concludes it doesn't look right, just standing there hoping for customers. She decides to try harder to look engaged, absorbed, completely lost in something—but not so lost that she couldn't hop to help a customer.'

The Staff Picks bookshelf (all Delphine's picks, of course) is right next to the desk. Scooter studies it a moment and lifts a slim volume of poetry, *Circles on the Water,* by Marg Piercy. She thumbs through it briefly and stops at the poem "*To be of use.*" Her lips move minutely, as she reads the poem to herself. Soon she is whispering, then reading louder.

The work of the world is common as mud.
Botched, it smears the hands, crumbles to dust.
But the thing worth doing well, done well
has a shape that satisfies, clean and evident.

By the end of the poem, Scooter is gesturing avidly, book raised in one hand, the other hand flung over her head, exhorting her would-be audience to join her.

Greek amphoras for wine or oil,
Hopi vases that held corn, are put in museums
but you know they were made to be used.
The pitcher cries for water to carry
and a person for work that is real.

"And so say all of us." The young man's smiling face hovers in the open doorway.

Scooter closes her mouth abruptly and brings the book close to her chest. Her face flames with embarrassment. Her voice comes out a squeak. "Oh." Horrified at herself, she adds, "Can I help you with something?"

The young man steps fully into the bookstore, still smiling. "My friend Joey said you had a community bulletin board. Can I post something?"

Scooter studies the man as he steps closer, proffering his stack of posters. "I've seen you. You were at our house with Joey last night."

"Yeah, we spent all night making posters for a workshop I'm doing. Can I post one?"

A frisson of panic flits through Scooter. Delphine never mentioned the rules for posting on the board. Attempting nonchalance, she stretches out a hand. "May I see one?"

The young man hands her a poster. "My name is C, by the way." He uses his free hand to form the letter 'C' to clarify what he means.

She looks up. "Just C?" When he doesn't offer any explanation, she returns to studying the poster. Scooter rubs at her jaw reflexively. "Okay. This is a free workshop that happens this weekend. All this is good, but I'm not sure I understand what you're teaching."

"Is it imperative that you understand it? I thought it was a free community board?"

Scooter considers for a long moment. "Do you live around here?"

"Nooo."

She consults the poster, gathering her thoughts. "Learn to create the Diva persona locked within you—from perfecting your makeup techniques, to appropriate wig selection and consummate wardrobe consultation." Scooter locks eyes with C one more time. "You realize this IS a feminist bookstore? I'm not sure how teaching women to become Barbies is exactly fighting the status quo."

C erupts laughing, flapping his posters and trying in vain to smother his reaction. "No, no, no, Scooter. You mistake my intent." He struggles to compose himself. "I'm not teaching women how to become Barbies ...I'm teaching men!"

A long silence ensues while Scooter refers back to the poster and then scrutinizes C intently. "You're shitting me?"

C shakes his head with gusto. "I am NOT shitting you, Scooter."

After another long moment, a smile splits Scooter's face. "That is fuckin awesome, C. That is so radical, it makes me want to sign up right now!"

C shrugs, "Well, normally I would say 'first come, first served...but."

"No, no. I totally understand." Scooter sighs. "Hey, but I can help you poster, if you want."

"You're kidding?"

"No, give me a bunch and right after work I'll do along Broadway for you. I imagine you've covered off 4th Avenue pretty well already."

"Wow, thank you. Joey was right…you are a keeper."

Scooter ducks her head in embarrassment. As C hands over a dozen posters, he adds. "What are you doing tomorrow night?"

Scooter's face shows an instant of panic.

"Oh, don't flatter yourself; you're not my type!" C smirks. "But if you've never seen drag, I will take you to a couple of clubs that will blow your mind, girl."

Scooter hesitates, blowing out a wary breath. *Strange man, strange invitation and alcohol too…all the things Janie warned me about.* "Ah, I dunno…"

C catches on right away. "Okay, what if Joey says he'll come along too? Will that make it easier to say yes?"

"YES!"

"Okay. You tell him C wants to go clubbing with you—but he has to chaperone. I'll pick you both up tomorrow night at nine, sharp."

"What if he has questions?"

C is already turning to leave. "He has my number; tell him to call me." He steps through the open door but bounces back inside again. "*You* are going to have so much damn fun…cow punching will look candy-assed compared to this."

As he disappears down the sidewalk, Scooter whispers. "I never punched a cow in my life, city boy."

• • •

The following night Joey and Scooter are vying for room in front of the bathroom mirror. "Fuck. What should I wear, Joey?"

"It doesn't matter. No one will be looking at you, to be brutally honest." He turns to scrutinize Scooter's choices. He picks at her shirt and makes to peer inside. Scooter cuffs his hand away. "Joey!"

"A bit of advice, Scoot. Clubbing is like hiking. You want to wear layers so that you can start shedding clothing the minute you get warm." He lifts his own shirt to show a bit of bare stomach. "I can just rip this off if I want. You, on the other hand, might want to have layers." He pauses meaningfully, "I'm just sayin'."

"Fine, fine. I'll go put on some layers." Scooter flees the bathroom. Moments later she thunders down the stairs as the doorbell rings. "C'mon, Joey, our date is here."

Joey takes the stairs two at a time and is at the door in a flash. It's barely open before he and Scooter are outside with C on the porch.

"Okay. Don't invite me in and introduce me to your parents."

Joey jumps down the three exterior steps. "Oh, shut up. Just drive."

When he sees Scooter's shocked expression, C explains. "He's always like this before we go clubbing. Can't wait to get there and then can't wait to leave—after he goes unnoticed by the legions of his crushes."

"We could just walk down the hill and take the little ferry, Joey," C suggests.

"Where we going?" Scooter truly has no idea.

"Oh girl. You gotta get out more. We're going to Davie Street, Honey." C puts his arm around her. "Your life will never be the same." He stops them at an old VW bug and opens a passenger door. "Your chariot, Princess."

FIVE

The three of them walk abreast down Davie Street. They haven't linked arms, but they may as well have. All three are excited for their own reasons; they are matching steps all along the sidewalk.

Scooter is awash in excitement, guilt, curiosity and a kind of benign bewilderment. Music blares from the open doors and windows of clubs and restaurants. A mix of people like she has never encountered before walk the streets, make catcalls and greet friends and potential enemies alike with a heightened bravado that is both foreign and deeply exhilarating. She can feel her heart racing, and she keep repeating to herself *fuck, fuck, fuck.*

Joey puts his arm around her shoulder. "You definitely are not in Kansas any longer, Scooter."

Everywhere they walk there's music. 'She Works Hard for the Money' blares from the windows of a restaurant. Annie Lennox croons 'Sweet Dreams' through the sliding glass doors of a dark and smoky bar a few steps farther along, and Freddie Mercury's falsetto wails 'Somebody to Love' from the interior of a passing car. Scooter starts singing along with it, as it passes by them. Joey frowns, but she just shrugs. "How can you not love that song?"

"Well, I totally agree," Joey chimes in. "Where to, C-meister? This is your little parade."

"Let's go to Celebrities first and kill some time until the drag shows start." C walks confidently across the street. Cars that had been coasting along at cruising speed slow to let him pass—but not without some verbiage thrown at him.

"What's wrong, Honey, did he leave you for a dame?" This because Scooter and Joey stayed on the sidewalk. "Although, she's not much of one, if you ask me."

"I'll take you, sweetheart. C'mon over here." This from a man leaning out a car window.

C stops to blow kisses to the men. On the sidewalk, Scooter mumbles, "What did they mean, *not much of one*?"

Joey holds her closer. "Girl, lighten up. They're trying to get C's attention, not yours."

A long pause, then Scooter turns to Joey. "They're flirting? Just like that?"

"Why do you think we all come down here every night we can?" Joey gets her walking again, "To flirt, to flaunt, to fly away from our humdrum closeted existences." They take a moment to cross the street to join C. "This is our real world, baby, and welcome to it! That patriarchal construct will be waiting for you first thing tomorrow morning. Don't waste one minute of this one tonight."

Scooter follows C and Joey around like a puppy out for its first walk. Daunted at first, she rises steadily to the challenge, while her two buddies grow less and less steady as the night wears on. Scooter props first one up and then the other as they wander from bar to bar and drink to drink.

In the depths of a smoky, ginny joint, Scooter vacates their table for a visit to the amenities. When she returns, she can't help but notice a woman has taken her seat at the table. She approaches cautiously, being uncertain of the protocols involved. As she waits at a polite distance, weighing her options, the club DJ cues up a song that was one of Scooter's all-time favorites. No one could listen to the Pointer Sisters' 'Jump' and remain immobile.

Never taking her eyes off the table, Scooter begins to snap her fingers in time to the music and sway her shoulders. Moments later, behind her, a hand touches her hip lightly and she hears a woman shout, "You should be dancing."

Scooter turns abruptly, a quick retort ready to stave off any further misconceptions about her presence in the club. Maggie stands inches away, a smile on her face.

Speechless, Scooter flounders. "Ah…that's one of my favorite songs." She takes a step away from Maggie and nearly topples a passerby.

Maggie closes the gap between them. "Even more reason to dance before the music stops. C'mon, 'fraidy cat."

Scooter looks around her, eyes a little wild. "I can't seem to find the dance floor. And besides, I have my boots on."

Maggie graciously takes Scooter's free hand and starts dancing. "Dance right where you are, if you can't find the dance floor." Maggie inexplicably JUMPS right when the Pointer Sisters tell her to.

Scooter laughs out loud in surprise and then jumps too. When the song ends, they both stop and simply stare at each other.

"We should probably head home," Maggie whispers. "Why drag this out?"

"What about the boys?"

"Believe me, they'll understand." Maggie grasps Scooter's hand firmly and tows her across the dance floor and out the front door into the velvety night beyond.

SIX

What lies beyond this moment, Scooter does not know, or even really care. All she can think of is the warmth of Maggie beside her and how that warmth has changed her life forever—in a profound and completely unexpected way.

During the night she had heard Joey come in and close the front door, then cross the living room to his bedroom. Scooter had lain in Maggie's bed and listened to the sounds of the night around her. Maggie's breathing, the sound of Joey's footsteps and a siren somewhere off in the distance, heralding an unknown calamity.

Then suddenly, a piercing and hair-raising scream ruptures the early morning and sends Scooter vaulting from the bed. "What the fuck…?" She rapidly pulls on her jeans and t-shirt and bursts out of Maggie's room.

She vaguely senses Hayley appear at the top of the stairs, and then Joey catapults out of his room just as the agonizing scream of someone in desperate pain echoes through the house again.

Hayley starts screaming too, trying to be heard over the din. Scooter races across the room to join Joey and they both hurtle towards Jacob's bedroom door. Scooter raises her hand to knock, but Joey shakes his head no and simply barges into the room, with Scooter close behind.

Sitting up in bed, Jacob screams again and again. His arms are wrapped around his torso, as if he's in horrible pain. "Please stop, make them stop. No, no, not again. Please."

Joey and Scooter's eyes meet for a moment, then Joey leaps onto the bed and wraps his arms around Jacob. "Jacob, it's Joey. Wake up, Jacob." Joey starts rocking Jacob gently, back and forth. "Wake up, Jacob. It's just a dream."

Joey motions Scooter closer. "Talk to him." He continues to rock Jacob.

"Jacob, it's Scooter. Can you open your eyes?"

Jacob's eyes flutter open and lock on Scooter's face. Then he notices Joey next to him and he screams again, this time furiously. "Get out of here, both of you. Get out of my room." He scuttles to the far side of the bed. "GET OUT NOW!"

Joey levitates off the bed and begins to backpedal towards the bedroom door. He makes placating gestures towards Jacob, trying to assure him. "It's okay, Jacob. Just a bad dream. Don't worry. We're leaving now."

Joey jerks his head towards Scooter, encouraging her to leave. They both exit and gently close the door behind them. Maggie and Hayley are waiting on the far side of the living room, watchful and utterly silent. Joey opens his arms and herds them towards the stairs. "Hayley's room, right now, you guys."

At the top of the stairs, they can hear sobs emanating from Jacob's room. Joey opens the bedroom door and they all troop inside. At the corner farthest from the doorway, they arrange themselves on Hayley's rumpled bed.

"What the hell was that?" Maggie whispers hoarsely.

Joey shakes his head slowly, a grim look on his face. "Bad dreams. Jacob has suffered them for a couple of years now."

Maggie interjects, "It sounded like he was being murdered. Or tortured."

"I know." Joey's eyes tear up. "I've haven't been able to get him to talk about the nightmares."

"Obviously it's something horrific. But you don't know what?" Scooter whispers.

"No. Not a clue." Joey slumps onto the bed. "It's happened before, and lately I've noticed that it often happens around holidays—or days connected to a family visit. He's due to go out to Abbotsford for Thanksgiving tomorrow."

After a protracted silence, Hayley offers. "Maybe he's embarrassed to talk to a guy about it, Joey?" Joey turns raised eyebrows to her. "I never thought about that, Hay."

"I could maybe sound him out. If the right moment comes up?" It's clear Hayley is dubious, hoping Joey will try to dissuade her.

Instead, Joey looks relieved and offers up a deep sigh. "Could you please? I feel so bad for him...We palled around a lot as kids, camping and all that stuff, and I don't ever remember anything like this happening then."

"Clearly something's happened in the interim that's really affected him deeply." Maggie sounds genuinely sympathetic. "Let's stay on top of this, okay, you guys? No one deserves to suffer like that, right?"

They all nod their heads in agreement. After a moment they all stand up, unsure how to adjourn their impromptu meeting. Joey turns and looks at the girls. "I don't think I can go back to sleep after that. I'm going to go for my morning run, but I don't want to leave him alone. Will one of you stay here?"

Maggie nods. "I'm going to try to go back to sleep. It was a late one last night."

Joey grins, "I bet." And heads for the stairs.

Hayley turns to Scooter. "You want some tea, Scooter?"

Scooter turns and sees Maggie leaving the room without glancing her way. She hesitates, wanting to run after Maggie—but has no real reason to do so. She pastes a smile on her face and shrugs. "Sure, Hayley, tea would be great. I won't sleep for a while after that anyway."

Hayley leads the way down the stairs and whispers,

"Where were you last night? I waited up, thinking we could plan something for today. Ya know, sister stuff?"

Scooter blushes furiously, grateful Hayley's leading the way to the kitchen and can't see her face. While Hayley sets the kettle to boil, Scooter leans over the kitchen sink and slaps cold water on her face to minimize the blush. She grabs a tea towel and pats her face dry. "I ran into Maggie last night at a club Joey took me to, and it was really, really late when we all got home. So, I just slept on the sofa rather than risk waking you up."

Hayley laughs, "Well that's both dumb and really thoughtful. Did you sleep at all?"

Scooters laughs too. "Agh, very little. Today might not be the best sister-pal-around day. Do you want a rain check?" She pulls out a kitchen chair and drops onto it.

"You're working tomorrow?"

Scooter buries her face in her folded arms atop the table. "Yeah. Delphine is letting me open the store all by myself."

"Wow, that's fast." Hayley pours the boiling water into the teapot. "You want some peanut butter on toast?"

"Uh-huh." Scooter lifts her head, eyes bleary. "Thank you, Hayley, you really are a peach!"

Hayley pops bread into the toaster and then puts a big mug of tea in front of Scooter. "That's what big sisters are for, Scoot." The rasp of a knife on toast accompanies her next question. "What do you think the deal is with Jacob?"

Scooter sits up and sips her hot tea carefully. "Fucking hell, that scared the crap out of me. I felt like those cartoons where the character's hair stands straight up in fright."

"Me too." Hayley takes a place at the table at right angles to Scooter so they can talk quietly. She takes a bite of toast and chews thoughtfully. "I'm going to go up to the Uni to study for a while—since you're a total write-off." She punches Scooter's arm. "I think I'll pop into the library and see what articles I can find on nightmares caused by trauma."

"Good idea. I'm going to have a hot bath and try to get a few hours' sleep. If the day works out, maybe we can go down to the beach before dinner, hey?"

Hayley finishes her toast and gets up to ferry her dishes to the sink. "Can you wash up?"

"Sure 'nuff, that's what little sisters are for, Hay."

Hayley stops and wraps one arm around Scooter's shoulders and kisses her cheek. "It is just the very best thing that you decided to stay in Vancouver, little sister."

"Oh, go on with ya…ya mush pot." Scooter pushes Hayley away, but she's grinning as she does so.

• • •

Scooter arrives at Athena Books early, of course. She sets her take-out coffee on the lid of the garbage can out back of the store and looks quickly around to ensure no one is watching. She carefully tips the edge of the old newspaper box next to it. Beneath it in the right-hand corner sits a red rubber heart. Scooter grabs the heart, drops the box and then squeezes the rubber change purse so it splits down the middle to reveal the key. She shoves the rubber heart in her back pocket to return the key later.

Once inside, she flips on lights, unearths the float tray for the till in a box labelled 'book returns'. No one would ever look there. It's Sunday, so Scooter's not expecting much traffic for several hours. Once the till is set up to make sales, she checks the paper tape to ensure it's adequate for the day and retrieves the dust rag and spray bottle from beneath the desk.

She starts at the bookshelf right next to the desk and works her way systematically around the whole store: dusting, facing books out, adding new stock, sipping coffee. Scooter loves the cozy silence bounded by acres of books and the smell of coffee. She has discovered that Delphine loathes mornings at Athena in equal measure.

Scooter finds herself grinning at the thought of Delphine. They really are such distinct opposites, and yet they get on seamlessly. Maybe it's because what Delphine avoids like a plague, Scooter is happy to wade into up to her waist. Scooter loves when boxes and boxes of books arrive from the distributors. Loves counting and comparing against the invoices, loves reorganizing the overstock once new stock has arrived.

Her favorite job is doing the window displays. Sadly,

this is the one area where she and Delphine are apt to clash. As the owner, Delphine's word is law about the store displays. But Scooter has come to realize that Delphine is imminently distractable. If the phone rings, or a friend drops by, or Scooter happens to mention a controversial new review she has read, Delphine will leap into the new thing that catches her attention, leaving Scooter to sort out the window displays all by herself.

Scooter is both amused and left feeling somewhat guilty by this bit of subterfuge. She recalls a bit of wisdom gleaned from Janie, her mother. 'If you really cared, you'd do it yourself, Scooter.' Scooter thinks Delphine likes the idea of input into the displays but likes even better having someone else start and finish them without hesitation.

As if summoned by Scooter's thoughts, Delphine breezes in through the back door and wafts into the bookstore proper. She casually places a coffee and brownie in close proximity to Scooter—but says only, "Damn, this is looking good."

"Thank you, Delphine. To what do I owe the honor of both a coffee and a brownie?" Scooter breaks off a hunk of brownie and places it in her mouth. She stops as if frozen in place by the morsel. "Really, they make the best brownies on the planet, Delphine."

Delphine nods agreement and snitches a small bit for herself. "Yes, they do. My largesse, Ms. Wells, is due to the fact that I was slated for a meeting downtown at SFU

Harbour Centre this afternoon. I can no longer attend this function …so you will go in my place."

Scooter nearly spews her coffee. "ME?"

Delphine sighs theatrically and seats herself on the stool behind the cash register. "Yes. Alas my Machiavellian plot must be revealed too soon, I fear." She eyes Scooter appraisingly. "Eat up, you've only got minutes until you have to leave." She opens her backpack, pulls out her car keys and slides them across the desktop towards Scooter. "I confess, I had ulterior motives in hiring you so promptly. I needed some muscle."

Scooter bursts out laughing. "Muscle?"

Delphine nods avidly. "But not stupid-as-a-bucket muscle. I needed someone who was young, strong and smart—someone that could grasp the particulars of book-selling rather quickly." She shrugs towards Scooter and the store interior. "You have done all those things and more, Scooter."

"Go on…" Scooter is now a tiny bit unsettled.

"In ten months, Vancouver will be hosting one of the biggest events the feminist, lesbian and gay community have ever seen. It's called the Gay Games and we are going to be selling books as if they were slushies at the beach during a heat wave."

Delphine rubs her hands together in anticipation. "And you are going to be the face of Athena Books during the five-day literary festival that is part of those games. Half our stock will be out and about at all the various readings and book signings. And it will be *you*, Scooter, who is scooping up all that cash."

Scooter takes a step back as if to get a better perspective on Delphine's announcement. "ME?"

"Yes you! I mean, honestly, you can't see me doing it, can you? Lugging and toting boxes of books all around the city? You'll be setting up little kiosk sales areas at nearly every venue, and then tearing them down again, to move on to the next."

"Ahhh, Delphine?"

Delphine smiles coquettishly. "Yes dear?"

"Maybe we should talk about this a bit more."

Delphine nods agreeably. "We will, we will. Just as soon as you get back from the tour of SFU Harbourfront. That's where most of the panel discussions and seminars will take place. So, go." She pushes the keys at Scooter and waves her away. "We'll talk more after."

"And I'm getting paid for this tour time?"

Delphine nods, "You sure are …on the job training."

Scooter exhales a huge breath to steady herself, picks up the keys and moves towards the back of the store. "Okay then…" she shouts uncertainly over her shoulder.

SEVEN

Downtown is a maze of one-way streets, and Scooter gets lost multiple times. But the big flying saucer on a pole at the top of Harbour Centre makes it easier to pinpoint how lost she is or isn't. Then there is the issue of finding parking for Delphine's incredibly big and brassy red Lincoln. Scooter feels insanely self-conscious driving it. If she had time, she'd pin on a sign that says, 'This ISN'T mine!'

Luckily, she finds a loading bay attached to the Centre in which she is allowed to park for free, using Delphine's pass to attend the meeting. The moment she's out of the car, Scooter feels as if half the weight of the world has been lifted.

There's a steep hill leading to the front of the building; Scooter is hyperventilating from the climb by the time she finds the front door. Light pours into the lobby, which has glass on three sides. It's beautiful...and huge. But then, compared to Regina, most buildings in downtown Vancouver are huge and new and beautifully enclosed with glass. Regina's biggest building was seven floors, maybe eight, if you count the cupola at the top of the government building.

Scooter introduces herself to the woman staffing the reception table. She ticks off Delphine's name on her clipboard and hands Scooter a sticky badge with Athena Books emblazoned across it. Scooter heaves a sigh of relief and steps aside to allow the next woman in line to check in.

As Scooter watches, the lobby rapidly fills up with women. As far as her eyes can see there are women—short, tall, stocky and thin. Some are young like her; many are aging and some downright old. But they all seem to know each other, and they all seem alight with ideas and information to share.

"No, no, no. Go back and read Shulamith Firestone again. *The Dialectic of Sex* will sort it out for you." The speaker leans past the woman she's speaking to and taps another woman on the shoulder. "Right, Gloria?"

Scooter watches as a wizened crone of a woman turns and locks eyes with the first. Her torso is bent and twisted, but her eyes are as bright as a hawk's with a field mouse in its sights. "Don't get me started on *The Dialectic of Sex*, Arianna," Gloria says. "I swear to God when I first started reading it, I thought I was not smart enough for this book. But I'm so glad I finished it."

Scooter feels completely out of place. She feels herself drawing farther and farther away from the bubbling cauldron of feminists gathered in the lobby. *What the hell is a dialectic anyway?* she murmurs to herself. *Fuck, what am I doing here?*

"I was just going to ask you the same thing!"

Scooter turns to discover Maggie at her elbow. For the first time since arriving, Scooter smiles broadly. "Maggie."

Maggie smiles back and nods in the direction of the jostling mass of women. "It is a bit much the first time you throw yourself into an event like this. Everyone seems to know everyone else—and they've all read the same books." She stands on tiptoe to whisper in Scooter's ear. "But they hardly agree on anything at all."

Maggie puts her hand on Scooter's forearm. "Which brings us to dialectic, which simply means a way to find common ground in a situation where people hold really varying opinions on something." She grins up at Scooter. "Like sex! Imagine how far apart a man's views on sex might be compared to a woman's. Throw a roomful of women like this together....Well, hell will freeze over before they find consensus."

Scooter looks as if a light has gone on inside her. "Ohh. So, Shulamith Firestone's book is just a discussion about sex?"

Maggie laughs out loud. "Well, kind of. But read it and then tell me what you think."

Scooter nods agreeably. "I will then."

• • •

Moments after, the lights in the lobby dim and brighten and then dim and brighten again. Maggie instinctively turns to face the stairs that lead to a mezzanine level. Scooter follows suit and is gratified to see a slim woman in a tailored pantsuit atop the stairs, holding a microphone.

"Good afternoon, everyone. Thank you for coming." The woman pauses to scan the faces in the room. "On behalf of the Belzberg family, head librarian Karen Marotz and the entire staff we'd like to welcome you to our first physical planning meeting for "Words Without Borders', the literary component of the Gay Games taking place right here at SFU Harbourside this coming summer."

Scooter looks at Maggie for confirmation. "So, it's true. There is going to be an Olympics for gay people here in Vancouver?"

Something in Scooter's voice compels Maggie to look in her direction. "Are you okay?" she whispers. "Is this the first you've heard of it?"

Scooter shakes her head lightly back and forth. "Second. But I thought Delphine was putting me on." She grimaces, "I am a bit of a yokel, ya know. I think she considers me fair game for all manner of pranks and such."

Maggie pats Scooter's arm and whispers back, "Well,

let's navigate this information session together. Afterwards you can ask me any questions you want. Okay?"

"Maggie Embridge, you are such a lifesaver!"

Maggie smiles at her with genuine affection, then nods, indicating the concourse where the group is assembled. "Okay, for starters you'll want to know what the square footage of this concourse is. Also, how big a marketing or bookselling space will each store be allowed."

Scooter nods, "You're right, it will make a huge difference to how much I can stock."

"Don't look at me! Ask her."

Scooter hesitates a nanosecond and then thrusts her hand over her head, waving it to get the woman's attention.

"Sorry, I can't see your name badge, woman in the blue chambray shirt. Go ahead."

Scooter awkwardly blurts her question, quickly rephrases it and then, suddenly, finds her comfort zone. All of them are in the same boat. No one in Vancouver has ever worked at a Gay Games before. This is the *first* gay literary festival in Canada.

Two hours later Scooter is driving Delphine's boat of a car back along Burrard Street. "Do you want me to drop you at home?" she turns and asks Maggie. "Or will you come to the store and walk home with me?"

Maggie purses her lips, suddenly solemn. "Let's go see Delphine and then walk home together, okay?" Scooter can't hide her smile.

Once they make their way down 4th Avenue and park the car, they enter the store to drop off the keys. Delphine appears to be deep in conversation with a university professor. She shoos them both away.

"Do you want to head to the beach for a walk before dinner?" Scooter struggles for nonchalance.

Next to her, Maggie stops abruptly and turns to face Scooter. "Scooter, I really need to make my position clear to you. I realize it was a big deal for you when we had sex the other night." Maggie hesitates, but then bulldozes on. "It was not a big deal to me. It has been years since my 'first time.' For you it's hardly been 48 hours. The gap between us is a chasm."

Scooter raises one hand as if to stop Maggie, or to ward off anything else she might say. Maggie takes Scooter's hand in her own and forces her to look into her eyes. "Scooter, you are a sweet, funny, really bright woman who is tough enough to face the truth. We are not 'girlfriends' because we had sex. We are not 'lovers'—what we did was have sex. There is no relationship between us except that of housemates and sisters in feminism. I know this hurts you terribly to hear it, but I owe you the truth."

Maggie turns to walk away, but Scooter trots to catch up. "Someday, I'm sure I'll thank you for your honesty, Maggie. I think." Scooter matches Maggie's step for a couple of strides. "But I'm telling you—you don't know what you're missing." She hesitates a moment and then breaks into a run, shouting over her shoulder. "Race you to the house, Mags!"

Maggie is left staring at Scooter's rapidly retreating figure as she jets down the hill to their communal house. *Did Scooter Wells just flip me and pin me and then leave me on the mat?*

EIGHT

Scooter makes it home to the house first. She runs up the stairs and bursts through the front door shouting, "Sis, I'm home." When there is no answer, she shouts again. "Hayley, I'm home. Where are you?"

"We're in the kitchen, Scooter," Hayley shouts back. "Be out in a minute."

In the kitchen Hayley rises from a chair and puts her hand on Jacob's arm, silently urging him to stay. "Let me talk to her, I'll send her on her way. We should finish this discussion." As she steps away from the table, Hayley turns back a moment. "In fact, let me make you dinner, Jacob. Okay?"

Hayley captures Scooter before she can cross the living room to the kitchen. She grabs her arm and pulls her back towards the door, whispering. "Bad timing, Scoot, really bad. I just got Jacob talking and really want to take advantage of this to try and figure out what's going on with him."

Scooter looks blank for a moment, then recalls Jacob's horrible nightmares in chilling detail. "Oh crap. Sorry. What should I do?"

Hayley's face softens as she realizes Scooter is onside without having to be pushed. "Can you give us some time alone? I've offered to make him dinner."

Scooter blurts, "What about me?" She winces, acknowledging how pathetic she sounds. "I mean, I was looking forward to our date together tonight, Hay." What she couldn't say was that she had been looking forward to Maggie coming home and seeing how happy Scooter was in the company of her dear sister.

"I know, I know. I'll make it up to you, I promise." Hayley can't help glancing back at the kitchen towards Jacob. "Can you make yourself scarce just for tonight?"

Scooter shoves her hands in her jacket pockets and mumbles. "Oh, okay." Outside thundering footsteps sound on the front stairs. Hayley panics. "Oh my God...who now?" Scooter peers out the door window and smiles. "Just Joey."

"Can you grab him and haul him off somewhere? I'm sure you two can find something to do for a few hours. Pleease, Scoot? I'll owe you forever!"

Scooter grudgingly turns and opens the door. "You owe me big time, Hayley Wells. And I won't forget it!"

Hayley's relief is palpable as she gives Scooter a quick hug. "I won't either, Scooter, I promise!" She heads back to the kitchen, trusting Scooter to get the situation in hand.

Joey is bent over untying his sneakers to leave them on the porch. Scooter quietly closes the door behind her as she steps out to join him. He looks up, a quizzical expression on his face. "Was that Hayley pushing you out the door?"

Scooter deflates appreciably. "Yes. She's got Jacob actually talking to her in the kitchen and wants me and you to disappear for a few hours."

"Oh. Well, I had planned to go out later, but we could go now if you don't mind stopping to get something to eat on the way." Joey reties his sneakers.

Scooter snorts a laugh. "Great! I had no idea what I was going to do—and I'm starving. Hayley was supposedly going to cook."

Joey stands up and grins wickedly. "Well, have I got a surprise for you, girlfriend. Let's go." He immediately trots down the stairs, not even waiting for Scooter to respond.

Scooter follows after him only seconds later. "So, what have you got in mind, Joey my dear?"

"Oh, you'll see." Joey rubs his hands together in delight. "And I guarantee, it will be a night you will not forget, Ms. Wells."

• • •

Night has fallen by the time Scooter and Joey have eaten and then boarded the little False Creek Ferry to hop a ride to the West End. A ten-minute walk along the seawall leads them to Bidwell Street and they climb the hill to Davie. As always, the street is busy with shoppers, dog-walkers, prostitutes, old folks and a veritable smorgasbord of gays. Joey leads her into a back alley where a lone lightbulb shines over a much-battered door. Joey tries the handle, finds it unlocked, and pushes the door open. They step into a very dim hallway.

"What is this place?" Scooter says inquisitively.

Joey's teeth flash in the dim light. "By day a coffee-house, by night it's Cheek-2-Cheek, a drag school and performance bistro."

Scooter's eyes widen in surprise and trepidation. "I've never seen a drag person before."

"Sure you have. You know C, he's the instructor here and headliner on the performance nights." Joey holds a heavy curtain aside and pushes Scooter through. He follows quickly after, running his hand along the finish on a jewel of a baby grand.

They tiptoe towards the back of the stage, a small, raised platform surrounded by folding chairs. Across from them a more brightly lit hallway beckons.

"The nouveau queens are likely downstairs in the

dressing room—raising a ruckus, no doubt, while they suit-up. Let's just wait up here."

Suddenly a trill of soft piano notes skitters across the stage. Joey and Scooter startle and hastily turn towards the piano behind them. An attractive older man in a black swallow-tailed tuxedo is adjusting the bench minutely to finesse his playing position. He sends another ripple of notes across the stage.

"Show doesn't start for another few hours," he says in Joey and Scooter's direction. He hums a melody and then plays it softly.

Joey smiles. "We know. We're here to meet up with C. Do you mind if we hang out here?"

"No. Suit yourselves." The man turns all his attention to the keyboard at his fingertips. A cascading rill of notes follows. "C's supposed to bring me a final set list for rehearsal."

Right on cue, C appears at stage left and crosses to the piano. "Adam, how are you?" When there's no response, C lays the sheet music on the piano case. "Good to see you again."

Adam merely nods, his focus completely on the piano. He slides the sheet music in front of him and casually riffles through it.

"Is it okay?" C leans towards the man, pretending to study the music over his shoulder. He places a tentative hand ever-so-lightly on Adam's upper back. "Conchita decided at the last minute to throw in an extra set. Can you make this work?"

Adam locates the song in question. He blocks out the melody with his right hand, still holding the music in his left. He slips the sheet back onto the piano deck and adds in the left hand. Moments later he's nodding. "Yeah, this'll be fine." He actually looks up at C and smiles. "It'll be fun to see what she can do with it."

Off to one side, Joey leans in closer to Scooter and whispers, "Just like that, Adam has it down—he knows instantly how he's gonna make Conchita look her best."

C looks over at them and grins as if he's just met Miss America. He turns his attention back to the pianist. "Terrific. I knew it wouldn't faze you."

Joey giggles quietly, "Oh man, C is totally stricken."

"What? What are you talking about?" Scooter mumbles.

"C. Oh my god, if he was any more blatant, he'd be in the man's lap." Joey can see that Scooter is still confused. "C has a raging crush on Adam, the pianist." Joey loops his arm through Scooter's and drags her out to one of the empty chairs in the audience. "Men *and* women—every-one—swoons over Adam. But as far as anyone knows, he remains oblivious. C is definitely barking up the wrong tree."

They sit down, pulling up empty chairs to rest their feet on. When a server comes by to see if they want drinks, Joey orders a Guinness and Scooter nods and says, "Make that two."

Several men wander into the room, request drinks and find seats. Scooter eyeballs them. When one of them meets her eye, he winks. She brings her attention back to Joey and leans over to whisper to him. "So, Joey...umm like— are you gay too?"

Joey cocks his head and arches an eyebrow at her. "*Seriously*? You have to *ask*? If so, I am doing something fundamentally wrong."

Scooter looks down at her feet, embarrassed. "Well, I did just move here from the prairies. I'm not sure they even have gay people there."

Joey lets out a loud, deep blast of laughter. Everyone in the room, even Adam, looks in their direction. Scooter slides down in her chair, piling her arms over the top of her head. When the room has quieted, she sits back up and turns back to Joey. "Okay, do not laugh this time. Promise me." When Joey nods, she adds, "Do you think I'm gay?"

Joey slips his arm around Scooter's shoulders. "Honestly, Scooter, that's a question that only you can answer for yourself. Don't listen to what anyone else thinks...Listen to what you know is true for you. That's all that matters."

Scooter is silent a long time, then whispers, "I slept with Maggie the other night."

"Annd?"

More silence as Scooter tries to imagine what to possibly say. "I thought my heart would break, I felt so alive, so open, so full." Joey merely raises one eyebrow as comment.

"And then I thought I would die when the next day she told me it meant nothing to her."

Joey can sense that Scooter is broken up all over again at the memory. He whispers, "Maggie said it meant nothing? That sounds pretty harsh, even for the ever-truthful Maggie."

"Well…She said we were at really different places in life and implied I needed to have a lot more sss…"—she almost says sex—but changes it to "experience."

Joey's titter echoes through the mostly empty bistro. "Now that sounds like Maggie." He notices Scooter's stricken look and softens his voice. "She's right in a way, Scooter. No one ever stays with their first fling. Maybe a day, or a month or a year, but how can you call yourself a gourmand if you only ever dine on hotdogs?"

There is a long pause before Scooter offers, "Well, isn't that all you eat?"

Joey jumps to his feet. "Holy fuck! Did you just make a gay joke?" He sits back down and places a discreet kiss on Scooter's cheek. "Welcome to the tribe, Honey. I knew I liked you."

Their drinks arrive and Adam's noodling at the piano turns into a real tune. Scooter sips her Guinness and a small smile spreads across her face. She's found her tribe. As the house lights go down, the stage lights brighten and a spotlight is focused on Adam at the piano. His overture turns into a raucous honky-tonk and a woman dressed as a man saunters onto the stage and begins to sing.

Joey leans over and whispers to Scooter. "That's Carly, drag king extraordinaire. Is she cool or what? She started out here with Jorge but is joining C's drag queen review."

"*Willkommen—Bienvenue—*Welcome! *Fremder, étranger,* stranger. *Glücklich zu sehen. Je suis enchanté!* Happy to see you…*Bleibe, restez,* stay. *Willkommen—Bienvenue—*Welcome! *im Kabarett, au cabaret,* to the cabaret."

The troupe of new queens marches on stage, lining up behind the MC. Each performer drapes their arm over the shoulders of the person next to them and begins a sensuous can-can as the MC launches into the next chorus. The last person to enter the stage is C, whose stage persona is Marilyn Monroe. He joins the MC and adds his soft-voiced silky tones to the duet. "*Im Kabarett,* au cabaret, to the cabaret."

As the piano accompaniment drops several levels, C steps slightly upstage of the MC. "Ladies and gentlemen, boys and girls, thank you for joining us for our dress rehearsal for tomorrow night's premiere." Every word is delivered in the blond bombshell's trademark whisper.

"We've worked hard to perfect our routines, our makeup and our clothes." She performs a little spin. "I hope you have as much fun tonight as I've had helping pull this show together."

The MC melts into the backstage chorus line of queens, which then splits in half to create a runway for the first exquisite impersonator to take center stage.

Marilyn breathes into the microphone. "Please join me in welcoming the West End's exceptional Rainy Daze." Marilyn backs off the stage daintily as the spotlight finds the first performer. Once she's out of the spotlight glare, she tiptoes over to the piano and sits down ever so smoothly next to the piano player.

Without missing a note, Adam turns to her with a genuine smile and whispers, "I've been waiting my whole life for this, Miss Monroe."

Caught a bit off guard, C bats his very long eyelashes at the man and whispers back. "You bet your very sweet ass you have, Adam."

NINE

December 1st, International AIDS Day, dawns cold, rainy and grim in Vancouver. Scooter stands with head bowed beneath the bare cherry trees that have become a living memorial to the first four men to die of AIDS in the city. Everyone had brought umbrellas, prepared for an hour in the rain—everyone except Joey. He squeezed in under Scooter's massive black arc, his head also bowed.

"Four years since James, Ivan, Gino and Randy were taken from us." The speaker is somber, of course, but also impassioned. He had known these men and knew others who now struggled with the disease. "The first fallen pink petals have already been followed by too many. Let me repeat their names so they may live in our memory." The man takes a breath to steady himself and then begins.

"This year Alex, Alvin, Amanda, Brian, Bruce, Darrel, David, Frank, George, Helmut, Hunter, Ian, Keith Haring,

Kevin, Kevin Brown, Jacqueline, James, Jim, John, Joseph, Mark, Michael, Norris, Paul, Randy, Robert, Ron, Ronald, Robert Mapplethorpe, Rock Hudson, Sidney, Sita, Steve, Steven and Warren were taken from our arms. These are Vancouver's brothers, sisters, fathers, lovers, daughters and sons. They have families who mourn them, friends who miss them—and far too much of their lives were left unlived. Hold them in your thoughts today, so they may live a moment longer in our circle."

A long, silent moment passes as the group stands and remembers those they had known—and tries to envision the ones they had not. If not for AIDS, they would all still be here standing in the rain with them.

Unbidden, an old protest song by Joan Baez slips into Scooter's mind. *'Show me the famine, show me the frail—eyes with no future that show how we've failed. And I'll show you the children with so many reasons why. There but for fortune go you and I.'*

Scooter takes a slow breath and softly sings the final phrase: *"There but for fortune go you and I. You and I."* The whole group sings along, and then they cry, like the rain that pours down around them.

• • •

The car pulls over to the curb in front of their house and Scooter and Joey slowly unfold themselves from the back seat. The driver calls out as they exit, "Thank you for coming, especially you, Scooter. That was a lovely way to end our gathering."

Scooter wipes rain from her cheeks and smiles grimly in response. "Next year may there be no names."

"Amen, sister. Amen."

Scooter shuts the car door carefully and cocks her head to Joey. "Are we ready?"

Joey loops his arm through Scooter's and tugs her forward towards their house. "Not really. But let's go fake it."

They trudge up the stairs to the front door, remove their shoes and furl the umbrella. Before Scooter can reach for the handle, the front door opens and Hayley fumes, "Where have you been, Scooter Wells? Look at you—you're an utter mess."

Joey deeks around Hayley and mutters, "See ya."

Scooter's expression is so woe-be-gone, she can only shake her head. "Not a good time, Hayley. Let it be."

Hayley swings the door wide and motions Scooter inside. "You better have something better than that, miss. I called the store and Delphine said you left at two. It's after six now and you come home soaking wet and not a word about where you've been?"

Scooter steps into the room and intends to keep schlepping towards the stairs, but Hayley grabs the back of her shirt and hauls her to a stop. She turns to Hayley and growls, "I said, let it be, Hayley."

"Scooter Wells, you're my baby sister and I have a right to know what you're up to. If you…"

Scooter cuts Hayley off. "I am not your baby anything, Hayley. I never was, never will be. I was at an AIDS memorial, if you must know, grieving the dead and dying."

Hayley is brought up short. "AIDS! That gay thing?" She takes an impromptu step away from Scooter. "You weren't with anyone who's actually sick, were you?"

Scooter's eyes meet Hayley's. "And if I was?" Her tone relays all Hayley needs to know about Scooter's feelings. But Hayley is deaf to the signs she's given.

"Well, you should strip off your clothes and toss them in the washing machine right now. Jump into the shower and wash all over really well. Wash everything."

"Hayley, you do know a person has to share bodily fluids to get AIDS, right? We didn't kiss, or fondle or fuck. We came together as a community to mourn those who have passed, to sing them home and to cry for our loss."

Hayley's eyes widen in surprise as Scooter's words blossom into her consciousness. After a long silence, she whispers, "You think you're gay, Scooter?" But before Scooter can answer, Hayley rushes on again. "Holy Christ, Scoot, you can't be gay. It'll kill Janie…and little Lana? Oh my God, Scooter, you can't be gay. It's not normal."

Scooter takes a step away from Hayley in shock. "Hayley Wells, for gawd's sake, who the hell have you been talking to? You can't really believe all the horseshit that straight people float about being gay!"

Hayley interrupts, grabbing Scooter's hand. "Talk to Jacob, Scooter, he can help you turn away from all this. His father, Reverend Skinner, specializes in helping gay people change. You don't have to be this way."

Scooter pushes past Hayley in dismissal. "That might work if the gay person thinks it's wrong, Hayley. I personally have no doubts at all that this is who I am. Get used to it." She pounds up the stairs to her room.

• • •

Wednesday is Delphine's day to open the store. Scooter appreciates the chance to sleep in, do laundry and generally just go slow before encountering the mayhem of delivery day at Athena's. Most Wednesdays she stops at the Naam on her stroll to work and picks up a coffee and treat for herself and Delphine to share.

Today is no exception; the Naam is busy but not crazy-busy at 2 p.m. Most people had already lunched and are either staying warm inside or playing checkers quietly. Scooter collects her treats and hurries through the rain to the store. As she pushes her way through, she can hear the CBC broadcasting on the radio from the shelf behind the cash desk. Delphine is busy knitting.

"Tough day, hey?" Scooter nods towards the clacking needles in Delphine's hands. "Want coffee?" She puts her goodies on the desk in front of Delphine.

Setting her knitting aside, Delphine picks up the coffee and smells it extravagantly. "Well, you are certainly going to earn your keep today, buster." Delphine sips from the cup. "My god, how did humans survive before they discovered coffee?"

"Oh goodie. If there's anything I hate, it's not earning my paycheck." Scooter saunters towards the back and lets out a low whistle. "Holy Gutenberg, batman—they may have emptied the warehouse for you, Delphine." Setting her cup on a nearby shelf, Scooter scrutinizes the boxes, looking for identifying marks.

Delphine calls from the front. "Most of it's overstock for Christmas…But some of it will be Gay Games stuff too. The European presses are starting to deliver." She appears in the doorway, "Which is good. I don't want to be caught short."

"Really? It's December!"

"Um-hum. And Little Sisters is still waiting on stock they ordered last August. I ran into Janine at a WAVAW fundraiser the other night. She can't even get Maupin's *Tales of the City* through Canada Customs these days. If you find a box of it, they're for her…so set it aside."

"Gottcha!" Scooter pulls off her raincoat and frowns at the stack of boxes. "Did you think to make a list of which publishers sent what?"

"Ha. I did one better—I made a list of publishers you

MUST open, names of ones that can wait and…" Delphine mimes tooting a horn and drops the lists onto the worktable with utter satisfaction. "People think I can't be organized. "I even have a list of which ones are GG books too."

Scooter scowls. "Governor General nominees?"

"No, from now until August 4th GG becomes our acronym for Gay Games…Unless you want to use LG&G instead."

"Umm, I like the short one."

"Don't you even want to know what the other means?"

"No. 'Bye now, Delphine. I have work to do." Scooter bends over, lifts a box and tosses it three feet away. She looks again at the list on the table.

Delphine plasters a petulant frown on her face. "It's Wednesday, it's raining…no one has come out to play all morning."

"Do you want this done, or not?" Scooter turns to face Delphine with a serious frown on her face.

"Fine then." Delphine flounces back to the front of the store. Once seated at the cash register, she calls back through the open stockroom door. "See, still no one here!"

Scooter is already deep into her inventory. All that can be heard is the plok, plok, plok of rain, the thud of boxes being sorted and the murmur of the radio at the front. After twenty minutes Scooter is smiling again, liking the way the day is turning out, thinking about what to have for dinner.

Suddenly Delphine screams loudly, bloody and long. Scooter drops the box she is holding and races across the stockroom, jumps over a short stack of books and barrels into the store.

Delphine is on her feet, both hands gripping the bookcase which holds the radio. She's shaking like a leaf. Scooter bolts across the space to her side and only then sees that tears are running down her cheeks.

"Nooo." Delphine's chin is wobbling, and she sucks up a trembling breath. "This can't be happening."

Scooter immediately wraps her arms around Delphine and starts murmuring platitudes. "It's okay, Delphine… Whatever it is, we can fix it. Just tell me what's going on." Delphine looks at Scooter and opens her mouth, but only sobs come out.

At that moment the phone rings. Scooter isn't certain if she should let go of her boss, who pushes her towards the phone. Delphine leans against the bookcase as Scooter reaches over to pick up the receiver.

"Athena Books, how may I help you."

The woman on the other end is sobbing into the phone. She manages to whisper, "Is Delphine there?" Which is followed by a new wave of sobs.

By now, Scooter is utterly rattled. She hangs up the phone. "Delphine, what the hell is going on?"

The front door bursts open and Renee Rodin from a small used bookstore three stores away stumbles into the store. She's soaking wet and looks as if she's barely holding herself together. She immediately spots Delphine sobbing against the bookshelf.

"Oh FUCK, it's true. Isn't it?"

"WHAT!" Scooter's composure is starting to strip away. "Renee, what the hell is going on?

Renee walks right past Scooter to face Delphine. She picks up two books and slams them together. The ensuring crack shocks Delphine into silence and tiny Renee roars at her, "Shut up, Delphine. Pull yourself together."

Surprisingly, it seems to work. Delphine pulls away from the bookshelf, wipes her face with the palms of her hands and releases a huge sigh laden with unshed tears. "You're right, Renee. Thank you." Delphine reaches up and increases the volume on the radio and then crosses to the desk. She takes her place on the stool, pushing aside her knitting.

"Okay, so first off, Scooter." Delphine's lower lip trembles dangerously but she continues. "The CBC has just announced that a man with a gun has shot and killed fourteen women in Montreal at the *École Polytechnique*. They were targets; he was hunting feminists."

The shock punches into Scooter like a blow. Tears instantly fill her eyes, but she wills them not to fall. She stutters—floundering, searching for words. "That's impossible. How can we verify this?"

Renee blurts, "WAVAW." When Scooter looks confused,

Renee explains. "Women Against Violence Against Women. They'll know for sure if it's true."

Before Renee can finish, Delphine is already dialing. She listens a long moment. "It's busy." She hangs up, and the phone immediately rings. "Athena Books. Yes, this is Delphine." Her bottom lip begins trembling again, so she presses her lips together. "Yes, we'll keep our doors open. Once you have more details, call us. Talk to anyone who answers, and we'll pass the news along." Delphine sets down the phone gingerly, as if it were a bomb.

Scooter studies Delphine with dismay. When she doesn't speak, Scooter nods. "It's true then." A statement. "So, what's the plan?"

Delphine adopts a trembly smile. "Action, of course. Athena is now the West Side hub for a rally and vigil." She quickly starts pulling out ledgers and receipt books. "I'll start making posters letting people know to meet here."

"What can I do?" Scooter enquires.

"Scooter, I want you to take the car and run up to the Safeway at the top of 4th. I need you to buy crackers, cheese, mild sausages, baguettes, cookies and tea and coffee—really anything you can think of to feed people."

"How many people?"

"Start with snacks and drinks for twenty-five. That should get us going." Delphine pulls her keys from her purse and a wad of bills from the cash register." She slides everything across to Scooter. "Go. Be quick, we have a lot to do."

As Scooter turns to leave, Delphine reaches out for her hand, and she stops. "Best thing, Scooter, is don't think too much. Do the tasks ahead of us to get us to the vigil tonight. Okay?"

Scooter pulls in a shaky breath. "Yes ma'am." She hurries out the back door towards the car.

By 7:30 that night hundreds of women had made phone calls, created posters, fed each other, consoled each other, bought candles and flowers, and gathered silently *en masse* at the old Robson Street courthouse where an impromptu stage had been erected.

The stage is ringed in candles. Both ends of the street are blocked to traffic and the ever-growing mass of women spreads like ripples of sadness down Hornby Street and Howe Street and down the stairs to the ice rink below ground. Every woman holds a candle and someone's hand.

Earlier, Scooter had driven Delphine downtown with the posters. Renee and two students from UBC Women Studies came along to help poster. Scooter couldn't help but wonder where Maggie was, how she was doing. She felt an inexplicable need to see her face, to know she was safe. Would any of them ever feel safe again?

Scooter is glad she had arrived early. She got to witness the amazing power of women firsthand. They began to arrive shortly after regular working hours ended. They walked to Robson Street in twos and threes and fours. Everyone wore black or had a black armband or scarf. And as the crowd grew in size, the single mourning women became a warm knot of concerned friends and family. Each was determined to help the others through this moment, this vigil, this horror.

As Scooter looks out across the crowd, she feels a warm hand slide into her own. Looking down, she sees Maggie's safe but tear-streaked face. She can't stop herself; she draws Maggie to her and wraps her arms around her, whispering, "Thank god you're safe. I was so worried, Mags." Maggie wraps her arms around Scooter's waist in response.

Promptly at 8 p.m. a tall, massively imposing woman steps onto the stage and keys a microphone. The crowd turns expectant eyes as she speaks. "There is nothing good about this evening except our willingness to come together to comfort each other. Thank you for coming tonight. My name is Frances Wasserlein, and like most of you, I have no words." She pauses to let that thought sink in.

"Our thanks go out to Gary Cristall at the Vancouver Folk Music Festival for helping us organize sound and stage for tonight." Frances releases a heavy breath and continues. "We are so fortunate tonight to have a singer, a cantor, who can help us take that first step through our grief." Frances holds up one hand, "Please, no applause. Like us, Ferron, too, is in mourning."

A single light is turned up to illuminate the lone singer. She begins strumming her guitar, and slowly the crowd settles and is pulled in closer to each other as comfort against the night. The guitar finds a melody, as if by accident, and the player explores it while the women settle.

And then, she sings—voice faltering at first, tamping down her tears. *"They say slowly / brings the least shock / but no matter how slow I walk / there are traces / empty spaces / and doors and doors of locks."*

A universal sigh slips from every woman in the crowd at the rightness of Ferron's choice. They spontaneously join her, adding their voices to hers at the chorus. *"And by our lives, be we spirit. And by our hearts, be we women. And by our eyes, be we open. And by our hands be we whole."* They sing it again and again and she keeps strumming her guitar until she feels the energy change slightly, and then she adds her voice to theirs as the song comes to a close.

"Sing their names with me now." The melody changes slightly but is still as familiar as a lullaby. Each woman in the gathering repeats the names of the dead, fitting them seamlessly into the tune. "Geneviève Bergeron, Hélène Colgan, Nathalie Croteau, Barbara Daigneault, Anne-Marie Edward, Maud Haviernick, Maryse Laganière, Maryse Leclair, Anne-Marie Lemay, Sonia Pelletier, Michèle Richard, Annie St-Arneault, Annie Turcotte, Barbara Klucznik-Widajewiscz."

As each name is sung, a candle on the edge of the stage is blown out. The singer strikes the last chord and then mutes her guitar with her hand before it's done ringing in the silence. Surrounded by the candlelight cast from the women nearest her, Ferron whispers, "Go now quietly, thoughtfully…being gentle with yourself and others. And sing their names."

TEN

It is 6 a.m. on a dismally cold and rainy Vancouver morning. Scooter has pulled the receiver for the house phone, which hangs on the kitchen wall, out the back door. She sits on the covered porch bundled in a duvet and dressed only in her pajamas. She intends to go back to bed, but it's New Year's Eve and she wants to wish her mother Happy New Year.

Scooter understands she will be in no condition to do this call tomorrow morning, or potentially not any time during the day. It's now or never. The phone continues to ring. Scooter wonders if service is down from snow or wind in Regina. Finally, someone picks up.

"Hello. Wells residence."

Scooter grins; it's Lana, her baby sister. "Lana, Happy New Year, it's Scooter in Vancouver." All Scooter can hear is a piercing scream at the other end of the phone.

"Mama, mama...It's Scooter. She's calling us. C'mon, hurry up."

Scooter raises her voice, trying to make herself heard over his sister's excitement. "Lana, I can talk to you too, ya know."

A very out of breath Lana returns her attention to the call. "Oh Scooter, this is so exciting. Tell me all about Vancouver. Have you got snow? We have tons. And Freddie Cooper pushed me into a snowbank yesterday, but I tripped him on his way past me and rubbed snow in his face. And..., "

Before Lana can add any further gruesome details, Janie arrives and rescues the phone. "Hello Scooter, is that really you?"

Scooter can hear the delight and a thread of fear in Janie's voice. "Everything's okay, Mom, I just wanted to wish you and Lana a Happy New Year. I figure it'll be awful trying to get through tomorrow."

"Oh, Honey, that's so sweet of you. It is just so wonderful to hear your voice. You got my last letter? How are you doing? How's Hayley?" Janie pauses to catch her breath and then laughs at herself. "I've missed you, Scooter."

Scooter can feel tears pushing at her, but she sniffs them back. "I miss you too, Mom...and Lana."

Janie interjects, "Honey, can you afford this call?"

"Yes, absolutely. It's cheaper before eight anyway—another reason I called early."

"Fine then. Spill the beans, Scooter; you never call me mom or mama unless you're hurt or upset." In the pause that Scooter doesn't leap to fill, Janie adds, "Are you and Hayley getting along okay?"

"Well, no worse than usual. We room together, which was maybe a bad idea—but it was the room that was available. And she still has moments when she is just so friggin bossy, which really gets on my nerves." Scooter lets the sentence hang for a long moment. Her voice is low and a little creaky. "And somehow she feels like she has the right to tell me what to do, who to be."

At the other end of the line, Janie 'hmms' into the phone. "None of this is really new, Scooter. Hayley's always been like this. Talk to me—what's really going on?"

Scooter twists the phone cord around and around her finger. "Well, it's me. I'm changing, and Hayley doesn't like it."

"Go on, you've never let Hayley push you around before. Why now?"

Now the tears really are pushing their way forward. Scooter takes a deep breath to steady herself. She almost whispers, "It's because I might be gay. Hayley says I need to fight it, go to counselling. She says I'll go to hell if I don't."

"Well." This is all Janie can manage for a long moment. "Let's be clear, Scooter. I don't think either you or I believe in hell. We've lived it with Hanson, so honestly, that's not much of a threat, is it?"

Now Scooter does cry softly. "It's okay then? You don't mind?"

Janie is crying a bit now too. "Honestly, Scooter, what I care most about in life is that you're happy. You deserve it. *We all deserve it*—but you more than anyone I know. So maybe you're gay, maybe you're not. But as your mother, Scooter, my only concern is that you find yourself. *Be yourself.*"

"Really? You're not mad or horrified or going to make me come back to Regina?"

Now Janie laughs, a choking kind of crying laugh. "Oh Scooter, as if anyone could make you do that." Janie sniffs and blows her nose. "So, this is costing you a fortune, please write me more about all this, okay?"

"I will, of course. Although it's all a bit confusing. I'm not certain I know how to be gay, Janie."

"Honey, who would?" Her voice suddenly becomes more serious. "Scooter, just focus on being yourself. Hold true to that, okay?"

"Yes, Mom."

"But remember, Hayley has her own path too. It just may not be yours." Janie blows her nose again and adds, "And will you do me a favor and talk to Lana for a minute, she's rabid to hear about the beach." There's a pause. "Scooter, you know I love you...more than mittens in winter, Honey. Now talk to Lana before she dies of anticipation."

Scooter can hear the phone being handed off to her

little sister. Even though she's freezing out on the porch, she's grinning like a love-struck monkey. *My mom loves me, really truly loves me.*

"Hi Scooter, Janie says you live really, really close to the beach."

"I do. And you're going to come see it—just as soon as I can save some money."

When Scooter hangs up the phone, she feels lighter than she has in months. She shakes her head in disbelief as she unwraps herself from the duvet and drapes it over a chair. *Janie was so cool about the gay thing; who would have ever expected it? I really have the greatest mom in the world.* Scooter wasn't oblivious to the emotion in Janie's voice as they talked. *But that didn't stop her from letting me choose for myself. Wow, I am so incredibly lucky.*

Scooter looks around as if seeing the kitchen for the first time. Dishes need washing, coffee isn't yet made. She jumps into the work, even makes pancake batter and starts frying flapjacks to offer to Hayley for breakfast. She figures any truce with Hayley will be most appreciated with food.

It isn't long after the smell of coffee begins circulating through the house, coupled with the aroma of fresh pancakes frying, that Scooter hears her housemates emerging for the day. The first to poke his head through the kitchen door is Joey.

"What's up, babe?"

"Nothing, if you ever call me that again. Dude."

"Is that coffee?"

"Uh-huh. And pancakes."

"Oh, my heart be still." He steps into the room and bows regally to Scooter. "Oh, Queen of the Morning, what can I promise in return for a full steaming cup of black coffee?"

"Set the table…Do the dishes afterwards."

Joey capers over to the dish cupboard. "Done. Do I have time for a quick run before you serve it up?" He says this as he's pulling dishes from the cupboard and placing them on the table.

Scooter nods, laughing. "Yes. I'm waiting to surprise Hayley. You likely have a half hour or so. Either way, I'll save you some."

"Terrific. See you in thirty, then." Joey blasts out of the room and Scooter hears the front door slam. "Better than an alarm clock, Joey. Thank you."

Scooter has barely placed the tray of fresh pancakes in the over to stay warm when she hears the thump of feet on the wood floor. Her heart picks up a beat; it could just as easily be Maggie who's up and moving about as her sister. Scooter pastes a unconcerned smile on her face.

Hayley pops her head around the doorframe, sleepy-grumpy. "What the heck…I was trying to sleep in."

Scooter makes a face of sisterly concern. "Joey took off for his morning run with a fair bit of enthusiasm. Come

sit down and have some coffee. It'll make it all better."
Scooter lifts a pancake on the spatula, saying, "I have
pancakes to go with it—with real maple syrup!"

Hayley waves a hand in negation of the offer. "No time.
I'm heading downtown to serve breakfast at the Mission
to street people."

"What! It's New Years, Hayley...I thought we could
have a sisterly moment together."

Hayley sighs in mock disappointment. "You snooze,
you lose, Scooter. If you had only said!" Hayley shrugs
acceptance of the status quo. "Jacob asked if I wanted
to go...and I thought it would be a nice gesture to start
the new year."

Scooter's disappointment is plain on her face. Then she
brightens, "Well, have a quick bite and then you can run
off. Get some fuel in you for the day?" Her face is hopeful.

Hayley is oblivious. "Sorry, Scoot. I really can't. Jacob's
outreach team meets and shares a meal together before
the street kitchen opens. Tradition..." Without another
word she turns and leaves her sister holding the pancake.

Scooter stands a moment longer at the stove, waiting for
the last batch of pancakes to finish cooking. Once they're
done, she piles them on the plate in the oven. *Okay then,
no Hayley for breakfast; obviously no Jacob either.* She sets
down the spatula and crosses the living room to Maggie's
bedroom door. She taps gently on the door. When there's
no answer, Scooter opens the door as quietly as possible.

She peers into the room and notices the bed hasn't been slept in at all. *Okay then, no Maggie either, apparently.*

Scooter turns and crosses back towards the kitchen but stops when she hears pounding feet on the front stairs. The door is flung open and Joey appears silhouetted against a glare of morning sunlight. He crows, "Wow, what a run—what a day!" Scooter picks up the nearest sofa pillow and throws it at him. Hard.

• • •

It's nearly 11 p.m. when Scooter and Joey hop off the Stanley Park bus and cut across the hill. The glowing lights of the Vancouver aquarium guide them down the hill to the party. Joey has assured her multiple times that no one arrives at a party of this scope early. Still, she's anxious.

At her core, Scooter is a little scandalized that the gay men who organized this party are holding it at the aquarium. *I mean, it must be costing a fortune. And what will the fish think?* She is filled with apprehension as they step inside. The lights are dim in the entry and the foyer, but the massive floor-to-ceiling fish tanks are fully lit and offer an astounding ambient light. The fishy silhouettes and shadows they cast on the walls and floor create a magical atmosphere. Scooter stands with mouth gaping.

Joey reaches over and pushes her jaw shut. "You look like a trout, Scooter."

"My god, I wish I was one. This is astounding…I'd dive right in if I had gills."

Joey beams. "I know, eh. I will say one thing about our tribe: gay men really know how to throw a party."

They are greeted and get an ink stamp applied to their hands, allowing them to come and go as they please. Scooter scrutinizes the stamp on her forearm. "What is it?"

Joey gives it a cursory look and laughs. "The Gay Games logo. I guess they recognize a marketing opportunity when they see it. There aren't that many people here right now but in twenty or thirty minutes the foyer will be packed right up to the tank walls." He motions Scooter forward as the sonorous notes of a piano weave into the shadows on the walls around them.

In the main concourse, a white baby grand piano has been set up. Seated at the bench and already warming up is Adam. His fingers fly across the keys with equal amounts of showmanship and aplomb. He spots them crossing the concourse and picks out a lilting, mincing tune that matches their steps perfectly.

"Nice…" Joey reaches the piano first and smiles at Adam. "Not very often I get my own soundtrack to life."

Adam nods his head in acknowledgment. "A pleasure, Joseph." Adam turns the lilting melody into something far more elegant and lyrical. "Who's your friend? She was at the dress rehearsal the other night, right?"

Scooter leans forward and offers her hand to shake.

"Scooter Wells, Mr. Heber. You play beautifully." Without missing a beat, Adam reaches up and taps her palm with the fingers on his right hand and smoothly drops it down again to the keyboard to continue the piece. Then his face lights up with utter delight and both Joey and Scooter turn to find the source.

Across the concourse, Marilyn Monroe appears from behind a closed door. Dressed in a form-fitting bright red sheath, she glides towards the piano. Adam half rises from his bench seat, nodding his head in welcome.

C, as Marilyn, reaches over and smooths a stray lock of hair off Adam's forehead. She whispers, "Play something for me, Adam. Let's give the boys something to talk about tonight, shall we?"

Adam skillfully segues his improvised overture into a Big Band tune from the late forties. Marilyn looks over his shoulder at the music and hums the melody a moment before accepting her cue from Adam's intro.

"You made me love you, I didn't want to. I didn't want to do it."

C's sultry Marilyn voice gains assurance as some of the early arrivals drift towards the piano. Apparently C is oblivious to their presence as he leans on the piano, singing directly to Adam.

Scooter shakes her head in amazement. She whispers hoarsely to Joey, "My god, C is brilliant as Marilyn." All Joey can say is, "I know." Scooter watches a moment longer and then mouths, "Am I allowed to ask what C's real name is, Joey?"

"Ask me, yes. C never. Good choice, Scoot." Joey catches C's eye and raises his drink to her. "C was christened Connor, and he seemed to be headed towards a union with Christ, but a Bible camp counselor got there first."

Seeing Scooter's shocked expression, Joey shakes his head. "C will tell you he has always been very clear about what he wants. And he was lucky, he had educated parents who weren't at all offended that their son was gay. But the other boy wasn't quite so lucky. C believes he was sent for conversion therapy by his father."

"Holy crap, Joey. Even I know that is totally barbaric." It's clear to Scooter that this conversation is hard for Joey. She puts her arm around his shoulders and gives him a quick hug. "Thank you for saving me so I don't put my stupid foot in my mouth. Very much appreciated."

Joey punches her arm lightly. "Well, I can't always be here to save you…but I'll do what I can." He smirks. "Oh, I see my guy."

"You got a guy, Joey?"

"I live in hope, Scooter." Joey bounces off across the room.

Scooter watches him cross the concourse and grins. She realizes with surprise that she loves Joey. Loves his good nature, his buoyant spirit and the fact that he's always up for anything. She studies the people in the room, which has filled up considerably in the last twenty minutes. *For the first time in my whole life I am in a room that is filled with gay people. And frankly, I'm happier than I can ever remember being in—well, yonks. What the hell…*

She watches as a small, well-dressed group surges to the open space near the piano. Adam obliges with a flourish to announce their arrival, and the whole crowd claps spontaneously. Everyone in the small group basks in the applause for a moment and then Adam leaves the piano and moves to just upstage. With his microphone he captures the attention of the crowd, waiting until they quiet.

Adam nervously clears his throat and begins. "Ladies and gentlemen, dykes and fags, gay women and gay men—thank you for coming tonight to help raise funds and awareness for the Gay Games coming this summer.

"Beside me are many of the people who convinced the Gay Games committee in San Francisco that Vancouver could pull this off. Mark Mees, Betty Baxter (an Olympian in her own right), Richard Dobson and Bill Amundson have been the guiding lights of the games. But hundreds of volunteers have been working for years already to ensure both the Gay Games and the Cultural Festival that will run concurrently are a hit. Please show the committee your appreciation for their service to our community in bringing the Gay Games to Vancouver."

The concourse erupts in applause. Over the loudspeakers Queen's 'We Are the Champion' bursts forth.

Immediately everyone is clapping in time and dancing in place. After a minute or two of frivolity, Betty Baxter steps forward with the microphone and the sound technician fades down the song.

From the far side of the concourse, Scooter looks around and observes the crowd. The people all seem so relaxed and happy and present in this moment. Scooter suddenly recognizes how tense she has been since the night when she and Maggie had sex. In some ways it had confirmed a lifelong suspicion for Scooter—but it left her feeling so incredibly *visible*. Everyone must know, just by looking at her, that she's a homo. Except here! Here everyone is a homo and no one cares a whit. *What a relief!* Here she fits in, here she is one among many. Here is her tribe, right in front of her face.

Now she understands the passion Joey always exhibits when he speaks about the Gay Games. The rumor was that thousands of gay folk from around the world were coming to Vancouver. For a brief moment in time, they would *own* their little corner of the city. Instead of being a tourist curiosity, they would be more vast, more visible and varied than anyone had thought possible. They would control the streets of their home. There wouldn't just be Davie Street homos anymore—there would be French and Irish and Italian and American and British. And everyone in Vancouver would come to understand that there aren't just a few local gay yokels; gays are everywhere in the world and thousands are coming to Vancouver to help make that statement.

This thought sends a frisson of excitement through Scooter. She lets her eyes wander around the room again. C is standing next to Adam, running his fingers through the hair at the nape of his neck. Joey is across the room practically vibrating as he talks to an incredibly handsome man, suavely leaning against a wall.

Scooter catches herself thinking: *For this brief moment, we are all happy. What we desire most is right here where we can all see it. For this moment everything we want feels possible.* She wants to be alone with this thought, to give it the space it needs to settle and take root in her.

Janie was right, she only needs to be herself without fear, without hesitation. She waves across the room to Joey and points towards the exit. He waves back and Scooter turns and walks away. Unnoticed, Maggie elbows through the crowd and catches sight of Scooter, following her with her eyes as she heads for the door.

ELEVEN

"Good gawd, Delphine, you've ordered way too much stuff. There's no room for it all. Not in our little kiosk, not here—even if we use the trunk of your car." Scooter stands, hands on her hips, exasperated and glaring at the pile of boxes.

"I know, I know." Delphine wears a look of contrition. "Renee said we can store some in her back room. We just have to be sure to itemize anything we leave there, so we don't forget it and order more." Delphine pastes a completely false smile on her face. "Maybe you could do that while you unpack everything and pull stock for the kiosk venue. It has to be there tomorrow before the Games open."

Delphine quickly scuttles back through the doorway. "I'll handle the cash desk while you toil in the trenches back there."

"And you'll buy treats and coffee to placate your grumbling worker."

"Right-o. Watch the front, I'll be back in a minute, oh grumbly one."

Scooter hears the brass bell on the door tinkle before she can ask Delphine how she is expected to be in two places at once. She schleps to the front of the store and perches on the stool, reviewing some packing slips while waiting for Delphine to return. The bell tinkles again. Scooter doesn't look up as she growls, "Wow, that was fast. What'd you bring me?"

A moment of silence follows, and then a timid voice answers, "Ah, tickets to the opening ceremony of the Gay Games." Scooter looks up and finds a very young, very nervous woman standing still in the doorway.

"Crud, I'm sorry. Come in—I won't bite, I promise." Scooter sets aside the packing slips and stands up. "I thought you were my annoying ne'er-do-well boss."

The young woman offers a hesitant smile and approaches the cash desk, obviously still not certain of her welcome. She extends her hand, offering the envelope she's carrying to Scooter. "The passes. For the opening ceremony."

Scooter reaches for the passes and raises her eyebrows, questioning. "So, what's your name?"

"Cory."

"I'm Scooter, Scooter Wells. Is this your first time in the store, Cory?"

"Yes ma'am."

Scooter snorts but realizes instantly she's just made Cory even more nervous. "Sorry. I always think of my boss, Delphine, as the ma'am here. You can call me Scooter." She comes around the desk and motions Cory over to the Staff Picks shelf. "Do you read much, Cory?"

Cory brightens considerably and smiles as she nods an eager 'yes'.

Scooter reaches for a book and turns to Cory, handing her Alison Bechdel's *Dykes to Watch Out For*. "This is one of the authors everyone is looking forward to seeing at the Literary Festival. She might be someone you'd enjoy."

Scooter returns to the desk, leaving Cory to examine the other books on the shelf. "Have a look around, Cory. May as well see the sights while you're delivering tickets, eh? And let me know if I can help with anything, okay?" She picks up the packing slips and starts highlighting the books she wants to leave at Renee's store a few doors down the block. When she notices Cory is preparing to leave, she says, "Hey Cory, if you're not doing anything tonight—want to come help us paint glitter all over the streetlights on Davie Street?"

Cory stops, hesitating. "Uh, is that legal?"

Scooter shrugs. "We own the street for the next ten days until the Games are over. Really, our village could look way more gay than it currently does. Want to help?"

More hesitation. "Sure! Where and when?"

Scooter smiles in delight. "Meet me and a gaggle of other gay folk at the corner of Davie Street and Bute at nine o'clock We'll work our way west, painting as we go."

"Okay," Cory blurts with enthusiasm mixed with trepidation. "See you then." She opens the door just as Delphine is returning.

"Why thank you, kind sir."

Cory looks at her blankly. Uncertain how to respond, she simply hurtles through the door.

Scooter looks up at Delphine. "Don't pick on the baby dykes, Delphine. You make them nervous."

"I'm an actor; it was a line from Shakespeare." Delphine sets down the coffee and obligatory brownies. "Really? I make you nervous?"

Scooter scoffs. "Gawd NO! You do make me tear my hair though. How did you do this job without any muscle all these years?"

Delphine smiles her sweetest smile. "I have begun to wonder that myself lately, Ms. Wells." She raises her coffee cup. "Cheers. And let the Games begin!"

· · ·

Scooter is the first to arrive at the corner of Bute and Davie. As always, summer or winter, the intersection is busy. Busy with cars, shoppers and the guys and dolls of the 'hood. It's especially vibrant on this gorgeous summer evening that has coaxed people outside in hoards. At nine o'clock long shadows lace across the street from the trees and the posts of streetlights. At the far end of Davie, closest to the water, the sky is edging towards amber, umber and gold. Scooter sighs. She really does love this place.

She carries a backpack full of cans of spray paint in all the primary colors. Her bravado in talking to Cory about tonight was just that. Bravado. Honestly, she'd never intentionally done an illegal thing in her life. It was scary and thrilling at the same time.

Cory turns up five minutes later, and then Joey. Scooter scans the street a moment longer. "I thought you were bringing the troops."

Joey grins like a spaniel who's been caught doing something bad. "Be patient, oh wise one. Many hands will make light work."

Moments later, Delphine's bright red Lincoln careens into view and slides into a parking spot across the street. Within minutes she and five towering drag queens hit the street and jaywalk across to join them.

"Sorry. We had to detour. The city crew is putting the bollards in place across Burrard Street to close off Davie to traffic. We had to sneak around to get in before they closed the gap."

Joey's eyes are dancing with excitement. "Okay, boss. What's the plan, Scooter?"

"Delphine, have you delivered on your promise?" Scooter challenges.

Delphine turns to the queens behind her and yells, "GIRLS, she wants what we got."

Like a top drill team, the queens snap out five matching clear plastic handbags each filled with glitter in a primary color. "We couldn't decide if we should just mix it all together or maintain color integrity in case a situation called for it." Delphine and queens are clearly quite pleased with their array.

Scooter nods her head sagely. "Good call—I think maintaining color integrity is going to serve us well, ladies." Titters greet her pronouncement. "Okay, I believe we can cover the most ground if we split into two units." Scooter checks with her troops and they're all nodding in agreement. "I can cover one side of the street and Joey will lead the others directly across from us and paint that side. Try to stay reasonably in sync with each other." She hands out whistles on chains to each of her troops. "IF anyone sees the cops, blow your whistle and immediately disperse. Meet up at the Pump Jack afterwards and we'll decide if we can redeploy to finish our mission."

"The Pump Jack?" Delphine croons.

"Well, we'll have no trouble spotting each other amongst the leather men, eh?" Scooter smirks. "And you can admire the wares while you wait, Delphine."

Everyone applauds with obvious excitement. Joey heads across the street with Delphine and two queens. Cory stands around with her hands in her pockets, waiting for instruction. Scooter catches her ambivalence out of the corner of her eye. "You okay, Cory?"

"Yeah. What do you want me to do?"

"Relax, for starters." Scooter pops her in the arm. "I'll do the first couple, then you take over from there. Okay?"

"Sure." Cory is both excited and nervous.

Scooter shouts to Joey. "Let's do this!!" And the spray painting begins. Scooter approaches a light pole and aims a can of neon orange at it. She only succeeds in painting her own t-shirt as the wind blows it back onto her chest. "Oops. First lesson—know which way the wind's blowing!" Scooter tries again and manages to coat a three-foot length of the pole. The three drag queens step forward and toss glitter onto the wet paint. *Voilà*, gay light poles.

They move on. Once Cory sees how it's done, Scooter hands her several cans of spray paint. "Mix it up as much as you can." As they move along the street it's inevitable that they attract a following. A number of people offer to help, so Scooter divides up her paint supplies and sends a drag queen along with each new reveler who joins their troop.

"Can we use rainbow condoms to decorate too?" This from a lanky dude leaning against a wall as they pass. Cory and Scooter and their glitter gal lock eyes and shrug. They all chorus, "Sure! Whatever." And then they paint and spatter another light pole.

The street is alive with music spilling out of the windows and open doorways of the clubs. The painting party has added a festive aura to a perfect summer night, and people are reveling in the freedom of owning their little corner of the world. Scooter is practically skipping with delight. Around her people are singing along with the music and dancing in the street.

Cory turns to her, absolutely glowing. She shouts, "This is the absolute coolest thing I've ever done. It's brilliant." Scooter nods in speechless agreement.

And then a high-pitched chorus of screams pierces the levity. A second scream quickly follows. Scooter looks across the street to Joey, who mutely throws up his hands in bewilderment. The crowd directly in front of them rapidly thins and grows ragged as an old pickup truck inches its way through the throng. It begins honking its horn loudly, drowning the laughter and music as people scatter in confusion and fear.

Scooter shouts to Joey. "Fuck, they're going to kill someone. C'mon." They sprint up the rapidly clearing street, running towards the truck. "They must've gotten through before the bollards went up and now they don't know how to get out."

Joey and Scooter slow down to a walk as they approach the pickup. A man stands up in the back of the truck and raises a bullhorn to his mouth.

"The time is nigh, ye sinners. For the Lord sayeth, thou

shall not lie with a male as with a woman; it is an abomination." He turns to point his megaphone in the other direction. "Hear unto me, you fornicators and adulterers. The Lord God has spoken. Leviticus—Chapter 1, 8 verse 22."

Joey and Scooter both stop and look at each other as if to say ,*You've got to be kidding.* Scooter watches the crowd in the street in front of the truck. Some people are trying to get out of the way; others are clearly wanting to stand their ground and dispute this incursion into their space. They can see two men in the front of the cab, windows down, jeering at the people scurrying in front of them.

Someone in the crowd tosses an empty plastic pop bottle at the cab. The driver bats it away and keeps his truck moving forward, laughing.

"Joey, someone's going to get hurt. We have to do something," Scooter yells.

"Whaaat?"

Scooter takes a deep breath, closes her eyes a moment to settle herself and says, "Okay. Wait here, I'm going to cross the street and when I'm in line with the truck cab you have to do something—anything—to draw their attention for a moment."

Joey's expression turns to horror. "Scooter…"

"I'll wave at you when I'm ready," she calls back over her shoulder as she sprints across the street.

Joey watches as she threads herself through the crowd on the sidewalk.

The man with the bullhorn blasts them again. "If a man lies with a male as with a woman, both of them have committed an abomination. Know ye the Lord God is good, He is the light everlasting."

Joey edges closer to the truck and sees Scooter's wave. He has no idea what to do but he's determined to do something. He hesitates, then takes a running leap and dives onto the hood of the truck and pulls himself up using the windshield wipers. He is face-to-face with the men inside. He beats on the window.

On the other side of the street, Scooter watches Joey run towards the truck. "Oh shit, Joey." As soon as she sees the driver's attention diverted, she takes a flying leap herself and lands on the running board on the driver's side. She quickly thrusts her hand inside and finds the ignition keys and turns off the engine. By the time the driver notices someone is hanging onto his door, Scooter has the keys in her hand and is falling away from the vehicle and melting into the crowd.

The driver shouts, "Hey. Stop." Then he suddenly realizes what a precarious position they are now in. "Roll up the windows," one of the men shouts. "Roll up your friggin windows, man." The windows go up, but the man in back is still shouting into the crowd. The driver scowls, "We should try to shut him up."

The other man in the cab looks dubious. "It will be as God wills it." He slinks down in his seat.

Scooter weaves her way around to the front of the truck. She climbs up to join Joey on the hood and waves her hands to get the attention of the crowd before them. When people begin to turn to face her, Scooter holds aloft the set of keys. "Well, first problem solved. Now, who wants to help me put the trash outside our door for the city to pick up?" Everyone laughs and applauds.

"I'm not kidding, you know. All of us, working together, can push this old crate back to Burrard Street and leave it for the cops. Who wants to help?"

Before either she or Joey can slide off the hood of the truck, people gather in front of them and start pushing.

At the front of the truck, Cory shouts, "What about the old guy? Can we shut him up?"

Scooter and Joey look at each other briefly, then Joey shouts back, "We could drown him out."

Scooter starts pounding on the hood of the truck, a deep rhythmic bass beat that everyone knows. The crowd starts clapping, keeping time—and singing. "We will, we will rock you." Many people on the sideline pick up trash can lids and start pounding them in time to Scooter's beat. "We will, we will rock you." They sing and laugh and shout the lyrics as they follow the pickup all the way down the street.

Scooter is filled with a love for these people that can't be described. While she pounds on the hood, she looks out at the throng below her. C is there as Marilyn, and Adam.

She can see other drag queens pouring out of the bars to add a glittery accent to their march. The leather men shoulder their way to the front and push. And everyone is laughing and singing in response to the attack.

As they near Burrard Street, Scooter can see a cordon of placards and people moving towards them on the other side of the bollards. There are two motorcycle cops on each side of it, cautioning traffic. She motions to Joey, who has climbed onto the roof, to take over the beat. He does so, and Scooter shouts to Cory, "Jog ahead, past that group approaching us, and make sure the police know what the situation is here." Cory nods, laughing, and shoots off like a rocket.

Scooter takes up her station once again on the hood of the truck and watches the group approach. It's a small group, and she dismisses it completely, taking a moment to survey her tribe again around her. Together. Moving, if not mountains, at least an irritating and life-threatening pickup truck. She has never felt so proud...AND SO GAY!

As Scooter turns her attention back to the placard-waving throng, she is struck speechless by seeing her sister Hayley at the forefront carrying a large sign with burning flames depicting the message SINNERS. Beside her, Jacob is holding a Bible aloft and shouting, "Ye shall reap what ye sow—thus sayeth the Lord."

Joey sees Scooter's reaction and leaps up, shouting. "Let the cops handle this now. Just move the bollards, so we can get them out of here. C'mon, everyone. Move the bollards."

The crowd surges forward and creates a gap through which to shove the old truck to the other side. Joey grasps Scooter's hand and pulls her down off the truck and away from the crowd.

Scooter turns to Joey in shock. "Did you see Hayley and Jacob? Together! They held a sign that called us all sinners." Scooter can't stop the sob that escapes her. "Joey, that's my sister."

Joey wraps his arms around her, nodding his head. "I know. My mother and brother stand shoulder-to-shoulder with them in their hearts." He pulls her forward another few steps. "This is why we need each other, Scooter. Why we build our own family, our own community who better understands the price we pay every day to be ourselves."

Joey pulls her farther from the fray. "My personal philosophy is to live well, LOVE lots and organize, organize, organize." His smile is incandescent. Scooter studies him a long moment, then grasps his hand in hers and raises them over her head in triumph.

"Ow!" Joey yells as Scooter presses his hand too hard. He pulls her hand down and turns it over, disengaging his own. Pressed tightly in Scooter's palm are the truck keys. They both look down in surprise. Joey laughs. "Should we find a way to give them back?"

Scooter looks at Joey and shouts, "Never! After all that work? We've earned the keys to our kingdom tonight. I'm keeping 'em!" She tosses him the keys playfully and Joey tosses them right back.

Suddenly fireworks fill the night sky and everyone on the street turns to look.

"Quick, down to the beach. They're testing for tomorrow's opening ceremonies."

They join the hundreds of gays and lesbians running to English Bay, thrilled that the party has begun.

ACKNOWLEGMENTS

First and foremost, I want to thank my amazing, kind, knowledgeable and patient editor. She edited my first novel, *Scuttlebutt*, and has been a reader and punctuation tutor for all of my work over the last five years. I am so very lucky to have her!

My youngest sister, Regina, has also doggedly read everything I write and given me the benefit of her broad knowledge of story. How lucky can a writer get?

As well, I've been blessed to find a terrific cover designer in Arjuna Jay at 99designs, and an excellent interior book designer, Tara Mayberry, TeaBerry Creative. I just provide the words; they create beautiful books.

And finally, I wish to thank my co-creator of the 1990 *World Without Borders* Literary Festival, Rick Marchand, as well as the Gay Games Board of Directors and the countless extraordinary volunteers who made the Games possible. Last, but definitely not least, the amazing LGBTQ+ communities of Vancouver.

ABOUT THE AUTHOR

Jana Williams published her first novel, *Scuttlebutt*, in 1990 and has been writing avidly ever since. Her work includes stories, screenplays, science fiction books, blogs and writing manuals.

The Truth about a Girl took at least a decade to find itself and gel into its ultimate format. Each of these stories was complete in itself, but they were set aside for years before they were expanded into a novel.

One day Jana had a flash of understanding: these stories are stronger together than apart. Voilà! *The Truth about a Girl* was born. And in short order, one of the stories, *The Tenant*, was optioned by a Vancouver film producer to be adapted to film.

Jana's science fiction novels, *Freefall and Shadowfall,* and the forthcoming *Windfall*, have all had individualistic journeys into being too. Each in its own way has a been a joy to write!

Visit Jana at https://www.janawilliams.ca

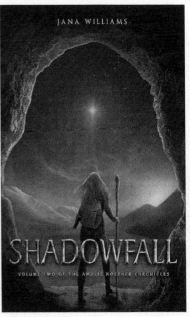